The Sea Flower

A Novel

Also from Ruth Moore

Spoonhandle

The Weir

Second Growth

Candlemas Bay

Speak to the Winds

The Walk Down Main Street

Cold as a Dog

The Sea Flower

A Novel

RUTH MOORE

ISLANDPORT PRESS

IsLANDPORT PRESS

Islandport Press
P.O. Box 10
Yarmouth, Maine 04096
www.islandportpress.com
info@islandportpress.com

Originally published in 1964 by William Morrow & Co.
First Islandport Press Edition: March 2024

ISBN: 978-1-952143-84-7
Library of Congress Control Number: 2023946352

Dean L. Lunt | Editor-in-Chief, Publisher
Shannon M. Butler | Vice President
Emily A. Lunt | Book Designer

For Mimi and Cheni

Table of Contents

Part One: Marney

Marney Lessard's Uncle Joe was killed at two o'clock on a summer Sunday morning, riding home on his motorcycle from the Blue Feather Inn. He had been happy-drunk when he'd left the roadhouse bar, clipping along well over the speed limit and singing at the top of his lungs; but the wind in his face and the jounce of the motorbike sobered him up some, and half-sober, Joe was always mean-drunk. When he got to the Gorge and saw what he took to be an old tomcat crossing in front of him, he grinned, aimed straight at it, and stepped on the gas. The road-cut in the Gorge had been blasted out, leaving steep rock faces on either side; signs were always up there: LOOK OUT FOR FALLING ROCK. What Joe had taken for a tomcat was a roundish gray rock, about cat-size, lying in the road. He didn't hit the rock; he jinked to miss it as soon as he saw he was coming up on something that was likely to fight back. It was the jink that threw him.

The motorcycle wasn't hurt much—some dents, some paint scraped off—as the state police found when they came to examine it later. It spun around on its side a few times and came to rest on the road shoulder, its hind wheel slowly turning and its headlight on, pinpointing Joe where he sat, as if braced against the opposite rock face, covered with blood and still grinning.

The accident had made a brief, clattering racket enough to scare up a big night bird which had been sitting peacefully in a tree high on the rock face. It flew away with a heavy clapping of wings and quiet settled down. Young Denzil Fairchild, coming home from a dance and a late date, had no warning whatsoever. He was hurrying, in case his father woke up and found he'd come in at two instead of twelve o'clock; and he drove right up onto a sight which was to give him nightmares for months to come—a blood-covered dead man with a spotlight on him, sitting grinning against the ledges.

1

Denzil's brakes let out a stuck-pig squeal as he tromped down; the car bucked, but she stopped all right. As soon as he could, for shaking, he got out to see if he could do anything. He couldn't; no one could have told who the man was, not by looking at him. But that big red motorbike, fixed up with all kinds of gadgets and the real leather saddlebags, he had seen a good many times. It was the envy of every kid in town. You couldn't mistake it. The dead guy over there against the rocks had to be Marney Lessard's uncle, Joe Dondin.

He hit that rock, Denzil told himself. Going like a bat. Drunk, too, I betcha.

Teeth chattering, he piled back into the car, drove on into town, and at the first phone booth he came to, called the state cops. Then he called his father. What better excuse could a guy have for coming home late than something as horrible as this happening practically in front of him?

His father took some time to wake up; when he did, and finally got through his head what had happened, he blew up.

"Why in hell didn't you come home when I told you to? Then you wouldn't have run into it. I'll be darned lucky if they don't lay the blame on you. You didn't do it, did you?"

"Oh, my gosh, no, Pop. I—"

"Well, you could have, the half-witted way you drive that car. The cops know it, too. All right, dammit, you stay put, I'll be down." He hung up with a crash.

Denzil himself hung up, but dignified and slow. He stuck his little finger into his ear and wiggled it. That slam had darn near busted his eardrum.

Well, the old man was going to be unreasonable, so get set. Sure, he had been in trouble once or twice with the car, but not his fault, and the old man's insurance had paid for it anyway. As for getting blamed this time, there was the rock in the road and the cops could read skid marks. What was the matter with him?

Thinking of the rock, the skid marks, the scene, made his stomach turn over; for a moment he thought he was going to throw up right on the phone-booth floor. Cheest, the poor guy. Was he ever mangled!

2

Denzil folded back the door of the booth and stood breathing the fresh night air. The street was shadowy, with pools of light under the street lamps; not a soul stirring, not a sound. It was awful, standing around here, nothing to do but wait.

Well, one thing, he could call Marney Lessard. Somebody ought to, seeing Joe Dondin had been the only relative he had. They lived up a back road in on the edge of the mountain; Joe owned a ramshackly house in there. At least it was ramshackly on the outside, as a front; Denzil had heard that some of the rooms inside were fixed up for the booze parties and poker games Joe ran there—kind of an offbeat roadhouse. Denzil himself had never been inside the house; he was forbidden to go there. Decent people didn't. That was one thing the old man would've torn Denzil's head off for—if he'd known, which he didn't and never was going to, how Denzil and one or two other guys sneaked up there sometimes and bought a bottle from Joe. Wow, dog, if the old man ever heard about that!

The last time they'd gone there, they'd run head-on into one of Joe's parties. It had been a corker, too: crumby drunk dames going in and out, and a lot of Frog millworkers from over back of Bristol. Denzil and the other guys had stayed out in the bushes for quite a while, watching. With all that going on, they figured they'd better not try to buy the bottle—might be somebody in that crowd that would know them; but it was a moonlight night, and you could see about everything that went on. All at once an upstairs back window over the porch went up, and some guy came out of it carrying a big bundle of stuff that looked like—yes, it was—bedding. You could see the stripes on the pillow that didn't have any pillowcase on it. The fellow went footing it across the porch roof and climbed out of sight into some kind of a gutter connection between the house and the barn.

One of the guys nudged Denzil and whispered, "Hey, that's old Marney. Gone to sleep out under the stars, what'd you know?"

Denzil said, "Betcha one of those yellow-haired lassies tried to crawl into bed with him." And the idea of that—that guy and any dame—struck them all so funny that they got to laughing and had to haul tail out of there before someone heard.

The next day Marney showed up in school with a limp and a fine, oozy black eye; he sat in class like a lump. The teacher asked him if he felt all right, and he said sure, but at noon he vanished and didn't come back till the next day. Then he showed up again, as standoffish as ever. So far as Denzil was concerned, he hadn't been missed.

Denzil couldn't have liked the guy if he'd tried. Someone comes to your school, a stranger, he's the one to do the trying. No one was going to fall all over a fellow who apparently didn't feel it was worth his while to turn his hand over; didn't seem to like any of the fellows, wasn't interested in any of the girls. Oh, he had a brain somewhere; he got straight A's, got them without trying, it looked like. He never did any work. Never took books home, though you could see why; who could do homework in the middle of Joe Dondin's rig? Asked how he got by without studying, he just said he'd been over that stuff last year in the school he'd gone to. The way he said it, he might just as well have said right out that Spancook High was a backwoods shebang not worth his time. Made you want to haul off and take a poke at him. Except you know he wasn't anybody to fool with. He had a good build and he had height—six-two, around there. The Spancook basketball team sure needed height last year, too. But Marney Lessard made it clear, first off, he wasn't going to play any ball. So that was him, and so far as Denzil was concerned, you could have him.

Still, whether you liked the guy or not, you could ring him up, couldn't you, when it was something like this, his only uncle? Joe Dondin might not be much of a loss; he was sure one bad actor, as everybody knew. Marney might not have made a go of it at the school anyway, even if he'd tried, because of Joe. Most parents were pretty leery about letting their kids have much to do with anyone who was that close to Joe Dondin. Don't get mixed up with that, they said.

Thumbing through the phonebook, hastily, so that he wouldn't get back to thinking what Joe Dondin looked like now, Denzil suddenly got a picture, almost like a snapshot, right before his eyes, of the red motorbike. Lying up there in the Gorge; didn't look to be damaged at all. What would become of it? Well, sure. Marney would get it, if

Joe turned out to be the only relative there was. Wow, dog! Denzil found the number and dialed it.

The phone answered at once. Cheest, the guy must've been sitting right by it.

"Okay, Joe. What is it?"

"Look, Marney. Is that you, Marney? This is Dence Fairchild."

"Oh? What are you, drunk or something? Kind of late, isn't it?"

"No, look, Marney. Joe's had an accident."

"He has?"

"Uh-huh. He hit a rock with the motorbike."

There was a short silence. Marney said, "Is he hurt?"

"Oh, God, yeah! He's—I found him, coming home from the dance. He's up there in the Gorge covered with—" Denzil ground to a stop, confronted by the word *blood*.

"You mean he's dead?" Marney said.

"Yeah. I guess he is. He sure is."

Again, nobody said anything. Denzil waited. After what seemed to him to be a properly respectful time, he said cordially, "But look, Marne, the motorbike's not smashed, didn't look to be."

Marney said, "Okay. First things first." He hung up.

Outraged, Denzil took the receiver from his ear and stared at it. Then he hung it back on the hook with a crash.

That guy! The way he turned things hind-side-to, slapped you right in the face with them. And cold-blooded, too, skin like a walrus. News like that, and all he did was make kind of a dirty crack. Cheest, he ain't normal!

From somewhere down the highway, a siren snarled briefly and he twitched at the sound. The cops. Coming now. And what if the old man was right? What if they did blame him?

The state troopers needed no story from the likes of Denzil. What had happened to Joe was written on the highway for experts to read, and they were experts. There was the rock; there were the skid marks;

and there was Joe, even after his sudden translation, smelling very high of alcohol. They weren't even surprised. Long ago they had taken bets on how soon they'd be taking Joe to the mortuary, the bike to the junkyard. Whoever had bet on the bike, though, lost; it was only scratched. But they did take Joe to the mortuary.

Marney cradled the phone, stood for a moment leaning against the wall beside it, slowly rubbing one big, bony bare foot against the other. He was a tall boy, with long, good bones, but so thin that his pajamas looked as if they had been made for someone several sizes larger; one sleeve had been ripped out and pinned back in with safety pins. They were actually his own pajamas, brought with him when he had come downstate a year ago to live with Joe Dondin, at a time when he had been heavier by some twenty pounds. He was too thin now for his height and, also, for his looks; he was at that stage of adolescence when a boy's face is not a unit: the mouth too large, the chin too long, the forehead either too low or too high; nothing is pulled together—all seems about to fly off in different directions. Marney's thinness accentuated this look. A haircut would have helped a little. He needed one badly; a long lock of straight black hair drooped down nearly over one eye.

He stared at the telephone. He had been so sure the voice would be Joe's; at this time of night, it always was. Joe had lived his life from nightfall to daylight, like an owl or a rattlesnake. Darkness was his natural time. He'd never thought anything of hauling Marney out of bed to run errands, which might be anything from delivering what he called "a package," to fetching him down a different jacket or some money out of the box. At any time of night the phone could ring, and did.

"Hey, kid, I'm at the Feather Inn"—or wherever; it could be anywhere within a radius of thirty miles—"I need so-and-so. Hop in the Chevy and bring it down."

Tonight Marney had known a call would come sometime, because Joe had gone off and had forgotten his wallet. After he'd left, Marney had found it on the table when he'd been clearing up the supper dishes. Joe would need it. Not that being without his driver's license would ever bother him, but his money was something else again. Joe had a game going somewhere, though he hadn't said where. Marney had thought, Well, maybe if I look around downtown I can spot the motorbike, find him, and save being yanked out of bed later on.

He'd stuck the wallet in his windbreaker pocket and gone out to start the Chevy, but as he'd backed her to make the turn out of the driveway, something had let go in the engine with a racket like a washboiler full of tin cans, and she'd stopped dead with the engine running. So that was that. He'd been telling Joe all summer that something was wrong with the Chevy, but Joe hadn't bothered his head about it and he wouldn't now. So the poor old boat had had it. The clutch probably. One thing, Joe would have to do his own errands, unless he had it fixed.

Marney had been going to clean up the house—it was like a pigpen. The poker game Joe had gone out to had started here last night and had gone on until nearly daylight. Joe had won—quite a lot, Marney had gathered, hearing the talk. Ordinarily when Joe won, that was the end of the game; but last night Paul Maddocks, the town chief of police, and his deputy and boy friend, Elman Atwood, had been in the crowd and had lost. There'd been a lot of kidding, all palsy-walsy and nice, with no doubt about what was meant. So Joe had said sure, he'd give them a crack at winning it back tonight. The party had left an outsized mess in the front room that Joe had had fixed up as a game room; Marney looked around at the spittoons, overflowing ashtrays with chewed-up cigar butts, stinking glasses, beer bottles, half eaten sandwiches, and suddenly realized that if he touched anything, if he didn't get out of here and into the air, he was going to be sick. He went out and closed the door of the game room behind him.

Joe was going to be sore—he liked things cleaned up as long as he didn't have to do it himself. But a night's sleep would be worth a slamming around in the morning. No one could have slept here last night, there'd been too much noise. Anyway, if you went to bed, sooner or later you'd wake up to find Ellie Atwood fumbling around; so Marney hadn't gone to bed. Sometimes he'd been able to get some sleep by sneaking his bedding out to the valley between the gables above the porch roof; but last night it had rained.

He'd have to tell Joe he'd been sick; and the way he felt right now, that was no lie.

Meantime he was going to get cleaned up, go to bed. He'd often felt filthy in this year he'd been here at Joe's, but tonight, somehow, seemed worse than ever. Joe probably hadn't left any hot water. Even if he hadn't, there was water; there was soap. And he'd dig out some pajamas; there might be a whole pair in the bottom of the drawer.

He was so tired that he almost went to sleep in the tub in spite of the chilly bath; then, after he had got into bed, he felt as if his eyelids were stretched open with wires—as if he had a great big crack right down between his eyes.

One thing was these pajamas. Set him thinking. Gram Lessard had made them; once they had had his initial, M, embroidered by hand on the pocket. The pocket was long gone, ripped off in some hassle or other with Joe; Marney'd had to pin one sleeve on with safety pins. Most of his underclothes now had had it. Joe wouldn't shell out anything for clothes. He and Marney were near enough the same size, he said. What the hell, he had plenty of hand-me-downs, not worn out, either; so pick up some of the stuff around the house. Joe's discarded jackets and pants were often pretty nice—they looked sharp. His shirts were beautiful, but mostly of silk. They were too fancy for school. At school they were a big joke, and they were a living advertisement of his link with Joe.

In a way, he wished he hadn't put on these old pee-jays. They were too big—he'd sure lost weight; but mostly, lying here, feeling Gram's careful stitches, it seemed almost as if he could smell the clean, lined dresser drawer where his things used to live. So far he'd been able to stop himself thinking about home; but tonight he couldn't. What had started him off, he knew, was the Chevy. Losing her was like one more door slammed between now and then . . .

The Chevy had been Grampa Lessard's car; he had driven it for years, being a man who liked old, useful things, and saw no necessity for change so long as care—taking pains—could keep them so. The Chevy had always been well cared for and she ran like a watch. At twelve Marney had learned to drive her; she was as familiar to him as an old basketball shoe. First on back roads—where nobody would see them and complain about a young kid driving—with Grampa Lessard sitting straight as an arrow, his mop of silver hair standing on end, scared white in the face while Marney was learning; then, two years later, when Grampa was beginning to get blind and a little too shaky to drive himself, on the main highways. Nobody complained anyway, because Marney was big for his age, and Grampa, after all, was old Judge Lessard, who ought to know the law if anybody did, and who did know it, but winked at it just a trifle in this case. He himself had taught Marney to drive, and he knew Marney was good; he wouldn't be caught dead letting anyone else drive him. Grampa Lessard had been a good driver—there probably hadn't been a better one in the whole county of Carrington—but all his life he had been scared to death of an automobile.

The county, two hundred miles upstate, and the county seat of Carrington where Marney had lived, and Gram and Grampa Lessard had gone out of his life as if they had been washed under by flood-waters. Gram had waked up one morning to find Grampa dead on the bathroom floor; he had apparently gotten out of bed in the night and had just dropped down. She hadn't been able to stand the shock; she had keeled over alongside him. Marney found them there, with Toughy, Gram's cat, curled into the crook of Gram's arm. Terrified, he had snatched up the cat and called the doctor. Gram wasn't dead, but she might as well have been. Oh, Doc Bradford was careful telling Marney. Cerebral accident, he called it; he could have called a spade a spade. She had never come back to herself and never could; she had had too much brain damage. She was in a mental hospital upstate now;

Marney had written there, once in a while at first, always getting back the same answer. No use to write; she couldn't read or hear his letter.

That had been summer, a year ago. Ever since then there had been Joe.

You couldn't have asked for a nicer, more respectable-looking fellow than Joe the day he arrived in town for Grampa's funeral. He rode into the yard on his motorbike—the one he'd sold last summer, which wasn't a patch on the big red one he'd bought later, but still a pretty impressive machine. The first thing he did, he apologized to Mrs. Crawford, the neighbor who was staying in the house with Marney, for being so dusty and dirty. He'd driven two hundred miles in a hurry, he said, because the word that the old Judge was gone had only got to him that morning, and he'd wanted to be in time for the services. He was. He sat with Marney all through the funeral; he even cried—or if it wasn't crying, it was a darned good show.

The boy, Marney, he said, his older sister's son, he hadn't seen for years—was about eighteen months old, Joe guessed, whenever it was that his sister and brother-in-law had got drowned in that Adirondack lake. Oh, yes, Joe'd been here for the funerals then, had seen the baby they left—cute little devil he was, too. The reason Joe'd never been back all these years, his job had been in the Merchant Marine, mostly out of the country. He'd only been back a few months, getting settled down in business at home, busy, but planning to come and see the only relative he had left in the world—"and I guess that goes for you, too, eh, Marney?"—when he'd heard the old Judge was dead. You could have knocked him over with a feather.

Even then, Marney was a little puzzled. If he hadn't been so numb, so knocked out, he might have started wondering. But what he thought was, I guess I must be mistaken about what Grampa said once about Joe Dondin—"your uncle, your mother's brother . . . somewhere. No one knows where. He may not even be alive, because if he were, he'd either have shown up at your mother's and father's funeral, or sent us word. He's probably dead."

Anything to do with his parents had always been vague to Marney. They themselves were not much more now than their names. He had been too young to remember them; he only knew the story of the fatal weekend at the Adirondack camp and the overturned canoe. Grampa had still owned the camp; for a long while afterwards, he and Gram hadn't gone there. Then, as the years went by and the tragedy faded into time, and Marney got big enough to be taken places, they began taking him there; and the lake became again a quiet lake in the foothills, the camp a place where the three of them had a good time.

Well, Joe had been at the funeral.

Maybe Grampa forgot, or I misunderstood him. Anyway, Joe's here now.

Everybody thought it was so wonderful that Joe had showed up. Mrs. Crawford, the neighbors who had been helpful, and Judge Jameson, the executor of Grampa's estate, they took Joe right in—and, you could say, vice versa. He seemed so honest; he had that grin. A nice looking fellow, thirty-five or so, a neat, quiet dresser. Marney's mother's brother. A relative, responsible. The neighbors told each other, told Joe, how lucky it was for Marney, he being underage; and here was somebody who could take over.

"Well, I sure do feel a responsibility toward that boy," Joe said; and he took over.

He got the Judge to appoint him Marney's guardian; and then he started in, all legal and aboveboard, to see how Grampa's estate could be settled—"What would be best for the kid and for the sick old lady, all that jazz, Judge." If it was hard on him that Grampa's money had been left in a trust fund, he didn't show it. He nodded and told Judge Jameson that was fine; it would take care of the kid's schooling, later on. In the meantime—well, Judge Lessard must surely have arranged for Marney's living expenses; he, Joe, wasn't well off, just getting established in business—if he could have some of that, say a monthly check—? Judge Lessard had made arrangements; there was a generous monthly check—of which, in all the time he had spent with Joe, Marney had never seen a cent.

That would take care of the expense, Joe said. Great. Now, what about the house? What had he ought to do about that? He couldn't live in it himself, his business interests were all downstate, and he'd of course take the boy with him when he went. But there looked to be some nice stuff in that house that ought to be taken care of. What did Judge Jameson think—sold or something?

Well, it seemed the house couldn't be sold until the old lady died and the boy was of age.

Oh, sure, sure, anything legal the old man had wanted was okay with Joe. Still, those things were pretty valuable, some of them, it seemed to him. Since they were going to have to close the house up or rent it, what about storing everything in a safe place, for the kid later on?

The trouble was, Judge Jameson was old. He was in his eighties; a good deal of the time he was sick. Since his stroke, he fumbled a lot, and he heard about a third of what was said to him. Years ago, when Grampa's will had first been made, Judge Jameson had been a man in the prime of life. Neither of the two, as old men often do not, had realized that the other was getting on, that changes should be made. Judge Jameson had sole responsibility; he was relieved enough to hand some of it over to Joe.

Things began to vanish out of the house: the old furniture, Gram's Lowestoft, Grampa's lawbooks and stamp collection.

Marney asked Joe about the lawbooks. For while Grampa Lessard, in his lifetime, could and did talk about anything under the sun—make history and even geography sound like something out of the movies— his first love had been the law. He had talked law from morning till night, and everywhere—out riding around in the Chevy, fishing on the lake before daylight at camp, at meals—Gram sometimes accused him of talking law in bed. And Marney had been fascinated with it, from beginning to end. Of late years, it had never entered either of their heads that he would do anything but head for law school when the time came. The law library was valuable—one of the best in the country. It was now, of course, Marney's. And the man who had come and hauled everything away had been, according to the sign on his truck, an antique dealer.

Joe said, Oh, sure, sure, he was; but he was also the local representative of the Metropolitan Museum in New York, where everything was going to be kept in a vault until Marney needed them.

That, on the face of it, had been absurd. Who ever heard of the Metropolitan Museum having a "local representative" anywhere? Joe hadn't even bothered to lie very well. Or was he kidding? Marney couldn't be sure. Later on, he was to find out that this was a thing about Joe; he would tell you some yarn a fool or a child wouldn't believe, say the first thing that came into his head whether it made sense or not. He wasn't even contemptuous—it wasn't anything as strong as contempt; it was more like disregard. As if he said, "You don't amount to anything; why should I bother?"

Well, he liked Joe, trusted him. He kept telling himself he was lucky—he wasn't alone in the world; he had Joe. But seeing the house dismantled, piece by piece, the whole familiar foundation of his life being knocked down and carted away, jerked Marney, for the first time, out of his apathy of grief. He began to wonder, to question. Then came the business of the cash from the locked drawer in Grampa's desk.

The locked drawer, of course, was a farce; it was seldom locked. If Grampa did remember to lock it, half the time he'd lose the key; so the key hung on a nail driven into the side of the old roll-top desk, in plain sight of any thief. Not that anybody in that house ever considered the possibility. Grampa liked to keep cash on hand; since he'd retired, he'd been busy, had had a lot to do with his time. He couldn't bother to run to the bank, he said, whenever he needed a ten-dollar bill. He was old-fashioned; he liked to pay his bills in cash, get a receipt marked "Paid" for his money. On the Saturday closest to the first day of the month, Marney would drive him around town in the Chevy, and Grampa would take care of all the bills. He enjoyed handling the money; besides, he said, it gave him a chance to gossip with everybody and see what hell had been raised around town since he'd retired as Judge. Sometimes he would have four or five hundred dollars in that drawer. Liked to have enough on hand, he said, so that Ma could go to the desk and find the price of a standing ribroast, if she wanted to serve one.

Some days after the funeral, Marney came to enough to remember that Gram had told him to take some money out of the drawer and go buy himself some new socks.

"I've mended and mended till there's nothing but a darn to stick a needle into," she'd said. "The next thing'll be blisters, if those heels of yours aren't made of cast iron, which I suspect they must be. You go get yourself some new ones. I've chucked out the lot."

Dressing that morning, Marney realized that she must have. He hadn't a whole pair to his name. For a moment, he sat on the edge of the bed, staring dully at his bare feet and swallowing hard. So far he hadn't cried; but if that lump in his throat came up any higher, he would. He'd put back his head and howl like a wolf, if it would do any good. It seemed that he could almost hear Gram saying that about his socks, that if he were to listen just a little harder, he would be able to hear the sound of her feet, in the knitted bedroom slippers because of her sore bunion, scuffling softly on the stairs. He caught himself listening, pulled up with a jerk. It wasn't possible he'd never hear her again; that she'd never mend any more socks. Still, it was. That sound downstairs was Joe. The smell coming up the stairwell was from Joe's cigarette. Funny, a smell of smoke in the house that wasn't Grampa's pipe.

Get going. Go buy socks. It'll be something to do.

But when he went to the desk drawer, it was empty. There weren't even any slips left in it. When he or Gram had ever taken money out of the drawer, which they could whenever they'd needed some, they'd left a slip of paper, saying. Not that Grampa cared, he'd always said; he just liked to know how much he had in there.

Joe, behind Marney, said, "You looking for something?"

Marney jumped.

"Anything I can help find?" said Joe.

The voice was smooth, silk-soft.

"Oh, yeah, hi, Joe." He looked at Joe. Joe wasn't dressed in his neat dark suit this morning. He had on tight dungarees, with a tan cashmere sweater and a black leather jacket. Made him look different, somehow; not so . . . so solid.

"Some dough," Marney said. "I know there was some. Grampa used to keep it, here in the drawer. Somebody must've—"

"Uh-huh," Joe said. "Somebody did. Me. I had to." He waved a hand. "All stuff like that—cash, dough, lettuce—is part of the estate. Judge Jameson's got it."

"Oh. Well. Okay, sure. I guess I don't know . . . much about how things're supposed to work." He turned stiffly away, thinking, I'll have to have some socks. I can't go around barefooted.

Joe said, "We got to think of your gramother, you know, kid. Till the estate's settled, cash is a scarce article. Any loose dough that's around has got to go to her. Little comforts, stuff like that." And he sounded as phony as a three-dollar bill.

Perhaps it was the way he'd lowered his voice to make it sound reverent; and it didn't—it sounded oily. It sounded, Marney realized with a start, exactly like the bogus preacher who'd come into town last spring to stir up a revival, and who'd got caught good and stoned out behind Dick's Bar. He'd turned out not to be a preacher at all, only an operator from downstate trying to make a fast buck out of camp meetings. He hadn't; he'd got a jail sentence. But before they'd caught him, he'd been going around town sneaking up on girls and women, putting his hands on their shoulders and saying, in this creepy voice, "My daughter, why don't you come into the church with me?" Marney and his friend Hal Baker had practiced mimicking him; they had worked up a pretty good act, and Marney couldn't help recognizing one like it now.

What am I—nuts? he thought. This is *Joe*.

Aloud, he said. "Sure, I know. I was only going to buy socks."

"Socks, you want? Hell, just ask me." Airily, Joe pulled out his billfold, which was stuffed. Stuffed so full it wouldn't bend. It wasn't often you saw a billfold stretched out an inch and a half thick. "I was going to ask you," Joe went on, "if you'd like to come out on the bike today with me. Teach you how to ride it, if you want me to. How about that? Well, come on. We'll stop by downtown, get you some socks."

In a week's time, Joe had the house rented, cleaned out of everything valuable, and the "transactions," as he called them, turned over to Judge Jameson. So he said. Any valuables worth keeping, he said, were all now in a safe place. But the trunk and the back seat of the Chevy were packed full of stuff out of the house. Almost none of it belonged to Marney; some of his personal things he wanted to take, there wasn't room for. He mentioned this to Joe.

"Gee, kid, I thought you'd rather have these keepsakes to remember the old folks by. Thought I was doing you a favor, doing the best for all concerned." A man misjudged; a man a little hurt in his feelings. "None of this stuff amounts to much, but you don't want to leave it for those bums' kids to bust up, do you?"

By "those bums" he meant the new tenants of the house, who weren't bums at all, but decent people, the Fessendens from the other side of town. Mr. Fessenden was the manager of the woolen mill.

"Well, it's just . . . there're things I'd rather take," Marney said.

But Joe didn't appear to hear. He was all wrapped up today in his project of selling the motorcycle to a fellow down at Fred's Garage. "We won't need her," he told Marney. "We'll drive down in Grampa's old tin washboiler. I guess she'll hold together long enough to get us home. I've been going to trade in the bike, but this guy's a sucker for her. He'll do me better than a trade-in, and I'll get a new bike down home."

Up to now, Joe had always referred to Grampa as "the Judge," sometimes "the old Judge." Grampa, huh? And he hadn't any right to call the Chevy an old tin washboiler, either. It riled Marney, perhaps unaccountably, but he spoke out.

"Look, Joe. That Chevy's no washboiler. She's old, but she's been taken care of. Her engine's smooth and cool as—"

"Yeah," Joe said. He seemed about to say something more, then broke it off. "Shoot, kid, she's a swell old gal, I know it. That was just a way of speaking. You can have her when we get down home to drive back and forth to school in. I guess I told you I live kind of out back, a ways from town."

Oh, yes, Marney thought. School. Spancook High now, instead of Carrington High. Well, he could get used to that, though the way he felt now, tired as a dog all the time and without a brain in his head, wasn't going to help much. Maybe he could get Joe to let him skip school, anyway, for a while. He couldn't see that it would matter much if he did enter a little late; he was nearly through the work for junior year, anyway, because Grampa had been coaching him all summer for College Boards. When he thought of it, he dreaded school. A lot of new people. Nobody he knew. And the nearer the time came for him and Joe to pull out, the more he dreaded that, too. It seemed that once he left this town, the last brick would be yanked out of the foundation; his whole life would collapse.

But they did go. They left at night, on the day before the first of August.

"Be less traffic on Nine late at night," Joe said. "And with the old tin—with your Chevy, we aren't going to make too good time. We ought to get started by eleven. So, say goodbye."

He went upstairs to pack his grip. Marney could hear him walking around up there, going from room to room. Singing.

"Say goodbye, say goodbye," sang Joe. "Say goodbye to the old apple tree. If my Pappy had of knowed it, he'd be sorry that he growed it, for they hung him on the old apple tree!"

So sing, Marney thought. Go ahead at the top of your lungs, while you look around up there and see if you missed anything worth taking.

He stared around him. The living room, in spite of the raucous caroling from upstairs, was already a dead room, silent and dead. What had been here was gone; it was just four walls with nothing between them but a few sticks of discarded furniture. The place where Gram's cherrywood china closet with the glass front had been was a rectangle on the wallpaper. Other things, too—faded rectangles. Traces of Joe were all over the room: his ashtrays scattering butts; his cashmere sweater, hauled off wrong side out and balled up in Gram's rocking chair—the chair considered by Joe to be too dilapidated to store, sell, or whatever he had done with the rest of the stuff; but as anyone ought to know, the most comfortable place to sit in the house.

Marney picked the sweater off the chair and gave it a fling across the room. It landed on the floor, arms sprawled, in a kind of flattened-out shape of Joe. He sat down in the chair himself.

Who is he? he thought, suddenly. What is he? Why did he, after all these years, when nobody even knew if he was alive, all at once show up here? How did he know about Grampa? Well, Grampa had been a state senator in his day, and a pretty well-known judge. Joe must have seen his death in the newspapers.

Through the door Marney could see the kitchen table. The dirty dishes were still on it, even the frying pan, crusted with dried-on egg and grease, where they had had bacon and eggs, hours ago.

We can't go and leave the place like this, not with people coming into it. Better do something, get it cleaned up before we leave.

Leave? I don't want to go with him.

Toughy, Gram's cat, came through the kitchen door and jumped up into his lap. She turned around a couple of times before she curled down, with her black plumey tail over her eyes, and he realized with a sudden pang that since that morning in the bathroom, when he'd picked her up, taken her away from Gram, she'd scarcely been near him. She'd always been a smart little cat—Grampa'd always said smarter than most people. His contention had always been that if she didn't speak English, she certainly understood it. "Independent as a pig on ice," he'd said, grinning, because he liked that. "Try to pat her, if she isn't in the mood for it at the moment!"

Well, that was true, all right, as the three of them had found out, even when Toughy was a kitten. She was peppery with friends; with strangers, she was a lion. "Better not," Grampa would say briefly; he'd never been one to stress a point if it wasn't necessary. But there would always be visitors—ladies, mostly—who just had to pick up the cat, and nuts with children who thought it was cute when the kids began to maul the kitty. Toughy would take care of it. Out would come the claws—r-rip! and she would be gone, leaving someone holding out a bloody stump. She was all right, though, if you didn't mishandle her dignity; and if you let her make the advances, you couldn't ask for a more affectionate little cat.

She's thin, Marney thought, smoothing his hand down the black-satin length of her head and body. You could feel her backbone, where you never could before. And her white vest and four white paws looked ratty—kind of dingy and gray. Well, she'd been moping; and she hadn't eaten much. Times he'd seen her wandering around the rooms, sniffing at places Gram's furniture had been.

"You lonesome, too?" he said to her, and stopped short. Don't think about it now. Do something. Anything. Maybe Toughy was hungry; maybe she'd eat.

He got up, feeling as if every bone he had creaked at the movement. Oh, gosh, he was tired! What he'd like to do was go up and fall into bed, sleep for a week. Only, no bed. The last of the beds had been hauled away today. In the kitchen he poured some milk into a saucer for Toughy; she lapped it as if she were starved.

"Good girl," he told her. "Get your old belly full, because we've got a long drive coming up." Two hundred miles, Joe'd said.

Make sure she doesn't get out of the house and take off, he told himself. And better get her carrier down.

The cat-carrier was on a shelf in the pantry; it was a nice one, with a fancy cushion in the bottom, that Gram had bought at a rummage sale. He'd leave it in here on the floor, out of sight, he thought, until they were ready to go. If she sees it, I won't be able to lay a finger on her.

Toughy hated the carrier; it nearly always meant a trip to the vet. She had ridden to camp in it three times, though. She loved camp.

She hadn't drunk all her milk, he saw as he went back through the kitchen. She'd left about half of it, and she'd gone in and curled up in Gram's rocking chair.

Marney emptied the ashtrays, wiped them out with a damp paper towel; he picked up the dirty plates and cups, put them to soak in the sink. He stared at the crusted frying pan, suddenly wanting to throw up. How on earth would you ever clean a thing like that? The white enamel top of the stove was black with burned-on residues from Joe's "quickie" meals. "I ain't much of a cook," he would say, "but I sure can get a quickie."

At first, I liked him. I liked him a lot. Everybody else still does. And I guess I would, too, if it wasn't for—well, at times, that voice, like the bogus preacher's; that feeling of something, underneath, that could break out . . . he's like Wolf. He's like Hal Baker's wolf-dog, sometimes.

Hal Baker and Marney had been in grammar school the year Hal's father had brought the wolf pup home from Canada. It had been taken from a den by a trapper, who had shot the old wolves and killed four of the cubs, and then, as a whim, had saved the fifth one for a curiosity. Mr. Baker had seen the trapper mistreating it, and had bought it to save it from that; he hadn't at first thought of bringing it home—it was half-crazy with fear of anything that looked like a human being. But it had been a magnificent little animal; the Bakers loved animals, and after a while, they'd seemed to be getting somewhere with Wolf. He was beautiful; he would romp with Hal, like a dog, and eat out of a dish; he got to be affectionate, too; liked to be scratched on the belly and around the ears. And then, for no reason anyone could find out, he would have a spell of going back to wild. The Bakers might be sitting quietly in the living room, with Wolf asleep on the rug in front of the fire, when all at once he would growl, jump up and back into a corner, and the family would be confronted with a snapping, snarling, unapproachable wild animal. After a while he would calm down and be a pet again. The Bakers tried hard, but Wolf grew big and he grew fast. After Hal got bitten, Mr. Baker took Wolf to the vet. It had nearly killed Hal, because Hal had loved him.

Marney remembered Hal, crying out behind the garage.

"It was his dreams," Hal sobbed. "He must've had bad dreams about the first human he ever saw."

Marney realized suddenly that he was standing at the sink poking blindly with a fork at some dried egg on a plate, and tears were running down his face. All that had happened to him, and he had got through so far without howling; and thinking about Wolf and Hal had finally done it.

Who could I go to? Not Judge Jameson. Mr. Baker?

But the Bakers had had him and Joe to dinner the other night, and Mr. Baker and Joe had got along like a couple of old-time pals. You'd think the Bakers, of all people, would have seen that smooth, bitter, you-be-damned-I'm-what-I-am look, close under the surface; under the tameness, under the beautiful exterior, the something that in Wolf had always said, "You look out for me."

He was aware of a chuckle behind him, that Joe was standing in the doorway. He had his grip in his hand, his black leather jacket on, his bike-helmet tilted on the back of his head.

"What to hell you doing, kid? What's the idea of the K. P.?"

"I . . . didn't think we ought to leave it filthy," Marney said. He had turned quickly so that Joe wouldn't see the tears.

"Shoot, I ought to told you. Forget it, I got a woman coming in, tomorrow. Come on, let's go."

Try once more. See if he's lying again. If I can tell . . . Marney said, "Who'd you get? What woman?" Because Mrs. Crawford would be one . . . if it was Mrs. Crawford . . .

But Joe had already forgotten the question. His eyes suddenly narrowed, sharpened. He said, "Oh, some woman . . . other side of town," reached past Marney to the glass shelf over the sink, and picked up Grampa's electric razor which was still lying there in its place under the kitchen mirror. Joe began rolling up the cord around the razor. "This thing got a case anywhere?"

"Look, that's Grampa's," Marney said. He saw the knuckles of his hands whiten as his fingers clenched on the edge of the sink.

"So what? You leaving it here for someone ain't related to him? You're going to need a razor one of these days. Pretty soon, too, by the looks of it," and reaching over with his free hand, he tweaked out of Marney's chin one of the downy hairs that, lately, had insisted on growing there.

Something seemed to explode in Marney's head. He spun around, his fists doubled, ready to fight. To run. Run to Judge Jameson. To anyone. Don't go away with him. And found himself up against Joe's hand on his chest, the fingers slowly, painfully twisting his shirt front and getting some skin with it, too.

"Come a-awn. Come off it. I asked you, where's the case for this gadget?" The voice. Silky soft.

"In the c-cabinet," Marney said.

"Okay! Get your coat on, we're going to make knots." Close behind, he followed Marney out to the car.

The moon was high in the sky as they turned into Main Street. It was about ten-thirty. The second show wasn't out at the movie house; the street was lined with parked cars. For the first few minutes, Marney hadn't been able to think. Inside, something seemed to be churning; he felt hot as if he had a fever; nothing made sense. Nothing made sense at all until the Chevy stopped for the red light in front of the drugstore, and there, sleeping peacefully curled in the drugstore window, was the druggist's cat. Even then, it took a moment to realize; then the words burst out.

"Joe! I've got to go back!"

"What's matter? Forget something?" Joe had apparently cooled off, but his mind was somewhere else, because after he'd spoken, he started whistling between his teeth and stepped on the gas when the light changed. The car shot through the intersection; but the crowd at the movies had had to double-park in the narrow street—they had left barely passing space, and Joe, almost at once, had to slow down.

"Joe, listen!" He's got to listen this time, Marney told himself, and he set his jaw and leaned over and turned the ignition key. The engine cut, the Chevy rolled to a standstill.

Joe let it stop. Hands on the wheel, he moved only his head, looking at Marney.

"I said I had to go back, Joe!"

"I heard you the first time. We ain't got room for anything else in the car."

"I can carry her in my lap," Marney said. "It's only Toughy."

"The *cat*?" Joe said. He was so incredulous his voice broke a little.

"Yes, I can't leave her. She's—" He had been about to say that Toughy was all there was left.

"Okay." Joe was silent a minute, looking out and up through the car window. "I see the old Judge is still in his office," he said. "I was going to mail the rest of this stuff"—he patted his breast pocket—"but I might as well leave it. So you canter home and get the cat, hey? I'll be parked somewhere along here. It may be a ways down. And step on it, willya? I want to get going."

He changes like lightning, Marney thought, loping back along the street. I thought for a minute he was going to take a poke at me. What could you do with a guy like that? You never knew how to take him.

Glancing back, as he crossed the street, he could see the light in Judge Jameson's office. The old boy must be working late. Well, that was nothing new; he often did. Living alone the way he did, except for a housekeeper, he didn't have much to go back to his big house for. Marney had heard him tell Grampa that, more than once.

Joe sure fixed it so I couldn't sneak in to see him, even if I'd planned to. Wonder if he really had stuff to leave, or was he just being two jumps ahead of me? Because I guess I'd have tried to, if I'd seen that light before he did.

And as he looked at it, the light went out.

I could maybe catch up with him on the street . . .

But no. Joe would be around here somewhere. I'd have to yell to make the Judge hear. He might not do anything, anyway. And if I make Joe mad again, he might not let me take Toughy.

So go. Don't take a chance on that. It'll be bad, but it'd be worse without her.

He broke into a run, took the shortcut between the A & P building and the bank, and pounded up the hill.

Toughy had been left alone in the deserted house and she disapproved of it. As he went up the front steps, Marney could hear her yowling behind the closed door. He'd have to open the door carefully, because she'd be ready to take off.

Toughy was ready. She was sore at Marney, sore at the whole human race. Lock her in, indeed, when she had night plans! As he knelt to scoop her up when the first sign of irate head and glaring eyes came through the door, she went through his hands like a streak of butter. He managed to get a grip on the long, fluffy tail, but she knew the treatment for that. She gave a great spit, doubled back on herself, and raked his hand with two sets of business-like claws. Marney said, "Ow!" and slatted his hand with pain; and Toughy vanished into her inaccessible place under the front steps.

Oh, judast, now what'll I do?

If he knew Toughy, she wouldn't come out for hours; maybe not till morning. He called, "Kitty, kitty, kitty," and "Toughy, Toughy, Toughy," but for all the response he got, there was no cat under the steps. A chunk of fish might bring her out, but there wasn't any fish. There were sardines, though. Those she would take or leave; but try anything.

He tore into the house, trying not to breathe in the smell of it, which was stale food and cigarette smoke, but mostly dead house, put on the light in the kitchen, and rummaged in the supply closet. There wasn't much left, because Joe had liked things out of cans. Apparently he had liked sardines, too. There weren't any.

There was a can of salmon, though. Sometimes Toughy'd eat salmon.

He cut his hand opening the can with an old-fashioned opener. Gram's electric one was gone; he hadn't noticed that before. He got a clean white saucer out of the cupboard, dumped the whole can of salmon into it, got the cat-carrier out of the pantry, and stashed it at the top of the front steps. Then he set the dripping saucer beside Toughy's hole, retreated to the steps, and sat down to wait.

The moon was high over the town; from the hillside here, you could see almost the whole town, laid out, with quiet lights, roofs black in the moonlight. Seemed as if it ought to be changed, but everything was the same. And nothing was changed here in Grampa's front yard—the moonlight silky on the leaves of the big maples, soft on the lawn. Gram's dahlias were big as platters along the white picket fence, all color strained out of them, but lit up so that you could pick out the individual blossoms. Gram had loved those big, blowsy old dahlias; he and Grampa always had kidded her about them. "Great splots," Grampa would say, when she'd bring them into the house.

Someone would have to dig the roots when the frost came; they couldn't stay out in the winter cold. It was one heck of a job; he guessed he ought to know, it had always been his—digging the dahlia roots all around the inside of the long picket fence. Would Mrs. Fessenden know about them, what had to be done? She wouldn't know as much as Gram had, that was for sure.

I could leave a note. I guess I'd better, while I'm waiting. It's going to take Toughy a while, I can see that.

In the kitchen again—it was a good thing he'd gone back in, he'd left the light on—he found a pencil and the back of an old grocery list. He jerked his eyes away from the old-fashioned, stand-up handwriting.

> Dear Mrs. Fessenden,
> Someone ought to tell you about the dahlias. The roots have to be dug after the first frost or they freeze. There is a bin in the cellar where they go, with a cover, and if you put some layers of newspaper and the cover back on, it won't be too warm from the furnace.

There seemed to be a lot to say. You'd have to write a book to get down all of Gram's instructions.

> They have to be set out as soon as the ground is warm enough in the spring, about the—

Well, when *did* they have to be set out? He had started to write "the middle of May"; now he wasn't sure. He racked his brain. First of May? April? No use. His head might as well have been stuffed with styrofoam. He crossed out "about the" and went on:

> I hope you will want to keep them. They are good dahlias. Each root has a—

What was it they had? They were darned expensive to buy, he knew that; Grampa had always grumbled a little. What was the word?

They had to be like any other living thing; if you stopped to think of it, anything alive now, in this year, this date, this night before the first day of August, had a long . . . thing . . . a what was it? . . . going back to the seed, the amoeba, the protoplasm where everything began. Like a kite-tail behind, of all like you that had gone before, reaching back forever. People, dahlias, dogs . . . Dogs! Yes. Pedigree.

He finished:

> Each root has a long pedigree.
> Sincerely yours,
> Marney N. Lessard

He anchored the note to the kitchen table with a pepper shaker, turned out the light, and went through the living room, where a square of moonlight lay softly on the bare floor. He said under his breath, "So long, Gram. That's the best I can do," and went out, carefully closing the front door behind him.

The salmon lay by Toughy's hole, untouched, There was no sign of Toughy.

He said, "Oh, Toughy, please come," but she wouldn't, he knew that—not when you called her. She had to be the one to say. But there was no time for that now. The car turning at the bottom of the bill was certainly the Chevy; he could tell by the sound of the engine. Joe. Tired of waiting.

He stared wildly around the yard. Once you started to lose what you had, it didn't stop; it was almost as if somebody had planned it, kept piling it on, until everything was gone. He might as well light out, get clear away from here. Because if you tried to buck it, all you got was tired.

He started wearily to leave the yard; and there by the fence, rolling over and over in the catnip bed, was Toughy.

She said, "Prr-t," forgivingly as be picked her up, and nudgeled her head against his hand. He said, "You devil, Toughy! You darned little black devil!" and had her back to the steps and into the cat-carrier before she could utter the first long, outraged, and furious yowl. She didn't like anything she saw through the tough mesh of the carrier window; she especially didn't like being jounced, as she was when Marney took off and ran down the hill to meet Joe.

"Sorry I . . . kept you waiting," Marney panted. He was shifting around in the seat, getting settled, with the carrier across his knees. He had thought he might put it on the seat between him and Joe, if Joe didn't mind, if it wouldn't bother his driving, but the space had been filled up with something—a fat, black, leather briefcase, Marney saw, as the car passed under a street lamp. Gold letters on it. *Carleton J. Jameson.*

"Nh-nh, you didn't keep me waiting," Joe said.

Thank the Lord, he was still amiable.

"You know what I done?" Joe went on. "Gah, what a dope!" He gave a short chuckle, shaking his head, a man amazed at his own stupidity. "I had this briefcase with a lot of my business papers in it in the saddlebag on the bike. Clean forgot it was there. So when you forgot something, I all at once remembered I had, too. So I had to go down to Fred's Garage, root it out of the saddlebag. Didn't even get a chance to call on the old Judge. He was gone, time I got back there."

"But—" Marney began. Because here, apparently, was the Judge's briefcase, and everybody knew Fred's was closed—it wasn't an all-night garage.

"And lucky me," Joe said. "The bike was out in the parking lot, so I didn't have to go root Fred out of bed."

My-daughter-why-don't-you-come-into-the-church-with-me, Marney thought. Well, let him lie. I don't care. I've got Toughy, anyway.

"What's that crowd?" Joe said. His voice sharpened a little, and he slowed the Chevy almost to a crawl, peering along Main Street. "Oh. Movies getting out, I guess. Well, we don't want to get mixed up with that, hey?"

"Take the first left," Marney said. "Gets you out around Main Street." How many times he'd done that himself, he thought. Grampa sure had hated to get mixed up in traffic.

As they turned, he caught a glimpse of the crowd. It wasn't the movie crowd. It was a little knot of people standing by the entrance to the Lawyers' Block, and an ambulance was parked at the curb.

"Hey," he said, sitting up. "Looks like some kind of an accident, Joe."

"Sure does," Joe said. "Wonder what it could be." He took off his helmet, let it drop on the seat, on the briefcase between them. "Oh, brother! Am I glad to get started away from this burg at last. Hang onto your hat, kid. Because good old Route Nine, here we come!"

*

August first, a year ago. Joe's ramshackly old farmhouse and barn, set on a hillside up a back road, seven miles out of town . . . for reasons, as Marney was to know. Joe's business needed seclusion. It flourished at night, sometimes, all night; and his clientele made noise enough to wake the dead. Also, he had to have places in which to hide his stock in trade, which was cheap liquor, cut and cheaply sold to anyone who came along wanting a bottle. Run-down old buildings were fine; they had unsuspected ancient manure pits and unused chimneys; holes all that would take some finding, in case he got raided. Not that Joe had to worry about the local police—Chief Maddocks and Ellie Atwood were good customers of his—but now and again the state troopers might come nosing around. Another thing, a house with no paint and a leaky roof was as good a sign as any that a poor guy wasn't making any money, was just getting by.

How much Joe made, Marney neither knew nor cared. He himself saw very little of it. Joe was tight. It was hard to pry enough out of him for a haircut, say, or forty cents for the school lunch. He did himself quite well—his new motorbike was terrific and so were his clothes; he spent a mint on fancy shirts. He had hidden away in the summer kitchen of the farmhouse a complete camping outfit, expensive stuff built to fold or to telescope or to collapse so that it would fit into the saddlebags on his bike.

"If I ever have to take off fast," he would say, "I'm not a man who yearns after being nabbed in a motel."

A week or so after he'd arrived at Joe's, Marney had a letter from Hal Baker. It was full of news and excitement—The Bakers' house was being sold, they were moving to California. Hal's father had one cool business proposition in Los Angeles. Hal would let Marney know the address as soon as he got it. How was Marney? And wasn't it too bad about Judge Jameson? The poor old boy had had a stroke and had fallen the full length of the stairs leading up to his office. Kaput. Hal seemed a little hurt because Marney had gone off without saying goodbye. So write. They were leaving tomorrow.

Marney stared at the letter. He was so tired, so dispirited, that it didn't seem to matter much if the last stone of the foundation had dropped out. He supposed he had had it in mind to write to the Judge, or to the Bakers, saying what this was like, here at Joe's. So now they were gone, all of them. The poor old Judge, wonder when he—could it have been the night we left? . . . the ambulance? If it had been, it must have been right after Joe'd left him; because Joe had seen him that night, no matter what he'd said. There was that briefcase. Oh, heck, he might have got it before . . . he certainly palled around with the Judge a lot while he was there.

It was too much to figure out; Marney was too beat. After a while he wrote Hal, marking the envelope "Please Forward," and Joe, headed for town, cheerfully took it in to mail. And that was that. He didn't hear from Hal again, nor from anybody else in Carrington. So it wasn't much of a chore to let things slide along. He did what Joe said—was errand boy, chore boy, waiter at the roadhouse. When school started, he went. Not that Joe cared whether he did; Joe slept daytimes. Nights were when he could use Marney.

School was rough. He got good grades because of Grampa's coaching and his own good memory; but being kept up late nights, he felt mostly logy and sleepy in school. He could get an occasional night's sleep by sneaking away from the rumpus and taking his bedding out on the roof; with Toughy to help him keep warm, it wasn't a bad place to catch up on sleep. But the thing at school was, he couldn't make any friends. About everyone there connected him with Joe. Big joke. Some of the kids' fathers he knew quite well; they sat in regularly on Joe's poker games. But when it came to their kids' social life, they were particular. So okay, Marney didn't care.

The present unwound, day by day. He didn't look ahead. Summer wasn't so bad; he could sleep daytimes. But in a month, school would start again, the class would be beyond the work he'd covered with Grampa. So lousy grades, because there'd be no chance to study. And what sense, now, did it make to read law? Or anything else. Maybe he could get Joe to let him quit school.

Lying in bed, tonight, Marney twisted inside the pajamas, twisted and turned. The bed felt hot and itchy.

Heck, a chance to sleep, and he couldn't. Maybe go out on the roof. Cooler out there. Go downstairs first and get a drink of water.

He had been in the hall, passing the game-room door, when the telephone rang; and he'd been so sure the voice would be Joe's . . .

He's dead.

He's gone. He won't be back. Ever. He's dead.

All right. I can take off now. And I will.

Not in the Chevy, though. The Chevy's had it. But on my hands and knees, if I have to. On foot.

Footie over footie, the doggie went to Dover . . .

I'm going. I'm going tonight.

Marney straightened up, drew a long breath. For the first time in a year, he felt like himself. Able to get his breath all the way down, strong in his hands and feet and in his body muscles, and his head not a lump of mush, but with plans clicking in and out, hot and fast.

Money. Joe owes me money. He stole five hundred dollars out of Grampa's desk; he's kept the checks that came for me. So okay. I'll take what's due me. It's not stealing from him. It's mine.

He got dressed, fast, put on his windbreaker, pulled Joe's wallet out of its pocket.

Forty-two dollars and some change. There'd be more in the box.

The box was a fireproof lock-box that lived behind some loose bricks in the summer kitchen chimney. Joe had always referred to it as his "hope chest"—it held his reserve of cash. Joe kept the box locked, but Marney knew where the key was. He had to know, because Joe, off somewhere on one of his night projects, often ran out of money. He never carried much with him; he'd always said that in his business, only a fool did that. Anyway, he could always call up Marney to bring some more cash down, out of the box.

"I know you're an honest little man," he would tell Marney. "But I know what's in the box, too. So don't let me miss a nickel, huh?"

Marney found the key, in the bureau drawer in Joe's room, between a couple of his clean shirts. The shirts were beautiful; there were thirty or forty of them, mostly new, in the shimmering colors Joe'd liked. The drawer was neat as a pin. You had to wade through dirty clothes on Joe's floor: shirts just like these, worn once or twice and then ripped off, buttons and all, thrown down; soiled underwear tossed on the chairs; wrinkled-up pants on the bed—but his clean things Joe'd liked kept nice. Marney took the key and went out to the summer kitchen.

The box was heavy with Joe's winnings from the game last night. Marney set it on the rusted-out stove which had once been the cook-stove in the summer kitchen, and began to count.

Grampa's five hundred; and what I needed for clothes and school. About eight hundred altogether. And not a cent more.

It was going to take a while to count out that much money. Marney was only halfway through when he heard the siren. Coming up the hill road to the house, wide open. Would it be town or state police? He cocked his head, listening. State cops didn't blow sirens unless they had reason to; and they'd have no reason to on the hill road. Even if they were chasing someone, they generally used that old flashing blue light. So that would probably be Chief Maddocks and Ellie Atwood. And he sure knew them.

His hand shaking a little, he stuffed the money he had counted into the stove, behind the damper. He hesitated, then took another handful from the box—a guess—added that, and clapped the cover on the stove. He closed the box quickly, fumbled to lock it, hoped he had; then he put it back in the hole in the chimney and thrust in the loose bricks. He had put the key back among Joe's shirts and was back in his bedroom upstairs, sitting on the bed, by the time the police car pulled up at the door.

The siren gave a couple of gobbling noises and died flat. Heavy steps came onto the porch; the door opened and closed. Chief Maddocks, all right. He said, "Kid must've gone to bed and left the light on," and Ellie Atwood answered him. "You want I should go up and tell him, Chief?"

"Nope. Anybody tells him, I will. You take it easy with your fun and games and don't be previous, Ellie. Let's look around first. Might be something poor old Joe'd want us to have."

Toughy, who had been asleep on Marney's pillow, woke with a growl and a spit. She flounced down off the bed and over to the window, where she stood waiting to be let out.

He thought, Gosh, if I let her out now, I may not be able to find her when I get ready to leave.

But she'd better go out; she knew it as well as he did. You never knew what dopes like these would do to an animal. Toughy had had some narrow escapes in her day, here at Joe's. Now when strangers came in, she made herself scarce, but quick. Marney opened the window screen and let her out, and she vanished along the porch roof.

Downstairs he could hear movements and rustlings; drawers being opened and closed. The sounds were reminiscent. You couldn't help but remember the sound of Joe, busily going from room to room at Grampa's. He could tell these guys were in Joe's room, because it was directly under his own; the voices were coming up the hot-air register, clear and strong.

"Hey, looka the shirts the guy had! Chrissake, Paul, looka them shirts!"

"What size? Yeah, sixteen. Won't fit me. They'll fit you."

"Joe won't miss 'em, that's for sure. You think old Joe'll mind me wearing his shirts, Paul?"

"Joe? He'll rise and walk."

Marney shivered. He couldn't help but make the connection—Joe was being paid off with interest. But it was grim to listen to.

"Old Joe. Must've been really rambling. Funny he didn't smash up the bike. What did they do with that, Paul?"

"Check it, the Sarge said. Just in case something besides a rock threw Joe. Then they'll bring it back here with the rest of Joe's things. All that stuff you're into belongs to the kid now, Ellie, you know that?"

"How about that?" Ellie said. He giggled. "Well, we might as well have first dibs. He won't be in any position to enjoy it."

What did he mean by that? They must know he was somewhere in the house, might be able to hear them. They weren't lowering their voices any, so obviously they didn't care if he did hear. So what . . . ? They had authority; they could swear you into any kind of trouble, into jail if they felt like it. Marney strained to listen, leaning over the hot-air register.

More rustlings and fumblings.

"Hey, what's this key to?"

"Well, well. Good for you. That's a part of what there is. The rest of it's here somewhere. The kid'll know."

The kid knew; so would they, if the kid stayed around to see what happened.

Marney peeled a gray army blanket off his bed, wabbed it up around his pillow, and followed the same route Toughy had taken, carefully closing the window and the screen behind him.

The long, flat, zinc-covered valley between the gables of the house and barn was sheltered on two sides; anyone lying on top of it couldn't be seen from the ground. The zinc was drenched with dew this early morning, but who cared? He probably wouldn't be here long enough for the dampness to seep through—only till those two downstairs got tired of looting and left. He plunked the pillow down, rolled himself in the blanket, and stretched out. And time began, slowly, to pass.

For a while they hunted for him. He could hear them calling, muffled, "Hey, kid!" inside the house, and once Ellie came out on the front steps and yelled, "Hey, kid, come on out. We got something for you." Then apparently they settled down to a long, leisurely ransacking of the house. He could hear thumps and bumps; once in a while, one of them came out to the Chief's car; the trunk would open and close. Whatever Joe's legacy might be, he thought, there wasn't going to be a whole lot of it left, not that he cared.

Just to get away in one piece, with Toughy. Anywhere, and fast. But how go fast? Fast enough to get away from them with their police car, their radio communications?

If I could have the motorbike. If I could get my hands on that, I could sure try.

Because it changed matters to realize, as he hadn't before, that he was, of course, Joe's heir . . . that any of Joe's possessions belonged to him. He could take the bike, legally, if he only knew how to get it.

Toughy came softly up the roof and landed on the blanket like a feather. He always enjoyed seeing that leap. She wasn't a kitten anymore and you knew she weighed something—you found that out if you tried to pick her up when she didn't want you to. If she wanted you to hear her, she could sound like an elephant crossing the bedroom floor. But, times, she would leap and you couldn't even feel her when she landed.

She clawed at the blanket and he loosened it, letting her come in with him, and she settled herself, heavy as a small, warm stone against his clammy chest, with her head pushed up under his chin.

"Little old heating pad," Marney told her. "I'm sure glad to see you."

He hadn't thought, before, how cold he'd been. Scared cold, until he'd begun to get warm.

The night, here on the roof, was quiet. He hadn't an idea what time it might be, but that vague gray streak in the east must be morning coming, sometime. The moon was way low in the west, its light cold on the thick leaves of trees. The apples on a Yellow Transparent tree outside the summer kitchen door looked like small dim moons themselves . . .

Marney caught himself, shook himself awake. His fatigue was beginning to catch up with him.

Gosh, I ought to have stayed cold.

A Yellow Transparent apple had to be caught when it was just right, and picked off the tree in August, or it tasted mushy. This farm must have been a good place to live once; you could see from . . . from the things that had been done around the place . . . The people who'd lived here and had gone away had liked it. Where had they gone? Died, probably . . . when you died . . . no matter what you had, what you left . . . the thieves got in . . .

*

R-rip! went the claws, right through the thin fabric of his shirt. R-rip! Come on. Next, it'll be skin.

"Hey," he said, in a mutter. "Cut it out. Ouch!" and shook himself awake.

Oh, gosh, he'd gone to sleep after all. It was daylight; the sun was coming up, low down, clear and red; and Toughy was tramping up and down on his chest, saying unmistakably that she wanted breakfast.

"Ssh," Marney told her. "I'll have to look around first. So wait, huh?"

There was a small silence while Toughy made known that she did not wish to wait; presently her small, outraged head appeared out of the blanket. In a minute she'd start yowling.

"Okay," he whispered. "Git. But keep out of sight, will you, till I look? For the love of Pete?"

He let her go, and she vanished up the slope of the summer kitchen roof. Cautiously, keeping his head down, he inched forward to the end of the gutter, took a quick look down into the yard, and as quickly ducked back. Chief Maddocks's car was still standing outside the front door, and he himself was just getting into it.

Oh, Lord, they hadn't gone. What had they stuck around so long for? Waiting for him to come out of hiding?

"Ellie!" the Chief said loudly. "Will ya for Godsake get a move on? It's time we rolled." He started his engine.

"Coming, Chief," Ellie called gaily from inside the house. But he apparently wasn't coming fast enough, for the Chief cut his engine;

Marney heard his heavy steps going across the gravel to the house, and the front door banged. At the same time, he heard other motors—cars coming up the hill from the highway, and something else that he had heard times enough to know what it was—the humming roar of Joe's motorbike.

There was a flurry and a scurry from below; two doors of the Chief's car banged, one after the other. A window was apparently open on the driver's side, because Marney could still hear the Chief.

"Goddammit, I told ya to hurry! For chrissake, look!"

"Gah!" Ellie said. "Old Uncle Tom Cobleigh and all!"

"I hope I get my hands on that damn kid. If we coulda found him, we coulda got it out of him, not had to spend three solid hours hunting. All right, you keep your trap shut, Ellie, let me handle it now."

Coming up the gravel road that led in from the highway was quite a procession. On ahead was Joe's red motorbike, ridden by a uniformed state trooper; next, a gray state police car; and last, a small black sedan. Marney lay motionless, keeping his head down. He could see them out past the eaves of the barn; if they looked up, they might be able to see him; he wasn't sure. They didn't; they pulled past and went out of sight into the yard below. Listening to the voices, Marney made out that one of them—must be the driver of the black sedan—was a woman.

The Law in the yard was cordial. "Morning, Mrs. Lewis. Welfare Department's out early, ain't it? H'ya, Sarge. See you brought the bike back. Find anything wrong with it?"

"Nope. Where'd he keep it, you know?"

"In the barn. Ain't no garage. Ain't this one hell—excuse me, Mrs. Lewis—heck of a setup, though? Ellie and me's been all over it, looking for that kid. Seems he's gone. And you ought to take a look in the house there, see what he done to it before he left. That's one tough kid, you know it, Sarge?"

"But where could he go?" said the woman's voice.

"Dunno, darned if I do. But we'll catch up with him. He can't have got far. Boy, and when we do—"

"When you do," the woman said, "I'll have to ask you to get in touch with us, Chief. What is he—sixteen, seventeen?"

"Oh, sure, sure, Mrs. Lewis, you know we will. Ellie and I's got to pull out, right now, got business downtown at nine. But le'me tell ya, Sarge, if you see a black cat around here with white paws, you catch her up and stick her into your car. Anything that'll bring that kid outa the bushes on the run, it's something going to happen to that cat. So long, see ya."

His motor started, gravel snapped under his wheels; he drove off down the road.

"Sergeant, is he drunk?" the woman's voice said.

"Well, if he isn't he's got a funny natural smell. What do you want to do, Mrs. Lewis?"

"That about the cat—that doesn't sound like a tough boy, does it?"

"Not much, no. But this place was a peculiar setup, you know. The federal boys were all cocked back for a raid when Dondin saved them the trouble. Look, why don't you go and have some breakfast, and we'll be in touch? I'm sorry we had to roust you out so early. But with Maddocks tracking around, we thought the sooner you people took the boy, the better."

"Yes, I know. Well, I'll be in my office, if you want me."

The black sedan started up, went out of sight down the hill. Marney watched it go. One gone, he told himself, and dropped his sweat-dampened face on his arms.

Below the voices went on.

"Maddocks, that son of a bitch! Would you take me up if I bet you that the bootleg, part of it anyway, is in the trunk of his car?"

"Nope. What's holding us back?"

"Not a thing. Not if we ease down around his house and garage, just riding around, say. Come on. Won't take long. We can come back here later."

"Brother, would it make my day to nab that creep, just one time . . ."

The police car was barely out of sight, before Marney was in at the window, scrabbling up the things he needed to take.

The house was a mess. The Law, seemingly, had left no stone unturned. But they hadn't touched Joe's fancy camp kit, stashed under the floor boards in the summer kitchen, nor the packages of canned and dehydrated food to go with it. Joe had sure had everything ready, in case he needed to pull out in a hurry—even a change of clothes, folded flat and neat and wrapped in plastic, and a waterproof, lightweight sleeping bag.

Marney raced the stuff outside. He wheeled the bike up the path to the back door, bundled everything into the saddlebags. It was designed to fit in there—nylon tent in a plastic envelope; camp hatchet; knife; collapsible camp stove and fuel for it; a nest of cooking utensils—but no time to pack it decently now. It bulged, and he fastened the straps of the bags with shaking fingers.

Toughy was yowling at the front door and he let her in and fed her, feverishly slopping some milk into a saucer. She'd stay with that till he got the carrier off the top shelf in his closet, he thought, tearing up the stairs. I'll get some canned salmon out of the kitchen to take along and a container of milk . . .

"Come on, girl," he panted, forcing the small, suddenly furioud, squirming body into the carrier. She wasn't used to being hustled, certainly not before she'd finished a meal, and she said so. He left the carrier by the door as he went to gather up the last few things. Matches. A set of Joe's goggles and a helmet; one of his leather jackets; gloves. And, oh, Lord, the money.

Chief Maddocks and Ellie had finally found what they were looking for. The loose bricks from the chimney were on the floor; the cashbox was gone. They had cleaned out Joe's temporary liquor supply, which had been in the partly collapsed Dutch oven, back of the stove. They had looked in the stove, because the covers were off; but they hadn't thought of feeling behind the damper. The money was still there. He tried to shove it into his pocket, but it was too bulky a lot even for two pockets. Sweating, he thought desperately, Where, then? and unfastened the buckles of Toughy's carrier, pushing back her outraged head as she tried to break free, and dropped the fat roll in. He heard her growl and spit as it landed beside her, and the ripping sound as her claws and teeth dug in; and he thought with dismay, Oh, Lord, she always tears up paper when she's sore, like Hitler chewing the carpet; but no time now to do anything. United States currency was tough and it was a big roll; she couldn't shred all of it. To the sound of a furious yowling, he kicked the motorbike's starter and rode out of the yard—not down the gravel road into the highway, but up it, into the woods, toward the mountain.

The state police that day were busier than they had expected to be. From behind a clump of bushes near Maddocks's garage, they watched the Chief and Ellie Atwood unloading loot. Along with Joe's shirts marked with his monogram, his hunting rifles and fishing rods, were other items plainly identifiable as his property, and a carton of plainly identifiable bottles. The stolen personal goods were enough to warrant an arrest, but since the troopers hoped for more proof of Maddocks's long-suspected connection with Joe's business, they waited, taking steps. Later in the day, federal officers caught the Chief and Ellie red-handed carrying cases of bootleg out of the old manure pit under the farmhouse barn.

They found more contraband in various hiding places in the house. They also found, in a hole in the summer-kitchen chimney, a battered, black briefcase stuffed with papers, and marked *Carleton J. Jameson*. Examination of the papers showed where they belonged; they were returned to Carrington, to the executors of Judge Lessard's estate. The papers, being in part Joe's "transactions," threw no light whatever on what had happened to Judge Lessard's household goods; they did show, later, to Carrington officials, why it would have been to Joe's great advantage to have Judge Jameson out of the way. The boy would be returned to Carrington as soon as he showed up. There was no reason to suppose he wouldn't show up at all; and he was, in a way, secondary to other official business taking place at the farmhouse that day.

It was late afternoon before anyone had time to notice that the motorcycle was missing; then, when word went out over the police radio, it went in the wrong direction. Because it entered no one's head that a skinny kid would try to push a motorbike over a near-mountain. Nothing across there anyway but an old woods trail that led down to some abandoned farmstands on the other side, into a washed-out gravel road. From there, eventually, you could make it to hardtop. But the woods trail was overgrown and the grade was rugged. A strong man wouldn't try it, not pushing a motorbike.

But a skinny kid, at times, will undertake projects which a strong man would not try; and a scared kid, streaking north on a motorbike, can go a long way in a night and a day.

By midafternoon Marney was over the mountain. He rested awhile, stretched out in the shade of one of the old farmhouses where the gravel road began. He mustn't stop for long, he knew; but he had to rest—he was pooped. And he had to let Toughy out and feed her, because it was going to be a long haul. She was still good and sore at him when he opened the carrier; she flounced out and vanished behind a patch of weeds, and he thought, horrified, What if she takes off—what if I can't catch her? But she was only behind there, digging, looking for privacy; she came back quickly enough when he opened a can of salmon. He gave her half the salmon and ate the rest himself, and took a long drink of milk before he poured some out for her into the empty can. Gosh, it tasted good! It had sure been hot coming over that mountain.

While she lapped the milk, he repacked his saddlebags, rescued the roll of money from the carrier. He had to grin, seeing it; it was scattered all over the carrier-cushion. Most of it showed signs of teeth and claw-marks, but she'd apparently concentrated only on one twenty-dollar bill, which she'd done her best to shred into pieces. He stuck the roll as far down as it would go into one of the saddlebags, made sure the straps were fastened securely.

He was going to need that dough; so take no chances on anything happening to it. Because he knew now where he was headed, and it was not back to Carrington. With all that had happened to him, and what was likely to happen if Maddocks caught up with him now, he couldn't go where he was known. And even if he could, he didn't want to. The thing was, get straight away; don't be found, don't talk to anyone. Stay by yourself, the only one you can trust. Because the support goes out from under before you can grab at anything to hold on to; the safe boat, where you've been sitting in the sun, goes down without any warning, and you're in black water, fighting with the sharks.

First stop, Grampa's camp in the Adirondacks. That was far enough off the beaten track. For a while, at least.

Take off. This gravel road goes downhill; it's got to come out on hardtop somewhere. It did.

He rode the rest of the day and into the night, without stopping, except for gas, and once, in a fair-sized town, at a pet shop, to buy a harness and leash for Toughy and to let her out in a vacant lot, firmly anchored to him by the leash. Because it would be like her to lead him a chase, and he couldn't take chances now—not on the main drag of a town, with who knew what police radio reports out. Toughy fought the leash; it was the final insult, and she left clawmarks on his hands.

Sometime before daylight, he had no way of telling when, he turned off the highway into the jeep road that led in to the lake. The jeep road was eight miles long, rough going for the bike. Awful for Toughy, he thought, but he gritted his teeth and shoved on.

The rougher the better, he thought grimly, because not everybody owns a jeep. It's a long way to pack in, and Grampa's is the only cabin on the lake.

The motorbike's headlamp began picking out familiar landmarks. Even at night, the road was familiar. Marney had been coming here summers since he'd been big enough to hold a fishing rod—except last summer, of course, when Grampa hadn't been well.

So nobody's been here for two seasons, Marney thought, sighting the shine of the lake through the trees. No knowing what's happened to it.

But there was the cabin—the same small, gray-shingled roof in the moonlight, the tiny screened porch, even, on the doorstep, a rusty can that had once held fishing worms.

He got off the bike, feeling as if every bone in his body were coated with grit, each one rubbing against the other, and unstrapped Toughy's carrier. Except for the weight of it, he wouldn't have known she was in there at all. She wasn't making a sound and she hadn't been for the last few hours. He'd worried, but there hadn't been anything to do—get here as soon as he could, was all. Now, when he opened the carrier, she didn't even try to jump out. She lay there without lifting her head; she'd been sick on the cushion and Marney's heart turned over.

"Come on, old girl," he said. "Sure, it's been mean. Rough on us both. But you know this place. You've been here before."

Toughy didn't move.

Marney slid his hands under her gently and lifted her out. She sat down on the floor, not looking to right nor left. Her fur was damp and rumpled.

"Oh gosh, Toughy," he said. "Please don't be sick. Look, water's what you want, I know; I'll get some."

He found a bucket and went down to the lake for water, but when he got back, she was gone.

Oh, gosh, he thought dully. What'd I leave the door open for? A guy can't think of everything.

Well, put some food down, build a fire, get this chilly, musty smell out of the cabin. Maybe she'd come back.

Thank the Lord, Grampa'd always left a full woodbox, with a lot of kindling.

He lit a fire in the stove, which at once began to give off a vile smell of hot lard burning—Phew! Gram must've greased it plenty, but of course you had to to keep the stove and pipe from rusting. He opened the door and all the windows. Each thing he did, he had to tell himself twice to do, and then do in a kind of slow motion.

Warm some milk. Warm some milk . . .

Make some coffee. Make some coffee . . .

Because if Toughy didn't come back, he'd have to go outside and hunt, and he didn't see how he could make it, and maybe coffee'd help.

Don't sit down . . . don't sit down, or you'll pass out.

But he had to for a moment; his legs had started shaking. He put his hands on his knees to steady them.

Toughy was all there was. If anything happens to her, I'll—I'll take a header into the lake.

When the milk was warm, he set a dishful of it on the floor by the stove, with a saucer of cat food. He poured out a steaming cupful of black coffee and couldn't drink it. His throat seemed to close. The first swallow gagged him. He set the cup down, or thought he did, but he had set it on the air; it fell to the floor and smashed with a wet, spattering sound. He started for the cabin door, stumbled blindly on something, fell into the bunk, and went out like a light.

The rest of the night wore away. Stars turned west and went out. Sunrise began to come, with a trail of small cumulus clouds which went trundling up the sky like a flock of pink sheep; a clear morning, with a high, blue sky. The lake was still—not a ripple, except an occasional quiet stir along the sand beach in front of the cabin. At sunrise a light puff of wind rippled the water; out toward the middle of the lake, a big trout jumped, coming all clear with a splash that sent concentric small waves out, to wash gentle as a brush of feathers along the beach.

The breeze set the open cabin door swinging, creaking softly on its hinges, and an old black bear on his way home from his night's ramble stopped dead still at the edge of the clearing to observe this phenomenon. This was unusual: he came this way almost every morning at daylight, not for a long time had that door been open. He padded across the clearing, sniffing. Human smell, sharp and strong, but good smells, too, and he was a nosy old bear.

No sound inside the cabin. He paused at the door, went in. Something wet on the floor, funny-smelling, not good, but two dishes of edibles, there. He scooped up the cat food with one gulp, and was lowering his tongue into the saucer of milk when he was taken aback by a wild-animal growl, a vicious hissing and spitting from underneath the stove. Whatever that was—some trap set by humans in case of bears, without a doubt—exploded in his face. Two sets of sharp claws raked across his nose; the thing went straight up over his head and across his back, making sounds that no decent bear had ever heard and certainly wasn't going to stick around to listen to. He doubled his hind legs under him and made it out of the cabin in two leaps, knocking over the water bucket on the way.

The chorus of furious yowls rising to a sustained squalling, and the slamming crash of the bucket hitting the wall, awakened Marney. He opened his eyes to see something, apparently a fifty-gallon oil drum, go charging out the door. Half paralyzed with fright, he had a split second before he could move; then he rolled out of the bunk and landed on all fours on the floor. Through the open door, he saw the bear making time down the lake shore, bouncing up and down like a ball. Toughy was on the doorstep. She looked to be double her size; her tail was a club six inches thick.

He yelled in horror, "Toughy, you darn little fool! That wasn't a dog!" but she only gave him a disdainful look and began to lick back into place her disturbed fur. As he bent to touch her, she squirmed away with a small, tentative growl deep in her throat, which plainly said, "And don't *you* fool with me either!"

Marney began to laugh. He collapsed on the step and roared, letting the loud peals go, until a loon some ways offshore in the lake, doubtfully answered him and took off in disgust and a shower of waterdrops that sparkled in the sun. Fifty yards off from the beach, the big trout jumped again.

"Wow!" Marney said, gasping for breath. "Get you, brother!" and he lurched back into the cabin, still staggering, hiccupping a little. Toughy, who at the first sound of his laughter had flounced back into the cabin—she hated laughing of any kind; it wasn't one of the things about humans she understood—gave him a glare, and then glared down at her saucer of milk.

"My *milk*," the glare plainly said. "That *animal* was after my milk!"

"Well, drink the silly stuff now," Marney told her. "And then come in with me to sleep. Later on, you and I've got a date with a trout, and he'll taste better."

Marney stayed at the cabin for three weeks. As his supplies dwindled, he and Toughy lived mostly on trout from the lake, though she varied her diet with wood mice and other small creatures, on which she thrived. She plumped out; her fur grew glossy and shone in the sun. Marney, too, thrived. At first he rested—slept a good deal, swam and fished in the lake, lay on the sand in the sun. He had meant to save on supplies, but that turned out to be impossible. He was hungry as a horse all the time. Even with the canned goods Grampa had left—and he always left some, just as he always left the key in plain sight on the frame over the door, in case some ice-fisherman or one of the wardens might need shelter—it was scary how the groceries vanished. He held off as long as he could going to get more, but the time came when he had to.

Toward the middle of the third week, he left Toughy at the cabin and went, not to the small village where he and Grampa had always bought their camp groceries, and where the storekeeper would surely remember him, but to a good-sized town twenty miles to the north. He shopped there in the anonymity of the biggest supermarket in town. As he had known he would be, he was sharply limited by what the motorbike would carry. Every so often, he realized, he was going to have to make a trip to town.

Not that he hadn't enjoyed it . . . or would have, if he hadn't felt so nervous—as if he ought to keep looking behind him to see if anybody was moving in his direction. But talking to people—it seemed so long since he'd spoken out loud to anyone but Toughy. He'd talked so much to the girl who was checking out his order at the supermarket, that once or twice she'd given him a curious look, as if he were some kind of a kook.

Riding home he thought, I'll sure have to watch that.

Up to now he had been living from day to day, hadn't looked very far ahead. Pretty soon he would have to decide whether to stay in the cabin through the winter. For one thing, the cabin was shelter; for another, where else was there to go? Toughy couldn't stand riding in the carrier on the back of the bike. A few hours had been as much as she could take, that was for sure. But thinking about winter on the lake made him shiver. It would be cold. And lonesome.

But not so cold and lonesome as being boarded out as a state ward, with strangers; or having somebody like Chief Maddocks catch up with you.

It might not be so bad, boarding with strangers, if you could be on your own, walk out when you felt like it. There must be people like Gram and Grampa somewhere. There had been in Carrington, or so they had seemed to be. But how would they be if you didn't have anybody, any place to go to of your own? If I went back there, who would I go to? Judge Jameson's dead; Hal Baker's people are in California. Fred, down at the garage, might give me a job. But who knew what lies Maddocks might have told? If the police were really after him, Marney decided that there was nobody he dared to trust in Carrington.

To stay in the cabin all winter would mean a lot of planning. Supplies. Kerosene for lamps, alone—how many trips to town? Firewood—how much? He'd have to cut a ton of it. He shivered again, thinking of the cabin at night, half buried in snow, the frozen lake. But okay. Get home. Make a list. Get cracking.

Meantime, first things first. Stop at a service station, gas up the bike, tighten up the lashings on the big carton of groceries on the carrier rack. For the last few miles, something back there had been flapping. It was a lousy way to have to carry a load like that, spoiled the balance of the bike.

He pulled in at the first station he saw. The attendant filled up his tank, stood watching while Marney fiddled with the lashings, trying to pull them tighter. But the carton itself was the trouble; its sides had buckled, slackening the ropes.

"That's a jackass rig, son," the man said. "You got far to go?"

Marney said yes, but he was taking it easy on the road.

"You'd better. Where you from—you don't live around here, do you?"

"No," Marney said. "I'm camping out, in on Settler's Lake." There he went, running off at the mouth again. He hadn't meant to mention the name of the lake. It had slipped out. And you'd never had the habit in your life of snubbing a pleasant guy who wasn't being nosy, only interested.

"Brother, you got enough stuff there for an army. You're going to carry loads like that, you need a sidecar. Wouldn't want to buy one, would you? I got a secondhand one I'd let go cheap."

Marney stared at him. A sidecar! Would that be the thing! Carry all the loads I'd need to; make a decent riding place in it for Toughy, if I decided to pull out anytime.

"I sure would," he said. "Take a look at it, anyway."

"Well, come on around back," the attendant said, leading the way. " 'Course, it's used. Been beat up some. Belongs to my kid, left for a summer job, upstate. Sold his bike and got him a car. Said sell the sidecar if I could."

The sidecar was in the parking lot behind the station, under a tarpaulin. It had been used, all right; its paint was scaled in spots; it had dents and scratches and its upholstered seat had seen better days. But it had a good windscreen and a practically new waterproof shield that fastened with toggles over the entire top. Its rubber looked all right, too.

"How much?" Marney said.

He pulled a roll of bills out of his pocket and paid without a word when the man named his price. And suddenly realized that he was stared at with a good deal of interest.

The money, he thought, and shoved the remainder of the roll quickly back into his pocket.

The garageman didn't say anything, though; he went to work busily and hooked up the sidecar to the bike. By the time the job was finished, Marney had the groceries transferred and the toggles refastened on the waterproof cover.

"This is one slick rig, you know it?" he said nervously, and when the man didn't answer, he went on, "Looks as though it'd be nice to ride in, too."

"Well," the garageman said, "that's what it's for, I guess, son." He stood up, thoughtfully shoved his wrench into his pocket. "Where'd you say you were camping? Settler's Lake, wasn't it?"

"I did?" Marney said. "No, I don't think that's the name of the place. I, uh, I'm not very well acquainted around here. Spruce Lake, I guess it is."

He straddled the bike, started the motor.

"Hey, hold on! You want some kind of a receipt, don't you?"

"I'll be coming by again in a day or so," Marney yelled over the sound of the motor. "Thanks a lot. See ya." He waved a hand and rode out of the yard.

The garageman stood looking after him.

Spruce Lake, huh? he thought. Well, if he's at Spruce Lake, he's sure headed in the wrong direction. That's to hellangone up in the mountains, and, anyway, it's backpack country.

You saw some real characters on motorbikes nowadays, raising hell up and down the highway. This one seemed like a nice-enough kid, but you never knew. That had been quite a wad for a kid on his own to have flashing around. Well, let's see if he comes back, like he said he would.

When in a couple of days Marney hadn't shown up again, the garageman telephoned a friend of his who happened to be a warden in the Forest Service. "Thought you'd like to know, Bill," he said. "You check that cabin in on Settler's Lake once in a while, don't you?"

"Not lately," the warden said. "But I will, right away. Thanks a lot. Probably just some camper, though."

Marney had spent the last two days closing up the cabin, packing for the road. Having the sidecar had helped him make up his mind to go, for the worst problem had been Toughy. Now he had the sidecar padded with blankets. It took him quite a while to figure out how to arrange for a circulation of air under the toggled cover. There had to be two air holes, or it would get hot enough to fry in there; but Toughy, of course, wouldn't be able to stand a constant draught. He finally solved the problem with the breadboard out of the cabin, fitting it in so that it partially covered the foot compartment of the sidecar, making a snug hole that could be crawled into; then he cut air holes in the cover, front and back, and stitched in two rectangles of old window screen.

He was proud of the outfit when it was finished. Toughy enjoyed holes of any kind; she'd always been delighted to find a hole in the ground, would stick around, in and out of it, for hours. She was nosy about this one, he was pleased to see. He let her find it by herself, and she vanished into the foot compartment and stayed quite a while. The padded bed in the bottom was nice and soft; apparently she liked it.

Cutting up that old breadboard had been a wrench. All the time he'd been working on it, it had reminded him of Gram . . . how she'd always insisted on bringing housekeeping stuff to camp, and how he and Grampa had always objected.

"Look, it's a *camp*," Grampa would say. "What do you want to do—put up curtains?"

"Yes, I do. And I'm going to. Now, look. You boys bring your tools here, why shouldn't I bring mine?" And she had put up curtains—nice, cool green ones that could be drawn to shut out the hot summer sun. She spent a lot of time in that cabin, she said, while they were out fishing or hiking—did they expect her to fry?

Good, peppery old Gram. A long way from here now. The hospital where she was, was over in the eastern part of the state, near the Vermont border. In answer to one of Marney's letters asking, some doctor had written that it was no use to come. "I'm sorry, but she wouldn't know you now, and you probably wouldn't know her. Best not to." Not that Marney had ever seen how, at Joe's, he could go there. But he could now.

He stared at the sawed-off pieces of the breadboard, lying on the ground by the sidecar. Silky, old wood, scrubbed many times; still with a good smell to it, faint, like an echo, a ghost of bread. Would the police have left word at the hospital, in case he went there?

No matter if they had, he told himself. Being sent to strangers, even to jail, couldn't be any worse than this—this lonesomeness.

He felt his eyelids starting to sting and pulled himself up with a jerk. He was ready to go. The bike was loaded; the cabin was cleaned up and closed; all he had to do now was lock the door. Wait for Toughy to come out of the woods, wherever she was; wait for darkness. Take off. Travel by night, until he was out of the state—it would be simpler.

He had gone a good deal of trouble to wipe out his tracks and traces around the cabin; no need to leave a trail pointing in any direction, in case someone thought to look for him there. He had done a pretty good job, he thought—not everything, of course; there were numberless footprints down on the sand beach and marks from the motorbike's tires on the jeep road. But the first good rain would take care of all that, and anyway, the tracks might belong to any fisherman who'd happened by. The cabin looked deserted again, even the curtains were pulled shut and Grampa's old boat was back under the screen porch, without a sign, so far as he could tell, of having been used and then put back again.

He had planned to build a small fire down on the beach and heat up a can of beans before he left, save unpacking stuff from the saddlebags or messing up the cabin again. He was gathering up some odds and ends of kindling from the woodpile when he heard, faint and far off, but unmistakable, the sound of a motor. He dropped the wood and froze, listening. Yes, it was; it sure was. A jeep or something, coming down from the highway.

Marney's heart began to pound; he stared wildly around.

What showed? The bike, of course. Well, he could fix that. The place where he always hid her when he was away from the cabin, wood-cutting or fishing, was behind the outhouse in a clump of bushes.

He had chosen the place because the ground was hard out there—he could slide her in without leaving a trail. Early on he had cut the middle out of the clump, and he had two small, thick-branched fir trees that he could wedge into the opening, making them look as if they had grown there. It was quick and simple, hiding the bike.

Panting, he came pounding back to the cabin. Looked deserted, all right. No! There on the porch rail were his damp sneakers set in the sun to dry; his shorts were hung on a string between two posts. He scooped up the sneakers, yanked down the shorts, string and all, and ran around the cabin. Nothing there. But Toughy—where was she? Nowhere, as usual. Well, maybe she'd have the sense to stay out of sight. At Joe's she'd learned a lot about the ways of strangers, sometimes, with cats. He lunged into a thick growth of bushes and lay flat on the ground. Just in time.

Through the trees he watched the jeep jolting along the road. It was one of the wardens—he could make out the Forest Service insignia painted on the jeep. This could be somebody who would know him, too. He and Grampa had been acquainted with some of the wardens. One of the things the wardens did was keep an eye on the lake cabins when no one was there. Could be this one was just checking. As the jeep halted by the porch, Marney tried to still the sound of his ragged breathing.

The warden got out and looked around. He wasn't anyone Marney knew; but he was checking, all right. He went up on the porch, tried the door, reached up to the top of the frame for the key, unlocked the door, and glanced inside. Then he locked up again, put the key back, and tried the windows.

Locked, thank the Lord I remembered, Marney thought. And he sure didn't see anything inside to make him wonder, either.

The warden came down the steps, walked around to the back of the cabin. As he disappeared from view, Toughy leaped up to the porch rail, sat down, and began washing.

"Oh, brother!" Marney breathed. "Oh, dammit! Toughy, get out of sight, can't you?"

She could have, but she didn't.

If he sees her—maybe he won't see her.

He did, though. He came strolling around the corner, glanced up, and saw her sitting, not two feet from his face.

He said, "Well, hi, sister. What are you doing here? You belong to someone?" And he put out his hand and scratched her on the head. And Toughy let him. She even showed she liked it. She nudged her head against his hand.

"Folks gone off and left you?" the warden said. "The dirty dogs. Well, you can't stay here alone all winter. You'll have to come along with me. I expect I can find a place for a nice cat like you." Then he made the mistake of trying to pick her up.

Toughy let him have it, claws of both front feet along the back of his hand. She went up over his shoulder, arched in a long leap to the ground, and vanished in the bushes.

The warden said, "Ouch!" and "Goddammit to hell!" He slatted his hand, pulled out a handkerchief, and sopped at the scratches, staring at the bushes with the put-out air of a man who had got something he didn't deserve. Then he shrugged a little and grinned.

"Okay, old lady," he said. "It's your nickel."

You bet it is, Marney told him silently. Now if she only had the sense to stay out of sight, not come plaguing around. Because the wardens always took care of pets that had strayed or sometimes were abandoned at lakeside cabins. Dogs or cats gone too wild to be caught had to be shot to protect wildlife.

If he starts to, Marney thought desperately, I'll have to show . . . stop him.

But the warden was through with the cabin—at least, for now. He glanced under the porch at the boat, went down on the sand beach, examined the footprints. Apparently he knew someone had been around there not long ago, but from what he'd said to Toughy, he thought that whoever it had been had gone. Presently he came back, leisurely whistling to himself, climbed into the jeep, and drove away.

Marney waited until the sound of the engine died away up the road to the highway. The guy was gone; he'd be back sooner or later to pick up Toughy.

So now I have to go. Not tonight. Now.

So where are you, as if I didn't know. Out of sight for hours, if I know you.

But when he went to get the bike out of the bushes, Toughy followed along behind him, rubbing against his ankle.

He glanced back once at the cabin, at the small, gray, weathered roof, as he rode away between the trees. It was just about the last link with home; he guessed if he never saw it again, he'd remember it for a long time.

Part Two: Liz

The three little girls walked single-file along the river road. The two smaller ones, who were about five and eight years old, were dressed to the nines in brightly colored big-and-little-sister dirndls; they had identical frilly blouses, hair-dos, and sandals. They walked in scowling silence, holding their flaring skirts away from the bushes and mincing with their feet, because the bushes were dusty and the river road, in places, muddy. The third child, in jeans and a not-too-fresh T-shirt, paced along a few steps behind. She was a skinny little girl, like a hard slat, who might have been eleven, no older, with a suntanned, pointed face and a tangled mop of fox-red hair. Whistling, she had both hands thrust as far as they would go into the pockets of her jeans, and a competent air of herding the other two along.

The eight-year-old skidded, barely saved herself from sitting flat in a patch of mud, and cast over her shoulder a glare of fury.

"You just wait, Miss Liz!" she said.

"Yah, wait for what?"

"You just wait till I tell my mother, that's all. I'm going to, the minute Melia and I get home from the party."

"Why wait? Call her up over old Bowker's phone. Maybe she'll come after you and I won't have to babysit you home."

"She'll give it to you! Making us spoil our dresses."

"I'm not the one got your sandals muddy!"

"You made us come this way. We didn't want to come by this ole mudhole."

The little one chimed in. "You made us. You're not a good babysitter at all. You don't care."

"You're so right," the redhead said. "I didn't ask to come babysit you. I was hauled there."

"Yes, and the lady said to our mother you were a good babysitter. She told a fat lie."

"Yup. She did. I'm a lousy babysitter."

The eight-year-old spun around, her eyes glazed with tears and fury. "My mother told you to walk us right down the sidewalk to Miz Bowker's front driveway," she stated. "And you didn't. And we're going to be awful late for the party."

"Oh, shad ap, Polly! It's your own fault. I told you to hop it or you'd miss old Bowker's ice cream and kisses. I don't care if you do. It's nicer down here than it is up on that old hot sidewalk."

It was, as anyone with half an eye could see; it was a great deal nicer than most places. The river ran soft and silky, with small ripple sounds near the shore; the New Hampshire sky was blue as a forget-me-not, and clear except for some big, puffy clouds drifting lazily over from the west. The only trouble was, it was hot; it was a very hot day, even for late September. The big hardwood trees, spaced along, offered an occasional patch of shade, but their leaves hung motionless and dusty. There wasn't a sign of a breeze. The little girls' faces were red and sweaty and the crisp skirts of the dirndls were wilting by the minute.

"You're nothing but an old popper," Polly said nastily. "You didn't even get ast to the party."

"Who wants to go to a runny-nosed kids' party?" Liz said. Whistling softly, she moved to one side, broke from a bush a long slender switch. "I may be a rotten babysitter," she said. "But I keep the babies in line. You can put that in your little pink pipe and smoke it. This is a stink-stick. They hurt worse'n any other kind. So you take back that crack about the pauper."

The smallest child, Amelia, burst into loud howls. She scurried up the road to be at Polly's elbow. The procession moved faster, with less caution.

"You see that path, there by the tree?" Liz said. "It goes right up to old Bowker's back door. So hop it!"

Polly said in a shaky voice, "You're supposed to take us there. You know you are."

"Can't you follow a path, for gleep sake? Big kid like you?"

"What if we get lost?"

Amelia's howls redoubled. "I'm scared. I don't want to be lost. It's going to thunder'n lightning."

"Well, if it is, you better run. Go *wawn!*"

She herded them up the path on the run. If the stink-stick snapped just a little too close to a bare ankle now and then, it wasn't any more than anyone had coming. These two kids were poison. Smarmy little liars and tattletales. You did what they wanted, or they told some fib that got you into trouble. Liz had tried in the beginning, but now she was fed up and bored. She'd seen real trouble in her day; and real trouble was something more than a bawling out from these two Boardman kids' mother, or a couple of snaps from Cousin Emily's thimble. So now, let 'em tattle. What she'd come down the river road way for wasn't to spite them anyway. She had a project of her own, to be attended to while they were at the party. She was going to see if the Bowkers' new houseboat was still tied up at their dock. They had a private dock here on the riverfront at the edge of their property; a week ago, the houseboat had been delivered and tied up there. Last Saturday, when Liz had for once got out of a babysitting job, she'd gone rambling. She had got away before Cousin Emily had been able to think up something else. Cousin Emily was always going on about Liz getting jobs to help pay her board and room—"Seeing," she would say, "that I've been kind enough to give you a home."

The two kids now were howling at the top of their lungs. It did Liz good to hear. But suddenly, around a bend in the path, a tall man stepped. He grabbed Liz by the arm and the switch out of her hand. The kids had stopped bawling at the sight of him; then they grabbed him around and tuned up again, twice as loud.

"She hit us, Daddy! She chased us! She got our dresses all muddy!"

"Where in thunder have you been with my kids?"

Mr. Boardman was boiling mad. He was yelling.

"Mrs. Bowker called up my wife, and she had to call me at the store, and with this storm coming, we've been half out of our minds! Come on, answer me! Where've you been?"

Liz said nothing. She twisted as hard as she could, but she couldn't break away. It might be just possible, if she waited a minute, to bite him in the hand.

"She made us go way down the river road, Daddy. She made us when we didn't want to," Polly sobbed. Amelia cut off in mid-yell, spread out the skirts of her dirndl. "Oh, Daddy, look at my pretty dress!" and began weeping again, this time prettily and pathetically, poor-pitiful-Pearl.

"You kids hustle up to the house, tell Mrs. Bowker to call your mother, say you're all right," he said, between his teeth. "I'll tend to this little—" He spun Liz front to back, gave her a good switching with the stink-stick. "There! Now, blast it, you beat it, and don't you ever show up near my house or kids again, you hear me—Ouch!"

Liz had done it. He had loosened his hold just enough. She had reached his hand and she had bitten it as hard as she could. He snatched the hand away. She went plunging out of sight into the undergrowth.

Safely out of sight and on the way to her project, Liz stopped to tuck in the tail of her T-shirt.

Brought the blood, she told herself with venom. If that old pot thought that was a licking, he ought to've seen some of the ones she used to get from Sarah Bigelow.

Sarah Bigelow was the woman Liz once had lived with, in New York City. Up until the day the gas oven blew up in the coldwater walk-up on Sullivan Street, Liz had always thought Sarah was her mother. Liz had sneaked out on school that day to go swimming off the East River docks with Charley Riccio. Charley had taught her to swim, and she was good; now he was teaching her swimming tricks, like fancy diving and stuff. He said if they both got good enough, they'd run away and get a job in a carnival. She'd been gone all day, and when she got home she'd thought the social worker waiting in the flat must be somebody—the truant officer, maybe—from the school. But the social worker took her to the hospital. And there was Sarah, though all you could see of her was her head, bandaged all over, with only a black hole for her voice to come through. The voice was hers—that was all the way you could tell.

"Is it Liz?" she said. "Well, look, Liz, I don't know how this is coming out, and I couldn't care less, if it wasn't for you. All I can think of is having peace and quiet, and if there's more of that coming up than I bargained for when I turned on that oven, I guess it's all right with me. You'll have to take it from here; maybe it's a good thing you do have to. I haven't done much for you. But even if you'd been my own kid, I wouldn't have, I guess."

Sarah lay in a high hospital bed, with metal slats along its sides. Like a baby's crib, Liz thought. But what for? She's grown up and she's not going anywhere; she's too burned.

The crib thing made it hard to see Sarah without standing on tiptoe; so Liz would bob up for a while and stand on tiptoe; but the sharp metal slat at the top hurt her chin, and she would have to bob down again. But when she bobbed down, Sarah couldn't hear her. She would say, "Liz? Are you there? Can you hear what I say?"

Well, if she wasn't Sarah's kid, whose kid was she? Maybe that's why she's never liked me much, Liz thought.

"You belonged . . . to . . . a friend of mine . . . I said I'd look after you . . . when she died," Sarah said. Her voice wasn't so loud now. She spoke with long pauses between the words. It was hard to hear.

"Liz . . . ? Tell Cousin Emily . . . you . . . belong . . . to me. She'll . . . take you in. Tell her . . . I'm sorry. I can't send . . . her any money . . ."

So who was Cousin Emily?

But the nurse had the address; and the social worker came and took Liz away. And that had been the last of Sarah Bigelow.

Well, her own mother was dead, Liz thought. She might as well cry for Sarah Bigelow. But it was hard to. Liz finally managed to work up a good crying spell by being sorry for the poor bandaged head, even though the hollow feeling at being left entirely on her own seemed so much worse. Sarah wasn't a great loss; it was no use telling yourself she was. She hadn't stayed home much, and when she had, it was usually because she'd been too drunk to go out on the street. Liz had been used to taking care of herself, scrounging her own meals. She hadn't spent much time at home either.

Cousin Emily was infinitely better than Sarah; she had a small house of her own and she kept it clean and served meals on time. You had to be there when the meals were ready or you didn't get any; and you had to take baths and do homework and talk nice. The relationship that Liz had established with Sarah's cousin, in the year and a half she'd lived with her, wasn't unbearable, but it was pull-devil-pull-baker—which were Cousin Emily's words for it. Cousin Emily was always arranging jobs for Liz around among the neighbors, for pay, and then taking the pay. She was a retired schoolteacher, living on a teacher's pension, which, she said, didn't allow for extras. Since babysitting was the job there was most of, she couldn't help it, she said, if that was the job Liz hated most. Extra money was extra money.

In Liz's judgment now, and going by what she had seen of people, there were two kinds. One kind was like Charley Riccio, in whom you could trust and believe, and whom you'd never see again; and the others were *Them*. One of *Them*, Liz would tell herself, gazing, deadpan, at somebody or other's face. She had to say that early on about Cousin Emily. Taking the money for the babysitting; all of it; she could have let you keep at least a quarter. Saying, every once in a while, that you ought to be grateful for such a nice home and glad to help earn your own living, "when I've been good enough to take you in." One of *Them* didn't deserve and didn't get out of Liz any more than Liz could help giving. She led Cousin Emily a chase, and she sneaked out on babysitting when she could.

Last Saturday, on the loose down by the river, Liz had spotted the Bowkers' new houseboat coming up. She had watched it from the shore, saying to herself, "Oh, lovely, lovely, I wish you were only mine!" and was enchanted to see it being tied up at the Bowkers' dock. When Mr. Bowker and his two boys and their chauffeur had gone away from it, Liz couldn't help herself—she'd sneaked out on the dock and gone aboard. She'd tried the locked cabin door; and then, wandering around the deck, she'd found, to her pleased surprise, an unlocked window, a way to get in. There were all kinds of fascinating things in that cabin: lockers full of bedding done up in cellophane; drawers full of clothes; a tiny kitchen with a stove and pots and pans;

and cupboards full of a million things to eat. If she'd only had a can opener! Lobster and crabmeat in cans, and mayonnaise; of all things, a canned plum pudding. All she could do, last Saturday, had been to drool, but today, among the treasures she carried in the hip pocket of her jeans was, just in case, a can opener.

The houseboat was even more wonderful than she remembered. She walked twice all the way around the deck. The deck was canvas-covered, painted slate-gray, beautiful and clean; the cabin was white, with dark, glossy woodwork around its rows of windows. At the back was a kind of sundeck place, with an awning which would roll back to let in sun, and canvas curtains to close on rainy days. The curtains were now closed, but it was easy to unbutton one and slide in. Why, it made a little room in there, full of gold light where the sun shone on the canvas. A little gold room! Wasn't it cunning!

Oh, if you only had this for yours! If only you had Charley Riccio here, what you could do! You could go around the world in it.

The cunning little room was very hot. Sun shining on the canvas had made it enough to boil you in there, but the big, fluffy clouds coming up in the sky would be over the sun in a little while, she hoped, and then it would cool off in here. She was about to slide out through the unbuttoned curtain, when she heard voices. On the dock. She peered out through the slit in the curtain.

The two Bowker boys. She knew *Them*. One was her own age, eleven, the other sixteen. They went to a private school somewhere, but were always home on weekends. You saw them around the town; you didn't speak to them, ever, because you didn't like the snotty old Bowkers, even if they did speak to you. Liz watched malevolently out through the slit in the curtain.

They didn't seem to be coming aboard the boat. What they were doing, they were tightening up the ropes that held the boat to the dock. The big one, the sixteen-year-old, was tying on some extra ones. He was bossy. Bossing the little boy. One of *Them*. They didn't stay long, only until the ropes were fixed; then they ran off the dock and out of sight where the path to the house went into the trees.

Well, good! Now she wouldn't have to bother about them.

But when she tried the cabin window which had been unlocked last week, she found it wouldn't open. Through the glass she could see that the catch was fastened. So were the catches on all the other windows. She tried every one.

If that wasn't just like the rotten old Bowkers!

She stood for a moment, scowling. It was only glass. It would break. Charley Riccio could always get into places by breaking a window. He'd said don't make any noise, though, someone'll hear it. She made a couple of stabs with the point of her can opener, but all it did was squeak and slide sideways on the glass. Well, how did you break a window without making any noise? If only this houseboat were out in the middle of the river, you could make all the noise you wanted to without anybody hearing.

So why couldn't it be? All she needed to do was untie the ropes and the houseboat would go. It wanted to, anyway, she could see it tugging.

The ropes the Bowker boy had put on were easy. She undid them, one by one, dropped them into the water. But the bow and stern lines were fixed in metal loops around posts sticking out of the deck; she couldn't budge them. They must untie from the other end. She would have to go onto the dock. The boys had done it, tightening them. What you did, you unwound them crisscross from the big pieces of wood nailed to the dock. It was easy.

When she cast off the bowline, it pulled right through her fingers. The boat surely did want to go—she swung around until she pointed downriver and Liz could see the name *Sea Flower* painted in black letters on her stern.

Wasn't that *pretty*? Just the right name, too.

The second line, pulled taut by the river current, was harder to undo. The tide must be going out, too, because the boat wanted so bad to go downriver. They always told you never to go swimming when the tide was going out, because it made the river run twice as fast. Cousin Emily had made a great yak about that. Nobody could swim against the current—you'd be carried down to the river mouth and right out to sea. Liz had never bothered about it; compared to the East River, this little old one wasn't much. She'd gone swimming all summer, whenever she felt like it. Not that Cousin Emily knew it.

The second rope came undone with a snap and started to pull through her fingers. She saw she was going to have to run and jump to get aboard at all, the gap between the dock and the houseboat was widening fast. She dropped the rope and took off with a long running jump; for a moment she thought she was surely going to land in the river. Her feet did; but she got her hands clawed firmly into the rail, scrabbled, feeling the water trying to pull, too, and climbed aboard.

So there!

The houseboat spun around a couple of times and started sideways down the river.

Now that she was out from under the trees that grew on the riverbank, Liz could see the sky low down in the west. Gleeps, it was yellowy-green and purple, just the color of a black eye!

Marney, heading south, had been watching the storm build up all afternoon. He had thought at first of locating a motel somewhere and holing up for the night early. Sleep in a bed for a change, have a roof over his head in case it rained, as it surely was going to before long. So far, he'd been lucky about weather—a couple of chilly nights and rain only once; the rest had been clear and warm—simple, camping out in weather like that. That one rainy night, though, had cured him of trying to beat wet weather, and Toughy hadn't liked it at all. So he figured, for tonight, a motel. Somewhere off the main drag, in a small town, just in case. But as the afternoon had worn on, and the low-lying bank of dark clouds hadn't seemed to move very fast, he'd kept on going. The weather system, apparently, was a slow-moving one. Why hole up in a motel with nothing to do, until you had to?

Since he had left the lake cabin, he had put a good many miles behind him. The night he'd stopped at the hospital near the Vermont border where Gram had been and had found she was no longer there—that she was with Grampa, now, in the cemetery at Carrington—he'd taken off blindly and ridden, in what direction he didn't even know, until sometime before dawn Toughy's yowling to be let out had brought him to himself. He had stopped then, and had made camp in a grove of trees near the road; but he hadn't been able to sleep any. The hope that he might find Gram better had taken quite a while to die; he supposed he'd had in his mind the kooky idea that if she didn't recognize him, she might anyway know Toughy. Brother! Once disaster drew a bead on you, looked like it never stopped shooting,

At daylight a farmer chased him out of the grove of trees, and he'd gone on again, and had found out he'd ridden to the Canadian border. After a while he'd found a job as a short-order cook in a small restaurant up there and kept it for three days until the boss, raving, found someone who was a short-order cook. Marney didn't in the least blame the man for firing him. He'd turned out to be a lousy cook. Besides, he'd had to leave Toughy in his room all day, and the landlady'd objected. She couldn't have a cat left in the room "messing," was the way she put it. The minute Marney'd left for work, she'd chased Toughy out. Toughy wouldn't be there when he'd get home; one night she'd been gone till morning, and she'd apparently been in a fight. One ear was torn; her fur was wet and dirty, as if she'd been rolled over somewhere in the mud.

That day he'd left her in her bed in the sidecar. She'd got to like the rig in the sidecar pretty well; she had room to move around and a bed out of the wind; she even seemed to enjoy riding. He'd taken the bike to the restaurant and had parked it around back in the shade, so that when he had a minute he could go out, make sure she was okay. But she'd had a night on the town—she slept all day; and that had been the day, anyway, that the man had fired him.

After that he'd taken a highway east for a while, and then turned south, not heading anywhere, not hurrying. He had learned a lot, by now, about riding a motorbike and about camping out. You didn't ride all day without a break, unless you wanted a stiff back; you got off once in a while and walked around some. As for camping, you used public campgrounds; if you couldn't find one handy, you pulled well off the road into the thickest cover you could find and screened the flame from your camp stove. Or you'd get chased off someone's property in a hurry.

He had come quite far south into—well, it must be New Hampshire now. The towns were getting bigger. He'd followed this river for a long way, down the west side, and finally had turned off the main highway on to what looked to be a new hardtop road, looking for a motel. But the new road went down to the riverbank and kept on following it, south, down into a summer colony kind of place—cottages on the river front, all with some kind of a boat dock. And no motels. And the thunderstorm, having dithered around in the west all afternoon, had finally made up its mind to move. The clouds were now nearly halfway up the sky; down on the horizon they were a vicious purply yellowgreen. Thunder was beginning to growl far off, with now and then an up-and-down zip of lightning. He had better make camp under the first thing he could find. Because if it rained to match those clouds . . .

The road turned sharp left and the hardtop at once petered out to gravel. It was hard gravel—had been used a lot—maybe it would go back to hardtop after it went around this small peninsula which jutted eastward into the river. He might just as well go on as go back, anyway. There'd surely be some place along here to creep under—a boat dock, maybe.

The road went on for a few hundred yards through big old hardwoods that were already letting go a few leaves to the gusts of wind making in from across the river. No shelter there—crazy to park a mess of steel like the bike under trees in a thunderstorm. Some old buildings up ahead, though, and what looked like—yes, it was. A Ferris wheel. Marney rode out of the trees into a clear space at the end of the low, sandy peninsula. A carnival or an amusement park, by the look of it, abandoned or closed for the season. There was a big long building—restaurant or dance hall—with shuttered windows; a shabby wooden walk led along a line of boarded-up concession booths above a sandy beach, to a one-story barnlike building, apparently a boathouse, with a walkway and dock and some paint-scaled small boats hauled up along its wall. A battered sign hung on the boathouse with some sun-cracked letters which could barely be spelled out: BILL'S MARINA. Bill hadn't done too well, it seemed; the place was falling down, deserted. But bless him, whoever he was, he'd built a covered jog on the western end of his boathouse above his boat-launching ramp, open on three sides but sheltered from the east; and Marney pulled into it with a breath of relief, just as the first scarf of rain began falling on the river.

He set up his tent in this lee, anchoring it to the corner posts of the structure. Toughy, let out of the sidecar, made off to a corner full of weeds where she dug frantically and then returned through the rain looking put out—rain being always a personal insult aimed straight at cats. She was used to this procedure. The tent with the camp stove burning in it meant warmth and dinner; she walked over Marney's feet, getting in the way while he opened a can and put down a dish of milk. She sniffed, glanced at him once, as if to say, "Salmon, h'm? Again? Where's the dinner?" and he grinned, watching her. "Okay, I know you. Go ahead, eat. Salmon's what there is, old lady." Then he heated a can of chili for himself, made coffee, and sat eating, watching the storm grow over the river.

Here on the waterfront, he could see now the way he had come. This low peninsula made with the mainland a small cove, sheltered by the big hardwoods; above the narrow beach, some thick-leaved bushes grew down almost to the water's edge. Behind the bushes, the hardwoods looked strange in the light from the sky—as if you could count every leaf on every tree. The river had turned a mean-looking ochreish green.

A flare of lightning lit the sky, followed by a thunderclap like gunfire. Briefly Marney hoped the top of his head was still on. One moment he could see a long way up the river; the next, the water, the stretches of shore, were blotted out by rain.

The roar on the thin roof over his head was so loud that it drowned out the thunder. The lightning kept up an almost continuous glare; against it, Marney could see the rain coming down not in drops but in streams the size of a pencil. He could see very little else. At the foot of the boat-ramp, the river water, sand-colored and oily, splashed up in peaks six inches high where the ropes of rain drilled into it. Beyond that he could make out some ten feet of the piles of the dock, with water running off its walkway like a waterfall. When a gust of wind struck, it would turn the perpendicularly falling streams into spray that looked like foam from surf. After a while he couldn't see even the edge of the dock.

A flash lit up the whole inside of the tent and snapped like a stick breaking; the clap of thunder on top of that one he did hear, and simultaneously, a tremendous rumbling crash, as if something had dropped from a height and landed hard.

Wow, that hit something! Marney thought, Not very far off, either.

He could even smell it—a queer, brimstone smell; so could Toughy. Spitting, she hunched herself into a ball on one corner of the sleeping bag. Every hair she had stood straight up, and in the dim light from the camp stove, her eyes were green lamps.

"It's okay," he told her. "Be over soon." But she found that no comfort. She hated thunderstorms.

Uneasily, he wondered what the lightning had struck. If it had been that big dance hall . . . brother! That would go like a bundle of kindling. "And we'd have to move out of here on the double go," he told Toughy. He stuck his head out around the side of the tent looking for any flicker of flames, but he could see nothing, only the murky sheets of water driving by the corner of the boathouse.

Maybe not much chance of fire, in this, he told himself. I'd better take a look, though.

The tent, pitched under the lean-to roof, was in fair shelter from the rain, though the wind whipping around the corners yanked and slatted it. He'd better tighten up the tent ropes while he was outside. And check the bike, though that was parked under the lean-to next to the wall and ought to be all right.

Marney crawled out of the tent and stood up. The lightning wasn't quite so sharp; that last crack must've been the center of the storm passing over; but the wind and rain hadn't let up at all. He still couldn't see ten feet. The rain now was like a sheet of opaque glass; when he put his head out to look around the corner of the building, he felt as if he had been hit in the face with that same sheet of glass. He jerked back into shelter; no use trying to see anything.

The tent ropes were as tight as they could be against the intermittent gusting of the wind; he'd have to put up with the slatting, and hope they held. The bike was okay, too—getting some rain blown in on it; that he couldn't help, either. The thing that worried him was a young river running down the slope from the higher ground in back of the buildings and along the outer edge of the boat-ramp. It was already three feet wide, five or six inches deep. If it rose much more, it would flood out the tent.

Worried, he looked around, wondering what he could do if it did. Nothing, unless he took shelter in the boathouse. But that would mean breaking in; and breaking in meant that sooner or later somebody would be trying to find out who had. So far, in his travels Marney had tried hard not to do anything that would give anyone a hold on him—bother anybody or call attention to himself. Even so, there'd always been jokers, some decent, some not, who'd wanted to know what he was doing, where he was going, who his people were; and you had to have a story ready or they got sore. When you saw the nosy look change to suspicion, brother! You'd better ride away from it, fast. So what had you done? You were a strange kid on a motorbike, with no story. But maybe this time he was going to have to break and enter. That young river was getting deeper, coming up on the ramp. A blackish oil spot on the tarred surface went under while he was looking at it. And the rain was coming down harder, if anything.

He looked speculatively at the nearest window of the boathouse. Streaming rain, blank, noncommittal, it stared back at him.

Okay. Here goes. I've got to.

The window wasn't locked. It went up quite easily for about four inches and then stuck. He put his palms under and thrust hard upwards, felt the punky wood start to give before he could get room enough to crawl through. The place smelt of dampness and must, of old rope and tar. It couldn't have been used for a long time. In the dusky light coming through the cobwebbed windows, he made out that the long, barnlike interior was empty, Nothing in here at all. The roar of the rain on its roof was terrific, and the roof leaked. In two or three spots the water was running down in streams. He saw also a sliding door, secured on the inside by a couple of hasps. It would open, he found, and he slid it back, letting in a great gust of wind and rain. There was a sloped platform leading up to the door, probably once used for hauling in boats. He thought, I can get the bike in here, too, if I can manage it before the darn roof blows off.

Toughy had snuggled down out of sight into the warmth of the sleeping bag, and he brought her first, bag and all, using the window so that he wouldn't have to race her through the rain. He put as much of the stuff from the tent as he could in through the window. The camp stove was too hot to touch, so he turned it out and left it till last.

The bike was already standing in water; he could hear water slosh in the sidecar as he struggled to push against the wind, and realized that he wasn't making any kind of headway.

Gosh, what have we got—a hurricane? he thought desperately. Because it's sure something besides a thundershower.

He wasn't going to make it, he saw. Unless he could start the motor. It wouldn't even kick over, and no wonder. Everything was soaked, including Marney. Then, suddenly, the ignition caught. He drove the bike up the sloped platform and bumped in at the boathouse door. Then he shut the door and leaned, gasping, against the wall.

He was wet through and cold; this big, drafty place wasn't a place to get warm in, either. He had better rig up the tent again, get the camp stove going inside it, and do it now, because the darkness was coming on by the minute. It would soon be night and he'd need some light to see by. Be a lot easier than working by flashlight beam. He found some corner stanchions that would take his tent ropes, got the tent up and the stove going inside it, along with Toughy and the sleeping bag. Now to get in himself, get warm.

Turning toward the tent, he caught a glimpse of what was going on outside the windows and, for a moment, stood awestruck. In the dusk there would be nothing at first but a kind of sand-colored murk, so thick as to seem almost solid; then lightning would rip through it, turning everything greenish blue. For an eyelash flicker he could see the parallel-blown sheets of water and about twenty feet of the river covered with a dirty-yellowish foam. Then murk again, and r-rip! the flash, the cloudburst, the roily, curdled foam. The river was higher than it had been. Well, no wonder, with all that pouring down into it. This far south, it would be a tidal river, too. Must be the tide coming in.

What was that?

Out on the river, at the edge of his vision, the lightning had flared on something that wasn't murk, something long and white, picked out with dark squares. Marney blinked, staring through the window. He rubbed with his clammy palm at the pane, succeeding only in smearing gritty dirt around, so that he couldn't see through it at all. He moved over to the next window and heard from outside a thick, bumping crash, with a cracking sound like the breaking of sticks. What he had seen had certainly been something; something big, too. Whatever it was had blown slam into the boat dock.

At the window he couldn't see anything. The murk was opaque, sand-colored as the river itself. If it hadn't been a boat, what then? It had looked like a long white shed. The black squares might have been windows. A house? Had it rained hard enough to flood somebody's house off the riverbank? Or maybe the river had come up somewhere that high? Had he better go outside and look?

But as he strained at the window trying to see, he realized suddenly that going outside wouldn't be necessary—whatever the thing was, it was coming to him. A horseshoe-shaped thing—a boat's stern, he saw briefly—was moving in fast, impossibly close to the window; he caught a livid, lightninglit glimpse of it again, just before it struck.

He had time to think, Get back from the wall, get back quick! and turning around from the scrambling leap that had landed him on all fours in the middle of the floor, he heard the crash of window glass, the splintery crackle of boards and studs, as the thing rammed through the wall.

Dazed, he got to his feet. He was all right; at least everything seemed to work and nothing had landed on him—yet. From the sounds going on, though, it might be only a matter of minutes before something did—say, the roof of this old shebang. So get out fast, rain or no rain. Get Toughy.

So where was Toughy? She wasn't in the sleeping bag; he felt all over it, feverishly. His flashlight was where he had left it when he'd unpacked. He snatched it up, circled the beam around the tent. She wasn't in the tent. Sick at heart, he thought, She got scared at all that racket; she's run somewhere.

He backed out of the tent, flashed the beam of his light around the inside of the boathouse. Toughy was high up on a collar beam, well out of reach. He didn't see how he could get her down without a ladder. When he called, she sat there and looked at him.

Don't push the panic button. Think. And he pulled himself together a little.

The roof wasn't buckling. So far as he could tell, it wasn't going to come down in the next few minutes, anyway. The boat had crashed through one section of the north wall; the overhang of its stern had crumpled three or four of the rotten floorboards. A houseboat, he saw, going gingerly a little closer, and a big one. She was grinding up and down, which meant that except for her stern jammed into the building like a plug, she must be still afloat.

How could that be? It meant the river had risen like crazy in the last few minutes or so; and, he thought, starting to shake inside his soggy clothes, If it's like that on the river side, how far is it up around back?

Cautiously, he slid the door open a little, a slit wide enough to stick his hand, with the flashlight, through. It didn't seem to be raining quite so hard. The lightning had let up, too. But he needed only one look to see that the boathouse was now an island. The water was within a few inches of the top of the sloping platform up which he had ridden the bike—how long ago? He tried to remember how steep the slope had been. A rise of a foot and a half on the land? Maybe more. Well, that was enough. He couldn't get out of here with the bike until the river went down. He slid the door shut and stood, trying to think what to do.

I could wade out of here now, all right. But I'd have to leave everything, and no place to carry Toughy but the front of my jacket.

Toughy, seeing that nobody was looking for her now, or calling, came down by way of a couple of stud-braces and took a long leap to the floor. She came over and rubbed against his leg. She said, "Pr-rt," anxiously, and he picked her up, rubbed his chin against her silky head.

Without the bike I'm stranded. And no place to go. The storm's letting up a little. The water'd have to come up a lot higher before I'd have to swim for it. I guess I'd better wait and see.

Maybe this was the thing to do, maybe it wasn't.

He put Toughy back in the sleeping bag—she was already showing signs of distaste for his damp jacket—and backed out of the tent again, worriedly flashing his light around the floor to see if there were any sign of water. As the beam fell on the stern of the houseboat, he saw she was riding higher. That meant the river was still rising. It also meant that she didn't leak.

As a matter of fact, she didn't seem to be hurt much at all. The railing around her stern gunnel had been torn off and was dangling. Dangling also was a stout cable—her stern line, probably, where she'd been torn loose from her moorings. Canvas curtains protecting her cockpit were still in place, though one or two of their supports were bent.

I'll bet she hasn't got much water in her, he thought. And inside that cabin, it's dry. I wonder . . .

If he could moor the thing—tie her up so she wouldn't go adrift; if he could get the bike down into that cockpit . . . it might not be too hard, either; the stern was only a little above the level of the boathouse floor. I could use a couple of broken plank ends to bridge that gap.

If I got the bike in there, how would I ever get her out? I don't know. I'd have to figure something. But at least, if the river should flood out the boathouse, I'd be in something that would float. Wonder if I could get aboard. Take a look.

Full of plans as he was, he didn't at first see the dark, moving object that came up out of the cockpit. He caught a glimpse of it as it passed through the flashlight beam, and heard the thump and the scrabbling sound as it landed on the boathouse floor. He turned just as something wet and knobbly ran full tilt into him, clutching on to his jacket with hands like claws, For a terrified moment, before a bawling, hoarse and continuous as a chain saw, started up and made him realize what this was, Marney tried to yank the hands away. The bawling stepped up a notch; he felt a round wet head burrowing into his stomach.

He said, "Oh, my gosh!" and "Take it easy," and "Hey, hold everything, you're okay now," and scooped one arm around, pulling the shivering, yelling, skinny object over toward the warmth and light of the tent.

Liz had not been scared at all up to a little while ago, for the simple reason that she'd been asleep. At first, aboard the houseboat everything had been lovely—better than her wildest and most satisfactory dream. Here she was, sailing away completely and forever from all the mean stinkers. She felt so happy at the moment that stinkers was the worst word she could think of. *They* couldn't get at her now, not possibly—because of the long stretch of river, all the time growing longer, between her and them. Sailing away to some place she didn't know and she didn't care where, just so it could be far off.

In deep content, she told herself, If anybody finds me where I'm going, I'll never, never tell my name or where I live, so they can't send me back there. Hooray!

She walked all around, exploring, as the houseboat drifted lazily downriver. Here was the place where the engine lived. Wasn't it a pretty one! Everything on it gleamed and shone. And here, up on top, was the steering wheel. On the wall was a little framed picture thing, saying the *Sea Flower*'s name and some numbers. It mentioned Charles Bowker, too. Well, this wasn't old Bowker's boat anymore; it belonged to 'Lizabeth Bigelow. She took down the picture thing and threw it overboard. She hunted all over the boat. Anything, any piece of paper that said "Bowker" on it, she got rid of. Into the river with it. Fix them.

Let it rain; let it be a thunderstorm. So who cared?

The *Sea Flower*'s motion on the water was lovely. Sometimes, encountering a swirl in the river current, she would turn in a circle, a wonderful, slow swing. She would zig toward one shore and then zag toward the other, coming in quite close once in a while, so that Liz could watch whatever interesting thing might be going on. Once she bumped quite hard on something underneath her and nearly stopped; then she slid along, still bumping, and went on. Another time she came quite near to a raft anchored out in the river, where a man with his outboard skiff tied up was pulling up the raft's anchor. He looked up to see the *Sea Flower*'s bow headed right for him and jumped into the air, yelling, as if somebody had stuck him with a pin.

"What in hell! Hey, sheer off, you blasted fool!"

And when the *Sea Flower* didn't, but kept on, he made a grab for the rope on his skiff. He was pulling it in, getting into the skiff, jerking at the motor cord. Maybe he was going to put chase.

Liz hollered as loud as she could. "Daddy, Daddy! There's a man going to come on the boat!" and cocked her head as if to listen for an answer. "My daddy says if you come near us, he'll tear your head off and throw it in the river!"

The man swore very loud; he yanked again at the starter cord on his motor, which didn't start. But just then the *Sea Flower* caught a current, sheered off, and went right out toward the middle of the river. The man shook his fist a couple of times; then he climbed back on the raft and began again to pull up its anchor.

Liz watched with satisfaction.

That had been just the thing to say. *They* wouldn't put chase if they thought your father was on the boat with you. From now on, he would be.

So now I-and-my-father am going into the little house to eat some of the stuff in the cans.

She giggled, then roared laughing. That man, hadn't he been scared? Good old *Sea Flower* did it on purpose, I'll bet, too.

She'd thought that to get into the cabin all she'd have to do would be break a window. But those windows had the toughest glass she ever saw. She pounded with the heel of her sneaker: couldn't even make a crack. And all the windows were alike, too.

If that wasn't just like those poison Bowkers to have tough glass in their windows!

So, okay for them. They can just wait till I find something heavy to pound with. I am going to get in.

She looked all around the boat. Nothing. Some tinlike chairs down in the little gold room; they weren't very heavy. Then, down in the room where the engine lived, she found a nice, heavy iron wrench. On deck again, she took a good hefty swing at a window; but all it did was make a round place with some little cracks like a cobweb. Try as she would, she couldn't break the glass. The only thing she got out of it was a jammed finger.

Holding her finger and hissing with pain, Liz made another tour of the boat. As she passed the cabin door, she turned the knob and gave the door a furious kick. It swung open with a smooth little click—hadn't been locked at all!

Of all the mean, dirty old tricks! Lock the door and leave a window. Next time, lock the window and leave the door.

Well, April Fool to *Them!* I-and-my-father's in.

Liz ate a lot out of the cans she opened. It was a temptation to start gobbling the moment she opened a can. Everything looked so good. But she wasn't going to have that. In a nice place that belonged to you-and-your-father now, you were not going to act like a pig. It was going to be kept nice. She set the cabin table for herself and her father. Two places.

On one plate she put lobster and crabmeat, mayonnaise, cocktail sausages, and pearl onions. In a dish by itself she laid out the plum pudding. Then she sat down at the table and ate the things on the first plate in the order set, all the time carrying on conversation.

"For once in our lives, Daddy, we are going to have enough mayonnaise, not just the mean little daublets people put on things for children," she said, ladling out a very handsome spoonful.

Daddy? That didn't sound right. It was how those poison Boardman brats talked. Not Daddy.

"Have some, Father?" she said, pushing the mayonnaise jar across the table. "It won't make you sick. That is one of the lousy lies they always tell the kids."

In the manner of Cousin Emily serving tea, Liz dished out the plum pudding. After all, you might not like Cousin Emily, but she knew what was what when it came to manners.

"This pudding is awful chewy and gooey," Liz said. She tried, but she couldn't stuff any more in. "Father, you haven't ate yours. So, okay, I won't eat mine."

It was certainly a disappointment. In all the stories Cousin Emily read around Chistmas time, the one about Bob Cratchit, that dope, when they had plum pudding they thought they had the dill. Well, they didn't; it stinks.

She made a face at the pudding and then suddenly discovered she was so thirsty she couldn't wait to get a drink of water.

She hunted. There must be some water somewhere. There were tea and coffee in cans; they had to have water to make tea and coffee. But anywhere she looked, she couldn't find any. She came across a rack of bottles, of the kind she had known well when she had lived with Sarah Bigelow—whisky, gin, sherry wine. One was open and she took the stopper out. Just that smell, like medicine, had always made her feel sick, and it did a little now. She put the stopper back, wishing she hadn't taken it out. She wouldn't have, either, if the stuff in the bottle hadn't been what Sarah and those people had always drunk when they'd said they were awful thirsty. So that was for *Them*; for Sarah Bigelow, who'd always had a stomach like a bagful of rocks—Cousin Emily said so.

But in the same rack with the other bottles was a big one, unmarked, full of water. Liz took it down and stood, admiring. Now, wasn't that a cute way to keep the water! It had a silver stopper, pretty as a gadget, with a lever to press, like a little pump.

She was so thirsty by now that she couldn't wait to be polite and pour some out in a tumbler. She put the spout in her mouth and pressed the little pump. The water squirted *bang!* into the back of her throat, went up her nose, all over her face, soaked her hair and her front before she could think to let go of the little pump handle.

Liz dropped the bottle. She choked and sneezed and gagged. She thought, I am going to throw; only the thought of wasting all that lovely dinner kept her from it. She sat down on a chair, holding her stomach and wheezing. After a while she felt better, but not so well as she had. Her hair was wet, dripping down her neck, very uncomfortable. Well, up in the front of the boat was the cute little bathroom. There were towels hanging on a rack. But even after she had rubbed hard with a towel and slatted her head, her hair just wouldn't get dry.

This was the nicest little bathroom. So clean. So complete. So everything. Inside the toilet seat was a slight sound, a soft glugging of water. Like company. She opened the seat and observed with satisfaction. And a medicine cabinet, just like in bathrooms ashore. Everything. Even a bottle of aspirin. If that wasn't nice!

I-and-my-father can live on this boat forever.

On one of the clean glass shelves was a pair of scissors. Well, good. Just what she needed to cut off this old cold wet hair. She cut it all off, as close to her head as she could. It felt wonderful. Raggedy, but nice. Not drippy anymore. Then she put the scissors carefully back on the shelf, cleaned up every strand of hair, and flushed it all down the toilet.

That had been the stingingest water. The back of her nose felt awful; but if she swallowed hard and kept swallowing maybe she wouldn't have to throw. Out on deck was the place, though. If you have a nice little bathroom of your own, you are not going to puke in it.

As she stepped out through the cabin door, she heard somebody hollering, quite close by, and an outboard motor sound.

"Hoy, the houseboat! Hoy! Anybody aboard there?"

Sure enough, there was a skiff, right alongside. The man in it had just opened his mouth to holler again. Liz hollered first.

"I-and-my-father's aboard here. What do *you* want?"

The man swung in closer; he cut his motor and grabbed the houseboat's gunnel. "Great Lord, son, I've been watching you drift downstream for half an hour. You all right? Had a breakdown?"

He thought she was a boy! Wasn't that a howl!

"My father's eating," she said regally.

The man looked astounded. "*Eating?*" he said. "Well, ask your old man if he's crazy. Tell him to stop eating for a change and come out and look at the sky. Don't he know there's hurricane warnings out all over? Ashore, we're all buttoned in! Hasn't he got a radio?"

"Sure. He's listening to it." Liz stepped back to the cabin door. She opened it and said loudly, "Father, there's a man wants to know have you got the radio on?" She listened a moment, shut the door, went back to the rail. "He says okay, don't worry. We're going right home."

"Okay, then," the man said doubtfully. He glanced upward at the sky. "He ought to know better than to be out on the river at all. And, goddammit, so had I!" He let go, started his motor, and headed for the shore.

"Crazy nut!" Liz said.

The sky did look black, with that big cloud coming, and the river had turned a funny greeny color. There were whitecaps on it, too. The boat was beginning to go up and down. It was scary.

That poison old squirt-bottle, she thought, gulping.

And all the lovely dinner went over the side into the river.

When she was through, she didn't feel better. She went back into the cabin, crawled into a bunk, and put two pillows over her head. Far off, she could hear thunder growling; but when you couldn't see anything, it was very much better. She was warm as toast; presently, she went to sleep.

A terrible crashing and pounding sound woke her up. And it was then that she really began to be scared. Her father certainly wasn't there. She was all alone.

✦

Inside the tent the kid kept on bawling, though it was more of a wheeze now than a bawl. What with the tears and water streaming down, he looked like a drowned rat. Marney mopped him off as well as he could with a soggy handkerchief, thinking, This outfit sure hasn't got much left that's dry.

Well, it was dry in the sleeping bag. Toughy could shove over. He could get the kid warm, at least; the poor little duffer was shivering like a dog. He said, "You want to take off your wet shirt?" but when he put out a hand, the kid slapped it away.

"Don't you dare to take off my shirt! My father'll fix you!"

"Oh, my gosh!" Marney said. Sure, the kid wouldn't have been on the boat alone. There must be somebody else. Hurt or worse, or he'd have been ashore by now. "Where is your father?" he said, trying to make it casual.

The kid darted a sideways glance at him. "He's there. He's sleeping."

"Okay," Marney said. Feeling icy-cold, he picked up the flashlight, and the kid began to bawl again.

"Where are you going? Please don't go anywhere."

"I'll be right back. Don't be scared. It's okay."

It wasn't okay. Outside the tent, Marney stared in horror at the black line of water creeping across the boathouse floor. In the flashlight's beam, it sparkled darkly; even as he looked, a small ripple curled over silently and flowed a little higher on the gritty boards.

See what's aboard the boat, he thought, and then get out of here somehow before we have to swim.

The boat had drifted out a few feet; he was going to have trouble getting aboard without going down into the water. He picked up a broken board from the floor, wrenched it loose, and just managed to snag the nails in the end of it into the mooring cable that dangled over the boat's stern. As he did so, it seemed to him that he must have, for a moment, fallen asleep on his feet and come to with a jerk in the middle of a tremendous silence.

The wind had stopped, and with it the rain. Through the smashed wall he could make out the squares of the boathouse windows, see her outline, even a little of the river, the water's silver-slick shine flowing swift and deadly. That was certainly moonlight; if he hadn't seen the moonlight, he'd have thought he'd gone stone-deaf. But the storm, thank God, was over.

Marney gave the mooring cable a good strong pull, felt the boat move, loose and free. She was adrift, all right; he couldn't take a chance going aboard until he was hitched to something, and he carried the cable end across the boathouse, passed it around a corner stanchion. It was wet, unmanageable; his fingers were stiff, all thumbs. He hoped the knot was a bowline, and turning, waded into the growing trickle of water.

The cabin door was shut. Opening it, he flashed his light around. Some stuff had broken loose and was lying around the floor. None of it was the shape of a man. Marney said, "Hey, anybody here?" His voice was a croak and nobody answered it.

He took a look around the boat to make sure. Nobody in the bathroom or in the small galley. Nobody in the engine room. Or anywhere. The man must have gone overboard.

So what'll I tell that poor little devil of a kid?

He went back on deck.

Black stormclouds were still ripping across the sky, but breaking through, in and out, was the moon, even a star or two. All kinds of stuff, dark objects big and small were tearing along downriver with the current; in the skimpy moonlight he couldn't make out details. Some things were big as houses; one, shaped like an upside-down V, looked like a gabled roof. He stared, awestruck, past the end of the boathouse at what had been the peninsula—the dry land he had ridden the bike over, and now a mass of curdled white foam. The foam must have blown there; somewhere under it must be solid ground, because it wasn't drifting, it was lying thick and still. Back a little from it, he could make out a mess of dark sticks or something, all jumbled together, as if someone from a place high up had dropped an enormous market basket.

That old Ferris wheel. I'll bet that was what the lightning struck, earlier on.

There was the road he had driven down last night. Like a happy fool. He could see in places the whitish strip of it, and as he looked, he realized with a cold clutch at his stomach why he could see so much of it. The row of boarded-up concession booths along the waterfront was gone—blown down, because he could see a few remains, sticks and timbers, thrusting out of water; and the big hardwoods he had ridden through lay in a tangle of black trunks and bare branches. Through them went the silver stripes, the foamy flecks of fast water.

Well, he didn't have to make up his mind now what to do. It had been made up for him. The peninsula, like the boathouse, had become an island. And if the water kept on coming up, it wasn't even going to be that. It was going to be part of the river.

The kid was huddled as close to the stove as he could get, warming his hands at the burners. He said, as Marney stuck his head into the tent, "Is that your cute little black and white cat?"

"Yeh," Marney said, startled. He'd come back wondering what to say and how to say it, and here was the kid not even interested in where his father was. Maybe it was a good thing. There wasn't time now for questions or for comforting.

He said, "We have to get out of this place. The water's coming in here. So come on."

"Where'll we go?"

"On the boat. Okay?"

"But the boat sunk. It hit a rock."

"No, it didn't. It's out there."

"No, I won't go. It's nice here."

Okay, there wasn't time to argue.

Marney scooped up the sleeping bag, making sure that Toughy was in it this time. He took off, running, across the boathouse, splashing up over the houseboat's stern. In the cabin, he put the sleeping bag in one of the bunks, shut the door behind him, went tearing back to the tent. The kid was still sitting there over the stove. He said, "Did you put the little black and white cat on the boat?"

"Yes, I did." He was frantically scrabbling stuff into the saddlebags, not stopping now for explanations.

"Then I'll go, too. I'll help you with your things."

"Well, you sure can, if you want to. If I boost you up on the stern of the boat, I can hand you things."

With the stove turned out, it was dark as pitch in the boathouse. No moonlight, now; the moon had apparently gone behind a cloud. Marney, trying to work by the flashlight's inadequate beam, suddenly realized that he had a fine source of light if he only had the sense to turn it on; and he wheeled the bike around, snapped on its headlamp.

"Here," he said, handing the flashlight up to the kid on the boat's stern. "I'll pass you stuff and you run it back into the cabin, okay?"

"You got a motorbike! And a sidecar!" the kid said. He was using the light to see where the headlamp came from. "Can I have a ride on it?"

"Yup," Marney said. If anybody ever can again, he thought.

He handed up the saddlebags, and couldn't help grinning a little at the spry way the kid rushed everything back into the cabin. Brother! At that age, a ride on a bike said a book full. Even on one marooned in the middle of a river. Well, the bike was next. He'd better take a look in that cockpit, see what it was like down there.

He unfastened the aft cockpit curtains, folded them back. By the headlamp beam, which shone out through the breach in the boathouse wall, he made out that except for three or four aluminum deckchairs thrown in a heap all anyhow, the cockpit was empty, and that it was fairly dry . . . maybe an inch of water sloshing around. Rainwater, driven in through the curtains, he hoped; if the boat had a leak anywhere, there'd surely be more of it by now. If he were careful, he could get the bike down in here. Ease her down. The kid could help.

As he climbed out of the cockpit, he saw shafts of rain slanting past the headlight beam.

Raining . . . again? And the moon was gone; the river was pitch-black. Rain from the west, though. West wind. West wind usually meant a storm was over. Didn't it? What about a tropical storm—a hurricane? When the second half could be just as bad, maybe worse . . . And this blow had been no ordinary thundershower. If that rain, that wind started in again . . .

Get Toughy, he thought, in a panic. Get the kid. Get out here, even if you have to swim, and knew, even as he thought it, that the only possible way he could make it now was alone.

So this boat is what there is. Cool off. There's always a shower or so at the end of a big storm. And now isn't the time to be scared.

But he was scared. He worked feverishly, ripping boards from the boathouse floor, ripping his hands, too, though he didn't know it. Some of the boards came up easily; the rusty nails pulled out of the wood. Some were rotten and broke. When he began laying his makeshift bridge from the houseboat's stern to the floor, he saw that now he'd have to ride the bike across. He couldn't possibly push her up there, the slope was too steep. The river had come up fast and was still coming. Every board he took, he had to feel for underwater.

Well, that would do it, or it wouldn't. Start the motor now, let her warm up. If she'd go at all.

The motor started at the second try. He wheeled the bike to the edge of the water, got on, and yelled, in case the kid might be standing too near, "Get way back, because when I come, I'm coming tooting!" and headed for the bridge.

Water fanned out under his wheels. The bike took the slope pretty well, then the engine skipped; he prayed, "Don't stall now, kid," feeling the makeshift bridge begin to buckle and crack. Let up on the gas, you fool, you're pouring it on, flooding her, and the engine caught and roared and he went racking up onto the houseboat's stern. Marney cut the ignition, but not quite in time. The front wheel fetched up against the cockpit cheeserind with a bump, bounced over it, kept on going down.

The bump threw Marney sprawling against the curtain stanchion nearest him; the folded-back canvas gave as he ploughed into it, but held, cushioning his fall. He scrambled up, desperately scrabbling on the slippery deck, peering, dazed, down into the darkness of the cockpit. The headlamp was out, probably smashed. The bike was bottom-up, sidecar and all.

He'd burned his bridges, all right; maybe he'd been an awful fool. But this was all he could do. He was finished. One more thing—fasten the canvas back in place; it was beginning to rain hard again now, and the wind was rising. Fumbling in the dark, he found the toggles, secured the curtains. And that was all.

He groped his way forward to the cabin, went in, and shut the door. Toughy was in the bunk where he had left her; the kid was in there, too. His hand, feeling for Toughy's silky fur, came down on top of the kid's hand, which was stroking it.

The kid said, "I was so cold and wet. I had to get warm."

"That's okay. You did just the right thing. You couldn't have helped if you'd stuck around."

"Your things in the leather bags are over there in the bunk. They're all wet."

"Yeah, I know."

"So I got you some of old poison Pa Bowker's stuff out of the drawer. Your little black and white cat and I's been keeping them warm."

He thrust a bundle into Marney's hands; Marney could feel warm, dry wool, and it felt wonderful. He changed, letting his dripping clothes drop to the cabin floor.

"I'll bet you look funny in Pa Bowker's pants," the kid said. "He's quite a fat man." He laughed, a high, clear sound in the darkness. "But I've got on Ma Bowker's pink ones. I'll bet we'll laugh at each other in the morning."

"Is Pa Bowker your father?"

The kid laughed again. "I wouldn't have him for my father if he really was," he said.

Something about the laughter, the sound in the pitchblack cabin, made Marney feel better. The morning. Sometime it would come. Sometime, the wind and rain would stop. We're moored to the boathouse. If the boat sinks, we aren't far from shore. We could make it. He told himself so, and thought, Lord, I ought to be scared. But . . . I guess . . . I'm too tired . . .

"Well, get in, why don't you?" the kid said. "I can hear your teeth chattering, and your little black and white cat and I's nice and warm."

It was fine in the bunk. Toughy moved at once into her place against his stomach; he lay feeling warmth come back, the dry comfort of the wool against his parboiled, shivering skin. His body seemed to be coming unshackled, a pile of unrelated muscles and bones, dumped down.

As sleep hit him like a club, be thought the kid said something . . . what? No matter. Sounded like, "You and your little black and white cat're a lot nicer than I and my father."

The eye of the hurricane passed over New Hampshire at around eight o'clock in the evening. By that time, nearly fifteen inches of rain had fallen on the land, poured down mountain slopes into lake and reservoirs, into streams carrying the flood to the sea. The spot of calm in the center of the massive circling clouds had lasted some twenty-five minutes. The moon had gone out like a doused lantern. The first gusts from the west had come tentatively, like a clearing wind, with a few shafts of rain. Then from somewhere back in the churning chaos, a howling throat let loose what for a few moments it had held back, in the design calculated to make its malevolence more fearful. Wind struck from the west at ninety miles an hour; again the thick pencils of rain roared down.

Upstate, at nine o'clock, a big dam, its spillways already overloaded, took the impact of the new deluge and collapsed; and the loosed waters of the reservoir lake behind it smashed down the river valley into a dozen waterfront cities and towns. If Liz had known it, she would not now, nor ever again, need to fear being pursued by Bowkers, by Boardmans, or even Cousin Emily. Aboard the houseboat, she slept; and Marney slept with Toughy huddled close to his warmth.

The flood and wind struck the boathouse together; and the boathouse exploded. Old timbers, already weakened, snapped and fell. The roof took to the air like a giant wing in the darkness. Three sides of the building, torn apart, spun out into the river current. The fourth side, moored to the houseboat by her stern cable, was towed out, as the boat heeled and swung. For a moment, she hung on the reef of the drowned peninsula, whose sign in the water now was a steep, glass-troughed wave. As she scraped across and the wind under her fantail drove her bow deep, she might have gone under then and there, if she had not fetched up against the sea anchor of the boathouse wall, towing behind. It steadied her long enough; she plowed through the wave and shook free. In midstream the *Sea Flower* joined the massive debris of the ruined countryside—the smashed houses, the dead livestock, the drowned bodies of the unlucky—driving downriver through the screaming darkness to the sea.

Part Three: Arvid

The hurricane called Fanny, which had dumped twelve inches of rain in the Poconos, washed out dams and roads from Pennsylvania to Maine, and devastated southern New England, had been a "sneak" storm in many areas, not behaving as it should have done, and creating no reasonable pattern which the Weather Bureau could have forecast. In the beginning, Fanny was no sneak. She had been spotted eight hundred miles off Florida by Airborne Early Warning, and tracked up the east coast for four days before she zeroed in on North Carolina, where she had raised a moderate amount of deviltry. Advice at first had been to get ready, anything might happen; but conditions ashore, it appeared, were unfavorable to Fanny. With diminished winds, she had crossed Virginia to eastern Pennsylvania, and there so nearly died that she was designated merely a low pressure area by the Weather Bureau in Washington. In the central Pennsylvania mountains, she got "lost." Nobody expected anything further from Fanny, certainly not the Weather Bureau, and they were not to be blamed. Fanny was a devil, hiding her tricks. The Weather Bureau forecast rain.

Somewhere above the mountain foothills, Fanny encountered a low-pressure trough. Into it she went, pouring her great air mass which was still tropical—warm, heavy with moisture—into head-on collision with cold upper air. She built up winds and rumbled out over the eastern states, spreading ruin. And dumping rain.

Free of the land and out on the sea again, her worst was over, but she was still a rip-roaring northeast rainstorm. She drove north into the Gulf of Maine, raising tides from Portland to Eastport, drowning in white water the ledges of the offshore islands. For two days before her coming, her barometric outriders blanketed the coast in fog, with moisture drops heavy as rain and as hard to breathe, and strange along the shores at night, because the big rollers thundering out of thick, windless darkness were tipped with phosphorescence. A man standing on land could not see his own hand; a flashlight beam splayed out on fog and stopped three feet in front of his face; but he could see the crest of a breaker forming thirty feet out on the water, watch it peak, curl, and shatter into hissing sheets of luminous foam. There was no land, no ledges, no beach rocks—only the wild ghostly lines and planes of cold fire, moving as if they had been formed on fog and were fog-borne.

"And that is a sight," Arvid Small said, "that scares me something terrible, you know it?"

With some others, he had been watching the eerie sight for a while and listening to Freddy Fowler's transistor radio. The storm had been a howler from Philadelphia to Portsmouth—millions of dollars' damage, towns smashed, people dead; whether it would hit here or veer off out to sea, the radio weather reports couldn't say yet.

"It'll hit here," Arvid said. "I never knew it to fail, the sea firing on fog, and it's done it for two nights now. You wait. You'll see!" His voice a dismal croak, he waited for an answer. When nobody said anything, he went on. "And I am not going to insult my feelings by watching the goddamned thing any longer." He stumped off in the direction of the harbor shore, where his fishhouse was.

Everyone knew why Arvid was scared. He had been brought up by a superstitious grandmother who had had a sister struck by lightning, and who had believed that natural flames of any kind were omens. St. Elmo's fire and will-o'-the-wisps were the worst, straight out of the cemetery, and who was to say that the sea firing at night on a fog mull wasn't a part of the same thing? To hear Arvid on this theme, a listener might have wondered if he were not descended in direct line from those Elizabethans whose graves broke open, while hoot owls hooted and stars fell out of the sky to announce the murder of the king; and perhaps he was. No one could say that his premonitions didn't make a man somewhat uneasy—in combination with the peculiar weather and the radio reports, of course. Another one coming through now still gave no definite information about Fanny, beyond the fact that she had broken up New Hampshire, which was now drifting in pieces out to sea, and Freddy Fowler turned off his radio with a snap.

"Arr-gh!" he said. "Them boys don't know any more about it than we do. All they can talk about is what's happened, not what's going to. Listen all day and what do you know? Not a damn thing."

"In my opinion, she's a-coming," Simon Eldridge said. "Look at that!"

The fog, briefly, had flashed a pale greenish blue, followed in a few seconds by a long, low, distant roll of thunder.

"I'm going home," Simon said. "Standing here Old Dan Tuckering ain't going to calm them rollers down out on Thirteen-feet Shoal or in around General Remarks Island." He curled his fingers around his mouth and suddenly boomed out in a tremendous bass, "Good-by-ee to thee, a long farewell!"

Since every fisherman there had traps set in the shoal waters named, and had had no chance to shift them because of the two-day fog mull and the sea making up so fast without warning, no one questioned what Simon was saying goodbye to. By the time the weather cleared, if a man found so much as a buoy afloat out there, he'd be a made man. Someone remarked that be wished to God he could get his breath down; it was like trying to breathe inside a blister on his own heel.

Everything had been done around the harbor that could be done—moorings checked and strengthened, punts and other small boats hauled above high-water mark and turned bottom up, rickety fishhouses propped. The thing to do now was go home and wait; stick around, in case the wife and kids were scared. Glumly, the group started homeward.

"Arvid's punt still up on sawhorses, Freddy?" Simon asked as they walked along.

"I guess so," Freddy said.

"Think we ought to stop by and lift her down for him?"

"Nope."

"Uh-huh," Simon said. "Well, I'll see ya, Freddy." He walked away, up the road to the village, the beam of his flashlight almost at once smothered by the fog. Everybody knew why the punt was still up on sawhorses, from which position she might blow to kingdom come in the event of a hurricane. Three times this summer Arvid had started to paint her; each time he hadn't finished getting one coat on before the fog had come in. Three days ago, he had sworn by several sacred and unmentionable objects that she wasn't coming down off them sawhorses now until the weather cleared off. No matter what. So who was going to interfere with a man's private business?

Freddy walked along slowly in the darkness. Pretty soon, he'd have to make up his mind whether or not to go home. He ought to, he knew. In case the storm got bad, his wife ought not to have to stay there alone. Still, it was a big solid house; it had weathered storms since 1820. He doubted if it was going anywhere tonight. And Philomela would still be boiling mad; after the row they'd had at suppertime, she was going to be two or three days cooling off. And so was he. As for being scared by a storm, Freddy told himself bitterly, you couldn't scare Philomela with a rattlesnake.

He could, he supposed, go back and try to make it up one more time. He wished to God he could. It was damned forlorn, out here in the fog. A night like this, a man ought to have a place to go to and be welcome there. Three years ago, when they'd first got married, she'd been glad to see him, no matter what, no matter when. Tonight she'd probably go off to bed without speaking to him. So what was the use? Go back and start all over again? She must know by now, after three years, that he wasn't going to give in on this particular thing; and damn it all, she knew why, too. You'd think she'd listen to reason, knowing it wasn't, by God, a whim with him. She could give in herself for once, and . . . The more he thought about it, the meaner Freddy felt.

Well, after all, there was a place where he was always welcome. Old Arvid always had a drink for a man, and he was good company, too. If he'd heard that thunder rolling, he was probably scared to death by now and would be glad to see anyone. Arvid was, actually, Philomela's uncle and no relation to Freddy at all; but Freddy had always felt closer to him than to any blood relative of his own. His own family, so far as Freddy was concerned, had never been anything to care much about. Nine kids, of whom he'd been the oldest boy, living together all jumbled up in a house the size of a market basket;

racket and noise and screaming to drive you crazy all day long; crazy as a dog, when what you wanted was some decent privacy where you could study, keep your things. From his early boyhood, Freddy had found that place at Arvid's, in the rattletrap old fishhouse Arvid had fixed up on the shore to live in.

Judast, Freddy thought, walking along the beach toward the place, from the time I could run, I practically moved in here with him.

As soon as he'd been old enough, Freddy had got right out; he'd joined the Air Force, more to get away from his family than anything else. He'd been in Korea when the news had come about the automobile accident. His father, it seemed, had loaded the whole family aboard an old station wagon and had lit out for California, why, nobody knew; it was, Freddy'd thought, just about the kind of fool thing you'd expect of him. On the way, on one of the big turnpikes, he'd driven the wagon head-on into a concrete abutment, and nobody had walked away. The old man had never been much of a driver, mostly because he'd always been too poor to own an automobile, and if Freddy knew him, he'd probably been showing off at the time—letting everybody know he could drive just as well and go just as fast as anyone.

But Freddy's first thought on getting the news, and one that shocked him, because it seemed at a time like that he should have considered other things, was, "Where in hell did the old fool get dough enough to buy a car?"

Later, of course, he'd been sickened enough to lie awake some nights; but try as he would he couldn't recall any one of them he could mourn. Home was still what it had been, in his mind—nothing he'd want to go back to, even if it were still there, and full of the same people. When he'd got out of Korea, the place he'd come back to had been Arvid's, and up until the time he'd married Philomela and gone to live with her in her big house, where Arvid was had been home—as much as any place ever had been. Freddy had been a wanderer in his time. Now he was thirty-three and settled down. For two years, he'd been happier and more contented than he'd ever been. Up until a year ago, he told himself, he couldn't have had it better; up until Philomela had got this damned idea into her head and wouldn't get it out, and . . . oh, to hell with it! Freddy opened the fishhouse door, stepped in.

Arvid really had things fixed up in the fishhouse, which was not, however, his year-round quarters. He owned an old farmhouse off on one of the islands, where he lived from spring to fall. There had once been a village on the island; Arvid's people had lived there for generations. He and his brother, Vergil, Philomela's father, had been born in the house. But after World War I, the village had petered out; old folks died, young ones moved away. Vergil had gone at twenty; he had moved to the mainland, had married Old Man Heman's daughter and inherited his property and money, of which there had been a good deal. Both Vergil and his wife were dead now; Philomela was the only relative Arvid had left. He himself had never been able to abandon the island completely; but no one in his right mind would stay there alone in the winter. There were those who said they would not be caught dead on General Remarks Island alone at any time, especially in the dark, because those old folks buried in the cemetery out there walked nights. But ghosts weren't one of Arvid's superstitions. Those old people, he said, never harmed anyone when they were alive, so why would they dead? And there were two or three of them he wouldn't mind seeing again, anyway. No, what it was, winters out there were lonesome; after a while, a man found himself talking to the gulls. So, years ago, Arvid had bought the fishhouse and fixed it up to live in through the cold weather.

The place might look ramshackle, but it was certainly comfortable inside for a man. Over a period of years, Arvid had taken pains to see that it was. He had had to experiment. He was some old disgusted, he said, with the things you bought new nowadays. They didn't last to get home from the store, and modern people didn't know what comfort was. He had had a terrible fight with a mail-order house over a day bed, which, after several months of sizzling correspondence, he had bundled up and returned, mattress and all, with a final letter.

"I want you fellers to see," he wrote, "where on this contraption my weight has left its mark. And do not write me again, nor will I write you. Yours sincerely, Arvid Small. P.S. Keep the money and put it into your mattresses. They need it more than I do."

Since he weighed some two hundred and sixty pounds, he supposed, he told Freddy, that he would always have trouble with these newfangled mattresses and springs; they were some old shoddy-built, if you asked him. He wasn't a princess, he said, nor was there a pea; but what he liked was to sleep straight, not sag, in a bed. He had not licked the problem entirely; not yet, he said, and not enough to declare a holiday. Once a year he carted his mattress to the dump, where it was invariably picked up by the town secondhand dealer and sold to whoever came by the store needing a mattress. Quite a number of houses in town boasted mattresses, even springs, discarded by Arvid Small. "Perfectly good mattresses," the housewives said.

The problem with his bed was nothing, however, compared to what Arvid went through trying to find a stove. He now had a potbelly in the fishhouse, and the Lord only knew the trouble he'd gone to to get it. He had tried several kinds of stoves, even ordering one from a mail-order house—another mail-order house—which had advertised it as equipped with a modern draft and thermostat able to control a wood fire so automatically that it would last all night without attention; and this it might have done had it been up to the thermostat. Great pains had been taken with the thermostat, not any to speak of with the stove, which had been constructed of a sheet iron so thin that by the time a man got a chunk fire started ample enough to last all night, the stove was red-hot all over, even to the decoration on top shaped like a German soldier's World War I helmet. Since Arvid had seen action in World War I and was of a nervous temperament anyway, this spiked object, glowing threateningly in the dark with a ghostly radiance of its own, sometimes gave him nightmares. He had been known, between sleeping and waking, to leap out of bed yelling, "Over the top, boys! The bastards is coming!"

Finally, on a night of social communication with friends and a gallon jug of white port, Arvid had bet Simon Eldridge ten dollars that he could put his foot through that goddamned stove at any point Simon was mind to name, and had done so. Since there had been a fire in the stove at the time, quick action had to be taken—first to get Arvid's leg out before it burned off, and second, to rush buckets of water up the beach and douse the scattered coals before they burned down the fishhouse. The experiment cost Arvid; he not only melted the sole off of his rubber boot and had to buy a new pair, he was minus a stove. The next day he put his spoiled boots inside what was left of the stove, loaded everything aboard his boat, and sank the works out in the bay in forty fathoms of water.

He didn't mind saying, he told Freddy, that the matter had caused comment and that he was ruffled by the whole thing.

He next tried a boat stove, which was the only kind he could find made of heavy cast iron, and had the added advantage of an oven. It had been years since Arvid had seen an oven a man could warm his feet in. But when he got the boat stove home and set up, he found the oven door didn't open sideways; it latched at the top and let down—stuck out in front like a tongue. To get his feet anywhere near the oven, he would have had to blister his ankles. If he put his feet on the let-down oven door and bore down in the slightest, the entire stove had a tendency to tip over in his lap. The stove, being designed to fit a boat's cuddy, was too small; its firebox took a stick only six inches long and very few sticks at that. Stuffing it full to the lids, Arvid found he could get a fire that would last approximately twenty minutes. So, after a while, he put the stove in the cuddy of his boat, where it belonged.

"I would like to know," he said to Freddy, "what has become of them good, old, heavy iron stoves. My grandfather had a potbelly that for Godsakes would hold a fire for a week."

"They don't make them anymore," Freddy said. "For the reason that nobody burns chunkwood. People burn oil or gas. Why don't you put in an oil burner?"

"And suffer that stink? I'd just as soon dump a kerosene can in the middle of the floor, much less to wake up at night and find myself boiled in my bed. All you have got to do is read the paper to know how them oil stoves blows up in the middle of the night and sets the house afire, and nine-tenths of them, they burn up little children. I wouldn't have a minute's peace. Them old potbellies must be around somewhere. They never wore out, and they ain't took wing and flew off."

"Well, now, you know they did," Freddy said. "I'll bet you the antique dealers have rummaged two dozen of them old stoves out of people's barns, around about here, in the last five years."

"Antique dealers! For Godsakes, Freddy, them stoves was out of *my own boyhood!*"

"Sure. They run out of the old quite a while ago, so now they call anything an antique. Simon's got a cousin over Winterhill way that built a ox yoke and two butter molds out of an old beech tree laid in a brook all winter. He made his whole winter's work that way. You want a potbelly stove, Arvid, you'll have to go to an auction."

"Auction, hanh?" Arvid said. "Well, damned if I don't."

He went to an auction; as a matter of fact, he went to several before he came home with what he wanted. He became, in a way, fascinated with auctions, seeing what things people would pay good money for. Freddy usually took him in his pickup truck, and they had a gay time at the auctions, bidding things up and ducking out just in time. Freddy was better at this than Arvid was; he seemed to know instinctively when the time came to stop bidding. Arvid was more competitive and at times found it hard to let go. He got stuck with a maple table, not heavy enough to build traps on, and a hunting knife with a hairy handle made to look like a deer's foot and with steel that wouldn't hold an edge to cut butter. But put it down to profit and loss; he came home at last with a mushroom-topped potbelly stove nearly as tall as a man. For it, he had had to outbid a flock of summer women and three dealers; he had had to pay two fellows a dollar apiece to help him and Freddy load the stove aboard the pickup, and two others to help uuload it and set it up in the fishhouse. But it was worth every cent it cost him.

There it sat, day and night, all winter, giving out mellow, sweet-smelling heat. Around its stout middle was an iron ring on which a man could warm his icy feet—six men, if there were that many who wanted to all at once. On its wide top, Arvid's nickel-plated teakettle hummed a pleasant, continuous song, always ready for coffee or tea; and its cast iron was so heavy and thick that, Arvid swore, you stuff that stove with stumps, it would hold a fire for a week. And you could cook on it, too. Put one of those little tin ovens on the top and poke up the fire and you could bake the best biscuits Arvid ever saw.

Tonight, the night of Fanny, he had come in out of the weather and had lighted every kerosene lamp he had in the place. There were four of these, one on each wall, with polished reflectors, relics of former auctions. The room was nice and bright and a little too warm, for he had poked up the fire. He had then pulled down all the window shades. When Freddy appeared, he was lying on the day bed with his hat over his eyes.

Arvid was not, he said, sick. What it was, he was scared of a goddamned thunderstorm . . . always had been since his Great-aunt Lu had been struck by lightning. Burnt her head right off her body.

"It did?" Freddy said, interested. "You never said it did that before. Never told me that."

"Nor you nor anybody. I can't stand to think of it."

"Be damned. Really burnt her head off, hanh? Burn it all off or leave some?"

"Freddy, stop right there. I ask you. Is it still lightning outside?"

"Well, thing like that. Seems as though I'd have heard more about it."

"Happened before you was born."

"Well, seems as though I'd have heard someone say. Some of the old folks. I heard she was struck, but—"

"Oh, dear," Arvid said. "Oh, God. All right. If you don't want to be lied to, don't pin a man down. Is it still lightning outside, I asked you? You see any?"

"Couple of flashes."

"Two? You see two? We are going to get it, butt-end-foremost. That sea-fire on the fog, that meant something. Awful bad sign. I knew it."

"Meant you won't get your punt painted tomorrow. Why don't I just go out and take her down off the horses?"

"Nossir! I said what I said. If I take her down now and it never clears off again, people'll blame me. And rightly so, you let that punt alone." He took a deep, doleful breath, let it out in a blast. "Oh, dear! Oh, God! There is always something."

"Oh, come on, Arvid. Old Fanny's as liable to go out to sea as anything. Why don't we have a drink?"

"Well . . . I don't know. Right now, I don't know as I want one."

Normally, Arvid wouldn't have hesitated. He didn't, himself, care for strong liquor, but he did relish a drink of good wine, and certainly, at a nervous time like this, a man was entitled to anything that would calm him. Freddy, though, ought not to start in tonight, not the way he was feeling. Over on the shore, earlier in the evening, Arvid had noticed it. Others might not have, but Arvid had known Freddy a long time. Freddy got mad and he bottled it up; he might be boiling underneath and no one would know, until, all at once, out would come that cruel streak; then, cool and collected, apparently just talking off the top of his mind, Freddy would start to say things a man, at times, found hard to forget. He knew just what to lay his tongue to, too—the things that would hurt the most. With most men, in a state of mind like that, a drink or two would help, but not Freddy. He only thought it might; and when it didn't, only made him feel worse, he kept on—never did get really drunk, only sick. He wasn't a lush, with his set of insides he couldn't be; he simply didn't have the stomach. But let him get mad, liquor was the first thing he thought of, and then hell come Monday.

You'd think a man would learn, Arvid thought, hearing Freddy poking around in the cupboard. Well, it was no use in the God's world to try to stop him. He and Philomela had been catsing and dogsing it again, must be. Whatever ailed them two? Up to a while ago, they'd been as snug together as turtle doves.

"White port!" Freddy said, with disgust. "Hell with that. A whole gallon, for Godsake! What's the matter with you—getting stingy in your old age? Why can't you keep something around a man would want to drink?"

There it began. A man in his sixties wasn't old. And no one, in Arvid's life, had ever had cause to complain about his hospitality.

"Other cupboard, second shelf," he said, resigned.

Well, it was too bad. There was just about enough vodka left to make Freddy lose his lining. Half a bottle, maybe, Arvid didn't know. He didn't like the stuff himself—it was kept there only for company who liked something stronger than wine. In his concern, Arvid took his hat from over his eyes. "You want to go a little mite easy on that," he said. "That vodka, now, that's dynamite. And you'll have to be getting along home pretty soon, be with Philomela, this storm coming on."

"You want to throw me out, I'll go," Freddy said. He upended the vodka bottle, took a long drink. "If you don't, then quit bleeding, huh?"

Well, that could have stabbed a man, too. If you didn't know that drinking made Freddy sore at the world. Let him alone now. All you could do.

"Oh, dear," Arvid said aloud. "Oh, God. 'Tis a temptation." It was, too, with the thunder rumbling now, not very far off, so you could hear it. Almost continuous. A bad one. He reached over, picked up the gallon from the floor where Freddy had left it, took a long swallow. Seemed as though they both had reason.

"You know what's the matter with her?" Freddy said, suddenly.

"Look, you ain't even mixing that. Put some water in it, for Godsake."

"What for? She wants kids. Kids, for the love of God!"

"Well, kids is all right. You was a pretty nice one yourself, Freddy."

"Yeah. We all slept in the same room. Lucky if we weren't all in the same bed. Kids! Jeezus, I see myself! Look, I got shut of that once. I ain't about to start over again of my own free will. She knows it, too. What ails her, for Godsake? You ought to know, you're related to her. What's wrong with her, she don't listen?"

A bolt of lightning ripped the fog outside the window, so close by that it snapped. The crash of thunder that came on top of it was nearly drowned out by a simultaneous roar of rain on the fishhouse roof. Arvid gave a croak of horror and clapped his hat back over his eyes. "That hit," he moaned. "That hit close by. Is the place afire, Freddy?"

But Freddy wasn't listening. He emptied the bottle, let it drop to the floor. "You got any more this?" he asked fuzzily.

"No, I ain't!"

"Hand me over that jug, then."

"Nossir! I am not going to get up and cross this room, handing you jugs back and forth! Not in a thunderstorm!"

"No, but you lay there on a set of steel springs," Freddy said. "The lightning hits you, they'll fry your back into a checkerboard."

Steel springs! Oh, dear! Oh, God! The thought had never occurred to him. Arvid curdled inside. He began to shake and tried to roll off the bed and found he was so scared he couldn't move.

"Lights too bright," Freddy said. "Hurt my eyes." Hazily, he went about the room, blowing out the kerosene lamps. The last one went out before Arvid realized. "Cut that out," he moaned. "It ain't no time to touch the lamps." But the room was in darkness, and now he could see the goddamned thing.

While the harbinger of Fanny roared to its flaming peak, his tremors shook the bed. He lay there heaving and praying, holding the wine jug clutched in both hands, upright on his middle. Try as Freddy would, he couldn't pry it loose; every time the lightning flashed, he could see the shape of Arvid going up and down, the wine splashing from side to side in the jug, and the sight of its motion made him feel sicker and sicker. He was sure now that a drink of wine on top of the vodka would settle his stomach.

"You gimme that!" he howled. "Arvid! Cut loose of it! And quit pitching. You're making me sick as a dog!"

"*I* am?" Arvid said.

"Yes, you are! You look like a tugboat in a heavy sea. Cut it out, things're calming down anyway."

"They are?" Listening, he made out that the thunder might not be quite so loud as it had been. "Then I can let loose of my smokestack, can't I?" He made as if to set the jug down, and was aware that Freddy had snatched it away from him. "No, don't do it, Freddy. That mixing, that ain't good."

"Wine," Freddy said, "is good f'r the stomach," and he fell down in the middle of the floor.

Oh, dear, Arvid thought. When we are going to have to run out of here any minute, in case of fire. Then he pulled up short. No, that's only rain. Passing over to the east'ard, thank the Lord.

He got up, pulled out the bottom section of the day bed, arranged Freddy on it, covering him. Then he crawled back into the other side of the bed. He said, aloud, "God, Freddy, ain't it raining!" and turning over, went quietly to sleep.

On schedule, the rest of Fanny arrived. She was not now the harridan she had been, but she had enough punch left to do damage. She blew down trees and outhouses, knocked in a window or two on the exposed sides of buildings. Her winds followed their classic pattern, blowing northeast, then turning to blow northwest. Traveling more slowly now, she had time for whimsies. She picked up a tub of salted mackerel from Simon Eldridge's porch and flung it into the middle of his lilac bush; he woke in the morning to find the entire bush full of gulls. Among other things, Fanny ripped a corner off the roof of Arvid's fishhouse and replaced it with his punt.

The punt was a light boat of the variety known as a "punkinseed," which meant that she looked like just that. Fanny got under her with the same gust that tore off the corner of the roof, lifted her off the sawhorses and dropped her, bow-first, neat as a plug, into the hole in the roof.

Arvid, slowly waking in the morning, was aware of a spot of sunlight on the floor where none should be. He stared a moment, nudged Freddy with his elbow.

"Godsake, Freddy, ain't that my punt?"

And when Freddy did not wake nor answer, Arvid answered himself. "Why, yes," he said. "I believe it is."

If Arvid had known that Philomela was going to come to the fishhouse after Freddy, he would have stayed away; he wouldn't have gone back so soon with his bucket of water. The well was some way from the shore, at the end of a path, and Arvid had had some delay, due to a spruce tree blown down across the curb. Besides that, the morning was so beautiful he couldn't resist standing there and looking.

A high sky, blue as a baby's eyes, everything fresh and sweet-smelling from the rain. Fanny had gone past in the night, hellahooting; she had taken with her every fog drop, every impurity, every meanness out of the air, and left things looking like morning on the first day of the Bible. Off on the bay the water was calm, played over by little breezes, but out among the ledges and offshore islands to the east, big white combers were rolling in. Take a few days for that sea to calm down, most likely. It would be some old rough out on General Remarks Island. He certainly would like to be out there this morning to see it.

Well, everybody's traps out there had probably gone to glory in the storm, including his own and Freddy's; but if a man has come safely through great danger in the night, he is not going to spend the next morning repining. He is just going to feel good, and Arvid did.

Parting the tangled branches over the wellcurb, he bailed up a bucketful of water and drank deeply from the bucket. God, was that good! Sweet, ice-cold, with, this morning, a slight pitchy flavor where some spruce needles had fallen into it. He would have to bring up the ax and cut that tree back, or the water would be sour with spruce-spills. But the taste now was wonderful; it made a man want to make up poetry. He stood on the wellcurb among the feathery fallen branches and made up some.

> All in the lovely morning-o
> The coots and loons sang in the rockweed tree,
> And the boats went high and then went low,
> Over the bumps in the blue, blue sea.

Well, now, that wasn't too bad of a poem.

Ought to have a tune for it; it ought to be sung. He hummed, tried here and there, presently broke out into a song. By the God, that was it. That was the one. Play that on the accordion, it would walk a man right out through the side of a building. Go back and play it now, before he forgot it . . . No. Not now. Because of Freddy. Freddy might walk out through the side of the building, but not for that reason.

Oftentimes, he thought, walking back along the path with the brimming bucket, I could wish that Freddy had a stomach. Well, I will make him one gol-rorious, helmonious good cup of black coffee.

He said this as he walked in through the door. "Freddy, my boy, I'm going to make you one gol-rorious, helmonious cup of—" and walked head-on into the face and eyes of Philomela.

"Oh, dear. Mercy sakes. Philomela," he said. "You're up early."

"Yes," Philomela said. "I am."

Arvid set the bucket down. Freddy, he saw, apparently hadn't moved; he lay sprawled in the day bed with his eyes closed.

"Lovely morning," Arvid said.

"Well," Philomela said. "Nice overhead." Her glance swept over him, the bottles on the floor which hadn't been picked up, Freddy. "Nothing to speak of down below, as I can see."

"Hurricane, name of Fanny," Arvid said. "Eye passed right over the house. That's my punt, up there."

"Fanny's eye, if that is what it was, certainly looked down on a sorry sight."

"Freddy's feeble, I admit. Something he et—"

"Oh, for heaven's sake, Arvid. Don't bother with it. I know what's the matter with him. I ought to. The way I feel now, it couldn't happen to a nicer guy."

"Oh, now. That don't sound like you. Philomela."

"I don't sound like me to myself. I've learned a lot of new words and things since I was a poor simple schoolteacher. Some of them naughty. I hope he's good and sick and you have to nurse him out of it. You listen to his cussing and squawking and letting on he's doing you a favor by throwing up in the basin you're holding. I'm through."

She wasn't through at all, any fool could see that. She felt bad and was taking it out in being mad, the way a woman did.

When she's mad, he thought, her Indian blood shows. If it was Indian blood Vergil's wife always bragged she had. She'd certainly been one handsome woman, and so was Philomela.

Be couldn't help admiring, even while thinking he ought to get out of here, fast, and let the two of them fight it out. She was tall and slim and easy-moving; black eyes, black hair straight and neat; blue dress the same. Dark, smooth skin with a good suntan, right now dusky red under a kind of bloom. She had a mean look at the moment which wasn't natural to her, and she was talking very mean, which wasn't like her, either. She was, he thought, one of the nicest women he'd ever seen in his life.

When in her right mind, that is. And I would trust her with gold dollars, a lot sooner, he thought sadly, than I could ever trust Freddy.

Freddy stirred in the bed. "For chrissake, Philomela, cut out the yak. I'll come home when I get ready. Yon don't have to come crawling."

"I did come after you, I'll admit. But not on my hands and knees, don't forget that. I had it in mind to tell you that your boat is half full of rainwater and sinking on the mooring. If you care. But what I need you for, and that's all I need you for," she said, bearing down on the words, "is the kitchen oil burner's flooded. I thought you might come home and clean it."

"Oh, great," Freddy muttered. "Flood it on purpose, by any chance?" He turned over, his face to the wall.

"No. I'm tired. I didn't sleep last night. I don't imagine many did, except drunks, that is. But I had something besides Fanny on my mind, and I guess I spent the night thinking. This morning I turned the burner on and forgot it."

"I'll just bet you did."

Philomela regarded him. "What I was going to do," she said, loud and clear, "was make doughnuts. Nice . . . greasy . . . doughnuts."

Freddy rolled off the bed with an inarticulate sound which was part choke, and made for the door, slamming it hard behind him. The weakened wall where the corner of the roof was gone swayed and trembled; the punt slid downward six inches and stopped.

"Oh, dear," Arvid said. "Oh, God. Tch! You hadn't ought to have done that, Philomela."

Philomela said nothing. She stared out of the window at Freddy, legging it along the path to the outhouse. Her face was stiff and Arvid could see her eyes watering, but she wasn't going to cry—not in front of anyone. He said, "You want some coffee?"

"No, thank you. I'll go home and make some. I'll make those doughnuts, too."

"I don't know but I'd wait till Freddy fixes the burner."

"I can fix it. Don't think I can't."

She probably could. She was a smart woman with her hands; and anybody could have seen, anyway, that getting Freddy to clean out the burner had been an excuse to come. He wished he could think of something comforting to say to her, but as usual when he ran head-on into other people's troubles, only the most useless things came into his head. He said, "Awful good doughnuts, Philomela."

"Yes, they are, aren't they? You don't know what it's all about, do you? An idea wouldn't enter your head, All you think is, I shouldn't have done that to poor dear Freddy when he's hung. So go on, stick up for him. All I care."

"If I was going to blame anybody, I don't know as it would be you," Arvid said. He felt very uncomfortable, but he certainly had to let her know he wasn't taking sides like that. "What it is . . . well, what it is, a woman thirty years old wants a baby, she ought to begin it, not wait a minute longer!" He saw the change in her face. What he'd said hadn't explained how he felt, though; he ground foolishly on. "If that is what it is, if he hasn't been lying his head off, like of that. I don't know what is the matter with the poor slob—well, yes, I guess I do. That was a sorry mess he was brought up in. But any man would like to . . . Oh, no. Mercy, no. But awful becoming to you, being mad is, Philomela."

"So he's been talking," Philomela said. "Running off at the mouth." Her face had gone black with fury; she doubled her fingers into fists. "Damn him! Oh, God damn *him!*"

She spun around and departed. She, too, slammed the door. The punt slid down some more, hesitated, fell into the room with a thump.

"Oh, dear," Arvid said, after her. "Oh, God."

Well, he thought, staring absently at the punt, that'll save me winkling her down out of there, the least there is.

What could a man do? Nothing, until everybody cooled off. Maybe not then. Right now, get out of here. Get right away.

He filled the coffeepot, left it on the stove for Freddy, shoved a handful of biscuits, a carton of eggs, and some bacon into his jacket pockets, and went off to have breakfast aboard his boat. Hauling the punt out through his door, he was pleased to see that she had not been harmed by her journey through the house—a couple of heavy scratches in what new paint he'd been able to get on her before the bad weather set in. She didn't leak, which was a comfort, because there was no room in her for himself and any water. His ample frame filled her from side to side; she, being a punkinseed, was able to support his weight only because of his nicely calculated sense of balance. In fact, when he was waterborne, so little freeboard had she that at times in a slight chop, he seemed to be sitting flat on the water, rowing himself along with short, quick strokes of his oars.

He started a fire in the boat stove and while it burned up to cooking heat, pumped water out of the boat. The bilges had taken in an unmerciful amount of water . . . four–five inches. That rain. Freddy's boat was a little deep in the water, he saw, but far from sinking on the mooring. Trust a woman to say anything when she got mad. Well, anyhow, he would go over and pump out Freddy before he went ashore. Philomela'd mentioned it to Freddy; so now Freddy wouldn't.

Arvid ate his breakfast in comfortable solitude, looking around at what there was to see. The houses in the village were scrubbed and shining, as if they had been painted overnight, white with bluing in it. Looked pretty and gay. Over Simon Eldridge's house, for some reason, was a big flock of gulls circling. Must be something thrown out—garbage pail overset, maybe. That big hackmatack on the hill was over; too bad. A line tree, nice old-timer been there since a man could remember.

Funny thing, a tree live that long, go down in a matter of seconds in a single night. You would think a thing that tough would go down slow and hard; you would almost think it might scream as it went. Well, how did you know it didn't? Make some kind of a sound your ears weren't keen enough to hear. He'd often thought of that, cutting firewood. Got hard, sometimes, cutting down a living tree. It was too bad, in a way, a tree couldn't scream according to its size, and go on screaming until every bit of it was cut up and used and the waste burned up. Make some of those operators with chain saws think twice before they cut more than they needed to. And a lot of people would take more notice of pulpwood slash than they did, if it lay there making terrible screams of agony instead of just laying there.

Well, look at that! Matt Coffin's backhouse had got blown over flat last night, and the sign on his store that said GROCERIES was dangling by one screw. And Philomela had got her oil burner fixed and lighted. Smoke was beginning to come out of her kitchen chimney.

Things were certainly coming to a head betwixt those two.

And I don't know as I want to go back into it, till they cool down. That fishhouse ain't livable; I have got a good mind to stay off aboard the boat here, till I can find someone to fix that roof.

The cuddy of Arvid's boat had bunks with mattresses and bedding, as well as the stove. He often slept out here, for a change.

Still, I have got work to do. Repaint the punt. Work. An awful lot of it, and not a mite of it to interest me. What I'd like to do is go back out to the island for a while. Ought to anyway, to see if the house took damage last night. See if I've got any traps left.

By turning his head a little and looking off east, he could see General Remarks Island on the horizon. Six miles out; almost too far away to amount to anything. All the same, times he got downright homesick for it, and today, with a big sea running out there, was one of the times. Standing on the easternmost point, which stuck out into the ocean like a tough snout, a man could see the tide dividing; with the big rollers combing in on each side of him, he felt as if he were riding the bowsprit of the vessel of the world. And no people around with their troubles to frig a man up, spoil a nice, high, blue day.

Why didn't he go? It was only September. Looked like a good spell of weather coming up, too. He could stay out there till the winter broke—November, if he wanted to. He almost always had. October out there was about the nicest month there was. Only reason he'd moved in early this year, was because of Philomela. She'd persuaded him. Said a man of his age ought to know better than to camp out there alone, anyway. Suppose he took sick in the night? Well, suppose he did? He'd get well in the morning. What he'd really moved for was to be around in case she needed him, things being what they were. Helped a lot, too, hadn't he?

A big blackback gull flapped in, landed on the washboard of the boat, and stood cocking a cold yellow eye at Arvid's last biscuit laid on a coil of wet rope on the stern to see if it might absorb a little moisture and be edible. It had turned out to be one of a two-week-old batch he had been saving for a bread pudding; he'd grabbed it up by mistake. He didn't suppose he wanted it now, being full; had been going to eat it to save it, no sense throwing food away. But the situation developing had possibilities. The biscuit was four inches across—Arvid liked a big biscuit—and hard as a rock. He watched with interest.

You swaller that, he told the blackback silently, it'll sink you.

The gull took a tentative step, made a run, grabbed, and took off. It flew around in circles, stretching its neck in and out, but no use, the biscuit wouldn't go down. It appeared to be stuck.

Oh, now. That was too bad. Wouldn't want to strangle the poor critter. What could a man do?

If I brought my rifle up out of the cuddy, I could try shooting that thing out of his mouth. Be a hard shot, though; might kill the gull.

The gull had an idea worth two of that. He sat down on the water and dunked the biscuit until it broke into three pieces. Then he swallowed the pieces and flew off.

Now, beat that if you could. You want brains, you go to the creatures of the wild. See how they made out, it did you good.

Up in the village, the fire whistle let go, a long blast and a short one. Arvid jumped, twisted around to look. Philomela's, by the God! Smoke was pouring out of her chimney like a black cloud of anger against the sky. She had got herself one gol-rorious, helmonious old chimney fire.

Well, Freddy would have to bestir himself now.

I wonder if I ought to go.

But the tank truck was already barreling down the road. He could count one . . . two . . . six men around Philomela's house. That was enough. Plenty, without me splattering off that roof at sixty and some years of age.

The fire was of short duration. Watching, Arvid decided it couldn't be doing any harm—the boys were letting it burn out. Dying down it was, already. They didn't need hose apparently—hadn't called out the pumper.

But, my soul, a woman get so mad she'd gone home and touched a match to a flooded oil burner? Because that must be what Philomela had done. Or had she? No, it must have been something else—chimney was ready for a fire, maybe. She wouldn't risk burning down Vergil's old house. It was too nice a house, and hers now, too, inherited from her father. She had Vergil's money, as well; which could account for some of the trouble between her and Freddy, no way of knowing.

Time to get moving. Arvid eased himself into the punkinseed, rowed across to Freddy's boat to do the pumping job.

Funny thing, he thought, standing on the platform of Freddy's boat, working the pump leisurely up and down, that Freddy don't use some of Philomela's money to get himself a decent boat. Three years ago, when they'd first got married, he hadn't seemed to mind how much of it he spent. Bought that big garage over in Powell, and then, of course, lost it or sold it. Anyway, didn't own it now. Maybe this decrepit old boat was a part of the spite between them. Hard to say.

That old make-or-break engine, too. If Freddy wasn't a mechanical genius with all his brains in his hands, he'd never in the God's world be able to keep it running. Funny a feller like him would be contented to go fishing for a living, anyway, with all of the good jobs he'd had ashore. He'd run that garage; then he'd worked in it for a while under the new owner; then the manager of the woolen mill in Powell had offered him any amount of money to take charge of the machinery at the mill. Funny feller.

It surely was a lovely day. Blue as a baby's eyes, and them little breezes . . . H'm. Out on the island, a man would better in short order . . . stop wanting to kick somebody's pants up into his cowlick, maybe.

Arvid went back aboard his own boat and ran her in to the float at the town dock, where he tied up. He did not go into the fishhouse, but went quietly past it, stopping only to pick up his wheelbarrow. At the store he bought supplies sufficient, to his way of thinking, for a stay at the island, and walked leisurely back through town, taking his time. No hurry, anyway; anybody wanting to land on General Remarks today, with that sea running, would have to wait on the tide, which wouldn't be high till noon; besides there were a couple of things he had to do. One thing, if he didn't find out what all those gulls were doing over Simon Eldridge's yard, he'd be wondering about it all the time he was gone, and it was only a little bit out of his way.

Simon was hauling the keg out of the lilac bush and looking disagreeable as Arvid went by. He didn't glance around, and Arvid set the wheelbarrow down.

"Lost your mackerel," he ventured.

"See I did, can't you?" Simon said. He did glance around then and did a double take at Arvid's wheelbarrow load. "You going on a picnic?" he asked sourly.

Well, you could make allowances for a man who had responsibilities, and who probably hadn't slept last night, and had got routed out of bed this morning. Simon was the Fire Chief. Arvid himself glanced at his load. Fifty pounds of bacon, steak, lamb chops, baking powder and crackers and potatoes, twenty of flour, two ten-pound bags of sugar; eggs, lard; three pounds of cheese, Hershey bars and some other odds and ends of sweet candy; a five-gallon can of kerosene; and a ham. It rose a man's heart just to look at it. But not Simon's.

"Going out to the island," Arvid said.

"God, if I wouldn't like to go with you," Simon said. He came over to the picket fence, looked down in a blear-eyed way at the load of groceries. "I would sleep for a week," he said. "I am some goddamned old sick of being at every one's beck and call."

"Philomela have much of a fire, did she?"

"Cussed fool lit a flooded oil burner, was all. Where in hell's Freddy? He could have took care of that with one hand," Simon said. "Call me out, rout out the Department . . ." His voice died. He was a tired man.

"Freddy's down in my fishhouse. He is in kind of a state of shock. It is a wonder he wasn't killed and mangled. Old Fanny blowed my punt right through the roof of my fishhouse last night. Just missed him."

"It did? For chrissake!" Simon said, amazed.

That had roused him up some; he'd have that to think about now instead of Freddy and Philomela's business. Arvid picked up the wheelbarrow and walked on. "I wish you'd tell Rodney to take some lumber down, fix my roof when he can," he said, over his shoulder.

"Well, sure," Simon said, staring after him. He said in a feeble voice, "Hurt the punt any?" and Arvid called back, "Not a damn mite. Warn't that lucky?"

So that was taken care of. The other thing was to walk by Philomela's; not to turn his head looking, appear to be nosy, but just to find out, if he could, whether Freddy had gone home yet. Besides, if she saw Arvid with this load of groceries, she'd know where he was going.

She was sitting in the glider on the front porch, staring straight ahead of her. The glare she gave him froze him down to his belt, and he went straight on without saying a word. No sign of Freddy anywhere, and the air all around, even out here in the road where Arvid was, smelt to high heaven of a burnt-out chimney.

✦

General Remarks Island had got its name in the early coasting-schooner days from a Nova Scotia sea captain with astigmatism, who had misread his *Sailing Directions for the Coast of North America from Cape Canso to New York*. He had trouble with parallel lines of print—without his knowing it, his eye sometimes skipped a line or two. Coming down out of the Bay of Fundy in a two-master loaded with dried fish and lumber, he had lost his bearings in a thick and sticky snowstorm, and in unfamiliar waters had scraped keel on some misbegotten place he couldn't identify. The schooner wasn't holed, but she was fast aground; to start her off he had had to jettison most of his deckload of lumber and wait for a rising tide. Later, trying to figure out where he had come to grief, he lost his place in the *Sailing Directions*. His eye went from Gay Head and Gedney's Channel in the Index, and slid right over Gem Island to General Remarks, which he wrote down in his report to the owners. The mate said afterwards that, considering the atmosphere about the time the lumber began splashing overboard and bobbing away on the tide, the title was appropriate.

The story got around among seamen and the name stuck. Gem Island had always been a place to give a wide berth to, and a fretful place to land; in a century and a half, the remarks which had been made about it could certainly be classified as general. It had been named Gem Island on early charts because of an unusual deposit of mica in some rogue boulders on its eastern shore which, given a certain angle of the sun on a summer morning, threw off sparkles. During the mining boom in the 1880s, when everybody on the coast who owned an acre of land expected to find gold or silver on it, the ledges at Gem Island had got a good going over. But so much for hopes and labors; anything that sparkled in a rock might look valuable, but nobody found anything except two crystals of black tourmaline which made good keepsakes. According to a later State Geology report, the boulders were undoubtedly gem-bearing pegmatite, carried down from some northern deposit during the ice age by a glacier. About what you could expect of the place, the disgruntled miners said. Anything that looked good there, wasn't. A general remark, if there ever was one.

General Remarks, in the summer, was a magical place where the ocean ended the climax forest seeded down from the north. Even a man sailing past it could smell it—a wonderful combination of wild roses, juniper resin, and salt marsh. But in the winter, the best that could be said of it was that its western side was a salt-ice bog, its eastern a mass of black foam-washed ledges, with the frozen forest between.

The island was a mile long and three miles around—four times that if you followed precisely all its indentations. It was six miles from the nearest mainland if you sailed north or west, three thousand if you made a mistake and by some mischance sailed east. The people who settled there were second-generation from England and Ireland, by way of Massachusetts; they disembarked in the spring and fell down and kissed the earth. They thought they had landed in a butter tub—a fine free place that smelt good—doubtless because of some race memory of what their ancestors had had to put up with. Their descendants toughed it out for nearly a century and a half before throwing in the towel and moving ashore.

In the years they had lived there, they had been proud of the place and they had taken care of it. They built some twenty neat gabled houses, with barns and outbuildings, painted them white and, for the most part, kept them painted; they cleared fields and kept them clear. They farmed their woodlots—on an island where every stick that didn't grow there had to be carried on by hand, a man didn't destroy trees needlessly, nor did he leave slash piles and wild undergrowth to catch fire and burn up in a dry season. In its heyday, General Remarks was as neat as a park, its fields and woodlands as pleasant to walk in. It was not now.

The hayfields, without care, had come up to running juniper; the woodlots were matchsticked with blowdowns; the spruces had moved into the village. Most of the houses, the church, the schoolhouse were gone, or going—either burned down or rotted into the cellar holes. The place now had the haunted look of any ghost town, by moonlight especially strange. There were those who swore that they had seen Arvid's grandmother and her lightning-struck sister Lu sitting, inside the naked studs of what had once been the parsonage parlor—which Arvid could have proved to be a lie, but didn't for reasons of his own. He let the story go, even added to it the horrid detail of Great-aunt Lu being headless in the moonlight, it being to his advantage not to have Tom, Dick, and Harry—or say, Ed Snorri and his two hellers of twins, Dewey and Truman—landing on the island at night, or at any other time when Arvid wasn't there. His own house was the only one left still livable at all; he did have to leave it alone all winter, and he liked to be sure his things would be there, untouched, when he came back in the spring. Besides that, there were always some irresponsibles who would leave a picnic fire burning; and the wilderness the island was now, a spark would set it off like a bundle of matches. The best way, he felt, was to let on, now and then, that General Remarks had little unpleasantnesses, unexplained. If people wanted to believe it, that is, they could.

Arvid's old farmhouse was in a sad state of disrepair; he was ashamed, he said, to have folks see it. But every stick of lumber, every shingle, every can of paint, had to be boated over from the mainland, and backed or wheelbarrowed to the house; he had nearly killed himself over the years keeping the roof tight. He would get in fairly good shape out there in summer; then, through the winter, everything would start to go to pieces. If the Snorri kids didn't, windows would break themselves, shingles would blow off, plaster would fall in the upstairs rooms. Arvid, of late years, had limited himself to two rooms—the kitchen and a downstairs bedroom.

He said it was only a matter of time before the goddamned shebang would fall down on his head and bury him; at that, it might be a better burial than being put with his folks in the island cemetery, which was nothing now but a forest of spruces, some of them a foot thick. He might not have much choice, he said, and it probably wouldn't be too bad once you got used to it, but he had a dislike of being sucked up into a spruce tree.

On the south side of the island was a pretty little harbor, sheltered on three sides, but unfortunately open on the side toward the ocean. This had fooled the early settlers, but not for long. It was one of the things about General Remarks dreamed up to drive a man crazy; it was a fine harbor in all kinds of weather except bad. An easterly would drive rollers in there eight to ten feet high, making it impossible to land anywhere or to hold a boat on a mooring. The only other place to keep a fishing boat was behind a chesil beach on the western side, a place called the Salt Pond. This, too, was a lovely little harbor, cupped between the beach and the salt marshes; that is, it was at high tide. At low tide, every drop of water was drained out of it, leaving some three acres of soft flats mud. The inlet to the Salt Pond was narrow and long with a tricky channel; unless the tide were unusually high, a man who didn't know his way around there was sure to go aground. The tide, too, went in and out like a millrace, filling and emptying the Salt Pond fast, and sucking in any kind of nuisances of driftwood, ice cakes, and rafts of rockweed that might be floating around the bay.

As a consequence of these natural resources, any fisherman who had ever lived on General Remarks had grown up as a slave of the tide. If some of them walked nights now, Arvid said, it wouldn't be surprising. When the weather looked all right and the tide was going to serve low in the early morning, a man would leave his boat on his mooring in the Outer Harbor. Then he would go to sleep with one eye open. If the weather changed—and it could in ten minutes—if the wind shifted "out" and started to blow, he would have to stagger out of bed, go get his boat, drive her around through the inlet in the dark, and put her on his other mooring in the Salt Pond. Then he would have to put her "legs" on; these being lengths of four-by-four nailed together in the shape of an *L*, which fastened to ringbolts, one on each side, in the washboard, and kept the boat from tipping sideways on her keel as the tide drained away under her. Without legs a boat tipped sideways on the clamflats, was likely to fill with water before she righted when the tide came in.

Oh, you live on General Remarks, Arvid told himself, you either grow patience or you go nuts.

He was coasting along the western shore of the island, coming up on the outside of the chesil beach on which blue water and high tide creamed a long edge of foam. It was not possible to land on the beach because of an uncommonly treacherous batch of rocks, barely covered with water at high tide; but, right now, the curved length of pebbles was a pretty sight. Them curves, he thought, is nice. Always reminded him of a woman. Nothing nasty, or like of that, just a half-mile of long, sweet curves, in-and-out. Pleasant. Like a woman.

Arvid felt fine again. The boat ride out had blown all the disagreeableness out of his head; he was looking forward to a campfire on the beach and a fat broiled steak, with a nap afterwards and not a soul to bother him. He was thinking absently that with the wind a different way, from the east, he could have smelt that good juniper smell, coming up this close to the island, when he heard a bumping sound from the cuddy and Freddy stuck his head out of the hatch.

"For Godsake!" Arvid said, looking at him, and all his good feelings blew away on the wind.

Freddy looked better; apparently he had gone aboard at the town float and had been asleep down there, and the sleep had done him good. He grinned at Arvid. "I ain't welcome, I guess," he said.

"Well, as to that, it ain't neither here nor there," Arvid said. "I supposed you'd gone home. Didn't you know you had a fire up to your house?"

"That where it was? I heard the whistle. What'd she do, get her doughnut fat too hot?"

"Freddy, you ought to go home. I've got a good mind to turn right round and go back."

"Why? She can burn the house down if she wants to. It's her house. She ain't going to let me into it until she cools off some." Freddy stared off over the water at the long inlet into the Salt Pond which was opening up ahead. "You know, this is one high tide, Arvid."

No use to talk to him, not when he got that you-bedamned look. So make the best of it. Out here, he might cool off himself—wasn't any use for him to go home now, anyway, feeling the way he did.

They were halfway up the long inlet before anyone spoke again.

Freddy said. "I don't think I ever saw the channel in here so full. Must be a couple of feet higher than normal."

"Fanny, that was," Arvid said. "Piled half the bay in here last night. You can see where it was—four–five feet higher'n this." He indicated the tidemark, piles of rockweed and debris along the shore.

"Ought to be a mess of drift up at the end of the marsh," Freddy said. "After dinner, we'll have to go on a hunt. Might even find a trap or two."

He sounded quite cheerful, as if the cooling-off process might have begun. Maybe this had been the thing to do after all. Shoot, you didn't mind company, so long as it was good company. Arvid's own spirits began to rise. What would be, would be, and no sense repining. Buckle down while you could, and enjoy.

He spun the wheel as the inlet opened out into the Salt Pond. "Pretty in here, ain't it?" he said. "And not a soul to bother a man. You wouldn't think that in the old days there was ten–fifteen moorings in here, would you? Where now there's but one—mine."

He ran the boat alongside his mooring buoy, gaffed it in. "I don't know as I feel like manhandling all them groceries up to the house, build a fire in a stove before I eat. I've got dry wood in the cuddy and we've got a whole skiff-full of steak, ham, and eggs, whatever anybody wants." He jerked a thumb at his skiff, towing behind. The punkinseed, of course, for a trip like this was no good; she wouldn't tow very well, and she had made the journey pulled up across the stern of the powerboat. "I thought I'd build a fire, eat on the rocks in the sun. That is," he finished delicately, "if the smell of the cooking won't bother you, Freddy."

Freddy grinned. "Well, as you know," he said, "I couldn't eat a raw rat. Like you could. But you know, I could eat."

Ham and eggs and steak wasn't enough, Arvid said, when he had the fire going. Why didn't they cook some potatoes? Wouldn't take long and, Godsake, the ham and eggs would keep and there was a lot of steak, so why didn't they have steak and potatoes? He prepared these items, while Freddy took a bucket and went along to the spring after water. When he got back, things were beginning to smell good even to him. He told Arvid so.

"Beats all about this island," Arvid said. "It'll bring even a dead man to."

"So I've been told."

"Shoot, they ain't nothing in that."

"I ain't so sure. I had a feeling up by the spring somebody was watching me."

Arvid grinned. "That so? You wait till I get the coffee going. You'll see angels. Gi' me a holt of that water bucket—Hey!" Glancing past Freddy, his eyes widened with surprise. "Heb'm sake!" he said. "Now, where'd that come from? Here, kitty, kitty, kitty. Look, Freddy, ain't that a pretty little black and white cat?"

Earlier that morning Liz had found the spring. She couldn't think how long it had been since she had had a drink of water, only sticky juice out of canned peaches from one of the cans rolling around the cabin floor. For hours, in the night, the houseboat had pitched and rolled so dreadfully that she and Marney couldn't stay in the bunk. He had braced his back and held on, trying to hold her and the little cat in; but sometime, she couldn't remember when it was, there had come a terrible yank and jerk that had thrown them out onto the cabin floor. She had fallen on Marney and wasn't hurt, except she bumped her face on the side of the bunk, and the little cat had hung on with its claws; but Marney had been slammed all the way across the cabin and had fetched up against the wall. He had hurt himself, too, for he'd just lain there for a minute, and hadn't answered when she called. Then the boat rolled the other way and brought him back.

He had hooked his fingers into the sideboard of the bunk, and she had held on to him. For a while, the only thing they could do was sit on the floor hanging on. Then the boat stopped pitching quite so much and the wind howling didn't sound so loud. They were able to get back into the bunk and stay there; but Marney didn't talk. He only lay making a faint sound that sounded like "oh" in the back of his throat.

Sometime in the night the boat stopped pitching altogether. She bumped against something, quite hard. Liz could hear water rushing along her sides, but she floated easy. Then there was a long, slithery, sliding noise on her bottom; she heeled and swung a little and finally stopped moving at all.

By that time, Liz was so scared and slammed around and tired that she could hardly move. If he's hurt, she thought, what'll I ever do? Let the old houseboat sink, if Marney was hurt, she wouldn't be able to care if it did. She began to cry.

But he moved a little, and said, "What happened?" His voice was hoarse, but he sounded all right. All she could manage to say was, "Did it hurt you? Are you hurt bad?"

He didn't answer for a minute. Then he said in a puzzled voice, "Oh. It's stopped." He raised up on one elbow and listened and she thought he was going to get up, but then he lay down again. He said, "We're aground, I think. We aren't moving, are we?"

"No. Can we stay here?"

"We'll . . . have to . . . wait for daylight. I . . . can't . . ." His voice stopped and she thought he had gone to sleep. Then he said, "Don't . . . cry. I'm all right. Just . . . got a bump."

Oh, good. He wasn't hurt. Just tired and bumped, the way she was, and wet from rolling around on the cabin floor.

Liz pulled the blankets, all the ones she could reach, over them both, burrowed close to his back, and slept.

When she woke up, the sun was shining. The boat was still. She could see branches of trees and blue sky outside a window. Marney was still asleep, at least he was snoring deep down in his chest. She poked him a little and he moved and opened his eyes. He didn't see her apparently. He just said, "Water. A drink of water," and shut his eyes again.

Well, he must be awfully tired. She decided to let him sleep. Maybe she could find some water, get a drink for him. She was certainly thirsty herself.

Where was the little black and white cat?

The cabin was a terrible mess. Its floor was slanted slightly uphill and its door was open, swinging on the hinges. Everything loose that had been able to move had rolled down in heaps to that side—cans with labels washed off, soggy blankets, mattresses off the bunks, broken dishes. Liz put her feet out of the bunk. She felt wet and shivery. Everything hurt. Her face was sore and swollen, her arms and legs seemed almost to make a noise, like creaking. But she got out of bed and looked all over the cabin. In the bunks. Everywhere.

Well, what could you expect? The houseboat had been nice, but when in all your life had you had anything nice, had it to keep? You could put up with the mess in the houseboat, you had put up with messes before, and it hadn't killed you. But now the little black and white cat was gone.

I suppose she fell overboard. Like my foolish father. But he wasn't anything, only something I thought in my mind. And she had a little silky black head.

The tears started to sting and roll down. It wasn't any time to cry, but she couldn't stop. She did stop the loud bawls when they began to come, because of waking Marney, who needed so badly to sleep. She tasted the tears running down to the corners of her mouth—they were salty and wet, reminding her of how terribly thirsty she was. And Marney, too. He had wanted a drink of water.

At least I have got him left. He is the nicest boy I ever saw.

In the galley all the pots and pans were on top of each other. Wiping tears with the back of her hand, Liz found a bucket.

The houseboat had driven up across what looked like a big swamp and had stopped some way up a sloping bank with her bow in a clump of alders. Liz had no trouble jumping ashore. At the top of the bank, she found a path.

It was an old path or maybe a cart road; she could see traces of ruts overgrown with grass and small bushes, as if wheels had gone there once, but not for a long time. It led across some swampy ground, with mud puddles. The puddles were foul with floating twigs and grass—you wouldn't drink that unless you had to. The path sloped up through some big old trees and down to the shore again. And there was a nice, clean, rock-walled-up spring, with a cover on it.

Liz drank for a long time. The water was so good, icy cold and sweet. In the overflow from the spring, she tried to wash her hands and face. Her face was too sore to touch; what was on it needed soap. She hadn't any. But maybe she could find some back at the boat. She filled her bucket again and carried it back along the path. She was just climbing aboard again when she heard, quite far off, the sound of an engine. A motorboat, somewhere.

Liz stopped, listening. People. So be careful. People, most often, meant trouble—or always had. Some were all right; but would you want *Them* busting in on you and Marney? What they did, they made you feel mean, and you hadn't felt mean for quite a while. So watch it, dope. They'll take over everything, too.

Marney was still asleep. She set the bucket down beside the bunk, put a cup beside it, within reach of his hand. He needs to sleep, he's awfully tired, she thought. She wouldn't wake him. She waited a little while, but he slept on, still making the snoring sound in his chest.

Well, she would go and see if there were any people—what they looked like. Maybe he'd be awake by the time she got back.

The man getting water at the spring was big and tall and skinny. He yanked the cover off and slammed it back on with his foot. He had a face brown from the sun, quite good looking, only his hat was pulled down. She couldn't tell whether he was one of *Them* or not. He went back along the shore with his bucket.

Liz followed at a cautious distance.

I and Marney, she told herself, can live by ourselves a long time on that boat. Dry things in the sun. And there's lots to eat left in the cans.

Because now, through the bushes, she could see the fire burning. On it was a big bubbling kettle and a frying pan with, in it, a great piece of browning steak. And *smell* it! Her empty stomach made a noise that almost sounded like flapping.

What an e-normous fat man! Big as a house and funny looking and—

Liz froze in her tracks. The fat man was calling, "Kitty, kitty, kitty"; he was cutting off a slice of the steak and blowing on it and holding it out. And there, coming along the top of a big driftwood log that lay there on the shore, was the little black and white cat. Was Toughy. There she was.

There was her little silky black head.

From over Liz, the shadow rolled away. She felt as if a great dark cloud had gone, and out had come the sun. She crouched in the bushes, grinning from ear to ear.

Maybe things would be all right. Something good at last had happened to Liz Bigelow. For once of all the world, she had got a thing back to keep.

They were all eating. Steak and potatoes. Toughy was stuffing. She was having steak.

That must be a nice man, to give a cat such a great big piece of steak. Wait, though. You never knew. He might not be nice at all. But her mouth was watering all the way down to her stomach.

The tall skinny man put his hand in a paper bag and hauled out a handful of Hershey bars. He stuffed them in his pocket. He took an apple and got up.

He said, "I'm going to take a look alongshore, Arvid, see if I can locate any castaway traps. You going to have a nap?"

"Well, don't know but I might cork off for a while," the fat man said. He lay down with his head on the log and his hat over his face and almost at once began to make loud snoring noises.

Toughy sat on the other end of the log, washing; she was rounded out, full to the brim. She must be full, or she'd be stealing the rest of the steak. The frying pan was right there on the ground in front of her, with a great big piece left in it.

Liz stared at the steak. She came out of the bushes an inch at a time, let herself noiselessly down the bank.

The steak was still warm, slightly greasy from the pan. Lovely! She couldn't wait to take a great bite, telling herself she would eat just half of it, save the rest for Marney. It was hard to chew because her face was so sore; but before she could stop, the steak was all gone. Before she knew it!

Liz Bigelow is a pig. A big pig-hog! But it had been so *good*.

There was a paper bag, though, that might have something in it she could take back to Marney. She leaned and peered into it. Mm-m, great big soda biscuits and some apples, and a lot, a great whole lot, of Hershey bars!

Silently, except for a discreet crackle of paper, Liz gathered in the paper bag. She turned to go, was halfway up the bank before she remembered Toughy.

How could I do that? Leave her here? What if the man went off with her, took her away? He liked cats, you could tell he did.

Liz hissed, "*Ps-st*, come on, will you?" Toughy didn't even stop washing her face.

The paper bag decided the matter. It had been sitting for some time on a patch of damp sand; its bottom was wet. It gave. All the things in it fell out, thump, thump, thump onto the beach. One apple fell into the frying pan, which gave out a loud tinny clatter.

The fat man's face came out from under his hat; he sat up with a jump, looked around every whichway, and saw Liz. He gave her one look and let out a great, roaring holler.

"Holy great shivering jazzus! What's that? Freddy! Help!"

Toughy went off the end of the log and made it to the bushes in two jumps; Liz made it in three. She vanished fast, but Arvid, in the second or so before he had come to his full senses, had been sure the dream he'd been having wasn't a dream. The sight of Liz would have been a shock to a nervous man awake, Her ragged-cut, foxy hair stood straight up all over her head. She had one black eye; her entire cheek on the same side was swollen black and blue, and she was dressed in a ripped, muddy T-shirt tucked into a pair of pink lace underpants.

To Arvid, who wouldn't watch television—unless he got roped in and had to, to keep from hurting some neighbor's feelings—because blood and thunder gave him nightmares, Liz was a TV show walking. Then he jerked awake and realized that that hadn't been it at all, nothing of the kind.

He heard a pounding of steps on the path, and Freddy burst out of the bushes. Seeing him, Arvid waved a reassuring hand.

" 'S all right, Freddy. Sorry I hollered. Had a bad dream, and then I see—"

Freddy wasn't interested in that. "Look, Arvid, there's a houseboat wrecked up the inlet, must've gone ashore in the storm last night. There's a sick kid aboard of her. The way he breathes, he's got a helluva case of pneumonia. If we step on it, we can get the boat up the inlet, take him off before the tide ebbs too far. Because that's one kid that sure needs a doctor fast!"

The tide today had been unusually high, but nothing compared to last night's, when the weight of Fanny had rolled water from the bay through the inlet and up to the top of the marsh. The *Sea Flower* had driven in at the height of the flood. She was high and dry on the bank. To float her would take another hurricane.

It was only a quarter of a mile up the inlet to where she lay, but by the time Arvid and Freddy made it in the powerboat, the tide had peaked and had already started to drain the marsh. The water, when it started to go, went fast. They had to hurry. They anchored the boat and rowed the last forty feet or so in the skiff.

Marney was awake when they boarded the houseboat. He was sitting doubled over on the edge of the bunk, but he did not look up when they came into the cabin. Arvid went over and put a hand on his cheek. "Helluva fever," he said. "Goddlemighty, no wonder. He's wetter'n a rat."

Marney flinched away from the hand. He said hoarsely, "Don't, Joe. Please don't!"

"Crazy with it, poor little duffer," Arvid said. "Freddy, if we take him out of here wet, it'll likely kill him."

"No time," Freddy said. "Look, step on it, Arvid. Come on, fella, can you walk?"

"Sure, I can walk," Marney said. "What's the matter with you?" His voice lapsed into a mumble, but he got up and stood swaying. "Toughy," he said, clearly. "And the kid. There's a kid . . ."

"They're all right," Arvid said. "I'll look out for them. You come on now, boy. We're going to see a doctor."

With help, Marney made it to the skiff, but he had to be lifted aboard the powerboat. She was not quite aground, but when Arvid started the engine, her propeller stirred up a cloud of black flats mud. Freddy didn't even try to haul up the anchor, he cast it off—easy enough to pick it up again on any low tide.

While Freddy steered the boat cautiously down the draining inlet, Arvid got Marney out of his wet clothes and into one of the bunks in the cuddy, wrapped in all the dry blankets he had aboard. Then he started a fire in the stove, got it going good and hot, shut the drafts and damper. There wasn't much else he could do, and by that time they were out of the inlet into the deeper water of the Salt Pond, where, briefly, Freddy cut the engine.

"You better take him right in to the dock at Powell," Arvid said, hauling up the skiff by the painter and climbing into it.

Freddy nodded. Powell wasn't much farther by water, and of course, the hospital was there.

"Tell them to send down the ambulance and for goddlemighty's sake, to handle him easy," Arvid said. "He's just about one black and blue spot all over."

"Okay," Freddy said. "I won't get back tonight, Arvid."

"No use to. You'll have to notify the Coast Guard, anyway."

"See you tomorrow then. About one."

"Good," Arvid said. "Bring some more steak."

Freddy eased the boat carefully out through the channel, watching on either side for mudbanks or rocks. It was a winding channel, difficult for anyone who wasn't used to it. Arvid, of course, could run it in his sleep; if he had been taking the boat in to Powell, he would probably have thought nothing of coming back tonight after midnight.

Not me, Freddy thought, seeing with relief the mouth of the inlet, with deep water, opening up in front of him. It was a devilish channel, even by daylight.

Glancing back, as General Remarks dwindled behind him, Freddy told himself he was glad he wasn't the one marooned overnight on the goddamned tide hole. Arvid, of course, had been the one to stay. He knew the island, all the paths and places where somebody would be likely to go; he had to hunt up that scared kid, in case the kid didn't show. Funny he hadn't. Too scared, maybe. Freddy had caught sight of him diving into the bushes alongside the path, and making time, too; and no wonder, because Arvid had let out an awful beller.

Besides, that ghost town up there was enough to give anyone the heebie-jeebies. Place didn't look friendly. Pretty, God, yes! Along the shore; nice to have a picnic on a sunny day. But all the time you were there, you had a feeling. Something nudging you to get out, go away, leave it alone. That was foolish, but nevertheless, Freddy had felt it. Or felt something. It had probably been those old ruined dwelling houses up there in what had been the village. That church, with the bell tumbled down out of the belfry, lying on the ground; hymn books helter-skelter all over the floor, rotted with rain where the roof was open to the sky; and the cemetery-trees growing up among all those old slate-colored gravestones. Funny about Arvid. Scared into the shakes by a thundershower, but cuddling down like a cat under a stove on General Remarks Island.

Down below, in the cuddy, the sick boy muttered something, and Freddy pushed at the lever, trying to push it up another notch, get a little speed out of the engine.

Well, he'd notify the Coast Guard about that wrecked houseboat, mention that they'd find her hitched by her bow cable to a tree. Where she was grounded out, no one was ever going to be able to launch her again, unless old Fanny came back, and if she happened to be abandoned for salvage, Freddy Fowler had a line to her.

Arvid rowed thoughtfully ashore. A skiff was all right, nice steady boat, but heavy. Rowing one against a running tide took it out of a man, He wished he could have taken his punt.

The damn gulls was into them spilt groceries. As he neared shore, Arvid hollered and splashed with his oars, and a cloud of them flew up. Then he was sorry he'd hollered, because that youngster must be around there somewhere in the hinterlands.

And I already scared him to death, hollering, when I come out of my nightmare. Poor little duffer, if I go hunting him now, he'll think I'm chasing him.

Arvid was worried about the boy. There were too many places even a grown man could fall into, running headlong around those woods—cellar holes, open wells. So never mind the gulls in the groceries; he'd have to start hunting right away. But as he landed on the beach and pulled the skiff up a little, dropping her anchor so she wouldn't drift away, he caught a glimpse through the bushes of the pink lace underpants, just disappearing.

Well, good. The kid wasn't in a hard way, he was still walking around. So first things first. Take the groceries up to the house. Open up windows and doors to let good new air through; build a fire in the stove. Then fix a gol-rorious old beef stew with a lot of onions and leave it in the oven. That youngster might be scared—and a lot of good I could do, chasing him—and he might be lost; but in time, what he'd be most was hungry. Where he would come to, seemed likely, was a lived-in house, smoke coming out of the chimney, and the smell of something good cooking.

He went up the bank to the clump of bushes, where, when he had left the island a few weeks ago, he had hidden his wheelbarrow. Each time he went to the mainland, he did this. While it wasn't far up to the house, still, if the wheelbarrow was down to the shore, you didn't have to go up and get it, make two trips. He didn't have to hunt far in the clump to find out that the wheelbarrow was gone. There was the place where it had been, he could see the mark of the wheel.

"Oh, blast it and damn it," he said. He backed out of the bushes, glancing upward into the treetops. Yup, there she was. Them damn Snorri twins again.

The wheelbarrow, being painted bright red, was easy to see. Someone had tied a rope to the wheel, flung the end over a lower limb of a big spar spruce tree, and hoisted the barrow up to it. It was a senseless trick, because they hadn't bothered to cut off the end of the rope—they had just tied it to the trunk of another tree. All Arvid had to do was to untie the rope and let the wheelbarrow down. He did so, thinking disgustedly that brighter kids would have made things a little more difficult; with the Snorris, this was about what you could expect.

126

The Snorri kids weren't bright; but they were bloodyminded little horrors. They lived over in town and went fishing with their father, Ed Snorri, who wasn't much brighter or older in his mind than they were. The three of them accounted for most of the deviltry carried on yearly in the Township and along the shoreline. If somebody pulled your traps and stole the lobsters; broke into a garage or a henhouse; swiped stuff out of the grocery in the daylight; or drove off in somebody's car and left it where they got out of it, the Sheriff didn't draw a second breath. He just went along to Ed's and found the stuff and arrested someone.

Ed was hauled in once or twice a year; once in a while, but not often, he served a short term in the county jail. Generally, if he could be let off without pinching the law too much, he was; because he had a wife and eight children under sixteen, who all had to be supported out of public money when Ed wasn't around. No use being shortsighted about such things. Another reason why he was handled so gently, he stuttered. All the Snorris did, except Ed's wife—the kids had got it from him—but he was the fanciest stutterer of them all. To see him before a judge would wring pity from a tough man . . . Ed Snorri, well-meaning but misunderstood, not responsible for his hard luck and times, ragged-coated, tears running into his whiskers, and above all, Judge, the father of small children. Ed worked hard at his stuttering; he could end up sounding like steam coming out of a rusty pipe, helpless and pitiful. He would return the stolen goods; his boys were hard to handle; as soon as he could find the money, he'd pay for the busted windows. Or whatever. He would get off; he could count on it.

The Snorris had played this trick with Arvid's wheelbarrow before; Arvid knew why. They figured that anyone who would paint a wheelbarrow red and name it *Buttercup* was half-witted and meat for them. They'd landed here at the island one day last summer—Ed and the twins were always landing around on islands to beachcomb, or to break into a summer cottage, or to bust a few windows for kicks. Arvid had just finished the red paint job, and was lettering the name, *Buttercup*, across the wheelbarrow's bow in bright yellow. It was a harmless matter, a lazy job for a summer afternoon, but the Snorris thought it was crazy. You could see how their minds worked. So whenever they landed here now, the idea was, before they left, pull some kind of a trick with *Buttercup*.

If they keep on, Arvid told himself, carefully lowering the barrow to the ground, I am going to have words with Ed.

He got the groceries up to the house and stowed, and his fire built. Half an hour later his stew was simmering, beginning to smell good. Give it a while, with the doors and windows open, it would stink up a patch a hundred feet wide, all around the house. It ought to toll that youngster out of the undergrowth, if anything would. Arvid took a deep, appreciative sniff. It would toll him, before God, it would.

But all the stew tolled in was the little black and white cat, who strolled through the door, smelled around the room a while, and then took up residence under the cookstove, as if she owned the place.

At least he had *her* cornered.

He put the covered stew in the oven to simmer, shut the kitchen door, leaving the screened windows open, and went out to hunt. By dusk, he hadn't found a sign of the youngster; it was as if he were alone on the island.

The reason Arvid hadn't seen Liz was that she had seen him first. She had followed him, keeping out of sight but watching where he went, which was, several times that afternoon, to the houseboat. The first time, she had peered out of the bushes at him while he climbed aboard and went into the cabin.

He's gone in there to snoop, she told herself. To see what he can steal. If he comes out with anything, I am going to throw rocks till he drops it. This boat belongs to I and Marney.

Marney was sick. They had taken him away in a boat, who knew where, to see a doctor. She had heard that much, listening from the bushes. Seeing them go, she had felt so scared and lonesome that she had almost run out on the shore and yelled to be taken along, too. It had been awful. And then she'd thought, right away, that somebody had to stay here with the little black and white cat and keep care of the houseboat and Marney's things till he got back. He would come back as soon as he could; he wouldn't leave Toughy and the motorbike.

The bike was still there, in the little gold room. It was probably broken. She couldn't tell; all she could see was one side of the handlebars, sticking out above the ripped and shredded remains of the canvas curtains. There wasn't much left of the little gold room either. The awning was gone and the pipe-things that had held it up were all bent and twisted.

If *They* would leave I and Marney alone, we could fix things. Marney could, and I could help him. So I am going to keep care. Let that old snoop come out of there with one single thing, he is going to get a rock in his big fat face.

But the big snoop came out without anything at all. He stood on the deck looking this way and that, fished a pencil and a little black notebook out of his pocket, and wrote something. He tore out the leaf he had written on, pushed it behind the doorknob on the cabin door. Then he got off the boat, grunting a little as he climbed down, and walked away into the woods.

Liz waited until she was sure he was gone, Then she went aboard and read the note he had left:

"I'm sorry I hollered so loud. I wasn't hollering at you. I was to sleep and having a bad dream when you come, all I hollered at was what I see in the dream. There is a fire in my house to get warm by, and there is a beef stew in the oven. Your cat is under the stove. Go in and help yourself. A. Small."

Liz stared at the note. It didn't sound too bad. She was hungry again, too, and m-m, beef stew. Then she noticed "P.S. (over)" at the bottom of the note.

"Your bother was sick, so we had to hustle him ashore to doctor. If you will come over to the house, we will take you to where he is tomorrow, and find your folks so you can go home. A. Small."

Igerant. Can't even spell "brother."

Well, that's what *They* would do, all *They* would think of. Send you back to Cousin Emily, who all *she* could think of was babysitting. And the Bowkers . . . !

So much had happened, she had got so used to thinking of the houseboat as hers, that she had forgotten all about the Bowkers, what they would do if she got caught here and sent back home. They must know, by now, what she'd done to the houseboat. They'd put her in jail.

Liz stared around her in horror. She went into the cabin and closed the door.

It was awful in the cabin. Everything was wet where the water had come in when the door had blown open in the night. It smelt wet. Horrid. She thought at first she would try to clean it up; but there was so much of it. She was tired and stiff, everything ached. If only the mattresses and blankets weren't so damp, she could go to sleep in one of the bunks. No, she couldn't. Mr. A. Small might come back. She looked hopelessly around the cabin.

Maybe there was something dry in the drawers or in the lockers; there had been lots of warm things there on yesterday, and one or two of them hadn't banged open. Oh, joy, there were! A dry sweater and some dungarees that must have belonged to one of the Bowker boys; if she'd found them first she wouldn't have had to look so awful in Ma Bowker's pink pants. She put them on. And in a locker, she found a big woolly blanket, dry as could be in a cellophane bag.

Where would she put it? Not here. Not in the cabin. Because of Mr. A. Small. He might come back.

She took the blanket out on to the bank into the thickest clump of bushes she could find. The ground was damp, but she could double up the blanket. She sat on it awhile.

Through the bushes she could see the houseboat. Even though it was so nearby, it wasn't very comforting. Past it was the whole length of the marsh, the water all gone out of it now, leaving patches of shiny, slimy-looking green stuff and great expanses of mud. It was suppertime. It must be. She was so hungry.

Everything was lonesome and gone bad. Marney was sick. He was gone. Maybe he would die and never come back. And Mr. A. Small had the little black and white cat.

Mr. A. Small. Mr. A. Big. Mr. A. Big Liar. Liz sucked a tooth. The little squeaking sound, even that, the only sound there was, sounded lonesome.

Mr. A. Small right now was probably giving Toughy some of that beef stew. All right, let him. I have got something to eat aboard I and Marney's houseboat. I'm hungry, that's why I feel so bad.

Cautiously, looking around, she crept back aboard the boat. She picked up one of the cans from the pile by the cabin door. She couldn't tell what was in the can, the paper was washed off, but anyway, it would be something to eat. Where was the can opener? It was lost amongst all that stuff, and not time to hunt for it, *he* might come. Then she saw it, lying all by itself on the floor.

Liz gouged and tore, bent back the cover of the can. The smell came up into her face; something deep in her stomach said, "Br-rrmp!" It was a can of crabmeat.

She backed away. She wasn't hungry anymore. She dove out of the cabin and back into the bushes, buried herself in the blanket, and howled. For a while she made noise, but there was nobody to hear it. The noise became sniffs and hiccups and then silence. She was asleep.

Mr. A. Small came back twice before dark. He saw his note was gone and knew the boy must have taken it; but he couldn't find anyone anywhere. Well, he would try again, later.

When Liz woke up, it was dark; that is, it was quite dark, but there was a moon in the sky. Something had waked her, some noise, a sound like a bump. Sleepily, she lay listening, then, suddenly, bounced wide awake, with a jump. The bump was footsteps on the houseboat's deck, and people were talking. Voices. Men's voices, making, not words, but a funny kind of noise.

Liz turned cold all over; she began to shake. It couldn't be Mr. Big; he was alone, nobody to talk to. Or maybe the other man had come back. But this wasn't real talking; it sounded like arp-talk.

"Pup-pup-pup-parp," one voice said. "Lul-lul-lul—" and another voice answered almost the same way.

Liz got out from under the blanket. She crept on all fours to the edge of the thicket.

The moon was high in the sky, some little clouds flying past it. Things seemed almost as bright as day. She couldn't see anyone; but she could hear them. They were down in the cockpit, where the little gold room used to be. The tide was high again over the marsh, which lay in the moonlight like a big sheet, silvery and still. Some men had come in a boat. She could see the boat anchored out in the marsh; she could see the skiff they had rowed ashore in, hauled up a few feet from the houseboat's stern.

The men kept talking; they were pulling things around, not caring how much noise they made, didn't know anybody was there. She made out at last what the talk was; they were all stuttering, and she could understand a little of what they said. Not everything, but enough to know that they'd come to take away anything on the boat that was lul-lul-loose; and that the first thing they were going to get was Marney's motorcycle.

Liz didn't stop for anything. She took a running jump out of the thicket and landed with a thump on the path. She landed running. Because Mr. A. Small would have to come and help. He was all there was and he would have to do something.

Not far down the path, she ran head-on into Arvid, coming along at a trot, with a bucket in one hand and a darkened flashlight in the other.

He said something like "Wha-rr-p!" as the breath went out of him, and then he set the bucket down, put his arm around her and held her, her face close up against his chest.

"Sh-h," he said in her ear, in a whisper. "Don't make a sound. Sh-h, now. It's all right. Keep still."

"But they're stealing . . . they're taking . . ."

"I know. Keep still. I'm here. I'm onto them. I know who they are." He rocked her gently back and forth, patting her head, she realized, with the flashlight. "Don't you be scared, sonny," he whispered. "I have got a thing here to fix them jokers with, and you are just who I need to help me. What I have got here in this bucket is a dough face."

Arvid had been lying on his bed, fully dressed and wide awake, when he had heard Snorri's boat come into the Salt Pond. He had lain down there to rest for a minute before going out to hunt some more, and was wondering where on earth to look now; before dark he had covered a lot of ground. By this time, he was really concerned; that poor little duffer must be lying out there in the woods and swamps, maybe lost, maybe sick the way the other one had been, and, if neither, then certainly scared to death. This island was spooky enough by daylight; but in moonlight, those old empty ruins would scare the feathers off a jaybird. He would go out again as soon as he could, but he would have to rest first. He must have walked ten miles, and his feet were killing him.

He'd been just about to get up when he heard Snorri's boat. No mistaking who it was . . . he'd know that gasping put-put anywhere. Old Ed and those two heathen savages of his, and it wouldn't take a bookkeeper to add two and two, either. Sometime during the day them bastards had spotted the wrecked houseboat from the water, and they were gathering in like buzzards. And what they would leave was about what buzzards would leave, too.

Arvid went to the window and saw Snorri's boat start up the inlet in the moonlight. The house was dark, so they couldn't see him. He hadn't lighted a lamp when he'd come in and tumbled down on the bed, and that was fortunate. They probably thought there wasn't anybody here on the island—must've seen Freddy taking his boat ashore this afternoon, and thought he'd gone, too. Well, it was going to be their hard luck.

What he'd like to do was take the shotgun and go out and let go with a little Number Five shot; but no, you never could tell with a shotgun; even rock salt had been known, in the old days, to kill somebody, and you wouldn't want to do that. Arvid's mind went back to a thing out of his boyhood, something that had been used to very good effect even that long ago.

Yes, by God. You couldn't think of three nicer people to try that on than Ed Snorri and his twins.

The Snorris had already been made a little apprehensive by the sound of Liz crackling away into the underbrush; at least the twins had had a jump taken out of them, and the old man stopped chewing his tobacco to listen, shifting the cud from one side to the other.

Dewey said, in the gobbling language that usually it took a member of his family to translate, "Juh-juh-jeezus, parp! What in hell's name was that?"

And Truman said fearfully, "What could it buh-be? Ain't nobody here, is there?"

Ed said that if they would shut their guh-guh-goddamned traps long enough for him to lul-lul-listen, maybe he could tell; but he heard no further sound, so presently he shifted his cud back where it belonged and allowed that it was some kind of a goddamned nan-nan-nanimal. They wasn't nobody on the island, that was for sure; hadn't they seen old Buttercup-Boy's boat take off for the mainland? Still, it might be better if they got a hustle on, guh-guh-goddamned island warn't but a graveyard.

✗

Back in the woods, Arvid had got Liz calmed down and interested enough to hold the flashlight for him.

"Now, look," he whispered. "I'm going to take this out of the bucket and put it over my head and face. It is going to look awful, but don't you be scared, it ain't nothing but a good flour dough mixed up stiff. See, I flatten it out, like so, and then put holes in it for eyes and nose and mouth . . . like so . . . and like so . . . and like so. And then I put it on. Now, it's just soft enough so's it'll dreel down some." Arvid's voice came, muffled. "See?"

Liz had all she could do to keep from giving a squeal. In the moonlight, he certainly did look dreadful! If she hadn't known what it was, she would have died, right there.

"Now, you take the flashlight and shinny over to behind that tree on the bank. You'll hear me start hollering. Then, when I stick my head out of the bushes, you turn that flashlight right on my head."

The ululation that started in a low key behind the bushes and climbed up, moaning and sobbing, to a shriek, was like all the lost loons that ever cried and died, or the last ghost that ever dug his way up through the clay of a graveyard. It throbbed along the lonely shore, died to a strangled moan. It froze the blood of the Snorri twins, stopped it flowing in their veins. They were still in the cockpit, not having been able as yet to tear themselves away from the motorcycle; but Ed was inside the cabin, piling up things. He thought, briefly, that the boys were making the racket, and he came boiling out on deck to tell them to shut up their guh-guhgoddamned foolishness, just in time to get the full benefit. Out of the bushes before his eyes rose a white, wavering face surrounded by eerie light, a face so decayed, so rotten, that it was running down off the chin.

Ed said, "Juh-juh-jeezus!" and took off over the stern of the houseboat in a flying leap and landed knee-deep in the salt marsh. The boys hadn't waited. They had already shoved the skiff off and were skuttering and scrambling after the oars; they didn't even stop to pick up their father. Ed put right out into the water after them. He had to swim twenty feet before he could grab hold of the stern of the skiff, and then, in spite of his hollering and cussing, they wouldn't stop rowing long enough for him to climb aboard. They towed him all the way across the marsh to the powerboat.

" 'N there!" Arvid said, with satisfaction. "I guess we fixed them thieving barstids."

The powerboat started up, sputtering and coughing, and made time down the inlet, leaving behind it on the water a trail of scattered moonlight.

"Well, now, sonny," Arvid said. "You will have to come home with me, because if you don't help, I ain't never in the God's world going to be able to get this dough out of my hair."

Luck, tonight, had abandoned Ed Snorri. Once safely aboard his boat and with the upper inlet between him and the horror, his first reaction after his scare was one of fury. Two boys, he said, a man's own sons, row off and leave him to whatever the guh-guh-goddamned thing it was that was walking ashore there; leave him to swim for it, right in the face and eyes of guh-guh-God and everybody. It would serve them right if he hove the both of them overboard right here in the Salt Pond, let them swim ashore for that thing to git and fly off with. They had better not git near enough for him to lay a hand on, or he'd buh-bang their heads together so hard their buh-brains would run out of their noses.

The twins were up on the bow, as far away from him as they could get. They showed no sign of coming anywhere near him, or even that they heard a word he said. Spitting sparks and soaking wet, Ed steered his boat down the lower inlet toward open water; at a bend in the channel, he came within a hair of ramming head-on into a Coast Guard launch which was nosing in cautiously, and stopped just in time, so close that the two boats rubbed gunnels. The launch stopped also; one of the Coast Guard sailors put out a boathook and hooked Ed's boat. Someone demanded sharply what he was doing without running lights.

What was he doing without running lights? Well, by guhguh-God, if they wanted to know they could go ashore and see what kind of a duh-duh-damned dead, rotten kuh-kuhcorpse was walking around through the bushes. He had had to get out of there, hadn't had time to set up the guh-guhgoddamned running lights, and they could take that or leave it. The twins joined in the story, which the Chief in command of the launch, a fellow named Ferris, was unable to make head or tail of, beyond the fact that all was not normal ashore.

"Take it easy," he said. "Come again, now? Just what did you see? And where was it?"

The coastguardsman holding the boathook murmured, "He seen something nasty in the woodshed," and leaned over to smell Ed's breath.

"You cut that out!" Ed said. "I ain't drunk, nuh-neither. I see the guh-goddamned thing's head, coming at me out'n the puckerbrush. If I and the boys hadn't run, it'd been right aboard that houseboat—"

"Uh-huh," Ferris said. He knew who it was he'd picked up. Everybody who had anything to do with law along the coast knew Ed Snorri. "Come off it, Snorri. You were aboard that wreck seeing what you could find, weren't you? How much stuff have you got down in your cuddy?"

He hadn't got a guh-goddamned thing, Ed said. They could look if they wanted to. The time had come to clam up, and he clammed, while they searched his boat. They found nothing.

"All right," Ferris said. "But if we find stuff stashed in the bushes, we'll know who to come after. You stick up some lights, or you'll be hearing from us about a fine. Unhook him, boys. Let him go."

The launch backed away and rumbled on, slowly, up the inlet.

Ed glanced balefully after it. Fuh-fine and be damned, they would have to squat blood out of a turnip. Hell with them, could take their fine and—

Ed froze in his tracks; his jaw dropped a little. Up there on the slope by the old village, a lamp had been lit in Arvid Small's house. A light there, anyway, whatever it was. Of course, that was the house where that old woman had lived, the one who was kilt by lightning; maybe it was her. But as he looked, Ed could make out a form a lot more substantial than any ghost, going back and forth behind the window.

That goddamned Buh-Buttercup-Boy! Old Small himself! He's been there all the time. I'll bet to guh-God it was him—barstid rigged something up. Well, I'm a-going to find out, and if he did, I am a-going to fix him for it!

*

Liz got washed up in Arvid's kitchen at his sink, in a big basin of hot water with lovely soap. He said if she wanted to she could wash all over, and there was one of his clean shirts she could put on to sleep in, after she'd had her supper. She didn't see how she could wash all over with him sitting there. He still thought she was a boy, and she was certainly going to let well enough alone. He liked her as a boy; he might not even like little girls. She soaked and scrubbed her face and hands, took the shirt and went into his bedroom to put it on. She shut the door, to Arvid's surprise.

Funny kid, he thought. Well, he's probably had a nice bringing-up.

The shirt was beautiful and white and it smelt good, but it was away too big. When Liz got it on, the tails touched on the floor.

"Well, darn," Arvid said, when she came back into the kitchen. "You know what you look like? The Jack of Diamonds. There's your supper. Dig in. I ain't had mine, either. Walking a ghost is hungry work, ain't it?"

They ate and ate. Toughy came out from under the stove, and, to Liz's surprise, jumped up into Arvid's lap and took a piece of meat right off his plate. He didn't seem to notice, just went on eating and talking.

Liz thought it might be nice if she called attention to it, where he hadn't seen. "Toughy's eating out of your dish," she said, pointing.

Arvid glanced down. "Why, so she is," he said. "Ain't that smart, though. Just like a person. Prettier'n most persons, too, ain't she?"

"Don't you care?" Liz said, a little shocked.

"Why, no, I don't know as I do. Nice, clean cat. Speaking of manners, I've forgot mine. I ain't even asked you what your name is."

Liz opened her mouth to say Elizabeth Bigelow, but stopped in time. Things had been so bad she couldn't bear the thought of his having to learn to like her all over again; but she had to say something. He was looking at her, beaming and waiting. She closed her mouth over Elizabeth, and what came out was "B-Bigelow."

"Well, now, Bigelow," Arvid said. "I guess you'd better hop into bed. Take whichever side you want to. Outside or inside, all one to me."

"Okay," Liz said. She wouldn't mind sleeping in the same bed, it would be company. But what if he snored, the way he had been when he'd had the dream on the shore today? What if he woke up and hollered? And, besides . . .

"Don't you have two beds?" she asked.

"Well, I do," Arvid said. "There's the couch, here in the kitchen. You rather sleep on that? I can make it up, if you want."

Liz couldn't think what to say. He was so nice; it would be mean to tell him how awful he snored. "It's so . . . so *warm*," she said. "I can make the couch up, if it's too much bother."

"Mercy, no. I guess I have got the stuff here to make my company feel like company." He had been unlacing his shoes, but he got up and went over to a big cupboard, his shoelaces ticking on the floor. "Blankets," he said. "Hum. Sheets. Hum, clean sheets. Now, where did I . . . ?"

There was one more thing. It wouldn't wait. It was getting to be difficult, being a boy.

Liz said stiffly, "I have got to go to the bathroom."

Arvid's voice came muffled. He had his head inside the cupboard where he was rummaging. "Well, now. If it's number one, I guess nobody'd care if you stepped out around the corner of the house," he said. He backed out of the cupboard, pulling along a pair of crumpled sheets. " 'N there! If it's number two, the backhouse is right out along the path to the barn. Better take the flashlight."

Liz took: the flashlight. She found the path and the little house; but the door was swinging open; inside was darkness. When she raised the flashlight beam, she saw a spiderweb woven right across the doorway. In the middle of the web was a black and yellow spider as big as a quarter.

Go in there? Nossir!

That kid, Arvid thought, dumping his armload of bedding on the couch, is still scared. And rambling out there alone ain't going to help him any. I had better look, see if he's making out all right.

He stepped outside, peered around the corner of the house. After a moment, he cautiously withdrew his head.

Well, set fire! he told himself. For the sweet loving name of God in the wilderness! If I'd of known that, there's several things I would have done different. I can't think what I may have said, but I do know I've been cussing now and again.

He couldn't recall anything special, but what he could recall made him blush.

Liz came pattering in, in a hurry, the tails of Arvid's Sunday shirt flying. She tore across the room and grabbed him around the middle, clutching with hot hands as far as she could reach, burying her face in his stomach. "They haven't gone! They're not scared of the ghost! They are down there in the harbor, their boat has got lights on it—"

"Whoa, now, hold on. Whoever it is, it ain't likely them. Let's take a look. Most likely it's the Coast Guard."

It was. From the kitchen door, Arvid could see the launch in the Salt Pond, turning in the moonlight and slowing to pick up his mooring. "Poo!" Arvid said. "Nothing to be scared of. Them is Uncle Sammy's men."

"Will they take the houseboat? Will they take I and Marney's things?"

"The only thing they'll take is care of you and me. Now, Bigelow, you go to bed." He picked her up, carried her into his bedroom, put her in his big bed. "You have had too g—" He stopped, gulped a little, went on "—too goldarned big a day. Too much for one, not quite enough for two. I'll put Toughy in here to keep you company."

He scooped a long arm under the kitchen stove for Toughy, who did not wish to be disturbed and was ready to let her wishes be known; but before she could square around and let go a claw, she was caught in a knowledgeable grip. "Ha," Arvid said. "Caught you napping, miss, didn't I? Don't you scratch *me*. She may not stay," he said to Liz, going back into the bedroom. "She likes it under the stove. Peppery, ain't she?"

But Toughy knew when she was well off. She settled down against Liz and began to purr.

"You all right now?" Arvid stood, peering down. "You got everything you want?"

"M-m," Liz mumbled. The bed was wonderful. She couldn't wait to go to sleep.

Arvid went over to the commode. Thoughtfully, he rummaged out a sturdy, china chamber pot with, on one side, a design of a big pink wild rose. He set it under the edge of the bed.

"No need to go traipsing out in the cold," he said delicately. "In case, in the night, you have to go."

The Coast Guard launch was not going to be able to stay long in the Salt Pond; she was a sizable boat and the tide had already started to ebb. Fellow wouldn't have tried it up that channel, unless he thought I had an emergency out here, Arvid thought. He hurried down to the shore to say there wasn't one, and to tell them to hustle out of there if they didn't want to spend the rest of the night and most of tomorrow on the mudflats.

Ferris knew about the mudflats, all right. He had just barely escaped spending twelve hours on a bank down the inlet, a half-hour ago, when he had missed the channel by a few feet and had scraped the launch's keel. It had taken some frenzied churning to get off, had slowed Ferris up, and had thrown out his nice calculations on the ebb tide. He was sweating to get gone.

"Understand you've got another sick kid out here," he said, jumping ashore from the launch's tender. "Where is he? I've got to make time."

"The kid's all right," Arvid said. "He's asleep in my bed, and sleep is all that's needed. If I was you, I'd come back on the flood tomorrow. About two p.m., that'll be. Because that channel is a job you need daylight for. I don't see how you done it by moonlight, in that craft."

"Neither do I," Ferris said. "All I hope is I make it out of here with the keel on. Well, I will come back tomorrow, if there's no emergency."

"So do," Arvid said. "Best thing, by far. That older boy, the other one—he going to make it, you know?"

"Nobody knows. He took a terrible slamming around and he's got pneumonia. Understand it's nip and tuck. They've got him in an oxygen tent. We had it from your friend Fowler that the wreck is the *Sea Flower*, out of Medbrook, New Hampshire, according to her name and hail, and we got that on the wire, but God knows when we'll find out anything. That town was darn near wiped out by the flood and hurricane last night. We tried to get some dope out of the kid in the hospital, but he isn't making any sense. He's a sick kid. Well, good night. See you tomorrow."

He said something uncomplimentary about the damned mudhole, and pushed off.

Arvid watched him go. He supposed that if he'd been willing to hustle, he could have got Bigelow down here in time, let them take her ashore, and save them another trip tomorrow. But their feet weren't killing them the way his were him. And another thing, that kid needs to get her sleep out. Wake her up now, she'd have to find out about her brother the first thing; and then there'd be that long, cold boat trip, and nowhere to go when she got there, except to strangers.

And she don't feel good about strangers, Bigelow don't. So I will be goddamned if I am going to have that.

He flopped around some on the kitchen couch, before he could get to sleep.

If she didn't want to let on she was a girl, it wasn't up to him to tell on her. It wasn't any of his business, except being a convenient thing to know. Besides, no knowing what that young fellow in the uniform's morals was—judging by the looks of him, they would be pretty stiff and upright. Any girl would be as safe with Arvid as she would be with angels in heaven. Unless she was grown up and didn't want to be. Why, that young fellow might have felt it was his moral duty to leave one of his men here till tomorrow. And that would have posed a goddamned problem—no more extra beds. And I would have to be the one slept on the floor, because he'd be company in my house. I might as well, for all of this couch, which ain't by half big enough for a mansized man.

As for his feet, they were so tired they were numb.

And the only reason they ain't killing me now, is they already done that an hour ago.

Whereupon Arvid fell asleep and slept well and loudly until morning.

For Marney, the highway seemed endless, the blacktop moving ahead of him forever. Lights and shadows shifted in, and out. The lights of big towns and small: neon, red, green; lines of electric bulbs spotted the gas stations. They shone on brick fronts, cement fronts, on rows of pennant-shaped colored flags blowing in the wind. He wished the flags would stop blowing, the movement hurt his eyes. They stood straight out, their ends snapped in the sky with a queer, sharp sound. He rode through a city, past a canyon of tall buildings with tiers of white, blind windows. Now the lights were strung in upside-down arcs on the cables of a bridge over a river, black and swooping against blown clouds and a plunging moon.

Out on the bridge, the motorbike went too fast, snarling in and out of traffic. The wind hurt his face. He couldn't stop. Toughy climbed out of the sidecar, ran along the guardrail of the bridge. She was going up one of the high towers, he could see her small black and white shape, up and up; he was climbing after her, not coming any closer. She was gone and all there was was sky with dark clouds like smoke, and down below, the abyss of the river, black water patched with running foam. He fell, over and over, pinwheeling down.

The queer, sharp sound was a buzzing in his ears. It was Grampa's electric razor in the kitchen at home and Gram—no, Joe—was making pancakes for breakfast.

In and out. The wild, wind-blown lights. The blacktop, endless. On and on. Riding.

A voice said clearly, "What's he been living on—Coke and hot dogs? Look at him—when's he had a square meal?"

Warm, steady fingers touched his cheek; a wristwatch ticked, close to his ear.

The Coast Guard came and went next day. This time, knowing better the navigation problems they had to contend with, they came prepared. They brought along a shallow draft tender with an outboard motor, in which they went up the inlet into the salt marsh where the houseboat lay.

Some things about that boat mystified Ferris, he didn't mind saying so. Who were the owners? What was their name? There wasn't a scrap of paper, a record of any kind aboard there to show, and not even a set of pilot rules. And what was an almost new motorcycle with a sidecar doing upside down in the cockpit? Well, of course a lot of things happened in a flood; somebody must have dumped the bike aboard there in a hell of a hurry. Its plate was registered New York State, and he could check; and now that he had the houseboat's number, the police could check that with New Hampshire. But Ferris would sure like to talk to that kid. Where was the kid, anyway? Ferris had orders to bring him in.

"Why . . . he's right around here somewhere," Arvid said. "Or was a minute ago. Hey, Bigelow!"

No Bigelow.

"Well, what's he told you? Anything we could go on?"

"He says his name's Bigelow," Arvid said. He looked from right to left, as if he expected, momentarily, Bigelow to pop out of the underbrush. "First name, I should judge. What it is, he don't seem to want to talk about what happened. Clams up, like. Might be shock. Terrible thing, a little child caught out in that storm in a boat adrift."

"If he's still in shock, he'd better come ashore with us and let a doctor look at him."

"That's right," Arvid said. "Maybe so. After that, where would he go? Would there be a nice place, ashore there?"

"Oh, sure, I guess so. The Welfare Department'll take care of him till they can find out who his folks are. Or maybe the matron at the jail. It'll be out of our hands, once I find him and take him in. Any idea where he is now?"

"If it's a matter of a place to stay till they find his folks, he's welcome here with me. He kind of takes to me and he likes it here. He don't seem to take to strangers."

"Well, I'll tell you, Mr. Small, it isn't up to me. The Commander at the Base says bring him in, so I'll have to."

"All right," Arvid said. "I'll help you hunt him up. He might be up in the old village, he goes there sometimes to play. But you know, Mr. Ferris, you ain't got all day."

Ferris knew he hadn't. The Coast Guard launch lay at Arvid's mooring down in the Salt Pond and the tide was turning again. He said something violent about a tide hole.

"That is right," Arvid said as they walked along. "And if you was to add your words to them that has been floating around in the air over this place for the last hundred and fifty years, about what it would all add up to is the name of the place. Now, I'll tell you. Freddy Fowler is due here today in my boat, and I'll round up Bigelow and bring him in, soon's I can."

Ferris agreed glumly that it might be a solution. He let out a bawl for Bigelow and got no answer. He and Arvid hunted; he sent the crew of the launch off in different directions. The crew returned shortly, looking affronted. A search was impossible—woods and swamps and old ruins all on top of each other—there'd be a million places. And the tide was starting to ebb. They all embarked and stepped on it out of the Salt Pond, because they had to.

Arvid walked slowly back through the woods to his house, He had got about halfway there when he heard footsteps pounding on the path behind him. It was Bigelow.

"Heb'm sake, where was you?" Arvid said. "Didn't you hear that nice young feller hollering your name?"

Bigelow's face looked very black. "He needn't think I'm going with him," she said. "I hate him."

"You do?"

"Yes, I do. I'm not going anywhere. I'm going to stay here and keep care of I and Marney's things."

"M-m, somebody has got to. I could do it. You could go ashore and let them talk to you. I would try to get them to let you come back. That young feller is going to be prodding around here until he finds you, you know it?"

"I won't go. And I'm not going to talk to them. I know what they'll do. What they always do. Say they'll do something to get you to do what they want, and you do and then it is all a fat fib, and they knew it all the time. They'll yak around and then they'll send me back there. And I won't go, and if they do, I'll *kill* her, and then I'll run away again—"

Bigelow's voice had risen to a howl; she stopped short, looking horrified. Then she turned and ran down the path toward the houseboat as fast as she could go.

Arvid stood, astonished, looking after her.

What in the world had gone on to make a little young girl feel like that about everybody? What kind of people, for heb'm sake, had she been with? Whoever it had been had certainly raised the devil with a real smart little young one, and a nice one, too, if let alone—if let to grow up in peace, and decent, the way anyone ought to have a chance to. Something in the Bible about offend one of these little ones, he couldn't remember what it was, it had been a long time since he'd thought to look anything up in the Bible.

He guessed though, he told himself, resuming his way along the path, he'd have to look up this. There was an old Bible around the house somewhere. That word "offend," it seemed, didn't mean quite what you took it to be, not at the first glance of it. Didn't mean just to make somebody mad. It meant harm them in their inside in a way they never got over. How many people did you see, well, not all, but an awful lot of them, grown-up, man-grown out of offended little ones, who might have been twice-three times what they were, if it hadn't been for that harm? They got it early and they kept it going, passed it along the way they passed the color of their hair and of their eyes, so it never died out, but got to be as much a part of the human race as legs and fingers. Look at the way they mistreated anything that couldn't fight back, give back a wound. Animals. Birds. Look, for Godsakes, at the way they mistreated trees. "Offend."

Well, now, that was real smart of the Bible. You go poking into that word, you came up with a bloodcurdler: what was probably the real work on earth of the devil.

I am a solitary man for the reason of that. I haven't ever been able to stand it. I saw it happen to Freddy. And I will be goddamned if I will stand around and see it happen to a little young one who ain't scared of man nor tempest.

The Coast Guard launch had gone. Arvid's mooring was empty. Freddy, if he were going to get in on this tide, would have to step on it. If he didn't come soon, he would have to wait till tomorrow afternoon. Or maybe he was thinking that if he waited till tonight, sundown, he could anchor in the Outer Harbor, land in the cove down there. But the sea hadn't quieted down on the east side of the island. From his doorstep, Arvid could see the Outer Harbor. It looked calm on the surface, no choppy water; but what was running in was some big, oily old swells from the southeast. He could hear them crashing against the shore. No landing there tonight; no safe place to leave a boat.

But Freddy did not come. The tide went down without him, the Salt Pond drained dry. By late afternoon worry about him had begun to take shape in Arvid's mind. Bigelow hadn't come back, either. Finally, Arvid took his clam hoe and creel and walked along the path to the houseboat.

Bigelow had evidently been busy. She had a clothesline up between two trees on the bank, and had hung it full of waterstained sheets and blankets, along with some pants and shirts and a heavy leather jacket—apparently the boy's clothes.

Arvid stood on the bank and called. "Bigelow? I'm going out after a mess of clams for supper. Like to have you come along, if you want to."

There was only a short silence before Bigelow came. She scrambled down the side of the boat, glancing at him not very pleasantly out of the corners of her eyes.

"I can see you've been busy as a bumblebee," Arvid said. "Them fellers left in a hurry, didn't they?" He waited until he was sure she was looking at him, and then winked at her. "I shouldn't be surprised if you and I could dream up to be gone, next time they come."

He didn't wait to see if she had thawed out any, but walked along the bank to a sandy place he knew about, where the wading out wouldn't be too muddy. "You'd better roll them pants up," he said over his shoulder. "We're going to have to wade some!"

"And take off my sneakers, too, hadn't I?" Bigelow said. "They aren't dry yet, but they're getting dry. I hate to get them wet again."

"H'm," Arvid said. This was a difficulty he hadn't thought of. "You have got to have something on your feet. On account of you might step on a whore's egg."

"On a what?" Bigelow said.

Arvid blushed. Done it again, he thought. "Well," he went on aloud, "I guess we have all got a lot to learn. That is a name that some people around call a sea urchin when they get put out with one. When they don't think in time, they say it. It gets to be a kind of a habit."

"But what is one?"

"Well, right there. See that round thing with the prickles? You step on that barefooted and them prickles go into your foot and it is God damn George Taylor to get them out."

He stopped again. Take it all in all, it wasn't going to be possible. But Bigelow only said, "Who's George Taylor?"

Arvid's face creased with delight; he began to rumble and chuckle and burst out into a roar. "Oh, he's an old man used to live around these parts," he said. "Them sneakers ain't real dry, and we can wash them off when we come in, dry them on the back of the kitchen stove."

"Okay," she said, paddling into the water after him. "And I wouldn't be surprised if they'll look better than they do now."

✦

"Now, you take Freddy," Arvid said.

They were back in the kitchen again, with a roaring fire going. The kettleful of clams was steaming on the stove. Bigelow's sneakers were drying on top of the water tank. Arvid had put out a big dish of cranberry sauce, and he was baking biscuits. The kitchen smelled like heaven.

"Now, you take Freddy. He is not really a lush. He is one of the smartest men with his hands that I ever knew on land or sea, but he is awful easy upset in his mind, if his wife does the upsetting. Philomela is a good woman and a pretty one, but she has got a temper. They both have. Tch! Awful!"

Worried as he now was, Arvid could no more have held back from talking than he could have held back from eating supper. And Bigelow was a fine listener; he could see she was interested. He went on.

"If Freddy, by any chance, went home last night after he was through over in Powell . . . well, he was awful hackled up when he came out here and I don't know how much better he felt when he left. If he went home and they chanced to break out fighting again, the Lord only knows when he'll set back out here with that boat!"

"I don't care," Bigelow said. "I like it here with just us."

"Mm, good," Arvid said, absently. "The thing is, Freddy, when all was over and the corpses counted, if I know Freddy, he went out and tried to tie one on."

Freddy had gone home; it would not have occurred to him not to. His temper had had time to cool; so much had happened now that he had almost forgotten the fight. If he thought of it at all, it was to be a little ashamed of himself for walking out on Philomela after that fire, which he could have prevented if he'd gone home with her in the first place. If she'd only let him alone till he'd felt better, he supposed he would have. She'd still be sore at him for that, but there'd be only one temper skyrocketing instead of two. She wasn't one to hold a grndge for long; at least she never had been. And maybe she'd be so interested in the news about the wreck, and his plans, that she'd simmer down the way he had. Anyway, he could try.

That afternoon in Powell, after the ambulance had come and gone and Freddy had phoned the Coast Guard, he had gone up into town and had looked up some salvage laws in the library. He hadn't found precisely what he wanted, but he had found enough to make him sure he had some kind of a claim. The craft hadn't been abandoned and derelict—there'd been someone aboard of her. But the salvors of life were entitled to a share of the salvage for the vessel, if any award were made. The amount would very likely depend on how much the salvor had done—if he had saved the vessel from destruction, or had salvaged property accessories aboard her, for instance. That last was what took Freddy's eye—property and accessories. The boat herself was probably a total loss, considering where she lay; it would take another storm-tide to float her out across that marsh. The hull itself didn't interest Freddy, nor did any of the miscellaneous property in her cabin. But what a project if he could only get his hands on that big, modern engine!

The one thing that spoke to Freddy in a clear and concise tongue he could understand, was machinery—pieces of metal that he could take apart and put together: the carburetor, the transmission, the steering gear, the ball bearings in their bath of oil. Parts to clean, repair, replace, drill, grind. He liked best something that had been used, or that had bugs in it, something that could be put into shape and made to run again. The ailing engine of an old car or a boat had always been his poetry and his child.

The pickup truck which he owned now and which ran like a watch, was one which he had salvaged from the town dump, its parts replaced from a Powell junkyard. He had owned many such. His boat, which most people thought didn't amount to much, had an aged make-or-break engine—his pride and joy. Nobody knew the skill it took to keep the old thing running. Other fishermen—including Arvid, who worried—might wonder how Freddy managed to make the harbor or haul his traps on a windy day: not Freddy. He had the old heap of nuts and bolts under his thumb now; it was no longer a problem. Right now he needed something else to put his mind on. That houseboat engine—it was new, might not even be damaged. But it was lying there in salt water, rusting. It might even be full of salt water. Who knew?

And to be able to work on it in that place, with nobody around to bother—only old Arvid, who never bothered anybody, anyway . . . Freddy guessed he could put up with General Remarks Island, under those circumstances. Who cared what the surroundings were—the lonelier the better, if you had a project. Any port in a storm, just so it kept the world out of your pocket. Early in life, Freddy had taken steps to keep the world out of his pocket. In his father's house he had

had enough screaming, squealing, thumping, slamming to last him his lifetime; enough of putting something down and coming back to find it had been pawed over, broken, scattered, or lost. Some people could function, do work, in the middle of turmoil, might even thrive on it. Freddy could not.

As a younger man, he had had jobs in garages, had even owned a garage; he had had responsible jobs around the machinery in factories and mills. They had meant bossing and being bossed, paperwork; they had been hell. As a ground mechanic in the Air Force, he had been miserable. Nobody ever let a man alone, somebody was always yelling. Do this. Do that. Leave what you're doing, do something else. Distractions that drove him wild, drove him into a fury, because when he was interested, concentrated, nothing else meant anything—not people, nor pleasure, nor comfort; at times, not even food—only the work in hand.

People might wonder why, with his ability, Freddy was content to piddle around with an occasional old car engine, or make his living lobster fishing in an old boat. Freddy could have told them. To work alone was the only way he could work; and he was not a man who could compromise. And when he had a project, the world not only had better stay out of his pocket, it had better stay completely out of his way—or get chopped off.

Leaving the library and walking back toward the wharf where he had left Arvid's boat, Freddy made his plans. If anybody objected to his salvaging that engine, that was too bad. Under the circumstances, he guessed nobody would. Just getting the salt water out of it would do the owners a favor. Well, anyway, worry about that later. He would pick up his tools and get back out there. Maybe he could persuade Philomela to come along, too; it would be too bad to leave her alone right now. There was any amount of room in Arvid's old house; all they needed to do was fix up a little and take along some bedding. She might like to do that; it would give her something to do, too. She'd been complaining lately about not having enough to do. Maybe the change would settle them both down; he wished something would.

If they could only get back to where they'd been before this battle started . . . He could remember the day it had started, just about every word that had been said. For two years they had had a wonderful time; at least he had, and he'd supposed she'd had, too. She was just right for him; she'd never questioned, never nagged. Even as a bride, she hadn't demanded every minute of his time. She'd always understood what privacy meant to him; she'd seen to it that he had it when he wanted it. That workshop in the barn—she hadn't cared how much he'd spent fixing it up, or what the power tools cost; if he came home late after all day away and spent the evening, maybe half the night, working on a project in the shop, she might be disappointed because she'd have been glad of his company, glad to see him, but it always seemed to him if he was happy, so was she. He couldn't see where the change had come, because nothing had changed, but all at once, that first time, she'd started to tell him what a wonderful time she'd had when she'd taught school.

She'd had a tough school, too. Times, she said she felt like banging the rackety, ill-mannered little devils' heads together, but nine times out of ten, the worst they could do was only funny. It depended on how frazzled her nerves got, and she had always been too busy keeping one jump ahead to get really frazzled.

"Raw material," she'd said. "I cleaned, polished, ground, drilled, put it back together, and tried to make it run. Often it did. I think I might have been quite good at it. You know, honey. The way you are with an engine."

No, he didn't know, he'd said. At least, working on an engine he wasn't wasting his time. He had something when he got through. He hadn't been interested—the whole idea had bored him. He supposed he'd shown it. He'd have been better off if he'd dropped the subject right there, but he'd gone on to say that so far as he was concerned, kids—any kids—were wild animals, which, if she wanted to know, he'd just as soon not have around his house. He'd had about all of that he needed to last him a lifetime, and he wasn't about to start all over again in his own home of his own free will.

He'd stopped then, realizing that she was staring at him in wide-eyed astonishment, as if he'd said something crazy.

"Why, Freddy Fowler! Of course we'll have children! Our house is big, and anyway, you've got your workshop. And we needn't have a—a litter! I know how you feel, it must have been awful when you were growing up, but kids don't need to be like that, and"—and then she had started to get mad—"I don't know what right you have to think your home and mine has anything in common with that—that cuckoo's nest you were brought up in!"

He had got mad, too. "So that's why you were so keen on my having the workshop, is it? Well, is there any reason why you can't keep on being satisfied with me? If I'm not enough, I'm sorry!"

"Well, if that isn't a silly, pompous thing to say!"

And she had gone out slamming one door, and he had gone out slamming the other.

Time had gone on and things had gone back to normal; at least it had seemed so. Philomela's house was beautifully run; Freddy had never been so comfortable in his life. Then, last spring, they had come apart again, and over nothing in the world that amounted to anything, a mess of barn swallows which had started to build nests under the eaves outside the windows of Freddy's workshop.

The birds had done the same thing the year before and made a nuisance of themselves—birdlime down the windowpanes and on the clapboards. They had swooped and twittered all day—enough to drive a busy man crazy. Freddy had made up his mind that he wasn't going to have that again this year; he had got out the broom and the hose before the mudcasts got really under way and had swept them all down. Then he had got busy on a job he'd had going in the shop everything else had gone completely out of his head. Coming out of an afternoon's concentration, a few weeks later, he'd suddenly realized that his shop windows were so befouled with birdlime that he couldn't see out of them. He went outside and looked. The damn things had come back. That stuff was all over the clapboards, too. Take the paint right off, if it wasn't cleaned up. Impatiently, he routed out the ladder and the broom.

He supposed he wouldn't have knocked the nests down if he'd realized that, by this time, they'd have young birds in them. But the thing was done before he'd noticed; too late now. He was hosing off the side of the barn, with the old birds flying around, dive-bombing, when Philomela came out and saw the dead young swallows.

She didn't say anything; she stood there, looking.

"Well, how was I to know?" Freddy said. "I'm no bird watcher, damn it, Philomela."

"So it would seem."

"God knows there're enough swallows around. Blasted things all over the place."

"It's too bad those birds didn't lay ball bearings instead of eggs," Philomela said. "Those would have been left alone to hatch and grow up, wouldn't they?"

"Oh, cut it out, will you?" Freddy said. For Godsake, wasn't he feeling mean enough, already?

"You don't really like anything alive and young, do you?"

"Well, I like you. Most of the time. When you aren't acting like a—"

But she didn't stay to listen. She walked into the house and shut the door.

And you're all I do like, he said, silently, after her. You're what I've got and I don't want any more. I only wish you felt the same way.

Kids. A houseful. She couldn't let it alone, could she? Any more than he could give in.

And so all summer they had fought. Off and on. Sometimes making it up, sometimes not. It had got so neither of them seemed to have any peace of mind anymore. So far as Freddy himself was concerned, he couldn't work, couldn't concentrate; and when that happened, he felt as if he were out of his mind. He'd taken to staying away from home evenings—spent a lot of time with Arvid. Drank some; not that that did any good. Last night, though, was the first time he hadn't gone home at all—had gone off somewhere without saying where. She'd probably still be pretty sore.

Maybe with this new project, this change . . . if he could talk her into coming out to the island with him . . . well, it was worth trying, anyway. If he could make her feel it was a kind of second honeymoon, a new start. God, he wished they could. Start all over again. Go back to where they were in the beginning.

But when he got home from Powell in the late afternoon, he found the house locked up and Philomela gone.

Freddy stood on the porch, looking around in a bewildered sort of way. He had no key; in his time, he had never known the doors to be locked. She had always been there. He walked around to the back. His pickup was parked in side yard where he'd left it. The garage door was open, and her car was gone.

Maybe she'd just gone grocery shopping or something; but why at suppertime? And why lock up the house, when she knew this was the time he usually got home? Even the barn door was padlocked; if he'd wanted to, he couldn't get into his workshop.

Well, new plans, a new start, trying to fix things up—what was the use?

He might as well take the pickup and drive into town, get some supper. And then? Well, hell, he could spend the night aboard Arvid's boat. No use trying to get back to the island tonight, but he'd sure take off for there tomorrow.

He was climbing into the pickup when he heard a car turn in at the driveway. Sure enough. There she was, getting out, arms full of books and papers, or something.

"Hello," she said, turning, hearing his footsteps on the gravel. "You decided to come back, I see."

Freddy tried a grin. "Guess I could say the same for you, couldn't I?"

"Mm. I'm sorry you found everything locked up. But I had to be away all day. And I thought I'd better not leave your . . . your tool shed open. Good thing I didn't. The Snorri kids weren't in school today."

"School?" Freddy said, staring at her.

"Mm-hm. One of the teachers is sick. I'm substituting. Will you eat leftover lamb stew?" Over her shoulder, as she unlocked the front door, she went on, "Or if you don't want that, I've got some chops defrosted. They'll take longer, if you're hungry."

"Why . . . anything you want to fix'll be all right," Freddy said, staring after her.

This composure, this quiet—maybe she was still sore, maybe she wasn't. He couldn't tell. He followed her into the kitchen.

"It's good of you not to want a complicated dinner," she said. "I'm pretty busy. I've got a mess of papers to correct for tomorrow."

Was it sarcasm? He couldn't say. Whatever it was, it wasn't like her. An argument, yes; a flaming temper he could have understood.

"Have an olive," she said, holding out the dish to him. "Supper'll be ready in ten minutes."

Freddy took one. He nibbled it.

"This school business," he said. "How long will it be? I was hoping we could—I had a plan to—"

"Oh, a week, maybe. And off and on all fall and winter. I've told the superintendent I'll be available whenever he needs a substitute teacher. What was your plan?"

"I've got a project out on the island. That wrecked houseboat—I want to salvage the engine. I'll have to be out there a while. I thought you might like to come too."

"Freddy, I—what would I do out there? While you fooled around all day and half the night with an engine? Sit on a rock and look at the swamp? I might as well stay in this house that I can run for the two of us with one hand, watching twelve commercials an hour. Thanks, honey. But no."

"Well, skip it," Freddy said. "Just skip it, will you?"

"Anyway, there's your supper. So eat it."

Freddy stared at the steaming dish. "To hell with it," he said. He looked at her across it, and started to get up. "Philomela, honey—"

"Freddy, don't. I'm too tired, and all I want in the world is to eat my supper and do my work and go to bed. So just don't, that's all."

"Well, all right!" In spite of himself, he felt his temper flaring. "What's the matter with you? I came home feeling sorry as hell, and I've all but laid down and let you step on my face—"

Philomela burst into tears. "You know what's the matter with me. You want me to sit around wasting time, wasting my . . . myself, my life. When I've got a talent, too . . . like yours. Only mine is with children. And all you offer . . . all you offer is what you think is the remedy. The great pacifier. To smooth me out and stop me crying, like giving the baby . . . a bottle of milk!"

She got up and left the kitchen, only this time she didn't slam the door. She closed it quietly. He could hear her footsteps going up the stairs.

After a while he got up himself and left the house, and he didn't slam any doors, either.

Freddy got back to the island on the afternoon of the second day. Arvid heard with relief the sound of the boat coming up the inlet.

"Well, thank the Lord, there he comes," Arvid said to Bigelow. "Looks as though you and me wasn't going to have to live on clams and flounders after all. Let's go down and meet him."

Bigelow said, "I don't want to see any people," and she closed her mouth tight.

Arvid glanced at her. "Why, that's only Freddy," he said. "He's a good little man. Brought us some steak, I should think likely."

But Bigelow went off by herself. She didn't take the road to the houseboat, either. She went in the other direction toward the ruined village.

Tch! Poor little thing, Arvid told himself, watching her go. She don't trust nobody. Well, maybe me, a little, now. But nobody else. And that's too bad.

He went alone down to the shore, rowed off in the skiff to meet Freddy at the mooring.

Freddy looked down in the mouth and shaky. He most certainly was hungover. Whether it was a little or a lot, Arvid couldn't tell. He didn't mention anything; he said, merely, "Hi. You bring the steak?"

Freddy nodded. "Couldn't make it yesterday," he said.

"Thought probably you couldn't. How's Philomela?"

Freddy said nothing. He finished mooring the boat, came down off the bow, and began handing over paper bags and packages. They came, Arvid noted, from the supermarket in Powell, which probably meant that Freddy hadn't been home at all. But the last bag was greasy on the bottom and Freddy didn't pass it; he set it on the washboard of the boat, climbed into the skiff, then picked up the bag carefully with his hand underneath.

"What's that—eggs?" Arvid asked.

"Nope. Doughnuts. Philomela's."

He had been home then.

Arvid said, "Well, that was nice of Philomela. They'll go good."

"Don't kid yourself," Freddy said. "There's no goodwill goes with them. I swiped them, goddammit."

"Well now, Freddy, I'm sorry you had to."

"Oh, I had to, all right. Why I'm a day late; of course I had business over in Powell, but what I really stayed over for, I thought I could maybe make it up with Philomela, try again. But I'd had some drinks in Powell, she wouldn't give me the time of day."

His voice shook. Arvid saw, with concern, that he was holding back tears.

Must've really tried to tie one on. Feels awful, Arvid thought. Coming right apart. Never saw him do that before.

"I told her she could do anything she wanted to," Freddy said. "And all she would say was go on, get out of the house, she was through. So I'm through, too. I started to walk out and when I went through the kitchen, I saw this goddamned great crockful of doughnuts on the table. So I dumped them into a paper bag and took them."

His hands fondled the paper bag, which was growing, Arvid could see, more and more greasy, more and more flimsy, too. "You look out for that bag, Freddy," he said. "You're going to lose the bottom out of it."

"I don't know why I did that," Freddy said. "Except I thought maybe she'd thought things over, made doughnuts for me to show it. Something I liked. And I think that's what did happen, only when she saw me tight she couldn't stand the sight. Or I said something to start her up all over again. So I took the goddamned doughnuts."

A tear dropped off Freddy's nose onto the paper bag, landed with a plop. "What a hell of a keepsake to a man's marriage!" he said. "And I couldn't eat one if I—"

Seeing what was about to happen, Arvid shipped his oars. He reached over and rescued the paper bag. "Go ahead, get rid of it, Freddy," he said, "You'll feel better."

Waiting, he thought: The poor duffer. Howling over a bagful of doughnuts. That was not all of it, of course; but it went to show what foolish symptoms a man could take to remind him. A married fight is a goddamned unreasonable thing.

He almost said this out loud, but changed his mind. Enough had been said. It wasn't for him to pudden-stick into it. The thing to do, get him thinking about something else.

Seeing Freddy felt better now and was straightening out some, Arvid began to fill him in on events here at the island. It took a while, but presently Freddy began to show some interest.

"A girl, hanh?" he said. "What does she want to make out she's a boy for?"

"I ain't found out one namable thing about her. She don't trust a soul on earth. All she'll say, her name's Bigelow, and that's all she will say. So that's what I call her."

"Won't say who owns the houseboat, either?"

Arvid chuckled. "She says she does."

That interested Freddy, you could see. He sat right up. Had made him kind of mad, you could see that, too.

"Well, hell," he said. "It'll be easy enough to yank out of her who her folks are, where she came from. A good slap on the kisser'll bring it out in no time."

"Nossir!" Arvid said. "You hear me, Freddy, we won't have any part of that. Been through a lot of horrors, that little girl has. She's going to have a chance to take her own good time."

"Well, don't be a fool about it, Arvid. If she's got folks, they think she's dead. They ought to be notified. What's the matter with you?"

Arvid said stubbornly, "There is more there than meets the eye."

"So what is it? The thing to do is hand her along to the Coast Guard, or whoever's going to send her back where she came from. That's their business. How come you're mixing into it?"

He wasn't, Arvid saw, going to be able to explain to Freddy. Freddy was not a man who could put himself in somebody's place. You might love him like a son, but you couldn't help but know that in some ways he was hard. Still, Arvid supposed, you loved people because they were them, not because of what they did or didn't do. And Freddy, at the moment, was salved up to the eyes in his own troubles. What it was, he didn't like the idea of a kid, anyway.

Well, when things got complicated, let them alone for a while. Half the time they unwound themselves.

"I'd take it as a favor, Freddy," he said, "if you didn't let on to Bigelow you know she's a girl. I had to tell you, in case you might do something you hadn't ought to, in front of her—swear, or undress, or—"

Freddy grunted. "Oh, hell," he said. "Okay."

Likely she wouldn't be here long enough to bother anyone.

Leave me alone with her for two minutes, he was thinking. I can find out her name and all about her, don't think I can't.

Arvid was going on talking. "I hope you don't mind sleeping off aboard the boat a night or so," he began. "There's beds upstairs, but I ain't got bedding that's fit—"

"I've got bedding," Freddy said. "You might as well know first as last, Arvid. I've left home. I'm going to stay here. Awhile, anyway. I may even spend the winter here."

"Oh, now, Freddy. That can't be."

"It's going to be!"

"Freddy, this place is a terrible hellhole in the winter—"

"Look, my boat is anchored off the mouth of the inlet, with all my stuff aboard of her. My tools, my clothes, everything I own. If I hadn't felt so goddamned fuzzy, I'd have towed her up the inlet. As it was, I was lucky to hit that channel with one boat, let alone a tow. If you close your house to me, I am before God going to fix up one of these old shacks here and live in it. I am going fishing from here and do my trading in Powell. I'm not taking any argument about it, Arvid."

"I don't know as I was giving you one, was I?" Arvid said. "I suppose, the shape you're in, you get a satisfaction out of making things out as bad as you can, but you know you're welcome to my house, the flowers in May couldn't be more so. But I hope you know about this island, what you're getting into. Sure, people have lived here winters, but they was used to it and there was more than one of them."

"I'll get used to it. If you'll unload these groceries on the beach, I'll row down in the skiff and bring my boat up the channel."

"And I am a goddamned good mind to let you do it," Arvid said, looking at him. "Row down, eh? You can unload them groceries yourself. I'm too fat to bestir, when I don't have to!"

He sat flatly in the skiff while Freddy piled the groceries on the beach. Foolishness like that touched him up, he didn't mind letting Freddy know it did. Freddy knew, it went without saying, that Arvid would run him down the channel in the powerboat. No man needed to take a long row like that against the tide, unless he was about to make a martyr of himself. Which Freddy would get over doing as soon as he stopped being hung.

Bigelow was sitting on the beach when they came back up the inlet in the two boats. She did not look at them or say anything when they came ashore with a skiff-load of Freddy's possessions. Arvid thought he could see signs of tears, but he said merely, "Hi. Want to help lug some stuff?"

Bigelow shook her head.

"All right. You don't have to. This is Freddy. He's going to stay with us."

Bigelow and Freddy sized each other up at once.

Freddy thought, Oh, Christ, a brat.

She thought, This is one of *Them*.

As he walked past her with his load of stuff and went on up the path toward the house, she put out her tongue at his back and made a small, undercover raspberry.

"What'd you want to do that for?" Arvid asked.

"I didn't do anything." She glared past Arvid at the load of Freddy's things.

"You give him about as mean a look as I ever saw in my life," Arvid said. "And he don't deserve it, let me tell you."

"I don't want him to be here. What does he have to come for?"

"That poor boy has left his home. He hasn't got any other place to go. And you act as if he was a crumb. I swear, Bigelow, I wouldn't believed it if I hadn't seen you. I never would have dreamt you was that mean."

Bigelow's control crumbled. She gave a long sniff; her eyes watered. "You went off with him and left me. I thought you weren't ever coming back."

"Well, you ought to known better. As I recall, you was the one went off and left. I felt bad, too. But we had to hustle Freddy's boat up here, or we'd lost the tide. We couldn't wait, and that's too bad, you missed a nice boat ride. If you was to help lug some of that stuff up to the house, I'd take it as a favor if you say hi to Freddy, like a little l—"

Arvid stopped. His grandmother had always used set phrases when speaking to children. Every once in a while one slipped out of him. He had almost said, "Like a little lady."

Well, no use repining. Perhaps she hadn't noticed. He left it lying where it was.

Halfway up to the house, each with an armload, they met Freddy.

The bedroom over the kitchen is the best one, Freddy," Arvid said. "We'll stow your stuff up there."

"Okay," Freddy said.

He didn't even look at Bigelow, just stepped off the path so that she could go by. She thought he might have noticed that she was helping carry his things, and not looked so ugly in the face. She didn't see how she could say hi to him. She glanced sideways at Arvid, but he had gone up on the path. The occasion certainly called for something; she had to let Arvid know she wasn't as mean as Freddy was.

"Did you really," she said to Freddy politely, "did you really go out and tie one on?"

After a few days, when they were settled in, with Freddy established in the bedroom over the kitchen, Arvid realized that someone was going to have to do some planning. Freddy was here to stay. Right now he said he was going to spend the winter. It was no use talking to him or trying to make him realize what he was getting into; he had set his mind as hard as a hammer.

"Look," Arvid said. "There's times out here, weeks sometimes, when the inlet's full of ice. You couldn't get ashore if you wanted to."

"So what?" Freddy said.

"Food is what. Something to eat. When people lived on this island, they spent three-quarters of a year laying up for winter. You stay here through the hard weather, got to be ready. It ain't like sleeping five months in a feather bed."

"What of it? I'll go to Powell and lay in some cases of canned stuff. Sounds like a simple thing to me."

Arvid moaned. "Live on canned stuff? By spring you'd be consti-pated as a cannibal. Now, Freddy, staying out here the winter ain't a responsible thing, look at it how you will."

Freddy grinned. "When have you been responsible, you old devil?" he said. "I'd have been nuts twenty years ago, if I hadn't learned from you how a man ought to live his life. Look, you can't get off the island, nobody can get on, get at you. Isn't that how it works, now?"

Arvid had to admit, but to himself only, that that was how it worked. Sometimes. He had to admit, too, that the more he thought about the idea, the more it appealed to him. Right now, there was Bigelow. But, also, there was Philomela . . .

He said aloud, feebly, that there'd be an awful lot to do before the house would even be safe to spend the winter in.

"Well, tell me what to do. I'll do it."

Freddy. He didn't have an idea in the world what he was getting into. Arvid tried to tell him.

The house hadn't been weathertight for years. They would have to boat clapboards and shingles over from Powell. They'd have to re-putty storm windows, bank foundations with rockweed and brush. At least five cords of stovewood would have to be cut for the kitchen, and if they were going to be really snug, they'd better bring that old potbelly over from the fishhouse, set it up in the downstairs bedroom. To burn a potbelly through the winter, they'd need coal. If they couldn't get the coal, they'd have to cut more wood, four–five cords of chunks.

Arvid got into his stride. God, would it be fun! Like the old days. Like the summer out here, only not alone. With good company. He brought himself up short. What would they haul all those loads with? Have to have a horse and wagon, maybe a sled.

"Horse be damned!" Freddy said. "I know where there's a junked jeep. Fellow'd probably pay me ten dollars to haul it off his property. With some spare parts from the junkyard, I could make it run like a—oh, yes, and of course some rubber."

He even knew where he could borrow an old scow to transport the jeep out to the island. "There's a place where we could land it, isn't there?"

"Pick a calm day and the right tide," Arvid said, "we land it down in the Outer Harbor cove. Road goes right to the beach."

He spoke absently, though, passing over a thing like a jeep. Who could drive a jeep? Only Freddy. What we need is a horse.

And he realized, suddenly, that now he was thinking in terms of "we."

Well, what else? The stubborn ox wouldn't be moved.

He won't go home, and there's no other place unless he goes off to a town somewhere. Do that, he'll go to hell awhooping. If I leave him alone here, he'll go crazy. He don't like it here; at night he's nervous as a nun. If we stayed here till spring, he'd have a chance to straighten out, figure how he could go back home without taking a bite out of his pride. One thing, he couldn't run to a liquor store every time he got low in his mind. This island always straightens me out. Likely it would him. And Bigelow—she's straightening out by the minute. If I can have her a little longer . . .

He supposed the time would come when he'd have to let Bigelow go back to her folks, if she had any fit to go back to. Somebody must have a legal claim on her. So far, she hadn't said any more; but from the way she felt, little things she dropped, her folks didn't appear to be very pleasant people. She seemed to think the world of that boy Marney; but Arvid didn't believe now that he was her brother. When he had undressed the boy, that day aboard his boat, he had found a soggy money belt with quite a lot of money in it, next to his skin. In the hurry, Arvid hadn't known quite what to do with it, but it needed to be dried out, so he'd shoved it into his pocket, and he had it now, ready to return when the boy needed it. There'd also been an identification card tucked away there. Marney's name was Lessard; which wasn't Bigelow, any way you looked at it.

Well, leave it alone. Things would work out in time.

But he wasn't going to be a part of sending Bigelow back into a sorry mess, if so be it was, if he could help it. Times she could be cussed as a witchwife, still, but when you got to know what was behind there, you found she was a pretty decent little kid. Independent as a pig on ice, hard to scare, too. Like that black and white cat. The two had a lot in common.

Now, say we could all manage to stay out here till spring. The three of us. Or, maybe, if that boy gets better, we'd be four. Have to think about that, when it comes to laying in. If I took her ashore, all I've got is that fishhouse. Wouldn't be room in it. Not decent for a little girl. And that legal crowd, the Red Cross, the police, that young Ferris—whoever wants to send her back where she came from—they'd be down on us like a flock of gulls. I would lose her. It occurred to him that he didn't want to lose her.

Yes. By all means, it wouldn't hurt a thing to lay in a winter's supplies for four. Have something to pull and haul on, even if the boy didn't come.

Arvid's notions of what would be needed for winter began to expand to a degree which appalled Freddy.

Dried fish. Salt mackerel. Barrels of potatoes, sacks of flour, a side of beef. Fifty gallons of molasses.

"Fifty gal—" Freddy said, staring. "What in the living hell would we need fifty gallons of molasses for?"

"Why, gingerbread," Arvid said, with a faraway look in his eyes. He was remembering the mountain of supplies of his youth, the things that, when winter was coming on, the islanders had stored. As a boy who had liked to eat, he had loved the idea of all that food in the house. The smokehouse. The cellar with its laden shelves. Real treasure.

"Gingerbread!" Freddy said. "Jeezus, you could even bake a pot of beans."

Well, better have plenty. Ought to have a horse and a pig, too, he went on. And he'd be on the lookout for a nice cow.

Freddy exploded. Didn't Arvid ever listen? And was he, for Godsakes, crazy? All those animals would mean feed. Hay. Where was hay coming from? Good God, they had to repair the house, did they have to start in too on that rotten old barn? Freddy would be goddamned if he would tend a mess of barn animals. It was bad enough with that cat around the house.

"We could gather enough winter apples from these old orchards to see us through," Arvid said, thoughtfully. "Good apples. And later on, after first frost, marsh cranberries'll be ripe. I wonder if I could learn Bigelow to make jelly?"

He glanced up, surprised, as the door slammed behind Freddy.

Now, it was too bad Bigelow and Freddy didn't get along better together. Maybe they would though. Give them time.

Freddy had two reasons for his impatience. When he had made big talk about staying the winter, he hadn't realized what was involved. He had had visions of settling in with Arvid, batching it around the house, relaxed in his underwear, or without it if he felt like it. But the way it was, that kid, with the cat, was underfoot every minute of the day. Let the cat in. Let the cat out. Feed the cat. It wasn't any kind of a pet, even if a man cared for pets, which Freddy didn't; but anyone, every once in a while, might like to pat a cat on the head. It was a habit—just something you did, not thinking. So what happened? You were likely to lose a hand. And once when Freddy had sat down on the kitchen couch without looking first, he had come near getting the seat of his pants clawed out. It wasn't that he had anything against a cat—but why put up with an unnecessary nuisance around a house? And as for the kid, you couldn't make water on a bush without a glance over your shoulder first. What he'd counted on was himself and Arvid alone, Arvid carrying on with his chores and minding his own business, while Freddy worked on that engine. And here he was, all wound up with a mess of shingling and clapboarding and puttying which didn't interest him in any way whatsoever. Freddy didn't believe for a moment that all that work was needed. It was silly to think he and Arvid couldn't keep themselves comfortable through the winter in that house just the way it was.

So far the Coast Guard hadn't been back, but they would be, any day—probably as soon as the check with the boat's owners came through and something was decided. Freddy thought he ought to have some salvaged property to show, just in case. A couple of times, he had sneaked off the job at the house and gone over to look at the engine. It was beautiful, or had been; but you could see where rust had set in. And another thing he hadn't thought of at first—that motorcycle. That, too, had been dunked in salt water. Unless it was taken apart and greased, it would set solid with rust. After the second trip, looking, Freddy decided that for a while, Arvid would have to get along without him. Plenty of time for all those junky jobs later on.

As he jumped down off the houseboat to go back, he realized that Bigelow was sitting on the bank, watching him like a cat at a mousehole. She'd done that the first time he'd come over here, too. Creepy darned kid, what was the matter with her?

"Look," Freddy said. "Why don't you just go play?"

She didn't say anything, just went off along the path.

The next morning, without saying anything to anyone, Freddy got up early. He had his breakfast by himself, took his toolbox, and went over to the houseboat. He had decided to overhaul the motorcycle engine first, since it seemed to be in worse shape than the marine engine. Besides, he thought, if he got that bike so it would run, they could use it, with the sidecar, to haul loads—temporarily, anyway, till he had time to go over to the mainland and round up that jeep. This was a pretty powerful bike; wouldn't do as well as a jeep, of course, but it would serve the purpose for a while—save a lot of backaches hauling.

He got the boat's cockpit cleared up, piling stuff in a heap on the deck. There was a lot of junk—a tent, a camp stove, rusty cans of this and that, you couldn't tell what, the labels were gone—everything soaked up, musty, jumbled together. How it had got here, what it was all about, was a mystery which they might find out sometime, if Arvid could get that kid to talk. But whatever the mystery was, it wasn't, right now, a part of Freddy's interest. This was some bike.

He had his work space cleared and the sidecar unhooked; and he was just easing the bike down over the side of the boat to the bank where he could have room to work on it, when Bigelow came tearing out of the woods, yelling her head off.

"Now what?" Freddy said. "What's the matter with you?"

From what he could make out, she was yelling to let that alone, it wasn't his, it belonged to her and somebody, and that he was an old fool and a thief and some other things that surprised Freddy to hear from a youngster.

"Look here," he said. "What kind of a way is that to talk? You ought to have your mouth washed out with soap. Go on, beat it, I'm—" and he had to duck as a rock whizzed straight at his head. It came within an inch of getting him right in the hat, and the whole thing made him red-hot mad. He leaned the bike against the bank and put chase.

He didn't catch Bigelow. She vanished somewhere in the woods, but he figured he'd scared her enough so she wouldn't come back. He was just settling down again, cooling off and getting his breath back, when another rock banged into the middle of his open toolbox. A light tinkle told him that something had broken—sure enough, the glass that held the bubble on his metal level.

Freddy gave a howl of rage; he'd rather have had the rock hit *him!* He put chase again, this time carrying a switch he broke from a bush on the shore; but the same thing happened—he couldn't find Bigelow. With the third rock—and they weren't pebbles, they were of a size that could knock a man out—Freddy stamped back through the woods to the house to find Arvid.

"Now, look!" he shouted. "By the God, Arvid, you've got to keep that kid out of my hair or I'll—"

He ground to a stop. For there, sitting on the doorstep, cool as a cucumber, was Bigelow. She was squarely behind Arvid, who was puttying storm windows and had one lying in front of him across a couple of sawhorses. Freddy couldn't very well get at her unless he picked up the window and threw it, which he was inclined to do, except that an attack would also involve moving Arvid.

"What kind of a kook are you?" Freddy demanded furiously. "Throw rocks like that at a man? Those could easy have killed me!"

"Those things belong to I and Marney," Bigelow said. "Nobody has got a right to touch any of them." She made it sound polite; after all, she had promised Arvid to be nice to Freddy.

"Well, who's taking anything? Who wants it? You nor Marney nor anyone else'll ever run that bike unless somebody cleans it up, gets the salt water off of it. Honest to God, Arvid, will you try to talk some sense into—" He glared at them both, choked, and walked off around the house in the direction he'd come from.

There was a short silence, which Bigelow broke. She said in a small voice, "I guess I made him pretty mad."

"Well," Arvid said, "now, Bigelow, so'd I be mad if you throwed rocks at me."

"I wouldn't throw rocks at you. He was—he was—"

"I kind of run of an idea," Arvid said, "that Freddy was doing Marney a favor."

"He was *stealing* Marney's—"

"No, he wasn't. What he was doing, he was going to clean up that bike, fix it so's it would keep good till Marney's well enough to use it again. He's right about that, Bigelow; it'll rust all to hellan—to the dev—to heck and gone, unless he gets some oil on it. I kind of think you've made a mistake about Freddy, Bigelow."

"Well, why didn't he say? Why doesn't he tell people? He just goes ahead, tramps all over everybody! And he looks at me all the time to make me feel mean!"

"It's just that he ain't much of a talker," Arvid said. He glanced at her, laid down his putty knife. "It's coming on for high tide," he said. "How'd it be if you and me went in the boat and yarned in a few traps, got us a mess of lobsters for supper? Have a nice boat ride, cool off some till we can talk over how to fix it so's you and Freddy won't keep on running a-foul?"

"Oh, good! Can we fish, too?"

"Sure. You round up the fishing lines, whilst I put on my boots. Bring what's left of that hodful of clams, too, for bait."

He was standing on the steps with his boots on, when she came back with the fishing things.

"I brought a can of corned beef and some bread," she said, holding out a paper bag. "In case we get hungry—Arvid, what is it? Is something—"

"Sh-h," Arvid said, holding up his hand. "Listen. I thought I heard the cat yowl. Can you?"

They listened. At first, they heard nothing. Some gulls were calling down over the harbor, and Arvid was about to say that he must have heard one of them mewling, when, unmistakably, from somewhere in the woods the sound came again. No doubt about it this time. A cat-yowl. And a cat in pain.

Bigelow dropped her armload and tore down the steps toward the woods.

"Hey, wait!" Arvid yelled. "Something's after her. Wait'll I bring my gun!"

But she was gone, out of sight in the undergrowth. Arvid grabbed the gun off the rack in the kitchen and went thumping after her, not making very good time in his heavy rubber boots.

After a few minutes, he had to stop. He couldn't hear which way she had gone, anyway, and she was out of sight. Breathless and panting, he stood looking this way and that, listening. The cat had stopped crying. Well, he thought, whatever was after her's made off with her, no doubt of that; but no, there she was again, weaker this time, and a crackling sound in the bushes. Bigelow burst out onto the path. She was bare from the waist up—she had stripped off her T-shirt to put around Toughy, whom she carried, wrapped, in her arms. Her face was white and her eyes were dark blue with fury.

"Somebody's poured something awful on her!" Bigelow gasped. "Some stinky stuff, like kerosene. It hurts her, Arvid, it hurts her terribly! Oh, Arvid, what will we do?"

"Turpentine!" Arvid said. He could smell it. "Now, what devil done that?" There wasn't time, though, to wonder. Something had to be done quick. He wished to the Lord he knew what. "Lard," he said. "Lard might help. Come on, Bigelow, hustle!"

Arvid tried. Lard eased the stinging tender parts apparently, but he couldn't put lard in Toughy's eyes, and the turpentine was all through her fur—whoever had done this had evidently upended a can of the stuff and poured. Toughy was wild with pain and fright. She fought every inch of the way. Every now and then, she let go with a wail of agony which, whenever it came, visibly broke Bigelow's heart. Arvid finally stopped sponging. His hands were bleeding from scratches, and he had a deep, bloody claw-mark down one cheek.

"This ain't helping," he said hoarsely. "There's a vet in Powell. I'll take her in there, right now."

"Well, I'm coming, too," Bigelow said.

"Oh, no, you can't," Arvid said. He couldn't take her in there. Suppose somebody saw her, somebody who knew about her, like that young Ferris? They'd keep her there, that was for sure.

"Well, I won't stay here alone with that—that awful devil, that Freddy," Bigelow said. "He did this to Toughy, you know he did. He was so mad, so he did this—"

"Oh, no," Arvid said. "He couldn't. He wouldn't, Bigelow. Not Freddy." But in spite of himself, his voice lacked conviction. Because if Freddy hadn't done it, then who? Freddy had a can of turpentine, Arvid had seen it. Freddy. There was no one else.

"He did! He did!" Bigelow said. "If you make me stay here with him, I'll kill him! I'll take your gun and kill him!"

"All right," Arvid said. "You'll have to wear my jacket, Bigelow. We'll buy you some more T-shirts in Powell."

He found a covered carton for Toughy and laid her in it on a folded towel. She was tired now; the fight had gone out of her. She lay quietly in the carton without even a whimper.

Bigelow said, in a grief-stricken whisper, "Is she going to die?"

"I don't know," Arvid said. "We'll just have to do the best we can."

It was an accident, he told himself. It's got to be an accident. That boy would never—no. He may have a cruel streak when he's drunk or mad, but he ain't that bad. Freddy. Not Freddy. Not on purpose.

Hauling traps off on Thirteen-feet Shoal, Ed Snorri saw Arvid's boat come out of the General Remarks inlet and head, full speed, for the mainland. Well, now, if that wasn't a chunk of luh-luh-luck. There went old Buttercup-Boy.

Two hours ago, Ed had landed the twins on the beach in the Outer Harbor. The sea had gone down there now; a boat could put in safely, and on the steep beach, a skiff could make a landing. The twins had been pestering Ed for quite a while to land them on General Remarks. They wouldn't let old Buttercup-Boy see them, they said. They could sneak over through the woods—not go near the house—and see if that motorbike was still there. Maybe, if nobody was around, they could pick up some stuff off of that wreck. They wanted Ed to leave the skiff for them, in case they were able to make off with the bike or, for some reason, needed to leave in a hurry. But Ed said, Nuh-nuh-nossir, a skiff on that beach was too easy seen; he didn't want to be noticed around there just now, he had plans for later. After he had rowed the boys ashore, he took the skiff in tow and went off on the Shoal to haul traps.

Seeing Arvid go, Ed thought, Fine. Nobody on the island now. He could land there himself. Do old Buttercup-Boy good to find some windows smashed out of his house when he got back. Fix him.

But when he came around into the Outer Harbor, he saw that the boys were on the beach, waving, apparently in a hurry to be taken off. Didn't appear to be lugging anything, either; must be some reason for that. So Ed didn't stop to anchor. He nosed the boat as close to the beach as he could and shoved the skiff in to them.

The twins piled aboard, breathless and panting. Seems they'd duh-damn near got caught this time. Freddy Fowler was up there working on that bike. He hadn't been there when they'd first peeked out of the bushes, but they'd known somebody was around, all those tools spread out on the ground. So they'd nipped in to grab what they could before whoever it was got back, and just then they'd heard him coming. So they'd just grabbed and run. Truman had got two good wrenches—luh-luh-look—but, as usual, poor old Dewey hadn't been able to lay his hand on anything that amounted to much. All he'd got was an open coffee can full of turpentine.

"Juh-juh-just shet your eyes and guh-grabbed, I s'pose," Ed said, looking at Dewey with disgust. "What to huh-hell good was that?"

"Had to guh-grab something," Dewey said sullenly.

"Well, where is it?" A man could always use turpentine.

Seems Dewey had spilt it. They'd taken off running. The twins looked at each other and giggled. Run right head-on into old Buttercup-Boy's cat, and old Dew had let her have it, dead center. Talk about a yipping.

Mollified, Ed grinned. Buttercup-Boy's cat, hanh? Well, good enough. He'd done that to a dog once or twice. In his opinion, it was more fun to turpentine a dog.

On the way back to the Shoal, he saw something that made him realize that this was sure his lucky day. Got out of there just about right—couldn't have timed it better.

The Coast Guard launch, with quite a few aboard, was coming around the east end of General Remarks, heading for the Outer Harbor.

The Coast Guard had ferried out to the island an insurance company appraiser and an engineer, to look over the wreck. New Hampshire had traced the *Sea Flower's* name and number in state records. She had belonged to a Charles Bowker of Medbrook. Medbrook's river section had been wiped out when a dam in the hills back of the town had let go. A good many people were dead or missing—Bowker and his wife and two sons among them.

Ferris told Freddy about this while he waited for the appraiser and the engineer to finish with the houseboat. They had found Freddy, in peace at last, settling down to work on the bank, on the motorcycle engine.

"Don't know as I'd touch too much till these boys get through," Ferris told him. "In my opinion, though, they'll abandon the works. Then you can probably go ahead, or anyway, make a deal."

The only relative this Bowker had had was a brother who was in South America, tied up on an engineering project. He wasn't interested in salvaging a wrecked boat which couldn't be salvaged anyway without heavy machinery to launch her and a dredge to dig a channel deep enough across that mudflat. What he wanted to know was if the two boys who'd been found aboard the wreck were his brother's sons.

"We know the older one, the one in the Powell hospital, isn't Bowker's," Ferris said. "His name's Lessard, comes from some place in New York. He's better, by the way. Still pretty weak, but able to talk. He was riding through the area when the storm hit and he got aboard the houseboat by sheer accident. He doesn't know who the other kid is. We had an idea it might be the younger Bowker boy."

"Well, it isn't," Freddy said. He was still sore—got madder every time he looked in his toolbox. There was that smashed level, and somehow, the Lord knew when—he hadn't seen her do it, but she must have, there wasn't anybody else—she'd got away with two of his best wrenches and his can of turpentine. "Because that kid is no boy," he went on. "She's a girl, and a little hellion. Name's Bigelow, or so she says."

"Well, that figures," Ferris said. He dug out of a pocket a paper on which he had a list. "Small mentioned the name, but of course we thought she was a boy. Here it is. Elizabeth Bigelow, eleven years old, listed missing. Lived with her cousin, who's dead. Body's been found. I don't know what other relatives there may be—the Red Cross will. We'll notify them. Have to send her back if we can round her up." Ferris grinned. "So far, we haven't had much luck."

"Take her along today, why don't you?" Freddy said, "She's easy enough found, right now. She's out in the boat, somewhere, with Arvid. I saw them take off—oh, might've been an hour ago. My guess is, he's hauling traps out on Thirteen-feet Shoal."

And that, Freddy thought, was that.

He had no qualms about giving the needed information—in his opinion, it was the right, the only thing to do. Of course the kid should go back where she came from, to her relatives and friends. What else? It went without saying. If Arvid was sore about it, Freddy was sorry. But the thing now had gone beyond Arvid's—or the kid's—preferences. Its legal side could be pointed out to Arvid, and what might happen if a man got hauled up on a kidnapping charge.

Right now Freddy was interested in what those two guys were going to decide about the houseboat.

𝄃

The Coast Guard didn't find Arvid out on Thirteen-feet Shoal; they hove him to a few miles outside of Powell Harbor, headed back for the island. Arvid saw them coming from quite a distance away. He knew what they were going to do; he supposed he'd known from the beginning that this would happen sometime, and that there'd be nothing he could do about it. Too bad that it had had to happen today, just when things had got smoothed out again. Or any day, be thought sadly, watching the launch circle to come up alongside.

They had had a fortunate time in Powell. They had caught the vet in, at his office; and he said at once that Toughy would be all right, though it was lucky they'd got her to him as soon as they had. She'd have a sensitive skin and sore eyes for a while; but a bath and some lotion would work wonders, So leave her for an hour or two and then come back.

They had been so relieved and happy that they'd gone downtown and had had a celebration. Arvid took the precaution of going to the bank first. He could see that people were looking at Bigelow, if not at him, and no wonder. They both looked like Willie-off-the-pickle-boat. After he had cashed a check, he headed for the department store.

They bought Bigelow an outfit of fall and winter clothes—under-wear, woolen shirts, T-shirts, jeans, and even a pair of high, lined rubber boots, like Arvid's own. Passing a display of little girls' dresses, Arvid paused hopefully, but Bigelow didn't turn her head. She was going, she said, to pick out something nice for him—it wasn't right for her to have *all* the new things. Her choice was a wonderful Hawaiian shirt in loud colors that made his head ache, and looked to him, from the size of it, as if it had been cut from the awning of the Congregational Ladies Outdoor Food Sale. But under the circumstances, he wouldn't have swapped it for the plainest blue denim workshirt he'd ever bought. He wore it out of the store.

They had haircuts. They had ice-cream sodas at the drugstore. At a pet shop they bought a new carrier for Toughy—the old one, Bigelow said, was all smashed and musty-wet from the wreck. And, mentioning the wreck, she came to a full stop. To Arvid's surprise, her eyes filled with tears.

"Heb'm sake," Arvid said. "What's the matter? What are you puddling up for?"

"I'm mean," Bigelow said. "I forgot." She looked at him out of a dismal face. "All I thought of was having my own good time."

Arvid nodded. He could guess. In a way, he'd been expecting this. He'd hoped she wouldn't remember until they were safely back aboard the boat; because the hospital was the one place they couldn't go. "Well, you've had a lot on your mind, today," he said. "And, you know, they're likely to latch onto you, if we go where anyone has to know who you are. But I can phone. We can find out how Marney is."

He came out of the phone booth looking pleased, if a little rattled. The nurse at the hospital desk had said Marney was doing as well as could be expected. That wasn't enough; that wasn't any kind of good news to carry back to Bigelow.

"Well, is he better?" he asked. "Is he well enough to have company?"

"His doctor can—"

"Look, this *is* Doctor Forbush. I want to know how the boy's doing today."

"Why, yes, Doctor," she said, in a puzzled voice. "He's better. Out of danger—who did you say? Doctor *who?*"

"Thank you," Arvid said. "Thank you, ma'am. Thank you kindly." He hung up. Doctor Forbush had been his grandmother's doctor, dead these many years, but his name had been the only one Arvid could think of. The old man had done people many a good turn in his time; Arvid guessed this one more wouldn't hurt his record any. He relayed the good news to Bigelow, and they went on back to the vet's.

There was Toughy, looking as good as new. She had had a bath and some lotion on her eyes; she had just come out from under the drier. Her fur was fluffy again and smelled good; and even when the vet brought her out, they saw her try to get him in the hand with a claw. She didn't care for the new carrier; she said so, loudly.

"She's a spunky one," the vet said. "Pretty sore at me now for dunking her in the bathtub. Going to have some kittens, too, before very long. Did you know that?"

They hadn't known it; but it was one more thing to make up for the bad of the day. Arvid had just money enough to pay the vet's bill.

So now, he thought, watching the Coast Guard launch, it's all good and lost. That young Ferris is aboard, though. I might be able to talk him out of it.

"Well, Bigelow," he said, "I guess they've outsmarted us. But you get down in the cuddy and lie low and I'll do the best I can."

His best, as he had known, wasn't good enough.

Ferris was decent about it, but he was firm. It wasn't his choice and he was sorry; but they'd have to take the youngster.

"Look, you don't have any claim or interest," he said. "How come you're bothering us like this? That kid's got to go back where she came from. That's the law. Nothing I can do about it."

"All right, I know it's the law," Arvid said. "But they ain't no reason Bigelow can't stay with me till they make sure who there is to go back to, is there? From all I've been able to make out, Bigelow's been a pretty miserable kid at home, wherever that was. Who's going to find out about that? Anybody?" He had noticed that Ferris had said "she," but he carefully avoided saying it himself.

"Look, I'm sure sorry," Ferris said. He was puzzled and showing it. "But you know it isn't up to me. The Red Cross'll take care of her, if that's what's worrying you. Oh, come on, Small. Hand her over. All we can do is come aboard and take her."

"Goddammit, you may have to," Arvid said. "But I'll talk to her about it." There! Darned if he hadn't said it, in spite of himself.

He went down into the cuddy. Bigelow had heard every word of it. She wasn't crying. She was huddled up in the peak of the bow as far as she could get. Her face glimmered white in the dimness of the cuddy and her eyes were enormous.

"Bigelow?" Arvid said. He put out his hand and she batted it away.

He couldn't stand it. Maybe she wasn't crying, but all at once he was. For a minute he couldn't say a word. Then he pulled out his handkerchief, wiped away his tears, and lowered his voice to a husky whisper.

"Now, Bigelow. You have not got to be scared by this, because I am not going to stand for it. By the G—by the angels, I am not. Now, listen. I will take care of Toughy. I will take care of the houseboat and your things, and I will take care of Marney when he gets out of the hospital. And now you hear me, because this is a promise. I am going to come after you and bring you back. You hear?"

She still didn't say anything.

"Bigelow," he said, "when I make a promise, I keep it. I am a man you can trust. You go with them and don't fight back and do what they say. And I'll come."

Bigelow reached out a finger and touched his cheek. She said in a wondering voice, "You're crying."

"G—goddammit, of course I'm crying. I feel godawful. If it would do any good, I'd start a fight right now. But we can't fight the whole United States Coast Guard, you and me, now Bigelow, can we?"

To his astonishment, she both arms around his neck and laid her cheek against his. For a moment, their tears ran down his cheek together.

She said, "Will you be long before you come?"

"No, I won't. I'll start tonight. Soon as I find a good safe place to leave Toughy."

"Don't leave her with that Freddy—"

"No. I know a nice woman likes cats."

From topside, Ferris called down. "How about it? Have I got to come aboard, Small?"

"No," Arvid said. "Won't be needed."

He took Bigelow's hand and they came out of the cuddy together.

The last he saw as the launch pulled away for Powell was the white face, the enormous eyes looking back, the huddled, small figure, desperate and forlorn.

Arvid did not go back to the island. He headed inshore for home and tied up at his old mooring. Simon Eldridge was just rowing ashore from his own boat, and Arvid hailed him.

"Left your punt out to the island, I guess," Simon said, pulling in alongside.

"That's right," Arvid said, climbing aboard. "Glad of a lift ashore, Simon. I'll try not to sink you."

"What's in the box? A mink?" Simon asked.

"Got me a cat."

"Company, I guess. Must be lonesome out there."

"Not too. With a nice cat," Arvid said. Simon was probing around, he knew that, and Simon knew he knew it. After a moment, Simon tried again.

"You heard the news?"

"What news is that?"

"Freddy left Philomela."

"Heb'm sake. Lot happened since I been gone, I guess. Thanks for the lift, Simon."

He got out as the punt touched the beach and trudged away, leaving Simon looking after him. Well, Simon had known, of course, that Freddy was out on the island with him. It was probably the talk of the town. Just wanted to hear Arvid's version out of inquisitiveness. Well, didn't.

As Arvid passed the fishhouse, he saw that Rodney had been down and had fixed the roof. Looked nice. For a moment, he couldn't help thinking of the quiet and solitude in there, of that good, comfortable old potbelly stove.

I have come a long ways since them old days, he told himself, and went on up the hill, carrying Toughy, to the only person in the world he was sure a man could trust—well, not the only one now. There was one other; there was Bigelow—who was Philomela Fowler.

✦

Philomela looked white and pinched. She had dark hollows under her eyes. She certainly showed how she was feeling, and Arvid looked at her with sorrow; but her mouth went tight at the sight of him, and she said, "Oh, it's you. What might you want?"

"This in here is a cat," Arvid said. "Kind of a nice one. I got a story to tell, Philomela. If you'd listen, I would appreciate."

"I don't know why I should," she said. "Or bother with you in any way whatsoever. I suppose it's got something to do with Freddy. If it has, I don't want to hear it."

"This ain't about Freddy. He is in it, but he ain't the main. I give you leave to draw a bead on me, Philomela, but listen first."

She reached over, took the carrier out of his hand.

"I suppose, manlike, you'd let the poor thing smother in there while you talk," she said, opening it.

Toughy jumped out on the floor. Philomela put out a hand and pulled it back just in time. "Well, for goodness' *sake!*" she said.

"Name of Toughy," Arvid said. "Has to get acquainted first."

That was Bigelow, too; and seeing Toughy standing there with her tail straight up, not scared but independent in a strange place, Arvid couldn't help it, his eyes watered again. He had to get out his handkerchief.

Philomela glanced at him. She looked away. "I don't suppose you two lunks have thought to feed her," she said. "I'll get her some milk."

She went off to the kitchen.

By the time she was back, Arvid was composed. His handkerchief was back in his pocket.

"What is it?" she said. "Tell me." And she sat down, waiting, ready to listen.

You could always count on her, that was the thing.

So Arvid let her have it, the story of Bigelow, all of it that he knew.

"And that is all I know," he said. "But there is more to it than meets the eye, Philomela. And this is what I've got to do."

"Oh, dear God," Philomela said under her breath, hearing him through. "Those two children . . . on that boat in that storm. Oh, dear God in heaven!"

She looked now, he was glad to see, not so tired and forlorn—as if something in the world might ever interest her again. She even had some color in her cheeks. "And the boy's in the Powell Hospital. With nobody to—"

"That's right," Arvid said. "This is his cat. Thinks a lot of her, Bigelow says. Might help if you went over to see him. Take Toughy, too."

"Oh, they'd never let her into the hospital. It's against the law or something, isn't it?"

"Well now, Philomela," Arvid said. He looked at her, his head slightly on one side. "H'm, well. She's had a rough time, too, got into a dose of turpentine today. Got some in her eyes. Here's the salve for it. Tells on the bottle what to do."

He certainly wasn't going to peddle that about Freddy and the turpentine—ever mention it to anyone, unless he was sure. And he had his own ideas about it now, anyway. Old Snorri, off on the Shoal today when they'd passed him, had been alone and he'd had a skiff in tow. Could be he'd landed them two hellions on the island. He'd certainly landed them somewhere. They were always with him when he was out in his boat.

"So break the law," Philomela said. She had managed a smile, which presently broke out into a chuckle. "You old pirate. Well, you always have been, it's too late to change you. I suppose you know that what you want to do is breaking the law, too, don't you?"

"Well, now, Philomela, what would you do?"

"I'd break the law. Take the truck. Take Freddy's pickup. Or the car, if you'd rather. Have you got any money?"

He hadn't. She got out her pocketbook and gave him some.

He looked a little green in the face, she thought, and she patted him on the arm. "Good luck," she said. "Bring her back here. If we have to, we'll hide her in the attic."

Out of the side window, she watched him climb into the truck, and suddenly stood frozen and appalled, seeing it start up and buck out of the driveway in a series of horrendous jerks.

Dear God in heaven! she told herself. I never thought! But I don't believe he's driven a car since that old Model T he had, years ago. And I know as well as I stand here that he hasn't got a license.

✦

Marney sat in a wheelchair in the sun porch at the Powell Hospital. The sun felt good; a shaft of it warmed his hands, which since he had got better, seemed all the time to be cold. He was able to sit up now, walk around a little, getting well. Give him another week, the doctors said, he'd be ready for the bus journey home.

Home? Where was that? He supposed they meant Spancook. That was where they thought he'd come from. They'd checked, while he was sick, the license plate on Joe Dondin's bike. So all that running had been no good; he'd run from nothing into nothing. Go back to whatever there was for him in Spancook; the way he felt now, he didn't care, and the way he was, wabbly in the shoulders and with his knees knocking when he walked, he sure wouldn't be able to take care of himself, get a job, or anything. And, of course, he'd lost the bike.

At least, he supposed he must have. After that wild night aboard the boat in the storm, when everything had broken loose and crashed around him, he'd be foolish to think there could be much of the bike left. What there was of it must be still aboard the boat—they'd been able to check the license plate. But by the time he got well enough to go and see, the motor'd be rusted solid, all that salt water.

But let it go. And let Toughy go. Nobody he'd talked to had recalled seeing her. So he'd lost her that night, too.

Everything about that storm was so hazy now. He could only remember parts of it, a picture in his mind here and there, like movies with part of the plot cut out. Getting the kid and Toughy and the bike aboard the houseboat; bracing himself and the kid in the bunk; getting slammed around—dim pictures sliding in and out. And then he didn't remember anything. He had been still foggy when various people had asked him questions—he recalled a man in some kind of a uniform, a policeman, maybe. Since then he hadn't seen anyone but the doctors and nurses, who all knew that the kid was okay and the houseboat wrecked on an offshore island; and that was all they did know.

The shaft of sun was creeping away from Marney's hands. He edged the wheelchair forward a little to find it again. At least the sun was the same; it was still warm.

From the wide sun-porch window, he could see the roofs of the strange town. The hospital apparently was on a hill behind it, overlooking its homes. A fairly sizable town; not pretty; about like other towns he'd ridden through and not stopped in. Crooked streets, beyond them, wharves stretching into a harbor, with fishing boats and a yacht or two. And beyond the harbor, blue ocean, dotted with islands, to the horizon.

He wondered if one of the islands was where the houseboat was, where the bike was, where he'd lost Toughy.

A nurse came by with a tray of milk and orange juice. She kidded him cheerfully while he took the glass nearest his hand. They were always trying to buck you up. The easiest way, the way to get them to let you alone, was to let on you were bucked up. Then they would go away happy. So he grinned and tried to kid back, and presently she went off, tray and all. But outside the door, and he couldn't help hearing, she said to someone, "That poor little devil, he breaks my heart. Makes me want to put back my head and howl like a dog."

Maybe she meant him, maybe she didn't. Didn't matter.

If you didn't drink the orange juice, somebody would make a production. Marney drank it. He set the glass down and sat looking across the monkey puzzle of ugly buildings, toward the wooded islands that were dark and mysterious in the westering sun.

It was Toughy, but not Toughy alone. It was just about everything.

"Are you Marney Lessard?"

A tall woman had stopped beside him; he looked up at her with a start. She was nobody he had ever seen before, not one of the Gray Ladies with books or jigsaw puzzles, and she wasn't being cheerful with that gaiety put on for the occasion, which jangled your nerves and made you want to hit out with your fists. She was looking at him with serious, matter-of-fact eyes, and she'd spoken his name as if she'd really wanted to know.

She said, "My name is Philomela Fowler. I have brought you your cat."

And looking down with a sudden start of wild unbelief, he saw what she was carrying in her hand—a pet carrier which he had not seen before, but with a familiar, outraged, and furious nose against the screened end.

"You had better not open it," Philomela said, putting the carrier on his lap. "She is very put out and, at the moment, flighty. And they don't allow animals in this hospital. I had to sneak her past the desk when no one was looking."

But she made no attempt to stop him, thoughtfully watching his shaking fingers fumbling at the buckles.

Toughy was not about to be glad to see Marney or anybody else. She had been put by a stranger into a strange carrier and toted around in a car. Before Marney had the second fastening undone, she had her head out and one claw; she let him have it, a good one, on the back of his hand, wriggled the rest of the way out, and flounced down out of sight under a cot on the sun porch.

"Well," Philomela said. "Now, pray who comes in here first. If it's a blue nurse, we'll have a chance. But if it's one of those white ones, you and I'll doubtless end up in jail."

"Toughy!" Marney said. "Oh, darn you, come out of there!"

He didn't care if his voice trembled, or if it went up high, the way it had been when he was young, when it was changing.

No one seemed to care if a cat had got on to the hospital sun porch. The hospital staff seemed more pleased than anything else, even the knowledgeable white nurse, who brought salmon from the kitchen, let Toughy smell it, and then set the dish inside the carrier.

"That's the first thing that's made that youngster show any signs of life since we've had him here," she told Philomela, walking with her to the door as Philomela was leaving. "I wouldn't care if that cat had been an elephant. I only wish you could leave her here. It's too bad he has to stay here himself any longer. He's well enough to leave, but, of course, he's got no place to go."

"He is?" Philomela said. "Isn't there anyone?"

The nurse shook her head. "Apparently he hasn't any people. He lived somewhere in New York State, but so far as we know, he's on his own."

"Nobody at all," Philomela said.

"Well, the Red Cross—I suppose they'll arrange to send him back to New York."

Philomela set Toughy's carrier down on the floor. "What do I do?" she asked. "Whom do I see, to find out if he can come home with me?"

POWELL—15, the road sign said.

Well, goddlemighty, Arvid thought, catching it out of the corner of his eye as the truck ground by. Fifteen miles, it can't be.

It seemed to him that he had already come one helmonious long ways. He had been to Powell, of course, a good many times with Freddy, in this same pickup, but not driving; and when you are not driving, you don't notice the landmarks. And you don't notice how the thing drives, either, what to push and what to pull. He wished to God he had. If he'd only paid a little attention to what Freddy'd done!

It didn't drive like a boat, which was what he'd counted on—one gear lever to push ahead, and then you put the gas to her. She had one gear lever, to be sure, but push it ahead as far as it would go, he couldn't get the speed out of her that Freddy always had. Put the gas to her and the engine roared all right, but the truck wouldn't go any faster. And she certainly didn't drive anything like his old Model T. Altogether different.

Well, she would go. And she would go ahead, if slow. He would get there sometime. And, at least, he told himself, she steers like a boat. I can steer the goddamned thing.

A car which had been trying to get past him for some time back, finally made it by running out on the shoulder. The driver, red-faced, hollered loudly as he went by. "For so-and-so and this-and-that, get that mess of junk out of second!"

Second? Second. I ain't doing it right.

It had been hard enough to get the thing going at all; he wasn't going to go through that again.

Squarely in the middle of the highway, pulling over when he had to for oncoming traffic, he ground along, building up behind him a kite-tail of cars with furious drivers and honking horns. Eyes glued to the road ahead, ears filled with the sound of his roaring engine, Arvid did not notice them until he hit the new highway a few miles outside of Powell, where the road widened to three lanes. Then they began to go by him in a stream.

Mercy, must've been a funeral. Going like bats, too. They better look out or they'll kill somebody.

It was late afternoon when he finally got to Powell. Supper traffic was in full flux. It was too much to expect of a man. Arvid pulled over to the sidewalk and stopped, just before a busy intersection.

Maybe if I just sit here awhile, all them jokers will get by and go home to supper, he thought.

He waited, tranquilly, while cars hesitated, pulled out around him, and went on. Presently, a state police car nosed out of traffic and stopped in front of him. The officer got out and came back.

"Look, what's the idea? You know you can't park here, bud."

"Well, now, son," Arvid said, "I am certainly glad to see you. I can't get her out of second."

"She stall on you? She go at all?"

"I don't know as she will. I can try her again."

"Where do you want to go?"

"Woolley's Garage, if she'll make it. You know where that is?"

"Oh, sure. See if she'll start. If she will, you pull along behind me."

Being Freddy's, and in excellent shape, the truck started smoothly; being in second, she jerked a few times. But a slight downward slope helped, and she crept out into traffic behind the police car, which, siren going, cleared the way nicely into town and stopped in front of Woolley's Garage.

"Well, I certainly appreciate," Arvid said. "Never would of made it on my own. Now, anything I can ever do for you, you let me know."

"That's okay, you're welcome." The officer grinned. On duty in this part of the country, he wasn't unacquainted with old gentlemen who still drove an automobile as if it were a horse. He lifted a hand and went his way.

Woolley's was the garage which had once belonged to Freddy. A fellow named Ed Woolley owned it now. Arvid knew him slightly; well enough, he figured, to ask a favor of him.

"You like to see if you can get this critter out of second?" he asked Ed.

"Sure," Ed said. "Shove over." He got in. "Ain't this Freddy Fowler's pickup?" he asked. "Mean to tell me something's wrong with it?"

"I don't know as I know," Arvid said.

He watched carefully while Ed started the engine, flipped the gear lever from low to second to high.

So that was how it was done. Haul it back, not forward, as far as it would go.

"Smooth as a baby," Ed said. He looked puzzled. "What did you figure was wrong with it?"

"Something," Arvid said. He shook his head. "Might be something I done. I ain't as good a driver as Freddy. Not by a long shot. You got a place I can leave her here, whilst I do some shopping?"

"Sure. There's a slot right there in the parking lot, between the two Cadillacs."

Arvid looked at the slot. It seemed narrow. Not for him to try. Not between two Cadillacs, even if he did know how to get her out of second now. He said, "Well, Ed, you're in the driver's seat," and got out hastily. "Thanks," he said. "I'll be seeing you after a while."

He sauntered off down the main street of Powell. At a drugstore he stopped and bought a box of chocolates; at a hardware store he bought a shining new jackknife with four blades, and had the parcels wrapped together. Then he went along to the Powell Court House, climbed the steps to the Department of Health and Welfare. If they didn't have Bigelow here, at least they were the ones who'd know who did have her.

The Welfare worker at the desk was just preparing to go home. She had had a difficult day and she was not pleased to see anyone at this hour. She said, "I'm sorry, sir, but the office is closing."

"Well, now, ma'am," Arvid said. "I won't take a minute of your time. I've just come in from General Remarks Island, and these is some things belongs to the Bigelow kid."

"Oh, yes. I'll see she gets them."

"Good, glad I caught her before she left. I didn't know but you folks might've put her right on the bus."

"Oh, no." The lady sighed. If only it had been that simple. Part of her long day had been the ordeal of Bigelow, who had had to have decent clothes to travel in; and Bigelow had fought every inch of the way. Seeing Arvid still politely listening and beaming at her, she went on, "We had to wait for an answer from the Red Cross in Portsmouth, of course. So we're putting her on the bus tomorrow."

"I see." That was what he wanted to know. "Well, thank you, ma'am. I appreciate." And he went his way.

Arvid stopped again at the hardware store, which also was just closing. He bought an outsize waterproof tarpaulin. He had had it in mind to buy a couple of blankets, but the department store, he noted as he went by, was shut down for the day. Anyway, the tarp would do just as well, if not better, and it would come in handy out on the island this winter, too.

Shaved it close, he thought, hearing the store door click shut and lock behind him. Never dreamt that pickup of Freddy's would take so long just to come over here to Powell. Made it, though. Never mind how close it was.

He went to a restaurant in town where he knew he could get a drink at the bar and a good steak supper. Then he walked back to Woolley's Garage, climbed into the back of the truck, wrapped the tarp around himself, and went to sleep for the night.

In the morning he was stiff in the joints. It had been a mistake to think he could sleep on the hard floor of the truck body without paying for it. He ought to have got a bed in a hotel. But he had had to be sure of getting an early start in case the bus left before a human hour, as buses often did. You couldn't trust the cussed things, they left in the middle of the night if they could manage it, and the Lord only knew how long he'd have slept if he'd had a good soft bed. Besides, he had to figure the way to get this truck down to the bus station. He had spotted that last night; it was only a few streets away—about a five-minute walk, he should judge, if he'd been walking it. But there was some way to make the goddamned pickup go backwards, and he had to find out what it was.

He got out of the back of the truck and climbed, cracking and moaning, into the driver's seat. The engine started all right; this was certainly second—goddlemighty, he ought by this time to know where second was—and down here to the right was what she run on. There was two other places, low left and high left. He shut his eyes, tried high left, trod hard on the gas. The pickup went shooting out of the slot between the two Cadillacs and was halfway across the lot, going at a good clip backwards, before he could collect himself enough to stomp down on the brake.

Stalled her, but by God, that was it! Give him time, he'd have her by the short wool.

The bus wasn't at the station, but there was a fine, empty parking place. It said BUS STOP all right; and there was a diner, open too, right across the street. What he wouldn't give for some breakfast and a quart of coffee!

He made a swooping U-turn at the intersection beyond, under the sign that said NO U-TURN, came to a rolling stop at the curb by the bus station. The truck might be a little bit up into the bus's place. One experience backing her up had been enough, though. He would leave the key in; if the bus driver didn't have room, he would know how to get out and move the pickup without much trouble. The station appeared to be open; Arvid wished he dared to go in and ask what time the bus left. But under the circumstances, he figured it wouldn't be too smart to be seen in there.

He went into the diner, sat down at a window where he could have a clear view of the bus stop. He had finished a plateful of ham and eggs and was on his third cup of coffee when the big Interstate rolled in. He could see it quite a distance away, coming up the street. Sign on it said BOSTON.

Sure enough, the driver was having his troubles finding room in there ahead of the pickup. Seemed to be put out about it; he was signaling to a young fellow on the sidewalk. Pretty soon the young fellow got the message, went along to the pickup, looked in, got in, backed her up about twenty feet.

Well, there. Wait long enough, things unscrambled themselves. Arvid finished his coffee.

The driver got out and went into the station with a packet of papers in his hand. A few people got into the bus. Arvid waited. No sense getting hassled up yet. The bus wasn't going anywhere without the driver. And presently, along the street, with the lady Arvid had talked to yesterday at the court house, came Bigelow.

Arvid did a double take. For the sake of the living Lord in the wilderness, look at Bigelow! If it hadn't been for the lady, whom he recognized, he would never in the Lord's world have known Bigelow. Now, wasn't that nice!

She had on a neat little dark blue hat and a coat over a light blue dress. Sandals and socks. In her hand she carried the bundle he had left for her; he recognized it, as she came closer. She still looked white in the face and big-eyed; her mouth was shut very tight. She walked along without turning her head one way or the other. It was good she didn't; she might have looked up and seen him in the diner window, and she might have shown something, recognized him in front of that lady.

If that lady is going to go with her, he thought, it is going to fud up everything. I will have to think of something else.

He waited with a sinking heart; but the lady was only putting Bigelow on the bus. She had got on; then in a few minutes she got off again and walked away up the street.

Arvid paid his check. He sauntered across the street and got on the bus himself. Bigelow was sitting halfway back, looking out the opposite window. She didn't see him at all until he sat down beside her. He heard her gasp, but he managed to shake his head and put his finger on his lips before she could say anything.

He said in a loud voice, "Is this the bus going to St. John?"

A man, farther back, lowered his newspaper. "Can't you read, bud? On the front, says Boston."

"Oh, blast!" Arvid said.

He got to his feet, slipping a folded paper into Bigelow's hand. Behind him, as he got off the bus, he heard her clear, high giggle and glancing back, saw that she had some color in her face now. Her eyes were wild with joy.

Arvid started the truck. He knew the road the Boston bus traveled—out of town on this street and five or ten miles down to the through highway that led west.

Better get a head start, he told himself. Them buses travel like bats.

His driving this time went better—only a couple of jerks starting. This early there wasn't much traffic. He was spudging along in the slow lane on the highway, when the bus went by him in a cloud of diesel smoke at sixty miles an hour.

The note he had written said:

I can't take you with me now, someone would see us. But you sneak off the bus at the first chance you can get. Don't hurry it. Try to get off with other people, act as if you belonged to them. Don't wait around the bus station. Walk back a ways. Stay on the sidewalk and be oful careful not to get run over. Make sure you stay in sight of the road so I can see you when I come by. I will be in a truck. Learn this by heart and then tear it up fine. Don't leave the pieces aboard the bus.

Yours lovingly,
You know who.

Bigelow read the note and memorized it. She not only tore it up fine, she chewed the pieces and swallowed them.

The first stop was a pause at a smallish town, where a few people got on. There was no chance to get off, because nobody else did. She thought of trying it, and got up; but the driver turned around and looked at her, so she sat down again. The second stop was no better; people got on, nobody got off. But the bus was filling up and that was good—all the more chance to get off in a crowd, when the time came. Bigelow fidgeted, waiting for a chance that didn't seem to come. The bus kept rolling along; it seemed like hours. Finally it pulled up in front of a big roadside bus-stop restaurant.

The driver got up, said, "Rest stop," and climbed down out of the bus. Everybody moved.

Oh, this was the place; this was lovely. There was a fine crush of people. Bigelow pushed in among them, forgetting that Arvid had said not to hurry. She bumped hard against the rear of a lady, who turned around and glanced down. She was an old, small lady, with beady black eyes behind glasses; when she saw Bigelow, the beady eyes brightened.

"Oh," she said. "You're the little girl who ate the paper. Now, what did you do that for?"

Bigelow stared back. "I was eating *candy*," she said icily.

The lady shook a finger. "Oh, no, you weren't," she said. "I saw you, you know. I thought, what a strange taste, and I could not *contain* my curiosity!"

The answer came right into Bigelow's mouth. She almost said it, out loud. You mind your own business, you old crow. But this was the place to sneak off the bus. Don't start anything to call attention . . . you don't have to sass the old fool. So shut up. She closed her lips tight and moved back a few steps in the bus.

She got off behind everybody else and waited until they had all gone into the restaurant. Then she ducked out of sight behind a corner of the building. And there was no place to go. She had walked into a back yard surrounded by a high wire fence that couldn't be climbed—it had barbed wire all along the top of it. And the only entrance was the one she'd come through. Which way? What to do? To walk back down the street in plain sight—somebody from the bus might come out and see her. Wait here till the bus pulled out? But while she hesitated, the little old lady came around the corner.

"Honey," she said. "Do you want to go toidy?"

Bigelow jumped. "What?" she said with a gasp.

"It isn't around here, dear," the lady said. "It's around the other side. This is the men's. Come with me, I'll show you." She took Bigelow firmly by the hand.

Bigelow started to twist away. She hauled back her foot to let the lady have it, a good kick on the ankle. And stopped. Make a row now, everybody would certainly look. They would know if she ran. Bigelow went quietly.

"See? There it is. 'Ladies.' Sometimes when we're all alone, we don't like to ask, do we?"

Go in. Shut the door. Maybe the old flounder will go away.

But the old lady stood outside, holding the door open a crack.

"You know, dear, I *saw* you eat that paper. I thought at the time, there's a foolish little girl who is eating paper, just to see what it tastes like. Because, you know, dear, we don't eat paper, ever; it is apt to make us sick. So I thought to myself, she will have a pain in her stomach and have to throw it up, and I had better keep an eye on her. You see, dear, I know children so very, very well. I have taught school for many, many years. Do you feel all right?"

"Yes!"

"Are you through? Because the bus is about to start, I see. Yoo hoo, Driver! Just a minute, there's a little girl here in the—there's a little girl here."

Silently seething, Bigelow got back on the bus.

The lady sat down next to her. She talked. She produced sandwiches and cake from a lunchbox and offered to share. Bigelow said nothing. She only shook her head. Even if she hadn't hated the woman so, she was so upset, so worried by now, that she couldn't have eaten anything.

"Oh, dear," the lady said. "I knew it, I just knew it. That paper is making you sick. Are you sure you feel well? How far do you have to go, dear?"

Bigelow muttered the first name of a town that came into her head. "Waterford."

"*Waterford!*" The lady gave a shriek that made everybody look up. "Oh, mercy! Oh, dear! Honey, this bus doesn't go to Waterford. Driver! *Driver!* This little girl has got on the wrong bus!"

"Who?" the driver said. He glanced casually up at the mirror over the wheel. "Oh, that one? Calm down, lady. I know where she's going. She gets off in Portsmouth. She's being met there."

"Oh," the lady said. She stared doubtfully at Bigelow, who was sitting with her head back and her eyes closed. "But what—?" She shrugged, with her palms up, glanced around at people with a little laugh. "Oh, well, children, you know. And I'm sure this one doesn't feel well."

The bus was going on and on, very fast. Farther and farther away. How far was Portsmouth? Suppose it got there before Arvid could find her? Somebody would meet her and take her back to Cousin Emily and the Bowkers and to jail. Oh, *They* had fixed everything just fine, so she couldn't possibly get away. That was what They *would* do, tell the bus driver. Somehow, somewhere, she had to get off of this bus. So think. Nobody was going to help Liz Bigelow now but Liz Bigelow.

But could anyone think, with this chatter, this rattle of talk going on, right alongside her ear?

The bus went on. Time went on.

Bigelow watched out the window through slitted eyelids.

ROUTE 209, the signs said. They were coming into a big city. And Route 209 was where Arvid would be, looking for her.

The old lady began picking up her belongings. She poked Bigelow with a sharp forefinger. Bigelow didn't move. She made believe she was asleep. The bus had turned sharp right into a wide street full of stores. Maple Street. Another turn left. Elm Street.

Bigelow prayed. Oh, God, please make her shut up. Because I have got to remember how to get back to Route 209. He can't ever find me in this city. Washington Street . . .

"Well, honey, I'm sorry I have to leave you, but this is the State Capitol, where I get off. I am going to the Teachers' Convention here."

Washington Street . . . Elm Street . . . Maple Street . . . Right on Maple Street. Or had it been left?

The bus stopped.

"Rest stop," the driver called. "Fifteen minutes." He got off. Everybody got off.

The old lady moved. "But you haven't much farther to go, dear, and the driver will take care of you. This bus goes onto the Turnpike here and hurries right along, nonstop, to Portland, and after that, the next is Portsmouth. I have made the trip many times. Mercy, I guess we have learned one thing today, not to eat paper, never, never, *never!* At our age, we *do* have to learn things!" She started away, oozing bundles, turned, called back, "Honey, you really ought to wake up and look at the State Capitol. The bus goes right by it, and any child should see it, it's such a *beautiful* building."

Bigelow didn't stir, or open her eyes. Then she sat up. Outside the window, the lady was going along the platform, her little feet tittuping past each other, nip, nip, nip.

Wouldn't I just like to trip her up with a . . . a rattlesnake! But don't think of that now. Everybody had left the bus. This was the time.

Bigelow got off. Slowly, carefully, she walked the length of the bus, ducked around it, put it between her and the station. Then she tore across Washington Street, through the traffic, ran as fast as she could back the way the bus had come.

Elm Street. Which way? Which way to Maple? She couldn't remember. Out of breath, she stood on the corner, looking this way, that.

A man coming along glanced down at her and she said, "Where's Route 209?"

He grinned. "Going somewhere on 209? You tell your mother to keep you away from there, or you'll get run over. That's the state highway, young lady." And he went along.

Old fool.

They. All right. I'll fix it. I know what *They* like.

She rubbed her eyes to make them look red. It wasn't hard, anyway, to squeeze out some tears. She stood, sobbing pitifully, on the corner.

A lady stopped at once. "Why, what is it, dear? What's the matter?"

"My father said to meet him on the corner of Elm Street and Route 209," she wailed. "And I can't find 209!"

"Why, honey, 209 turns off on Maple. Are you sure he didn't say Maple?"

"Yes, that was it! Maple Street!"

"That's just up that way"—she pointed—"a few blocks—" And stopped, looking after Bigelow, who had taken off like a rabbit.

She walked east along the gravel shoulder of Route 209, watching for trucks. Why didn't he say what the truck would look like? They all went by so fast. And where was he?

She walked and walked. The sun went past noon, started west down the sky. She was hungry. Her stomach kept rumbling. She had put Arvid's present of a jackknife in her coat but in her rush, she'd forgotten the box of chocolates on the bus. If she only had them now! The new sandals were stiff; they had pointed toes, not good to walk in. They hurt. They were like those sandals the two Boardman kids had and thought were so cool. Who ever would want the rotten things?

Sometimes a car would stop. Somebody would offer a ride.

"Take you where you're going?" or "That's not a safe place to walk, honey. Don't you want a ride?"

To all, Bigelow made the same answer. "My father's coming to get me. I'm just waiting for him."

Going along, she thought, here I am again with my foolish father, the one who fell off the houseboat.

Who'd have thought, after Arvid, that she'd ever need that foolish father again!

Where was Arvid?

It would be so easy to let the thought creep in that he'd given up; he hadn't meant what he said; he wasn't coming at all.

Nossir! Arvid *said*. He said, I am a man you can trust. And he cried. She walked along.

All those trucks. They were buzzing along. Maybe he would be buzzing, too. Going too fast to see her. What if he missed her?

She began stepping out, just a little bit, on to the hardtop, so that all the trucks had to slow down.

What would his truck look like? Would it be little? Or big?

A tremendous semi, truck-trailer combination was coming along, far up the highway. Was that it? Arvid was big; he did everything big, too. Maybe that was what he had found to come after her in . . . It really looked like him. She would just bet that was him. She stepped out into the highway and stood waving her arms.

The semi was barreling along. It was coming from Nova Scotia with a perishable cargo aboard; the driver was in a hurry. He yelled; he stamped on all possible brakes; he aged ten years in a second. But he managed to squeeze by Bigelow, barely flicking the skirt of her dress. Horrified, he looked back. She was all right, walking on along the shoulder now. She wasn't hurt, thank God. But, jeezus, was that close! Why couldn't people keep their damn kids off the highway? Brother, he hoped he'd never come any closer to jackknifing the semi. He drove on.

✦

At sunset, Bigelow sat down on the top of a concrete abutment by the side of the highway. She was so tired she couldn't walk any more. The sun was going down. Pretty soon it would be night.

When the dark came, how could she see Arvid; how could he see her? Where could she go? There was nothing around here but woods, and they were dark and cold. A small brook ran under the abutment where she sat. Whenever the stream of cars got by, stopped making all that noise, she could hear it trickling. It sounded lonesome.

Another truck was coming, a little one. Let it go on by. It wasn't Arvid. Probably he wasn't coming. Probably. But she waved, half-heartedly, out of habit.

The truck started to wobble. It went from one side of the highway to the other, just missing a car that was coming along, and crossed back barely behind another. Its brakes let out a great screech. Some ways farther down, it stopped right in the middle of the road. A man got out of it and started running back to her, and it was Arvid.

She went running to meet him. He scooped her up in a big hug, and she hugged back.

"Oh, dear!" he said. "Oh, God! Bigelow, ain't we got ourselves into the wilderness, though!"

He mopped her tears with his handkerchief, and then he mopped his own.

Bigelow grabbed his hand with both of hers. She couldn't say anything; there wasn't anything good enough to say. But everything was all right now, and this was the second time they had cried together.

Another car came tooling down the highway, slowed with a squeal of brakes and a furious blasting of the horn, pulled out and around, and went on.

"Mercy," Arvid said. "Blow their horns for half a minute, don't they? Come on, we'd better move the truck before another one of them traveling carnivals gives us a root in the tail."

*

The bus driver, at Portsmouth, was a bewildered young man. Sure, the kid had been on the bus. At the State Capitol he'd checked. She'd been sound asleep, but she'd been there, so she must have got off at Portland. He'd had a crowded bus and his hands full with a bunch of drunks from a lodge convention, and he hadn't checked again; but the bus was nonstop from Portland to Portsmouth. She couldn't have got off anywhere, he thought, without his knowing it. You could have knocked him over with a feather.

The police would have to look for her—and they did. But it was as if she had vanished in air, and not the air around the city of Portland.

Philomela couldn't think what she ought to do. Arvid had been gone for two days, with no word. She was half out of her mind with worry, and she wished bitterly that she hadn't let him take the truck. Of course she wouldn't have if she'd realized that he intended to go any farther than Powell, to see what could be accomplished there. But he wasn't in Powell now. She had found that out on the morning she had driven over to bring Marney back to her house, when she had dropped by the court house, thinking she might find out something by inquiring about Bigelow.

"I'm taking one of the castaways home with me," she'd said. "I'd be glad to take the other one, if she needs a place to stay."

The child had already been sent away, she found. And the Welfare people were in a swivet about her; she was missing. She had apparently gotten off the bus by herself. Somewhere, possibly at Portland. The police were looking for her and they would undoubtedly find her. It might take time. No knowing where she had got herself to, and she had been a city child.

Well, at least he got as far as Portland, Philomela told herself with a kind of grim satisfaction. He would. But where was he now? Where were they now? That had been two days ago. Aloud, she said, "Quite an enterprising child. I take it she didn't want to go back."

"Mercy, no. She was . . . difficult about it. And, of course, she had very little to go back to. The cousin she lived with was killed in the flood. Of course, it's New Hampshire's problem."

"Doesn't she have any people at all?"

"None, I understand."

"What will happen to her, then?"

"An orphanage, I suppose. A foster family. She'll be taken care of . . . they'll do what they can."

The child . . . she didn't bear thinking about.

I left my hand on the door on that one, Philomela thought, leaving the building. Surely, if we had had time, we could have thought of a better plan and stayed within the law. What was the matter with me?

Except, as far back as she could remember, Arvid had always been able to make something wild and foolish sound wonderful. And practical, too. The old palaverer, he could carry you away with him, because—because, she told herself, he is always on the—what would you call it? Perhaps, the human side. And he is now. Up until now, though, it had been convention, customs, folkways that he had walked over, if he felt the occasion warranted—never, so far as she knew, the law.

She didn't need to know, she could guess, what he had done. He had taken off after the bus, and, God knew how, had winkled Bigelow off of it. Without knowing in the least what he was getting into. Not only the traffic, a far different business from anything he might have encountered on the back road to Powell, but, now the police were looking for Bigelow, possibly a kidnapping charge.

But the darned old pirate, whatever happened now, you knew you were still on his side and would do what you could. And end up, if you had to, in the next cell.

Wait a little longer. Maybe he'd turn up. So far, he always had.

⭠

Dewey and Truman hadn't been able to forget that motorcycle. Whenever they were by themselves, they talked about it. It burned in their blood. If they only had it ashore here, they could take off and go. No more being cuffed around by the old man, having to listen to his guff, being bossed by him. They were both good and sick of him. After all, they were going on fifteen; it was time they left. Stay around this junky town, go fishing all your life, what would you get—maybe the old man's crappy boat when he kicked off? They weren't going to do that. Look at the half-baked people who did. Look at old Buttercup-Boy and his red wheelbarrow. Not Dew and Tru. They were going to amount to something in a bigger place.

Besides, they couldn't get to first base here—there wasn't a cop in the area who didn't know them by their first names.

They spent a good deal of time figuring ways and means to get the motorcycle off the island. They didn't mention any plans to Ed. He'd find out, but they'd be long gone. What they had to do was figure out how to get a boat to get out to the island in, and a tender big enough to take the motorcycle and sidecar. The best way would be to steal a powerboat and a tender, go out and get the bike, and tow it to some town down the coast. They could leave the boat there—the cops would find it and return it to its owner, so no harm done. It was a good plan, but it wasn't simple.

They'd counted on having only old Buttercup-Boy to deal with; but now Freddy Fowler was out there, and he wasn't anybody to fool with. They wanted desperately to go ashore on the island again, spy on Freddy, see if they could make out what he was doing. Suppose he fixed up that bike, brought it ashore, and sold it, before they could get going? But Ed wouldn't land them there again; he said they'd have to wait until the Coast Guard got through fooling around there. No telling when you'd run into them, butt-end-foremost.

Then fate played right into the twins' hands. They woke up one morning to see old Buttercup-Boy's boat back on its mooring. That would be the one they'd swipe. Serve the old kook right. Seeing it was him, they wouldn't bother to leave it anywhere when they were through with it, they'd just set it adrift. If he wanted it, he could swim after it. Freddy Fowler's boat wasn't there, which meant he was probably still on the island. But they could go by night when he was asleep. By the time he woke up, they could be long gone, miles down the coast. They were packing, getting together the few treasures they wanted to take with them, when something else, something better, happened. Word came that Ed had been arrested in Powell. He had got ten days drunk and disorderly. And their mother got right after the twins.

"You take your father's boat and go haul traps," she told them. "Somebody's got to bring in a little money whilst he's gone."

Dew and Tru couldn't believe their good luck. Here was the boat; now they wouldn't have to swipe one. And they could take their father's skiff, too, without a question. Two industrious kids out hauling traps, working to take care of their mother and family while their poor father was in jail, if anybody should ask you. They took off in high glee and whooped and hollered all the way out of the harbor.

Freddy had been having a wonderful time. He had had to spend a couple of nights alone on the island, which he didn't particularly care for; but he had expected that Arvid wouldn't be back for a while; he would have gone on in to Powell, to see what could be done about that kid. Old Arvid. He was a pushover for anything that cried on his shoulder, whether it was a cat or a dog or an animal with two legs instead of four. Freddy could grin to himself, recalling that once or twice, in the fishhouse, he had seen Arvid put out crumbs or cheese for the mice. Well, he and Arvid were two different people. Freddy wouldn't go out of his way to kill anything; but he didn't see why he needed to be bothered with it, either. Feed a mouse, and the next week there'd be ten mice into your breadbox. So, pow! Take care of it before it got out of hand. The only sensible way to do.

Freddy wouldn't have objected to Bigelow, he told himself, if she'd been anything a civilized man ever wanted to have around; but he didn't feel called upon to put up with her particular brand of deviltry, either. He still mourned the loss of his bubble-level and his two wrenches. After all, that kid didn't actually mean anything to Arvid; she'd known how to play on his sympathies, was all. Too bad it had had to happen just that way—that Freddy had had to be the one to tell the Coast Guard where to look. But Arvid probably wouldn't ever find out . . . Tenderly, Freddy began taking the parts of the bike engine out of the kerosene bath where they had spent the night; and tenderly, here and there, he poured on penetrating oil.

He had been working for quite a while before he became aware of sundry rustlings, cracklings, in the bushes behind him.

What the—? Well, something. What now? He'd thought that kind of business was all talked over. Unexpectedly, he rose to his feet and strode across the path into the undergrowth. For Godsake, the Snorri kids!

Dew and Tru were lying on their stomachs, peering out. They hadn't had a chance to scramble up, he'd moved too fast. They lay looking up at him with round, unblinking eyes.

"What in hell do you kids want?" he demanded.

They began sputtering and popping like bacon in a pan, both together, so that he couldn't understand a word.

"Well, go on, beat it out of here. Go on! Git! Or I'll take a stick to you!"

They got up, all anyhow, and ran. He stood, hands on hips, watching them go, and hollered after them. "And you scramble off this island. It's private property here. You let me catch you here again, and, damn you, I'll drown you!"

He could hear for quite a while the sounds of their feet thumping on the hard-packed dirt of the path. Blasted nuisances! Reform school bait, that ought to have been shoved there years ago. Catch them around here again, well, he wouldn't drown them, or any part of it, they only thought he would; but he would, sure as hell, dunk them in the marsh or something.

Dew and Tru raced along the path till they were sure Freddy wasn't after them. They had had experience with him before; no kid in town ever bothered Freddy Fowler twice. They dropped, sobbing for breath, behind a fallen tree.

"Guh-God damn him!" Dew gasped. "Le's sneak back and puh-put the rocks to him. Le's smash the winders in the guh-goddamn house!"

"Nope," Tru said. "Huh-hold on, Dew. Use your head."

"Head nothing. He's tuh-tore that bike all apart. We can't tuh-take it now."

"He's tore it down. He's fixing it. He's about the best mechanic in the world, remember?"

"So what?"

Tru was the elder by an hour; he sometimes had ideas that wouldn't have entered Dew's head. What it was, he said, Freddy would get that bike fixed to run. All they had to do now was wait till he did. Leave the island, make believe they were scared off for good. Then, when Freddy had the bike fixed, sneak back by night and take it. It would be tuned right up in shape; they wouldn't have to bother with a garage ashore, in case it wasn't. Risk getting caught, have to pay dough; they could take right off. "So throw down them rocks, what are you, some kuh-kind of a nut?"

But Dew didn't throw down the rocks with which he had filled his pockets and which he was still collecting.

"The old man'll be back before we can suh-spit," he said. "We got to take it today."

Stupidity was something Tru couldn't put up with. The foolishness of taking the bike ashore in pieces—anybody ought to be able to see that. He turned menacingly on Dew, but Dew didn't notice.

"What if he fixes it and takes it ashore?" he asked.

"Then he'll be the one to frig with getting it aboard a boat and off the island. It'll be at his house, won't it? Duh-damn, Dew, you come on!"

"I'm starving to death. I'm going back and bust a winder and go in and get something to eat. He's got stuff to eat in there—"

Tru turned around. He grabbed Dew by the front of the shirt and twisted, cocking back a big, dirty fist. "Drop them rocks!" he said. "Okay?"

Dew dropped the rocks. Half-choked by the twisted shirt, he managed to convey "Okay." By the time they had rowed off aboard the boat, he had got it through his head: Let the bike alone until Freddy had it fixed.

Darn good idea, he told himself. How'd I happen to think of it?

They went off on Thirteen-feet Shoal and hauled traps enough to get a bucketful of short lobsters, not paying much attention as to whose traps they hauled, though they did avoid Freddy's—no sense calling his attention to them, not right now. Then they went ashore on a nearby small island, built a fire, and boiled the lobsters in a bucket. This, of course, was something Ed would never have let them do. He never ate or threw away an illegal lobster. Some restaurants ashore didn't ask questions about the size of lobsters; the little ones made good sandwiches and stew and weren't half so expensive as the counters. But Dew and Tru weren't figuring about the old man's business now.

They ate until they were not quite conscious—lobster and the crackers Ed always kept aboard the boat. Then they dumped the five or six shorts they had left onto the fire, and went off, leaving the fire briskly burning. The island didn't belong to them or to anyone they knew, so if the wind came up later on and blew live brands around into the grass, what of it? Let the place burn over, it would make the duh-damn blueberries grow.

The boy riding with the stout gentleman in the truck was certainly no part of Elizabeth Bigelow. He was dressed in jeans, T-shirt, sneakers, warm jacket, and cap. Elizabeth's clothes, folded neatly and wrapped in a brown paper parcel, lay in the back of the truck, forgotten.

As soon as he could, Arvid got off Route 209—in case of a chase, he told Bigelow. No knowing who might be coming after them. This delighted Bigelow; it was exciting, like movies. She kept looking back, almost hoping to see a whole squadron of police cars; because there was no doubt in her mind, if they came, Arvid would know how to outsmart them all. They went rolling tranquilly along on a nice quiet secondary road, heading, Arvid said, north, according to the sun. If they were going home roundabout, they might as well go roundabout; he didn't doubt that somewhere they'd come across another road that turned east. When they did, he would take it. Unless it was running over with automobiles. The traffic on 209, he said, had been too thick for his blood. They went north for a long way, passing up several big highways, and one old walloper of a four-laner, which was the northern extension of the State Turnpike. Stay off of that, Arvid said, or you'd likely end up in Canada. He said thoughtfully that it was too bad they couldn't go to see Canada, now they had a chance to. He'd always wanted to and never had.

Arvid usually got directions from the small-town diners where they stopped to eat; but he nearly always made a mistake and turned off on some secondary road that petered out to gravel or was somebody's driveway. On the third afternoon, the road went into some woods and ended on the shore of a big lake. It was so nice there that they stayed a while, resting, under big trees by a sand beach which was warm as summer in the sun. They washed their hands and faces and their feet in the lake water; they rinsed out their socks and hung them on a tree to dry. Arvid said by that time he was so hungry that he could eat a fried rat—they didn't give you enough in those diners to make a meal's vittles, unless you had two. So he built a fire on the sand beach and cooked a big steak that he brought out of a box of food he had in the back of the truck.

One thing about a truck, he said, you had room to carry about anything you wanted to, didn't have to worry over there being room enough. Someday, he said, he'd like to have one fixed up with bunks and good mattresses; the mattresses in those roadside cabins curled up a man's back till it felt like a fifty-gallon oil drum.

They had steak sandwiches and apples and doughnuts and milk; and after they ate, they had a nap. When they woke up, it was still nice by the lake and their socks weren't dry, so they stayed a while longer, sitting on the sand and matching up their stories about what had happened since they'd seen each other. Arvid was fascinated by Bigelow's bus ride; he shook his head sadly over the silly old schoolteacher.

"Don't you dare to feel sorry for her," Bigelow said. "Oh, I hate *her*. I would like to throw a rock right into the middle of her skinny old—"

"Well, now, Bigelow," Arvid said. He stretched out his bare toes, wriggling them in the warm sand. "It ain't no use for a minute to hate foolish old folks, you know it?"

"She had her rotten old nose stuck into my business."

"Old folks is nosy, sometimes, I give you that. Awful hard to put up with. But a lot of them ain't got very much left of their own, is what it is. Why, I recall Art Swanson's old great-aunt, eighty-three she was, moping around his house, nothing to do, and driving him out of his mind. So Art up and bought her an accordion. Paid money for it, too. It was a good one. I know, I got it now, bought it after the old lady died. Has a lovely tone to it. Well, darned if she didn't study up and learn to play it; used to go around playing it to the school and church times, even got her picture in the paper playing it, and she lived to be a hundred and nine. It all goes to show. You take that old schoolteacher bothered you, no knowing what in her lifetime she's been through, had to put up with, and left her with no more head than if somebody'd cut it off, run round town with it on a pole. No knowing what she was once; might've been as pretty a little girl as you are."

Bigelow gave him a look. She kicked a lot of sand into the water.

"Well," Arvid said, "stay a boy if you want to. But I will have to let on to you that I like girls as well as I do boys, and I don't know but, in some ways, better. Now, that was your story about your trip; let me tell you mine."

He launched into it. The reason he'd got so far behind—well, there'd been several, really. He had finally got the truck into high and had got over into the fast lane; but the best he could do, he couldn't catch up with the bus—never once caught a sight of it after it passed him on the highway. That fellow was going like Jehu on a Roman candle. And then, slap in the middle of a woods a mile from anywhere, he'd run to hellan—to heck and gone out of gas. Forgot to look and see how much there was, have any put in; so he had to get out and walk to a gas station, hunt round, find one, get somebody to bring him back with a can of gas. It had all taken time.

"And when you started out, you didn't even know how to drive a car," Bigelow said.

"Oh, yes, I did. Many's the year I drove my Model T till she wore down. So I knew about a clutch. Well . . . I knew how to steer a car, let's say. Had to pick up what was different as I went along."

"Is it hard to?"

"Why, no. Not once you get the hang of it. Comes easier all the time."

"Could I?"

"I don't know why you couldn't. Got as many brains as I have, in some ways, more. Come on. Nice back road here, nobody on it. I'll show you."

They had to spend the night at the lake, sleeping wrapped Arvid's tarpaulin, because it took him till dark to teach Bigelow how to drive the truck.

✦

"I was just riding my motorbike along through the river area," Marney said, "and camped for the night. And did I pick the wrong place!"

He had been telling Philomela how he had happened to be on the houseboat. He hadn't, so far, offered any other information about himself, nor had she asked for any. If he wanted to talk, later on he would. He had been with her for four days now, and he was getting well. His appetite had grown; he had got some color back. Tonight he was lying on the couch in her sitting room, playing with Toughy, and three times Toughy had made him laugh. The last time she had somersaulted over his stomach, landing on her feet on the floor and walking away with great dignity.

"You look out for your kittens, old girl," he said. "That's no way." He looked up at Philomela with a grin. "You know, those kittens are going to come pretty close to being citizens of Canada. She had a night on the town, up there near the border."

Philomela laughed, too. She couldn't think when she'd known a pleasanter combination than this boy and his cat. He was a bright boy. Decent-mannered. She couldn't help wondering about his people.

"That's as clever a little cat as I ever saw," she said. "She's quite a different breed from our cats in this part of the country—that little pushed-up face she's got, where our cats all have Roman noses. Is she Canadian, too?"

There was a silence. Philomela did not look up from her sewing. She bit off a thread.

Marney said, "She belonged to my grandmother."

Belonged. In the past.

"Gram . . . liked her," Marney said. "She used to sit on Gram while Grampa and I . . . Well, he was helping me bone up for College Boards." He stopped. When Philomela did not say anything, he went on, his voice sounding a little hoarse. "Grampa was great on history—a great one for knowing stories that weren't in the regular textbooks. Like . . . like the one he told me about the exploration of Newfoundland, I think it was. No, it was Nova Scotia. The . . . the English, they were all cocked back to be the first nation to explore the new land and claim it. So they fitted out this big expedition of three ships and all kinds of men, blessed by the Church and anointed by the King, and away they went, the Admiral's yellow flag up on ahead; and they crossed the ocean with great hardship and ceremony. Only when they got to Nova Scotia they found thirty-nine fishing boats snugged into harbor, with fishing stages set up for a season's work. Seems the French and Spanish had been coming there for years. It . . . it was an annual custom with them."

"Well, that was a comedown," Philomela said.

"Sure was. Grampa laughed his head off. Said he'd like to have seen all those solemn British faces."

"Mm-hm. So would I."

"So after he died and Gram had the shock, I took Toughy. I . . . don't know what breed she is. She was Gram's cat, all I know."

"Your grandfather and grandmother—they were all the people you had?"

"No. There was Joe."

He was quiet so long that, now, she had to glance at him. He was flushed and his eyes were too bright, and Philomela said, "You don't have to talk about it, Marney, unless you want to. I don't mean to be nosy."

"I might as well," Marney said. "I've got to go back there, it doesn't make any difference now whether anyone knows." He went on telling the story of Joe: of his year with Joe, and Joe's death, and his own endless running.

"Dear God in heaven!" Philomela said. Some time ago she had put down her sewing because she couldn't see it. "Marney, did you have to run? Your grandfather left you some money, you said. Where is it? Did Joe get it?"

"I don't know. Joe got the checks that came every month. Judge Jameson—Grampa left him in charge of the trust fund, but Judge Jameson's dead. I . . . thought at the time that Joe killed him. Joe had his briefcase that night, the same night the Judge died. I think. I don't know. I'm . . . It seems so . . . as if it hadn't happened to me. Like a story I read. And not important now. I . . . don't know what he got. If I know him, he probably cleaned out everything. But no matter. Joe's dead."

Philomela got up. "You've been too sick a boy to go over this all in a heap," she said. "But look, no one can force you to do anything you don't want to do, I know that. You don't have to go back to Carrington, and as for Spancook—you haven't done anything those people can punish you for. You can stay here as long as you like; but it doesn't have to be decided tonight. Tomorrow we'll see a lawyer and get him to write some letters. There must be someone in Carrington who knows about this. So now, you go to bed. And stop worrying, because you don't need to. Take Toughy, and I'll bring you a hot drink before you go to sleep."

Marney drew a long breath. He got to a sitting position on the couch, and then, shakily, to his feet. "I . . . wouldn't know how to thank you, Mrs. Fowler."

"You don't have to. If you'll just get it through your"—she smiled at him—"your thick head that you're out of the woods at last, that'll be enough."

In the kitchen, fixing the hot drink, she thought grimly, Children! How is it possible to believe what can happen to them! I am mad enough to fight somebody. And I am going to fight. Because I won't

stand for his having to put up with any more. These are the best we
have, they are all we have, and—

A car turned in from the street, came up the driveway. Philomela
jumped a little and listened. It sounded like—it was. Freddy's truck.
She put on the porch light and stepped out to look, just in time
to see the two far wanderers returning. Arvid was on the front seat
sitting straight up, proud as a peacock, with Bigelow beside him. And
Bigelow was driving.

With a little shriek, Philomela plunged into the house and snapped
off the light.

"All right," she said. "Who saw you?"

They were in the kitchen with the lights on and the shades drawn.
Bigelow and Arvid were having a late supper.

"Because," Philomela went on, "if anybody recognized you when
you came through Powell and saw Bigelow with you, you—*we* are
in trouble."

Arvid glanced at Bigelow out of the corner of his eye.

Bigelow giggled. "He already thought of that," she said. She looked
proudly at Arvid. "He thinks of everything."

It seemed that when they had come through Powell, Arvid had,
to all observers, been alone in the truck. Bigelow had been under the
tarp in the back. So that was all right.

"What about between here and Powell? Anyone here in town
would know Freddy's truck. And with a child driving it—Arvid, what
a mess of foolishness! Whatever possessed you?"

Well, Bigelow hadn't got out from under the tarp until they had
got off the highway, and as for this town, they hadn't come through
it at all. They had come in over the old fire trail across Lovejoy's Hill.
Philomela didn't need to worry. Nobody had seen them.

"Lovejoy's Hill!" Philomela gasped. "A car hasn't been over that
in—" She couldn't think how long. "That old trail's all grown up,
Arvid. I don't see how—"

"Well, cracked off a couple of alders," Arvid said, "and come through a witch's topknot of puckerbrush."

"And the game wardens took the culvert out so the poachers couldn't get through there," Bigelow added. "Arvid said. So there's a brook running across the road. But we made it, didn't we?"

"Yessir! Bigelow's getting to be a damn—a darned good little driver."

"Bigelow?" Philomela said faintly.

"Well, she's better'n I am at it. We figured best driver'd better drive."

Philomela threw up her hands. They had had fun, she could see that. They had had so much fun that nothing was going to spoil it. At least, not tonight. But she couldn't help saying, "Well, I honestly don't know what to do, Arvid. I'm good and worried about all this."

"Now, Philomela, I don't know as you need to be. What it was, I was riding along in the truck and here was this little girl by the side of the road, flagged me down. Said she got out at the bus station to go to the you-know, and the bus went off and left her. Well, a little child. Lost in the big city. *She* didn't know what to do. The only thing she could think of was to hitchhike back here where she'd started out from. And she had got out on to the main road, all them automobiles roaring by, when I happened along in Freddy's pickup. What could I do?"

"It wasn't," Bigelow said smugly, "any place for a little child, was it, Arvid?" She shoveled in a great mouthful of egg.

"Mercy, no. It's a wonder she hadn't got run over before I come. Nothing in the God's world for me to do but pick her up and bring her back with me. Couldn't expect me to light out after that bus. Jehu on a Roman candle couldn't of caught it."

"Well," Philomela said. What could you do? "I see the two of you have put together a story," she said. "I don't dare to think what'll come of it. But we can't do anything tonight. I expect you're both worn out. I'll show you where to sleep. Arvid, you'll have to bunk in the back room, Marney's in the guest room."

Bigelow stood straight up out of her chair. Her eyes widened and shone. "Marney?" she said. "Marney's here, too?"

"Yes. The hospital let me bring him here to get well. He's much better, too, right now."

"Well, now, Philomela," Arvid said, "That was d-darned nice of you, you know it?"

"Somebody had to—" Philomela began. And then, looking at them, she thought, Don't be crusty. Don't spoil it. You brought him home with you because you wanted him, not because somebody had to. "I was so glad to have him," she finished. "He's such a nice boy and he's wonderful company, and I don't mind saying, I'm lonesome, Arvid."

Arvid looked down at his coffee cup. "I know you blamed me," he said. "But I tried to make Freddy come home, Philomela."

"I did blame you at first," she said. "I was so mad, I suppose I was kind of childish. But I blame myself and him mostly, Arvid. He would have gone somewhere, and it was best he went to you. I suppose it'll get worse before it gets better, now. Because somebody has got to take the responsibility for these children. They are not going to be pushed around from pillar to post any longer; I am not going to stand for it. You and I will have to do it, Arvid. I will come out to the island and talk to Freddy, but I don't—"

Bigelow had come around the table and stood at her elbow. As she glanced around, Bigelow leaned over and kissed her, a moist, scrambled-eggy kiss on the cheek. "You're nice," she said. "And you smell good, too."

"Atta girl, Bigelow," Arvid said.

Philomela was astounded by the kiss. It had seemed to her from the beginning that she and Bigelow weren't going to like each other very much, Bigelow being a prickly kind of child—and I, I suppose, a prickly kind of woman. We weren't long, I thought, in sizing each other up. Two prickly females. She burst out laughing.

"You two palaverers!" she said. "Bedtime. Come on."

She took Bigelow upstairs and arranged a hot bath, which Bigelow certainly needed, putting in some bath salts and saying, "Now, you'll smell good, too."

"M-m," Bigelow said. But she was almost too sleepy to smell anything. Nevertheless, sleepy as she was, she said when she was ready for bed, "Can I see him tonight?"

"He's asleep. But yes, if you're careful not to wake him. He needs all the sleep he can get."

Briefly, she put on the night light beside Marney's bed. He lay sleeping soundly, a lock of hair draped over one eye.

Bigelow looked, solemnly. Then she tiptoed away.

"He's all right," she whispered, as Philomela tucked her into bed. "He's well, isn't he?"

"Almost," Philomela said. "In a little while he'll be as good as new."

"He kept me from being hurt in the hurricane," Bigelow said. "So he got hurt himself. He is the nicest boy I ever . . ." She was asleep.

When Philomela got back to the kitchen, Arvid was still sitting at the table. He had ladled the rest of the scrambled eggs and bacon on to his plate, but he wasn't eating. Toughy had climbed up into his lap, and he sat absently patting her on the head and staring at his plate.

"Well, if I land up in jail," he said, as she came through the door, "I would rather, than lose her, Philomela. I could have lost her, easy. They ain't going to get her away from me again."

"You know they are," she said. "Do you think there's a judge in the world who's ever going to believe that pack of lies?"

"They will have to catch up with us first. I am going to start for the island with her before daylight tomorrow morning."

"And make it all that much worse? We have got to find out how to make this legal, Arvid."

"I don't trust any of them people. Wind you up in red tape till you choke. Who is going to know she's out on the island with me? Only us. And Freddy, of course."

Yes. Freddy. In the background, solid as a wall. You could not go around, nor over, nor through him. You only walked along beside, wondering how on earth you could.

"Freddy's not going to like Bigelow's being around, you know that," she said.

"Then Freddy will have to re-tittivate his ideas a little," Arvid said. "It ain't that I don't know how he is, and it ain't that I don't think he's entitled to what he wants, if he can have it without making somebody else shove over. When he is working, he is all wound up in it, and nothing else amounts to a damn. Ain't anything wrong with that, as I can see. It's about the only way they is to get anything done, when you come right down to it. And damn it, up to a point I'm on his side, Philomela."

"I am, too," Philomela said. "You know I always have been."

Arvid nodded. "He don't give no credit to the world or what it runs on," he said. "To him it's a big flophouse full of good-time Charleys, I've heard him say so. So stay out of my hair, he says. Well, 'tis a sloppy rig, any way you look at it, I expect. Everything living can't wait to make little ones out of big ones, too much and too many, and then dropping them to grow big themselves any goddamned way they can, a good part of them. Like, look at a wood lot. It ain't good, all them saplings. But that's the way it is, it's too strong for anybody to do anything about. Freddy thinks it ought to be put a stop to, so people, a man like him, can get along with the work of the world. And that is where him and I part company. He ain't going to live forever. And when he's gone, who's going to run his pretty engine? He's out there now, working on a big one, in a boat that ain't never going anywhere."

"I know," Philomela said. "I am going to swallow my pride and come out and talk to him, Arvid."

"Yes, you do," Arvid said. He drew a long breath. "I love the damn fool," he said. "All his life, I've wished he would get squared around. But he ain't going to shove over, no more'n the world is, that's for sure." He looked at her. "I hate to think so, much less say it. But he ain't. You want to come with us tomorrow morning?"

"No, I can't do that. Marney has an appointment for a checkup at the hospital in the afternoon. I'll get Simon to ferry me out, oh, sometime soon. And I want to make some inquiries, Arvid. See how much finagling it'll take to get you off the hook. I may see a lawyer."

"Now you be careful, Philomela."

"You know I will. The island's no solution for Bigelow, you know that. She's got to go to school, be around with people."

Arvid nodded. He even grinned a little. "Well, I guess I can trust you," he said.

"Yes, you can. I wish I could say the same for you—I never saw two such fibbers in my life. I'll do what I can. Arvid, the cat's eating out of your plate."

"So she is. Now, ain't that pretty? I never knew a cat liked scrambled eggs, did you?"

✦

Philomela set an alarm clock for three and got breakfast. She drove the two travelers down to the harbor and saw Bigelow safely aboard Arvid's boat, with, for warmth, not only the tarp out of the truck, but a woolly blanket from the house. The two set off joyously into the darkness; she sat in the car awhile and watched the running lights of Arvid's boat vanish behind the seaward arm of the cove. For a long time after they had gone, she sat thinking.

✦

Arvid was astounded when he got out to the island and saw Freddy. Freddy had a big bruise on one cheek leading up to a greenish-yellow black eye. He limped badly when he walked. He was equally astounded when he saw Arvid with Bigelow. He was just having an early breakfast when they walked in; he stared, set down his coffee cup, and said, "Oh, for chrissake!"

"Freddy!" Arvid said. "Goddlemighty, what happened to you?"

Freddy shoved back his chair and started out the door. Arvid caught up with him as he went around the corner of the house.

"Freddy, what hit you?"

"The goddamned Snorri brats," Freddy said, briefly.

"Why, the darned little skunks! How come?"

"They came out here one night, tried to steal that motorbike. I beat them both up." Freddy sat down on a bench by the wall. He stared morosely off over the harbor.

"They both tackle you at once?" Arvid asked, looking at him with concern. The twins were big boys for their age, too much for even a husky man to handle.

"Yeah," Freddy said. He went on to tell.

He had got the bike fixed and running, and hadn't wanted to leave it out in the weather to rust up again; so he had ridden it back here to the house and put it under cover in the barn. He hadn't locked the barn, hadn't seen any reason to. Six miles off the mainland, he said under his breath, and still the damn bastards . . . In the night, the twins had landed and apparently had snooped around till they found out where the bike was. They had made some noise getting it out of the barn.

"I woke up," Freddy said. "Took a jump out of me, I'll admit." He grinned wanly. "Kind of a spooky place when you're alone here. First, I thought it was some kind of an animal fooling around, maybe the cat come back. Hadn't seen her since you left and—" He stopped, after a pause went on.

"Then I realized that whatever the animal was, it didn't have but two legs, so I thought, I'll fix that."

He had gone downstairs in his pajamas and had taken Arvid's shotgun off the rack. He'd loaded it and had gone along toward the barn. When he'd stepped around the corner, both boys had jumped him. There'd been a late moon, just setting in the west, so he'd got a good look at them, could tell who they were.

"If the gun hadn't gone off when they jumped me," Freddy said, "I might not have made out quite so well. But it scared 'em stiff, just long enough for me to drop the gun and get a good hold on their scruffs. They got in a few kicks on my legs before I could bang their heads together good and hard, but that slowed 'em down some, and the second time I did it, they broke loose and ran. So I chased behind all the way to the shore, firing the gun near enough to their tails so they could hear the shot rattle in the bushes. I guess they figured I was shooting at them. God, it was hard not to. I had to hold back, let me tell you. Anyway, while they were getting aboard their skiff, one of them let go with a rock, got me right under the eye. Pretty nigh knocked me cold. If they'd wanted to come back, they could have finished the job right then, but I guess they were too scared to."

"You want me to have a look at that eye?" Arvid asked.

"No. It's sore, but it's all right." Freddy touched his cheek tentatively. "Sure is. Sorer'n hell. I think the cat's dead, Arvid. I'm sorry to have to tell you. One of those brats hollered out that they'd be back and fix me the way they fixed the goddamned cat. And she's gone. Hell," he said, "I even took time off and looked for the blasted thing."

"She's all right," Arvid said. "They throwed a mess of turpentine on her. That's where we went, took the cat to the vet. I left her with Philomela."

"Well," Freddy said, "at least that's one thing I don't have to fall over." He glared, menacingly, past Arvid's shoulder.

"Wouldn't hurt to put some red meat on that eye, take the puff out of it," Arvid said.

"Who do you think you are—somebody's mother?" Freddy said. He got up and stalked away.

Arvid turned around to see, just behind him, Bigelow, with eyes like saucers.

"N'there," he said. "I told you he never done it. I told you so, didn't I?"

✦

Freddy was gone all the rest of the day. Arvid took him over some lunch and left it at the houseboat, but Freddy was working down in the engine compartment, and he didn't speak or come out. He came back at suppertime, ate, said nothing except a few monosyllables in answer to Arvid's talk, and went to bed. The next morning he was gone before daylight, had got his own breakfast, and apparently had packed himself a lunch. Thus he was still over at the houseboat in the afternoon, when Philomela put her head down into the *Sea Flower*'s engine compartment and called his name.

Philomela had got Simon Eldridge to drop her off at the island. Seeing the boat come in, Arvid set up a yell for Bigelow, who came bounding along the path from the direction of the houseboat.

"What?" she said pleasantly. "What, Arvid?"

Arvid looked at her. She had apparently been squatting in the mud somewhere, and her hair was full of twigs. And, h'm, he thought. Butter wouldn't melt in her mouth, either. Aloud, he said, "You been over bothering Freddy?"

"No. I haven't been anywhere near him. I only watch him from the bushes."

"Well," Arvid said. "Anyway, I guess your job of watching that boat for Marney's about over. Look who's come, down there on the shore. Marney, ain't that, with Philomela? Toughy, too. That's her new box we bought."

She looked; she went tearing down the path ahead of him.

Arvid followed more slowly.

Nothing was working out with Freddy. Nor ever would, he told himself. And to be fair, I don't know as I can blame him.

"Well, Philomela," he said, as she came up the path. She looked quite happy, he was pleased to see. Maybe she had good news.

She was chuckling a little, glancing back as she came. The kids had stopped on the beach to let Toughy out of the carrier. Bigelow was doing the letting-out; Marney was standing, looking a little bewildered, his hands thrust deep into his pockets.

"Marney's overwhelmed," Philomela said. "Do you know this is the first time he's ever seen Bigelow in daylight? He wouldn't have known her, except he knew she'd be here. And she's welcomed him as if he were her best, long-lost, and dearest. Scared him, I think."

"When Bigelow likes, she likes," Arvid said. He sighed a little. "And when she don't, she don't. I swear, I don't know, Philomela. She's got Freddy about on the run."

Philomela sobered. "How is he?"

"Put out. I don't know as this was the time for you to come."

"Maybe no time would be. I don't know. I have to try, Arvid. Where is he?"

"Over at the boat. I'll show you."

"You'll be glad to know," she said, as they walked along, "that the game of cops and robbers is over."

"It is?"

"Mm-hm. The Welfare people know Bigelow's been found and that she's here with us. And they're delighted."

"You told them? You took a chance on that?" He looked so horrified that she had to laugh.

"I saw a lawyer first. If you'd had the sense you were born with, we could have gone over to Powell that night and brought her back."

"Now, Philomela, the way they took her in the first place—"

"She was their responsibility. What did they know about you or me? Good heavens, Arvid, they aren't monsters. If they can find a decent home for a couple of kids, they're the first ones to cheer. All it needed was a little explaining. And you're out of the woods, you old pirate. You won't have to go to jail for kidnapping."

"Well, I don't know as I supposed I would."

"You could have. I think I did quite well without fibbing, telling as much of the story as I know—and don't you ever dare tell me the rest of it, either. I said that Bigelow wanted to stay here so much that she sneaked off the bus when no one was looking and started to hitchhike back. And that you happened along in the truck and, fortunately, found her by the side of the highway. If you ever get asked any questions as to why you fortunately happened along, which I expect you won't, since everyone is so relieved at the way it's turned out, you can say what you want to—maybe that you were headed for Portsmouth to see what legal means could be taken, so that you could bring her back here. Anything, just so it isn't my fib."

"Mercy," Arvid said. "Talk about a pirate."

"Yes. Next time, you look out. I won't lift a finger to keep you out of jail. Look at you, I believe you're sorry it's all been made nice and legal."

"Well, I have had a kind of a good time."

"I'll just bet. Well, there's the boat, isn't it?" She stopped and stood looking at the *Sea Flower* high and dry in the alders and already beginning to seem like a wreck, the new paint discolored, the propeller sticking uselessly into the air. "I dread this, Arvid. I wish I knew what to say to him."

"Yes," Arvid said. "I guess the hardest is yet to come."

He turned and walked back along the path, leaving her to climb up the side of the boat, where there was no sign of Freddy but a light tapping sound, coming from somewhere out of sight.

At the sound of her voice, he came blinking out of the engine room into the light. He was covered with grease, his coveralls and hands black with it; even on his face it was hard to say where the black eye stopped and the grease began. "Oh, Lord, Philomela!" he said. "Am I some damned glad to see you!"

The welcome was what she had hoped for, though she had hardly dared to believe she would get it. She had been telling herself, after what we did to each other that night, when he left, when I told him to go, surely he'll pick up the battle where we dropped it. He'll have to. I—we both said awful things. Things I thought we'd never be able to forget. But it seems I have. And so has he.

He was simply glad to see her and showed it, and in her relief, she burst out laughing. "Freddy, what a terrible black eye!"

"Isn't it a corker? Haven't had one like it since I got hit with a pitched ball when I was in the ninth grade. You would," he said, grinning, "come around here looking like a new snowbank and look at me. I can't even kiss you."

"Yes, you can." She leaned over and kissed him on the mouth.

"Well, that was pretty brisk. I suppose I ought to be grateful for small things. It's about time you did that."

"Yes. You, too."

"Come to stay?"

"I hope so."

"Good. A man alone's a sorry mess, let me tell you. I haven't been cleaned up for days. But, by gum, I can be. Come on, let's head for the house. I'll get rid of this, and we'll go off somewhere. This island's been giving me the creeps, but right now it looks like the finest kind of a place for a man to—" He stopped. "To start his courting all over again," he said.

"Freddy—"

"Don't you want to?"

"Of course I want to."

"Then come on."

He jumped down off the side of the boat, held up his hand to help her, remembered in time, and turned it over. "Put your hand on the back of mine," he said. "Look, there's one clean place, right there!"

So how can I talk to him now? she thought, as they walked together along the path to the house. I thought by now we would be in the middle of a roaring battle, and of course, in two seconds, we could be. Because what I've done will start the final, the most intolerable battle of all. He'll never believe I didn't do it to get back at him. Out of spite; out of anger.

Out of loneliness, she told herself. But most of all, because of the needs of two desperate children.

"What's the matter?" Freddy said. He had been striding along whistling softly; now he turned to her with a sober face. "You aren't down in the mouth, now, are you? About anything?"

"Well, I—no, Freddy."

Later. The time could not be now. He would have to be talked to, because she was already committed; she had taken the responsibility for two children whom he did not even know.

I need time to think how to be careful, how, God help me, to make him understand why I did this—he'll say—behind his back. I have got to.

Because somewhere behind the quarrels, the black residues of resentment and anger, was the man she had fallen in love with and had married. She knew that now, surely, for today he had come back. He was here now, and she did not see how she could risk losing him again.

They came out of the woods into sight of the house. Three figures were on the grass-grown plot with the fallen fence where the barnyard had been. Arvid, Marney, and Bigelow had brought the motorcycle out of the barn and were looking it over.

"Who's that?" Freddy said. He brought up sharply, glanced at Philomela. "You didn't tell me you'd brought company."

"That's Marney. Marney Lessard. The boy you took in to the hospital."

"Never would have known him. What's he want here? Oh yeah, come after his bike, I guess. Well, she's ready. He can have her."

"I think he wants to say thank you, Freddy."

"How come you—how'd you get to know him?"

"I went to see him at the hospital. Arvid told me about him."

"Arvid taking him over, too? Brother, if he's any relation to that skinny brat, hold onto your hat."

"He isn't. He's a nice kid, Freddy."

"Well, that's good news. Anyway, if he's come for the bike, he won't be around long. Too bad you didn't ask Simon to wait. Save us a trip inshore with him."

"He isn't going yet, he isn't well enough. And even if he were, he hasn't anywhere to go," Philomela said. "Freddy—"

"Philomela, what is this?" He stared at her. "Because I'd really like to know what all this has got to do with you."

But they were too close now for her to answer him, even if she could have. The three beside the motorbike had already turned around.

"Hello," Freddy said. He had given Philomela a glance, then had strolled up casually, his hands in his pockets. "You look some different from what you did the day I took you in to the hospital, wouldn't have handed you much then."

"Well, hi," Marney said. His cheeks were flushed, his eyes shining. "I'm sure glad to have a chance to thank you, Mr. Fowler. And for the bike, too. Gee, what a job! I didn't think there'd be anything left of her but a heap of rust. And look at her, she's even better than she was when I first got her."

"Nice bike," Freddy said. "Fun to work on."

"I guess I owe you something for fixing her, don't I?"

"Nope. Glad to do it. Just a spare-time job. All I've got to do is hook the sidecar on, and she's all ready to roll, get you anywhere you want to go. Back to where you came from in jig time, I shouldn't wonder." His tone said, the sooner the better, and he went on, "Arvid, you got any hot water in there?"

"Plenty," Arvid said. "Tank's full."

Helplessly, Philomela watched his departure through the kitchen door. She heard the tinny rattle of the dipper as he bailed water into a bucket. She saw Marney's bewilderment and withdrawal—it was as if his face suddenly had closed—and Bigelow's look of cynical affirmation, the raised eyebrow, the expression that plainly said, What did I tell you? Didn't I tell you so?

"Arvid, I haven't had a chance. I haven't been able to talk to him."

"So I gathered," Arvid said. "You take your time, Philomela. The kids and I are, anyway, about to go fishing."

He led the way down the path to the shore, and watching them go, Philomela thought, I let this happen and now if there ever were a chance, I've ruined it. Oh, stupid! Stupid and irresponsible. She followed Freddy into the house.

Freddy lay on the bed, his arms behind his head, watching Philomela dress. He had not said anything at all, he had only listened, and after a little, Philomela herself stopped talking, feeling the silence in the room stretch taut.

"Can't we talk about this?" she said at last. "Please don't just lie there getting mad, Freddy. Because you know if you get mad, I do, too."

"Yes," Freddy said. "I know you do. But what is there to say? It's all talked over, isn't it? You and Arvid, between you, have got yourselves stuck with a couple of stray kids. All I'd know how to add is that the world's full of stray kids and full of agencies to look after them. What do you want me to do—bleed?"

"I didn't go out looking for this," Philomela said. "It came looking for me. When I was alone and had every reason to think I was going to be. After what we said to each other that night, I didn't suppose you'd ever come back. That house is big. And empty. And when Arvid brought me this—the story about this child, I don't think I could have lived with myself if I hadn't done something about it. And he—Arvid was heartbroken."

"Look, any hard-luck yarn can get Arvid down, and you know it. Good God, Philomela, he gets tears in his eyes over a chopped-up tree. And when he wants to he can talk the leg off a cast-iron Indian."

"I'm no cast-iron Indian, Freddy. Arvid didn't talk me into this. These kids—well, we don't know about Bigelow, only from seeing what she is; she's kept her story to herself. But Marney's would freeze your blood. At least it did mine. No one—not children—should grow up feeling the world is . . . is wild animals."

"I did," Freddy said. "Can't see but what I made out all right. Nobody coddled me. Seems to me the earlier you learn dog eat dog the better. What's wrong with growing up in a world of strangers? You live in one all your life, why not begin? Beat them off. Set up your own place and keep them out of it. If you don't, they're all over you, so what have you got?"

"I don't know whether or not you're right," Philomela said. "Partly, maybe, you've left out some. Arvid coddled you when you were a youngster. He still does. And so do I. I don't think I'd say coddled—it's your word—I think I'd say love. Everyone has to have someone, Freddy. These two children haven't. If you could think of your world without Arvid and without me, it would be what they have."

"Sure. But what's that got to do with me? Look, I don't want kids around. I don't like them. I can still wake up and hear that catfight at home, the old man and the old woman beating on each other, and the kids yowling and doing the same; even in a nightmare it turns my stomach."

"All right, I'm not forcing anyone on you, Freddy."

"What else are you doing? You've already committed yourself, you said. Or maybe you could back out of it. Why don't you do that?"

"No. Not with Arvid feeling the way he does. And me, I feel the same, I expect. Some kind of an arrangement, a decent setup somewhere, will have to be made. I don't know what or where. Where it won't bother you."

"It bothers me to be made to feel like a heel," Freddy said. "I do, if that helps any."

"It doesn't. Maybe it would, if I'd set out to make you feel that way. I got mixed up in this, not to spite you, Freddy, but because I couldn't stay out of it."

"Damn it, Philomela, all I want is my wife!"

"And I my husband. What I don't want is the old man and the old woman beating on each other. The way we do. And will, I expect."

"Well, arguments. What other way is there to settle them?"

"Compromise. The way we've settled this one."

"Settled? You think this is settled?"

"I hoped so."

"What you mean is, you've settled it. By getting your goddamned own way."

"I haven't!"

"Well, I will say, you've gone around Robin Hood's barn, but you've done it."

"Freddy, you know what my own way would be! Children of our own!"

"So you compromise by getting wound up into a tack with two kids I practically never saw before. And one of them hates my guts."

Freddy got up and came across the room. He kissed her briskly on the cheek. "I'm going to work," he said. "I'll be over at the boat till suppertime. Back then," and he went off down the stairs.

I didn't get very far, did I? Philomela said to herself, hearing his steps pass below on the gravel by the front door. I don't suppose I thought I would.

She knew well that bright, brittle, kiss-you-on-the-cheek-and-go manner, which always seemed to mean, look, this is only another one of your notions, so think it over while I'm gone and snap out of it, for heaven's sake. As the adult of intelligence and judgment might treat a silly person or a child. And as a punishment, we'll just take away the candy. You won't see me all afternoon, and we were going to start our courting all over again, remember? And walk out, and back at suppertime, to see if the spanking has done any good. And mad because it hasn't.

It doesn't work with me. It never will. Father-with-daughter, or when he is down in the mouth or sick, mother-with-baby. And I see myself growing silly, as time goes on, and more childish and unsure, and the future a jangle of fights, till at fifty, with my false teeth and my boredom and my nagging, I'll be the woman they write all the mother-in-law jokes about. And well they may. Because there are too many of us to be ignored, and we are a joke.

He doesn't want children and he has a right not to. I don't blame him. He's entitled to his preferences. He remembers his own childhood, and so he does his creating with his hands. I would go along with him on that forever, if that were the rock we split on. It isn't. And so now I know.

Voices from below warned her that the fishing expedition was back. I expect it would be nice if I fixed my face and went down and got some food together for this crew. Everybody's probably starving.

The voices were cheerful but subdued. They stopped entirely as she came into the kitchen.

"Hello," she said, trying to make her own voice brisk and cheerful. "My, what a wonderful lot you got." She glanced at the sink, where the splendid catch, dressed and filleted, lay ready for the pan. "Will I cook those, and will they taste good!" She realized that the brisk voice was a little unsteady, and turned to face the battery of silence, the three pairs of eyes.

"It's settled," she said firmly. "The worry's over. You two are going to stay here forever. With Arvid and me. It's all right. It's . . . settled."

"It is?" Arvid said.

"Yes, it is. And I think it's wonderful. I hope everybody else does, too. So you all go get cleaned up, wash the fish scales off, while I get supper."

"Don't you want me to, Philomela?" The children had already gone, but Arvid paused in the door. "I'm kind of used to batching it."

"Mercy, no, I can whip up a meal in no time."

But he still stood, hesitating, in the door; and presently she went across the room to him and leaned her head against his solid chest.

"Things in a stew, I guess," he said.

"Yes. But we are keeping the children, Arvid. I don't think we'll be able to adopt them, the agencies are fussy about having married couples for that. I can take them on a foster-mother basis, and I'm going to. Of course, I already have."

"Yes. Don't see how we could back out now. But this is going to bust you up with Freddy, Philomela."

"Not if I can help it. It's not the children, Arvid. It's other things, too. We were busted up, you know, before this happened. We couldn't have gone on the way we were. Maybe this'll make us try a little harder. It brought me here to talk to him, which I wouldn't have done on my own. So don't worry. We have to see."

"Well," Arvid said, doubtfully. "God, I hope you make out, Philomela."

So do I, Philomela said under her breath, watching him go slowly down the steps.

"What's that for?" Marney asked. He had been strolling along the path behind Bigelow, thinking hard, not paying much attention to where they were going or what she was doing. Now he saw with a start that they were behind the bushes on the bank where the houseboat was, that she had filled her pockets with rocks and had thrust a good-sized one into his hand.

"Sh-h," Bigelow said. She whispered urgently, "We are going to plug these at that stinker, hit him right in the middle of his mean, skinny, old face. Now, when I say, throw, and then run."

Marney dropped the rock. He caught back Bigelow's hand.

"Hey, cut it out! What are you, some kind of a nut?"

"He was mean to her. He made her cry. He doesn't want us to stay with her. I'm going to bash him with a rock."

"What good will that do? You think it'll make him like you any better? Come on away from here."

Bigelow's tongue was already out, in the well-known raspberry. She was preparing to stick her head through the bush and make it at Freddy.

"Oh, great!" Marney said. "You look like that dead monkfish Arvid showed us. And you've fixed everything up just swell for us, haven't you? I don't blame him. I wouldn't want us, either."

He turned and walked away. Bigelow stared after him, horrified. The "Prr-rp!" had died on her tongue. He thought it was her fault! It wasn't. It was that Freddy's fault.

I hated him the first time I saw him, and so did he me. But Marney was going, and Marney was mad at her. Something would have to be done. She would do it.

She marched out of the bushes and over to the houseboat.

Freddy had been sitting on the deck not doing anything. He had come back thinking he'd go to work again, dig into it, get covered up with grease again, maybe it would help. But he didn't feel like it now. Here it was, the old thing with Philomela starting up again. He'd tried his best, and it hadn't worked.

All we have to do is see each other, and bang! If she'd only listen to reason. If she'd even try to get it through her head. I try to explain that this isn't a small thing to me. God, I can't live in a house with kids, and there she sits, as if all I'd said was, look, I don't like mosquitoes. Kids, they're a dime a dozen, loose all over the world, one born every second, like leaves drop off a tree. So add to the multitude, and why? So the tree can have more leaves to blow away with the wind. Trot-trot to market. Trot-trot home again.

Take your pick, she says to me. Let me have these two kids, or lose your wife. I don't suppose she knows she's left it up to me, but that's what it amounts to. Be Daddy, Daddee. Old Daddy-with-a-kite-tail. What's that to look forward to? What kind of a choice is that to have to make? And what in hell's name am I going to do?

Thinking, he had not heard at all the whispers, the slight crackling sounds behind the bushes on the bank. He could concentrate, Freddy; he could shut away the world, now, if he wanted to, keep it out of his pocket. But suddenly, he looked down and saw the fox-red head of Bigelow within six inches of his foot. By standing on tiptoe on the ground and hanging on with her fingers, she could just lift her chin over the boat's gunnel. There she was, the head only, deadpan, saucer-eyed, staring at him.

Freddy recoiled. He said nothing, only silently, oh, God, and he stared back.

For a moment, Bigelow remained. Her mouth worked a little, as if she might have been going to say something, but no words came. Then she dropped down out of sight, scrambled along the bank, and he heard her go pounding into the woods.

On the path, a little way from the house, Bigelow caught up with Marney. He was walking soberly along, flicking with a stick at the heads of some tall grass beside the pathway. He had no time to say anything, or even give her one disapproving glance, before she flung herself against him and started howling into his middle.

"Marney, what am I going to do? I've got to do something. I tried to tell him I was sorry, but he only looked at me mean."

"Don't howl," Marney said. "It doesn't help." He pulled out his handkerchief and tried to smother the racket. "Sh-h, they'll hear you; it'll only make them feel bad."

Bigelow gulped hard. She made a major effort, managed to choke it back. "But what will we do, Marney? What will you do?"

"I'll have to go, Bigelow. Clear out, right away from here."

Bigelow's hiccups cut off in the middle. She stared at him in consternation. "You can't!"

"I've got to."

"And leave me? Leave Toughy?"

Of course he would have to take Toughy. He couldn't leave her behind. He started to say so, and stopped. This kid. He couldn't feel he knew her very well, he hadn't seen much of her outside of that wild night on the boat. But she knew him all right; and she had taken him over, as well as Toughy. She was a good little kid. Wilder than a hawk, sometimes, but she was on his side, and brother, was that welcome!

"Arvid likes us, Marney. Mrs. Fowler does. Why do you have to leave?"

"We couldn't live in that guy's house, Bigelow. Yeah, I know Mrs. Fowler wants us. But he doesn't. So I better go."

"But I want to stay here with Arvid. You can stay with him, too. He likes you. He said so. I want you to stay, Marney." She began to cry again, this time silently, the tears squeezing out and running down her cheeks. "I waited so long for you to come, and I took good care. Arvid's here. He'll fix everything."

Marney looked around him a little wildly. He felt bewildered, no place to turn; and for the first time since his illness, he felt wabbly again, a little sick. Trouble—if it meant a mixup for Mrs. Fowler, of course he couldn't stay. After all, the guy was her husband.

"Look," he said. "I can't go anywhere till I get the bike ashore. Help me think. Maybe"—he swallowed a little—"you will have to keep Toughy till I can go find a place and come back for you both."

"I'm going to tell Arvid."

"No, wait. Before we do anything, we have to make plans. . ."

When Philomela, after waiting supper a while, went looking, she found them sitting by the side of the path with their heads together.

"Hi," she said. "I wondered where you were. Supper's ready."

They looked up at her with bright, cheerful smiles, scrambling up.

"Gee, we've kept you waiting. I'm sorry," Marney said. "We got talking."

Ed Snorri took another swig out of his bottle and got madder by the minute.

Shot to kill, that Fowler had, had he? A grown man like that, firing off a shotgun at two little fourteen-year-old kids, if that didn't beat anything Ed had ever heard of in his luh-luh-life.

Ed had got out of jail without serving all of his sentence; his plaint about his family starving without their breadwinner had had its usual effect on the County Sheriff. He could see that it cost more than a trifle to support that family; cost something, too, to support Ed in jail. Not a very practical setup. And so Ed, unexpectedly, had arrived home.

He'd learnt his lesson, he said; the Law was not going to catch up with him again, for the reason that he was not going to do another goddamned thing that the Law could take a skunner to. He stopped in Powell to pick up a bottle—after all, celebrate, a man just getting out of jail—and by the time he arrived back at the family shack, he had had just enough of it to get good and roaring mad at the story of Freddy Fowler and the shotgun.

Why, there wasn't a man in the whole rat-tailed You-nited States big enough to get away with a-firing off of a shotgun at Ed Snorri's kids. Unless he wanted a charge with a card on it tied with a pink ribbon and writ with "Love and Kisses from Ed Snorri," right back, where it would do the most good. Man must be a guh-goddamned criminal.

Well, now, a trip out to the island after that motorbike was right down his alley. If two little kids wanted a bike that bad, buh-buh-by God, they ought to have one. They deserved it, too; hadn't they been shot at? So, come on, they would go out to that Godforsaken hole, and if old Buttercup-Boy walked any ghosts at them this time, Ed would fix him too. They would go out tonight and git that machine. By the so-and-so and the last thingumajig there was, if his kids wanted a toy, he was not a man to hold back. Couldn't ride it round town, of course, but they could hide it, sell it somewhere when the furor died down, git the money.

Ed stopped right there, and a glint came into his eye.

Tru and Dew looked at each other, deadpan. It was sure fun to get the old man on a string like this, good as a TV show. As for selling the bike, they knew about how much of the money they'd see, once Ed got his hands on it, but they had plans, too. Now that he was home before his time was up, the twins had had to decide to cut him in. They wouldn't have the use of his boat and tender anymore; and, besides, their first experience with Freddy had taught them that, on a jaunt like this, they really needed the old man. When it came to moving around somebody's house in the dark without making any noise, Ed was the one to do it. He had had plenty of experience all his life; he could travel like a cat in the dark; see like one, too. So that was all right. By the time they got back tonight, he would be drunk as a skunk; and once get that bike on shore, then heigh-o for Florida; and points west, if they felt like it.

Marney didn't know how long he had been asleep when something waked him. He stirred and turned over and jumped a little at the sight of the white-clad figure beside his bed. He had been sleeping on the couch in the kitchen—there had been a difficulty about enough beds for so many people in the old house, which Philomela had solved by saying that she and Bigelow would use Arvid's bedroom; Freddy and Arvid would have to use the double bed upstairs. It was only a temporary arrangement, for one night—they would be going back to the mainland tomorrow.

The kitchen was full of moonlight, and by it Marney recognized the small, shadowy shape. "Bigelow?" he said. "What—"

"Sh-h," Bigelow said. "Whisper, Marney."

"What is it?"

"Those men are back that tried to steal the bike. I heard them go by my window."

"Steal the bike?" Marney said. He was hardly awake, but he managed to remember to whisper.

"Yes, they were here before. Arvid and I scared them away with a dough face. They've come back. They're the same men, they stutter, that's how you can tell. They're out by the barn now."

Marney came out of bed, He made a grab for his clothes. "Go wake up the others, Bigelow! Hurry!"

"No," Bigelow said. "They're awful men. They'll hurt somebody. There's three of them, and the big one's got a gun. If I wake up Arvid, he'll go running right out there, I know he will."

"Well, gee, we can't let them—"

"Sh-h. They've come in a boat and it's low tide, so there's one place where their punt will be, the back beach. If we just sneak down and push it off, they can't get away."

"They'd still have the gun."

"Maybe we could scare them, think of something. And by that time, Arvid could be ready."

"Okay," Marney said. "I'll go. Wait for me here."

"But you don't know where it is, Marney."

He didn't, he realized. The back beach was somewhere on the Outer Harbor shore. He had seen it from the water, from Arvid's boat, but he didn't know how to get to it.

They crept silently out of the house, crossed the band of moonlight between the front yard and the woods. The path to the back beach had once been an old wagon road, fairly wide, but it was overgrown now with clumps of alder and hardback, and lumpy with ancient wheel ruts. It had been in its time the main road through the village, with hayfields and houses on either side. Tonight a patchy ground mist lay over the few clearings left; through it the ribs of the ruined houses thrust black and wet, the jungles of running juniper sparkled with fog drops; in the dooryards, the lodged timothy grass lay white as hair.

Marney felt an uneasy crinkle at the back of his neck as he ran, stumbling and panting, after Bigelow. He wondered if she might not be scared; he wasn't, not exactly. But it was a weird-looking place in the moonlight.

Bigelow went, lightfooted as a shadow. She had been here before; she had played here, and she knew that whatever ghost walked among these old houses would have a dough face. At the edge of the woods above the beach, she waited till Marney caught up with her.

There was the tender pulled up on the beach, its anchor bedded in pebbles. Beyond it, seemingly only a few feet off the shore, was a powerboat. The tender was not a skiff or a punt; it was a small, flat-bottomed scow, big enough, Marney thought as they came down the beach, to take the bike and the sidecar, too, which was probably why they had brought that kind. The powerboat was hitched to a ringbolt in the scow's square stern by a bowline; a stern anchor held her off from grounding on the shore. Marney could see the wet line in the moonlight.

The tide was dead-low; a few ripples washing lightly on the mud at the foot of the beach showed that it might be turning. But the scow lay on the mud; its waterlogged flat bottom clung stickily and only burrowed deeper as they struggled and shoved. Try as they would, they could not move the awkward thing.

"Oh, gosh, Bigelow, if only I hadn't been sick," Marney gasped. He stopped shoving to give his wabbly legs a new purchase, and realized suddenly that he had to sit down.

"We can't do it, can we?" Bigelow said. She, too, was panting. Her feet made a plopping, sucking sound as she pulled them, one after the other, out of the mud. "Oh, Marney, what can we do?"

"I guess . . . we can't."

Sitting, breathing heavily, on the wet beach rocks, he thought, Well, this isn't the way. What, then? There must be something . . .

The powerboat was much the same model as Arvid's boat, fairly good-sized, with a cuddy. Out fishing with Arvid, he had explored the cuddy, fascinated by the boat stove, the bunks . . . the space in the forepeak, big enough to curl up in. To hide, if you wanted to. The space was, apparently, a place for equipment, like extra lifebelts; at least that was what Arvid used it for. He got up.

"Put the scow-anchor back where it was, Bigelow," he said. "And then let's see if we can pull the big boat closer in."

He heard the *clink!* as she dropped the anchor onto the beach rocks, and then she was back beside him.

"We could cut the big boat loose," she said.

"No. Not yet. I think I've got a plan. I'm going to take a look aboard of her."

The stern line had a little slack from the falling tide, and it stretched enough. Marney waded out a few feet, got his hands on the bow gunnel, pulled himself aboard. It was pitch-dark in the cuddy and smelled horribly of dead fish and gasoline; feeling his way into the bow, he found the space. It was full of some kind of lumpy junk that could be shifted to make a place; there were some old oilskins and what felt like a couple of ragged quilts stuffed in; room to hide, all right, and no reason, unless something unusual happened, why they'd ever look under there tonight.

He hustled back on deck, up on the bow. Bigelow stood there holding taut the line that kept the boat close to the shore. Her face looked pinched and white in the moonlight. She said, "Oh, hurry, Marney. They might come."

"Look, Bigelow. This is the plan. We'll let them take the bike, take it ashore. There's a good place to hide down there. I'll go, too. I'll find out where they take it, get it back, if I can."

"I don't want you to. They might hurt you. And where'll you go?"

"Don't ask questions, there isn't time. You've got to help, or it won't work. You hide, and hide good, till we're gone. Then you hustle back and tell Arvid. He can take out after us, get the police—"

"He can't till the tide comes. The boats are aground. I won't go till you promise you'll come back. I don't want you to leave me and Toughy."

He would have to. "All right. I promise."

"Cross your heart?"

"Lord, Bigelow, yes! If I ever take off anywhere we'll go together. I'll be okay, they won't know I'm anywhere around. Look," he went on desperately, "you know if we leave these guys ashore here without a boat, somebody'll get hurt. This way, I can maybe keep the bike and nobody'll be clobbered. So go! And hurry!" He stopped. "Will you be scared going back alone through the woods?"

Bigelow dropped the rope. "What of?" she said disdainfully.

He watched the small, dark figure go tearing up the beach, dart away from it into the woods. He drew a long breath and his heart misgave him. What if something happened to her? It maybe wasn't such a good idea, after all; he had had to think too fast. But he was stuck with it now. He had left some muddy tracks on the washboard, he saw, and he scuffed them out with his wet sneakers as he moved back toward the cockpit, hoping the blurred marks wouldn't show too much on the scaly paint.

He made himself a fairly comfortable hole under the junk in the forepeak and stretched out in it. It wasn't too bad. He waited.

It was dead silent in the cuddy, except for a slight ripple of water outside the boards under his head, and an occasional small creak of the anchor rope as the boat swung with the incoming tide. Somewhere, far off, a night bird cried with a lonesome sound—from the land or out on the water, he couldn't tell. Those jokers were taking a long time. Where were they? Why didn't they come? The smell in here was awful—old bait, bilges, gas—so thick it was like heavy cloth over his face. He had better get a few breaths of fresh air while he could, he thought, or that flutter in his stomach was going to mean something before too long.

He crept out of his hole, picked his way over the cuddy's assortment of lumpy objects, thrust his head out into the air, breathing deep. It was wonderful—cool, sweet, almost as if he could taste it on his tongue; and he stayed where he was, leaning heavily against the hatch coamings, keeping his head down so that it could not be seen against the sky.

Not a sound anywhere. The moon was tipping into the west, making squiggles of light across the still harbor. The tide had come up a little, covering the patch of mud at the stern of the scow. But it was a silent flooding, without a ripple, as water rises in a deep hole, pushed from below. And there they came; and they had the bike. He could hear the pound of running feet, an occasional thump and rasp of metal on stone. Two of them, he saw, as they appeared at the top of the beach and came slipping and sliding down. I thought she said there were three. And only the bike, not the sidecar.

They were not trying to be quiet; they were jabbering excitedly to each other, and Marney could not make out a word they said. Two or three, however many, it was time to hide. He slipped back into the cuddy, crawled into his place and huddled, with his knees drawn up and his head down on them. And listened.

He heard the clatter as they loaded the bike aboard the scow, and thought, They'll be a while, launching that craft out of the mud. But it seemed they weren't doing it that way. He felt the powerboat move as they hauled on the bow line, heard splashes and thumps as they piled aboard. One went tearing aft; he was hauling up the stern anchor. The other started the engine. Over the roar of its sound, Marney could hear nothing more, but it was in reverse and laboring a little; he guessed they were using the powerboat to haul the scow out of the mud.

Apparently they'd done it, too, for the engine stopped, somebody went up on the bow, and Marney could hear the flap-flap of the rope directly over his head—the bow line being unfastened from its cleat. They would, of course, take the scow in tow; the man's steps receded along the washboard as he went back toward the stern to make fast the line there.

And then from somewhere, Marney couldn't tell where, but it would have to be on shore, came the muffled report of a shotgun.

There was a moment's silence, some jabbering, and the two broke out laughing, roaring their heads off.

So far, Marney hadn't been able to make out a word they had said; it was the worst stuttering he had ever heard. But now, one of them, gasping and chortling, said quite clearly, "Buh-buh-by God, did we duh-dish the old man! Boy, oh, boy, oh, boy, did we fuh-fix him!"

 ✦

Ed had got the bike out of the barn without sound or mishap. He had had to leave the sidecar behind; he didn't see how they could heist that down through the woods, wheel only on one side, and this annoyed him. After all, it was property, well worth a few dollars. His temper, always touchy when he was nearly at the end of one bottle and didn't have another handy, began to steam a little. He walked down the woods path behind the boys feeling pretty dissatisfied.

The twins had got the bike and had taken off with it. They were quite a ways ahead of him—he had to go slow, being now a little insecure on his feet. He was also nervous in spite of himself. Maybe he didn't believe in ghosts anymore, was on to old Buttercup-Boy and his tricks, but still, them rotten old houses with the studs sticking up out of that ground fog like somebody's bones didn't look good to a man. Anything could come out of one of them guh-goddamned suller-holes, too; and as Ed passed one, something did. A wavering shape rose up out of the ground fog and let go with a curdling scream—and vanished.

It took a terrible jump out of Ed. He lost his footing on a patch of wet grass, dropped his gun out of the crook of his arm, waved wildly out of balance for a second, and sat down hard.

It wasn't too easy to get back on his feet, he found. He scrabbled around some, before he remembered the bottle in his jacket pocket, that one last long swig he'd been saving for the long, cold boat ride home. He fumbled out the bottle, uncapped it, tilted it to the sky. Hah! That was the stuff! That put the good old into a man. And now, buh-by God, he was mad!

Old Buttercup-Boy, by the so, that was him! Up to it again!

Ed got up. He picked up his gun. He began to prance in the road and wave the gun. He was a-going back, he said, and shoot a charge through that bastard's front window, show him. Crazy old slob, going around yelling out of suller-holes, place like this, scare decent folks so their legs give and they fell down. And now, completely muddled, Ed put back his head and demanded of the sky why it wasn't good and well right to shoot the windows out of a man that went around firing off shotguns at little innocent half-grown boys.

In the milky dimness under the ground fog in the cellar hole, Tru and Dew nudged each other. This was great, couldn't have been better. This was just what the doctor ordered. If Ed went back now, they could load the bike and be gone before he could get halfway to the shore after them. Smothering their giggles, they watched him stomp off up the road out of sight, and didn't try to stop him.

Ed went back to the house and stood in front of it in the moonlight, trying to draw a bead. He finally got one on an upstairs front window, let out a yell, and pulled the trigger.

Doubled up in the forepeak of the Snorri boat, Marney was frozen with worry. Bigelow had been right about these jokers—there had been three of them, and one of them had been left marooned on the island with a gun. That gunshot. He kept hearing it. Bigelow, where was she? If anything's happened to her, it's my fault. I hadn't ought to have let her go into those woods alone. If I'd only had more time to think! What I should have done was to wake up Arvid and Mr. Fowler. But I thought I could get these thugs off the island without anybody's getting hurt and maybe save the bike . . .

Well, it had been a lousy plan. That gunshot. It was still sounding in his ears when the boat slowed entering the harbor and tied up at the float.

Tru and Dew hauled the scow up alongside the float and tenderly lifted out the motorbike. They left boat and scow where they were. Let someone else bother; they had other fish to fry now. Now was the time; now was the hour. This, at last, was what they'd waited for.

They wheeled the bike up the float walkway, one at the handlebars steering, the other pushing behind. They pushed it past Arvid's fishhouse into the road, stood the sacred thing in the road heading up the hill, and realized there was one thing they hadn't thought of.

"Nuh-now, how do we start the duh-damned thing?" Dew said.

To his astonishment, Tru said, "I dunno," and stood looking, bewildered, at hope standing in the moonlight.

At that moment, he lost face with Dew. Tru was always the one who figured out things. Dew counted on him. Now that they had got this at last, were all ready to roll, here stood Tru, saying he didn't know how to start the engine on it, and it wasn't possible. Dew didn't believe him. He stared at Tru through slitted eyes.

"Well, cuh-can't see nothing in the dark," Tru said. "Dew, you guh-go down aboard the boat and fuh-fetch up the flashlight."

So that was it. Come to think of it, Dew didn't trust him, any more than he trusted the old man. What Tru meant to do, he was going to get Dew a ways away from him, and then he was going to ride off alone and leave Dew stranded. Without even a ride on the lovely thing!

"You guh-go git it yourself," Dew said.

It was Tru's turn to be surprised. He glanced up at Dew, standing there, squared off in the moonlight. "Guh-goddammit, you do what I tuh-tell you!"

"Guh-git it yourself, I said. I ain't taking it from you anymore, Tru."

Then Tru made his mistake. He was used to slapping Dew, and so he slapped him. Smack! Right across the face.

Dew's nerves were already strung up as tight as they would go. He spun around, crouched, and swung from the ground up, a wild haymaker, which, for once, connected. Tru landed flat on his back with a howl of agony. The next moment the twins were rolling over and over on the ground, fists flailing, yelling in the tongue they used to each other, unintelligible, shrill as a pig-killing.

Now, Marney thought. Please God, let it start at the first crack.

He came out of the shadows by the fishhouse and straddled the bike. It didn't start at the first crack, but it started at the second, smooth as cream. He slid it into gear and rode away up the hill.

The roar of the engine, almost over their heads, separated the twins for the first time in their lives before Dew got licked. They sat up, stunned, staring after the swiftly moving shadow vanishing in the moonlight. They hadn't seen anyone; they didn't see anyone now, for Marney was bending low, hoping to avoid thrown rocks in case there were any.

"Kuh-kuh-krissake, what done that?" Tru gasped. "Whuh-what'd it do?"

In agony, Dew moaned. It was going; it was gone.

"Oh, you guh-goddamned fool!" he said. "You went and left sss-something *on!*"

But Tru knew he hadn't. He hadn't touched anything. "Ketch it!" he screamed. "It'll hit a tree and bust itself!"

They tore up the hill; but even the sound of its engine had died away. They thought it might have stopped itself the way it had started, maybe rolled into bushes or behind a building somewhere, and they hunted. All over the road, through the village; they went all the way to the main road that led to Powell. No bike. It had gone as if it had never been, and gray light was beginning to come into the sky.

It was a queer light, showing them each other's faces, white and strained, and Dew's hair full of leaves. It made peculiar shadows under the trees along the highway.

Dew stopped in mid-stride. He tried to say something that clogged in his throat, so that for a moment he stood making sizzling noises.

Tru gave him a shove. "Well, go on! What's the matter with you?"

"I know what it was. I bub-bub-bub-betcha I do! It was that walking dead man, follered us. I betcha he was in the boat with us all the time."

"What walking dead man? There ain't no such thing as a walking dead man, you duh-damn fool!"

"What if there was? We sure see something, out there that night on the wreck with Pa!"

"That was old Small. Old Buttercup-Boy."

But Tru looked around fearfully. That light was sure scary. After all, no one in the world had ever proved anything, had they? Pa believed in walking dead men. If old Small hadn't lit his lamp that night, Pa'd have gone right on believing he'd really seen one.

"I don't think that was old Small," Dew said. He was beginning to shiver. "How could he make his face run down off his chin? Nobody could. That was dead and rotten, that's what that was. And I suh-see it move."

"Arrgh! Them things can't cross water. It couldn't work nothing off'n that island."

"This one did. In our boat. It's come and took the bike back there. I betcha if you went out now and luh-looked in that barn, you'd see it right back where it come from."

The notion was so horrible that it lifted Tru's hair on his head. The bike was certainly gone, with nobody riding it. If it hadn't gone straight up into the air, where was it? He had a momentary vision of it, whirling through the sky with that thing riding it across six miles of empty water.

Tru shrugged the thought away; it was too foolish. But all the same, he wasn't going to stick around here any longer, not in a place where such a thing might, just possibly, happen.

"Come on," he said. "I'm hitchhiking. If we go home, Pa'll bore holes in us, and we was tuh-taking off, anyway."

At sunrise they got a ride on a truck which took them some way beyond Powell. After that, they kept on going.

Marney had not gone far. He had not planned to—only out of range of the pursuit which for a brief time he could sense coming along behind him. Gas in the bike's tank was low; he had known this beforehand, and he hoped there'd be enough to take him out of danger. When the twins went tearing by on the highway, he was in a lean-to at the back of the Fowler barn, with the bike safely stowed beside him.

He waited a while, hunkered down. He had no idea what time it was or how long till morning. The lean-to was damp and cold; he felt chilled through and still a little sick and dizzy from breathing the fumes in the boat's cuddy.

I seem to spend my life hiding around in holes, he thought. And half killing myself trying to hang on to this bike.

At home, at Grampa Lessard's, a thousand years ago, a motorcycle would have been a plaything, something for fun. If you had had one then, you'd have taken care of it, kept it greased and shined, defended it from thieves, perhaps, but not with your life. You did that now, though, and you knew why. Because this bike, now, was your last handhold on freedom. With it you could get far enough away to find the holes you hid in, while, behind, the sounds of the chase stopped.

Yesterday, if he could have got ashore with the bike, like this, he would have kept on going. Now, he couldn't. Tomorrow he would have to manage, somehow, to get back to the island.

Suddenly, the holes—the cold, the damp, the lonesomeness—were not to be borne, and did not need to be. The people out on the island, all but one, were his friends. Let those two thugs come back and find the bike, if they could; take it, ride off on it. It was nice to own, but it was, after all, a plaything. He didn't need it now; because friends meant that he was done with holes and hiding.

He got up, purposefully walked out of the lean-to and around to the back of the Fowler house. He found a cellar window that would open, crawled through, made himself a hot drink in the kitchen, and went to bed in the room that Philomela had already told him would be his. He was asleep there when she, with Arvid and Bigelow, arrived at the house in the morning.

The gunshot and the smash of window glass had lifted Arvid out of bed. He had been sleeping on the outside of the bed in Freddy's room, and he rose up groggily, yelling, "A thunderstorm! The house's been hit!" and staggered to the window. Freddy, behind him, shouted, "Get down, you fool! He's shooting through the window!" The solid impact of Freddy's body, slamming against his from across the room, knocked him out of the way as the second shot went off, but not before he had caught a glimpse of the crazy figure weaving up and down in the front yard. And then, just as Bigelow had told Marney he would do, Arvid went tearing out of the house.

Ed was shakily trying to draw a bead on another upstairs window, as Arvid's lusty kick from behind sent him sprawling. In this earthward plunge, Ed dropped the gun, which went off again with a hollow bang and a flashing streak as it fell. Arvid grabbed it, broke it open, and made sure there were no more live shells in it. Then he wound it around the nearest tree. He turned around with his fists up, but Ed was too drunk to get back on his feet. He lay there scrabbling slightly and making a sizzling sound, which now, in the darkness, let Arvid know who this was. So far he hadn't been able to tell.

"You damned half-wit!" Arvid howled. He reached down and got Ed by the collar. "I'm a good mind to slat your head off! Come in the night, shoot at a houseful of women and children!"

He realized, then, from Ed's slackness and the way his head rolled, what was wrong with him. Arvid undoubled his fist. He couldn't stop himself from giving Ed a couple of good, meaty slaps; but after all, a man couldn't beat up a drunk. All you could do was lock him up somewhere and go and get the Sheriff.

Because, by the God, this is the end of it. This is the last I'm going to take from Ed Snorri.

He bundled Ed along the path to the only place he had that would lock from the outside—the backhouse, which had a stout button on the door. Still, those two kids of Ed's were probably around somewhere; he would have to fix that door so that it would take a crowbar to open it. A hammer and some twenty-penny spikes . . .

As he turned to go back to the kitchen, he saw that a lamp had been lighted. Philomela met him at the door. She was white-faced, and her voice was shaking.

"Arvid, what's happened? The kids are gone. And where's Freddy?"

"Freddy?" Arvid said. "Why . . ." Where was Freddy? "I thought he was right behind me, Philomela."

He took the lamp and started heavily up the stairs.

Philomela stood where she was. She thought, Something has happened to him, and I can't move, I can't lift my feet from the floor. In a moment, I'll know, preparing herself for the cry, the shout from the upstairs room, which she was sure would come. Bigelow came tearing in a flurry through the kitchen door, out of breath and panting from her dash through the woods. She flung herself on Philomela and clung, telling, between gasps, where Marney was; and Philomela held her close, saying automatically, "Don't be scared, honey, it's over, it's all right," and listening for the cry, the sound from upstairs, whatever it would be.

But there was no sound, for the reason that Arvid could not make one. He had made one, some inarticulate words, spoken under his breath, as he set the lamp down and slid to his knees beside Freddy on the floor. "Freddy? Oh, my God. If only I hadn't been so goddamned fat!"

Because Freddy was lying in front of the smashed window; and the second charge from Ed's shotgun had caught him full in the chest.

They buried Freddy from a funeral home in Powell.

Philomela sat through the funeral service, trying to listen to what the minister was saying; something about voyagers to a far country . . . Columbus . . . Magellan . . . The words seemed not to have much to do with Freddy, and her mind slipped away from them. Her mind had had a way of doing that ever since his death; irrelevant matters crept into it. She could tell herself that she ought to grieve, and feel nothing but numbness. Grief was there. At times she could sense it, like a pinnacle of cold stone lurking in fog; when the fog cleared she would crash on it, she knew. But that time had not yet come. Sitting here, hearing the minister's voice roll on, she found herself thinking, almost absently, oh, poor Freddy, he'll be back with all those Fowlers, and how he'll hate it.

Arvid was the one who was grieving, she realized with a start, remembering that since that night, though he had been around for a good part of every day, she had scarcely looked at him. He sat beside her now, his face set and white, creased in deep lines around the mouth, his big chin lowered to the collar of his white Sunday shirt, giving his head and shoulders a heavy, hunched-down look, as if he were cornered by something and about to charge out of the corner at whatever the something was. She had known that look before; for many years, throughout her childhood, it had always meant that Arvid could not hold in—that he had action to take or words to say, and that he was going to do something. And as she glanced at him, she realized that he was going to do something now, moving, rumbling a little in his throat, getting to his feet.

In shocked amazement, she thought, oh, no, not now, Arvid! And put her hand on his sleeve; but he was already rearing up, standing, his head still held low.

The minister had stopped talking and was looking at him, but Arvid did not look back. He was staring at whatever it was he was seeing, with bloodshot and tear-stained eyes.

"It ain't right," Arvid said. "He wasn't Columbus and he wasn't Magellan, and he ain't gone to discover America nore yet the Straits of Tella del Few-o-go. He was Freddy Fowler, and he's gone on a trip he wasn't ready for, that he never had a chance in the God's world to put a few things together for. It ain't a trip you go on in a vessel, the vessel ain't made yet to take you. What a man is used to is a cup of coffee and his own shoestrings and tomorrow, and standing on the beach looking at the water and saying, God, ain't that pretty. It ain't right, it can't be, to have this . . . this grab you and say go, and don't look back!" His voice stumbled a little and stopped. He looked around blindly, seemed suddenly to realize where he was, what he was doing. "Excuse me," he said. "It's taken a lot out of me. It . . . it was too half-witless a way for a man to lose his life." He sat down and buried his face in his hands.

Freddy lay quiet and comfortable and lonely in his casket; he did not look back. The minister said, "Thank you, Mr. Small. That's better than I could do." The funeral ended. Philomela wept, realizing now her loss, like a blow over the heart. Freddy's neighbors filed quietly out. This would be talked about later, this unheard-of thing, this shocking thing, of a man's interrupting a funeral; still, there was no one there who did not agree with him.

✦

Somewhere over the western mainland, a warm current of air folding leisurely into valleys and riding upward on steep mountain

Ruth Moore

slopes, encountered cold—met the first wintry blast driving down from Canada. Rain fell, and snow, and a little hail; lightning began to flicker. In the night the storm blew eastward, bringing to the sleeping villages and towns and outlying country farms, the hollow distant rumble of thunder.

A late fall thunderstorm, Philomela thought sleepily. Oh, poor Arvid! and she put out a hand to the open window beside the bed and shut the sash.

Marney did not waken; he slept soundly in the room down the hall from Philomela's, the room now his, where all his things were; he did not stir even when the pages of the open textbook beside his bed began to flutter, or the rain from the windowsill splattered on his face. Out of this safety, it would have taken more than a thunderstorm to wake him.

In the downstairs bedroom, Arvid stirred uneasily, rolled over, realizing that the bed was going up and down like a ship at sea. Out of a cloud of sleep, he thought, Funny kind of a nightmare, never had one like this, and jerked awake as a brilliant white flash ripped out of the blackness, lighting up the whole room.

Arvid reared up in bed. "Thunder'n lightning! Hide! Git under the bed, git down suller—" and realized that he could rise no higher because of the heavy object bounding up and down on his middle, beating at him with frantic fists.

"Arvid, you have got to wake up! You have got to come! Toughy is on my bed and she's sick. Something terrible's the matter! Arvid, Arvid, please!"

"Toughy, is it?" he said thickly, and wakened still more. "Toughy? Great balls of fire, can't have that! You go back, Bigelow, put on all the lights. I'll be right there—"

He fumbled around for his pants and shirt, hustled them on, went thundering up the stairs.

At the door to her room, ghostly in a white nightgown, Philomela met him. "For heaven's sake, Arvid, stop yelling! It's only a thunder-shower, you big idiot, go back to bed!"

He tore right on by. "It ain't no thunderstorm, it's Toughy. Toughy's sick—" and stopped at the door to Bigelow's room, as if he had run into the wall, not the open doorway. Over his shoulder, he said to Philomela, "Oh, God! Oh, dear!"

The light was on in Bigelow's room. She was standing at the foot of the bed, clutching the footboard with both hands, staring, openmouthed.

"It's her kittens," Bigelow said, in a breaking voice. "She was having them! And I thought she was sick!"

"Oh, my dear soul!" Philomela said. "On the bed, Bigelow!"

But Bigelow was beyond all that, and what, anyway, was a bed? Like Arvid, unable ever to contain emotion, she lifted up her voice in a shrill yell, half-laughter, half-joy.

"Sh-h," Arvid said. "You'll bother her, Bigelow. She's awful busy."

But no sound, unless a threat, could have bothered Toughy now. Concentrated, with neatness and dispatch, she had the last kitten.

"I'll find a box," Philomela said. "And then we'd better leave her alone in it."

"Marney has to see! Wait, I'll get him!" Bigelow raced along the hall, shouting at the top of her lungs. "Marney, Marney! Come see Toughy's kittens! She's had them on my bed—" The voice was muffled as it went through the door of Marney's room. Presently Marney staggered in, his hair on end, looked, went staggering back to bed. No one, not even he, knew whether he had seen the kittens.

Philomela came back with an ample clothes basket, well-padded and comfortable, just the right sort of place; but nobody was going to touch Toughy tonight or come within reaching distance of those kittens. She was a small, fiery ball of fierceness; she growled like the echo of the thunder which had passed over to the east and which everybody had forgotten even to notice.

Watching her, Philomela thought, The blind principle. And she found herself forcing back a sudden rush of rears. Well, I have my own family now. It cost me more than I could afford to pay. But better loved because of that. It has to be.

Collecting her voice, she managed to say steadily, "We'll have to leave her on the bed, Bigelow. You come on and bunk in with me till morning. Come on now, enough's enough. Off to bed. Tomorrow's a school day."

But Arvid forgot. Proud as a father, he counted. "One, two, three, four. Didn't you do good, dear," he said, and leaned down to pat Toughy on the head. And the blind principle let him have it, the claws of both front feet on the back of his hand.

THE END

About the Author

Born and raised in the Maine fishing village of Gotts Island, Ruth
Moore (1903–1989) emerged as one of the most important Maine
authors of the twentieth century, best known for her authentic por-
trayals of Maine people and her evocative descriptions of the state. In
her time, she was favorably compared to Faulkner, Steinbeck, Caldwell
and O'Connor. She graduated from Albany State Teacher's College
and worked at a variety of jobs in New York, Washington, D.C., and
California, including as personal secretary to Mary White Ovington,
a founder of the NAACP, and at *Reader's Digest*. Her debut novel in
1943, *The Weir* was hailed by critics and established Moore as novelist,
but her second novel, *Spoonhandle* reached great success, spending
fourteen weeks on *The New York Times* bestseller list and was made
into the movie, *Deep Waters*. The success of *Spoonhandle* provided
her with the financial security to build a house in Bass Harbor and
spend the rest of her life writing novels in her home state. Ultimately,
she wrote 14 novels. Moore and her partner, Eleanor Mayo, traveled
extensively, but never again lived outside of Maine. Moore died in
Bar Harbor in 1989.